ALSO BY MATTHEW PEARL

The Last Dickens

The Poe Shadow

The Dante Club

THE TECHNOLOGISTS

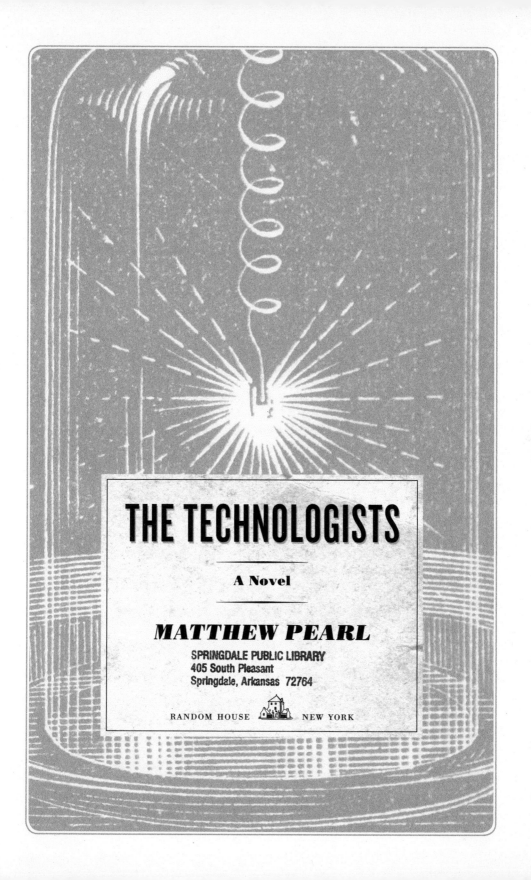

THE TECHNOLOGISTS

A Novel

MATTHEW PEARL

RANDOM HOUSE NEW YORK

The Technologists is a work of fiction. Many of the characters are
inspired by historical figures; others are entirely the author's
creations. Apart from the historical figures, any resemblance between
these fictional characters and actual persons, living or dead, is
purely coincidental.

Published in the United States by Random House,
an imprint of The Random House Publishing Group,
a division of Random House, Inc., New York.

RANDOM HOUSE and colophon are registered trademarks of
Random House, Inc.

Grateful acknowledgment is made to the Massachusetts Institute of
Technology (MIT) for permission to publish a reproduction of a
MIT diploma from 1868 incorporating the MIT Seal. Reprinted
with the express permission of the Massachusetts Institute
of Technology.

LIBRARY OF CONGRESS CATALOGING-IN-PUBLICATION DATA

Pearl, Matthew.
The technologists: a novel/Matthew Pearl.
p. cm.
ISBN 978-1-4000-6657-5
eBook ISBN 978-0-679-60507-2
1. Massachusetts Institute of Technology—History—19th century—
Fiction. 2. College students—Massachusetts—Cambridge—Fiction.
I. Title.
PS3616.E25T43 2012
813'.6—dc22 2011014628

Printed in the United States of America on acid-free paper

www.atrandom.com

2 4 6 8 9 7 5 3 1

FIRST EDITION

Book design by Simon M. Sullivan

FOR MY SON

Book 1

CIVIL AND TOPOGRAPHICAL ENGINEERING

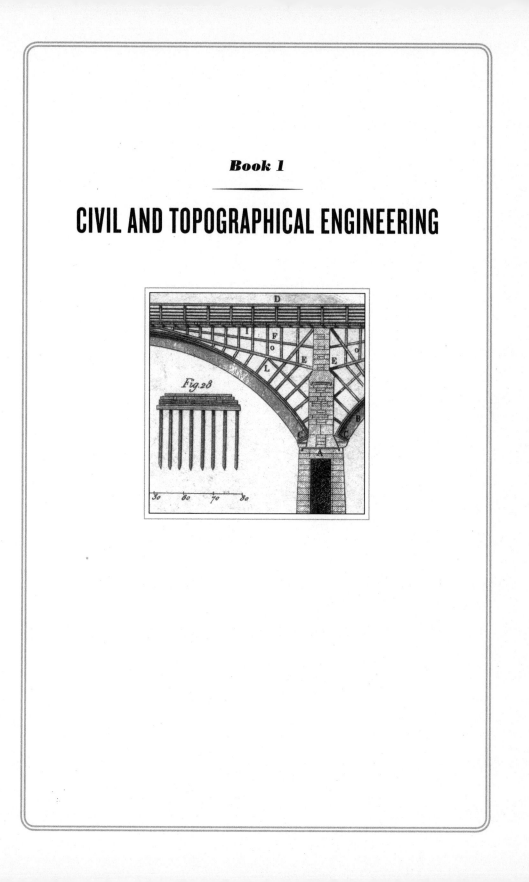

April 4, 1868

ITS PROUD LINES INTERMITTENTLY VISIBLE through the early morning fog, the *Light of the East* might have been the most carefree ship
that ever floated into Boston. Some of the sailors, their bearded faces
browned and peeling from too much sun, cracked the last rations of wal-
nuts in their fists or under their boot heels, singing some ancient song
about a girl left behind. After wild March winds, stormy seas, dangerous
ports, backbreaking work, and all the extremes of experience, they'd be
handed a good pay at port, then freed to lose it to the city's myriad plea-
sures.

The navigator held the prow steady, his eye on his instruments, as
they waited for the fog to disperse enough for their signal to be seen by
the pilot boat. Although Boston Harbor stretched across seventy-five
square miles, its channels had been so narrowed for purposes of defense
that two large ships could not safely pass each other without the harbor
pilot's assistance.

The *Light*'s austere captain, Mr. Beal, strode the deck, his rare aura of
high contentment amplified by the giddiness of his men. Beal could envision in his mind's eye the pilot boat breaking through the fog toward
them, the pilot dressed like an undertaker, saluting indifferently and
relieving Beal—for once—of his burdens. Then would come the view
of the stretches of docks and piers, the solid granite warehouses never
quite large enough for all the foreign cargo brought in by the merchants,
then beyond that the State House's gold dome capping the horizon—the
glittering cranium of the world's smartest city.

In the last few years, with so many men returned from fighting the
rebellion, even modest Boston merchants had become veritable indus-

trialists, beset as they were by excess hands. This city had prided itself on its history from the time it was little more than a quaint village, but Beal was old enough to know how artificial its modern visage was. Hills that formerly sloped through the city had been flattened, their detritus used to fill in various necks and bays, the foundations for streets and new neighborhoods and wharves such as the one that soon would welcome them. He could remember when the Public Garden was plain mud marking Boston's natural boundary.

A steam pipe bellowed from some unseen ship launching on its way or maybe, like them, gliding toward a journey's end, and Beal felt a solemn comradeship with all unknown voyagers. As he glimpsed the crescent moon and thought he would soon have enough light even in this nasty fog to lay course, his pleasant reverie was broken by a bright light flashing low in the water. When the captain craned forward, a lifeboat caught in the current, right in the path of their prow, sprang out from the mist.

His lookout cried out while Beal seized his speaking trumpet and shouted orders to change course. A woman's scream floated up. The schooner veered adroitly in efforts to avoid the small craft, but too late. The lifeboat's passengers jumped for their lives as their boat split into pieces against the *Light*'s prow, the screaming woman thrusting a small child above the waves. To the shock of the captain, another obstacle broke through the dense curtain of fog on the schooner's starboard side: a pleasure steamer, with its flags flying the signals of distress, and taking on water.

"Clear lower deck!" Beal shouted.

Light of the East had nowhere to go. The side of its hull grazed and then caught the stranded steamship, right through the forward bulkhead: Pipes snapped and scalding-hot steam rushed into the heavy air as the hold of the schooner was ripped open. Now it, too, took on water, fast.

Chaos reigned on and off the ships. Beal snapped an order to throw the cargo overboard and repeated it sharply when his men hesitated. If they didn't unload right now, they would lose not only their profits, but also the ship and likely lives.

"Captain! There!" called his lookout.

Beal stared in astonishment from the railing as a stray breeze parted the fog. The wharf loomed ahead, but it was now clear they were approaching it from the wrong angle, parallel instead of perpendicular. Incredulously, the captain extended his spyglass. A bark flying British colors had wrecked against the tip of one of the piers and caught fire, while another schooner, marked the *Gladiator,* had drifted against the wharf, where its crew feverishly tried to tow it in. As he watched, fiery debris spread to the *Gladiator*'s sails, which an instant later were wreathed in flames.

At least half a dozen ships were visible in those few moments of clarity, and all were foundering in various states of distress across the once-orderly harbor, reverberating with shrieking whistles, bells, foghorns, and other desperate signals.

Beal frantically stumbled and slid on his way to the navigational instruments. The needle of the steering compass, held under glass by the wheel, spun around violently, as if bedeviled, while on his pocket compass the needle was 180 degrees off the mark—north was south. He'd sailed by these navigational instruments—finely tuned with the expertise of nineteen centuries—for his entire life as a seaman, and he knew there should be no way for them to fail all at once.

The pleasure steamer they had crashed into suddenly lurched forward with a boom. In seconds it was entirely underwater. Where it had been, a vortex opened, sucking under those already stranded in the water, and then spitting them out high into the air.

"To the lifeboats!" shouted Beal to his thunderstruck crew. "Find anyone alive and get as far away as you can!"

Charles

SUBMERGED. As the waves soothed his naked body, his athletic strokes worked in concert with the rhythm of the current. The first week in April had not yet promised any warmth, the water still rather icy. But he willingly endured the chill ripping through his body for the better feeling swimming afforded him. It was a feeling of being alone but not lonely, a sense of freedom from all restrictions and control. Floating, kicking, somersaulting—try as he could to make noise, the water rendered him irrelevant.

Throughout his boyhood in a port town, he'd heard so many people spoken of as "lost at sea." Now it seemed to him the strangest turn of phrase. As long as he was in the water, he could not be lost. He could bask, bathe, disappear, and the water sheltered him as much in Boston as it had back home. Not that he ever felt homesick, as some of the other Institute students did who had come from outside Boston. He still traveled the forty miles back and forth to Newburyport by train every day to keep down living expenses, although it cost him more than an hour each way.

To his mother and stepfather, the Institute remained a strange detour from his good position at the machine shop, and a daily interruption to his help at home. His stepfather, James, had always been unhappy, plagued by a partial deafness in his left ear that made him shun all society and friends. He worked as a night watchman for a jeweler because he preferred the solitude and uneventful nature of the position. He assumed people were speaking ill of him because he could not hear what they said, which led him to the further conclusion that city life, being loud, was an evil cacophony of deceit. As for his mother, she was a religious zealot of the old Puritan kind who saw danger in urban life and no value to the son's studies in Boston.

Even now, when he was a senior, graduation a mere two and a half months away, they did not accept that he—Marcus Mansfield, of all people!—was a student at a college.

* * *

MARCUS PLUNGED his head back into the cool water, ears tingling as he surveyed the river—a tranquil and forgiving lane that ran between Boston and Cambridge, lined by a gentle, sloping green sward that would shade swimmers and oarsmen from the hot days to come. Unseen behind the thick weather, above the riverbank and the fields and marshes skirting it, there lurked the crowded brick and iron and gold-domed city, propelling Marcus forward with the powerful thrust of a gigantic engine.

At the shallow bend of the river Marcus took another big breath and sank, closing his eyes and relishing the drop. Down below, pieces of debris and lumber had lodged in the muddy riverbed. As he brushed against the foreign articles, he heard a voice beckon, distant, as though issued from the sky:

"Mansfield! Mansfield! We need you!"

Marcus bobbed up from under the water and then grabbed onto the side of a boat.

"Mansfield! There you are! You're late."

"How did you know I was swimming?"

"How did we—? Ha! Because I saw a pile of clothes back there on the shore, and who else would dare plunge into this freezing Styx!" The tall, blond oarsman dangled a suit of clothes above Marcus's head. "Actually, it was Eddy who recognized your clothes."

"Morning, Marcus," said the second, smaller oarsman with his usual open smile.

"And since Eddy and I were both ready," continued Bob, "we pushed out to find you."

"Then *you* were early," said Marcus, treading water toward the bank, "before I was late."

"Ha! I'll take that. Get dressed—we need our third oar."

He shook himself dry on the bank and climbed into his gray trousers and light shirt. His two companions presented a study in opposites as they helped him into their boat: Bob, with the quintessential New Englander's clear skin and crown of handsome curls, standing carelessly at the edge of the shell; Edwin Hoyt, slight and frail-looking, throwing the little weight he possessed to the other side in anticipation of a tragic drowning.

Despite knowing the water and boats pretty well, Marcus had not grown up indulging in such impractical pursuits as rowing for pleasure, with its arbitrary rules and catchwords. Some weeks before, Bob had announced one morning, "This is the day, fellows!" to Marcus and Edwin, their fellow Institute of Technology senior, as he bounded ahead of them on the way to a lecture.

"Which day?"

"Spring is here, Mansfield, and since it's our last one at the college it's time I showed you rowing just as I promised. Why, I hardly knew one end of the oar from the other until I was nine years old. A scrawny boy I was, the smallest Richards ever!" This served to emphasize what a commanding twenty-two-year-old Bob had become. Marcus could not actually recall Bob promising to teach them, but let that pass, given Bob's enthusiasm.

To his surprise, Marcus found rowing not to be the wasted time he expected, and it took his mind away from worrying about the looming future away from the Institute. It was at once calming and exciting, a thrill when the shell launched across the surface of the water as though alive. They tried to recruit more oars among their classmates to join them, but the few willing candidates never did find time.

As their small vessel pushed steadily along, Bob began laughing to himself. "I was just thinking of my brothers," he explained. "They used to warn me about the sea serpent of the Charles. Nearly one hundred feet long, they said, with humps like a camel and a cry like a braying donkey crossed with an elephant's trumpeting. You know how I have to take it upon myself to investigate anything in nature. Well, for three months I searched out old Charley, until I determined that the water wouldn't sustain a sea serpent's diet."

"But how did you know what a sea serpent ate?" Edwin asked seriously.

"Bob, would you mind rowing farther east today?" Marcus proposed.

"A quest! Where to?"

"I haven't seen the harbor since . . ." Marcus did not finish his sentence.

"Better not to, Marcus," Edwin said quickly. "I caught sight of it this morning after it was all over. The whole harbor was up in smoke. It was like looking into the face of a bad omen."

"Eager to see the destruction?"

"Actually, Bob, I was hoping to learn something from seeing how they begin the repairs," Marcus corrected him. "There is already some debris on the riverbed that must have drifted on the current." He stopped when he saw Bob's face narrow as he looked out on the water behind them. "What is it?"

"Just my luck," Bob said. "Faster, fellows! Go! Come on, Mansfield, faster! Well rowed, Hoyt! All clear, come on!"

A forty-nine-foot shell had shot out of the trees sheltering a narrow adjoining channel with the speed of a lightning bolt. Six flashing oars creased the surface of the river in synchronized strokes, throwing off white streaks behind them. The rowers were bare from the waist up, with crimson handkerchiefs wrapped around their heads, and their flexing muscles glistened in the strengthening sun. As Marcus peered back at them, they looked like highly educable pirates, and he knew it would be a lost cause to attempt to elude whatever this boat was.

"Who are they?" he marveled.

"Blaikie," Bob explained as the three of them pulled as hard as they could. "His is the best Harvard six there ever was, they say. Will Blaikie—he's the stroke oar. I'd rather stare into the mouth of the serpent."

Edwin wheezed between strokes, "Blaikie . . . was . . . at Exeter . . . with Bob and me."

The other vessel came on with a spurt too powerful to shake, now just a length behind.

"Plymouth!" cried the lantern-jawed lead rower on the lightning bolt. The boat went by theirs and then reversed and ranged alongside of them.

"Why, it *is* you, Plymouth!" said the stroke oar, Blaikie, to Bob with a gleaming smile. Even seated in his shell, he presented the particular mincing swagger of a Harvard senior. "It's been ages. You're not forming a randan team, are you?"

"We've been borrowing a shell from the boat club," said Bob, motioning for his friends to stop rowing. Marcus could not remember seeing his classmate so deflated.

"Don't tell me you're still dragging your heels over at that embryo of a college, Plymouth?" Blaikie asked.

"We are seniors now, like you."

"Tant pis pour vous," interjected one of the Harvard boys, eliciting chuckles from the others.

"I fear civilizing your classmates into respectable gentlemen will take more than teaching them to grip an oar," Blaikie went on cheerfully. "Science cannot substitute for culture, old salt. I used to agonize, Plymouth, what I would most rather be, stroke of the Harvard, president of the Christian Brethren, or First Scholar of the class. Now I know what it is to be all three." He was reminded by one of his oarsmen not to forget president of one of the best college societies. "Yes, Smithy! But it is best not to speak of the societies to outsiders."

"We are doing things far more important—things you wouldn't begin to understand, Blaikie."

"Just how many of you Technology boys are there?"

Throwing out his chest, Bob answered, "Fifteen men in the Class of '68. About thirty-five in the other three classes, and we expect more than ever in the next freshman group."

"Fifty. Fifty men and it is called a college! I call that cheek!"

"Mock if you like. When we are graduated on that glorious day of June the fifteenth, you can follow us in the newspaper columns as pathfinders."

Marcus was moved to see Bob align himself with his classmates instead of the fellows whom he'd grown up alongside in the snug parlors of Beacon Hill.

"*If* you're to be graduated," Blaikie said.

"What do you mean by 'if,' Blaikie?" Edwin asked.

"You hold your tongue, grayhead. You had your chance with us."

Edwin slouched in the boat, his hand reflexively moving to touch the light spot in his hair.

"You might want to hold your tongue now and then yourself, friend," Marcus said.

"What did he say to me?" Blaikie turned to his team, then to Marcus, as if noticing him only now. When their eyes met, Blaikie's shoulders tightened and he subtly recoiled. Marcus had that effect. His muscular frame was well built and solid. His thick brown hair and old-fashioned crescent mustache made his intense green eyes stand out. Most of all, the poise of an engineer clung to him, made him seem in control of any circumstance. "Who is this?" Blaikie asked.

"My name is Marcus Mansfield."

"Marcus . . . Mansfield . . ." Blaikie repeated speculatively, shrugging. He looked back at his men, who returned his shrug. "Sorry to disappoint. Never heard the name. Well, my men have much actual rowing to do, Plymouth. Some of the other sixes are too afraid to take their shells out because of the turn of events overnight at the harbor. They say there was a flash of fire, then ten, fifteen ships were crashing, and burning, sinking. Can you imagine what in the deuce those superstitious fools think of it? Black magic, perhaps."

"The city is in a panic about the whole thing, the industries scrambling to prevent losses. I've never heard of so many ships wrecking at once—the number of arrivals must have been too great in the fog," speculated Edwin.

"Too great!" Bob said. "There are more than two hundred wharves and docks in our harbor that would add up to more than five miles if placed end to end, Eddy. Even in much worse fog than that, our capacity for commerce—"

"Oh, who cares a fig!" broke in the Harvard captain. "It is not my business. But whatever it was, I'm not about to let it stop us from our practice, if we are to whip Oxford like we did Yale. Give me your hand, Plymouth. Godspeed to you Technology fellows."

"Godspeed, Harvard." Bob reached out to shake.

On Blaikie's nod, his team rammed their shell into the side of the

Tech boat. As Marcus grabbed their shell's sides to steady it, Bob went headfirst into the ice-cold water with a splash. Edwin, flailing to stop Bob's fall, followed him overboard.

"Cold day for bathing, Plymouth!" Blaikie shouted, as he and the Crimson pirates exploded with laughter.

Marcus grabbed his oar like a bat, ready to defend their boat from further indignity. Blaikie glared at Marcus, daring him to strike.

After another moment Marcus loosened his grip and let his instincts go quiet.

"Wise fellow," Blaikie said with an approving nod. "Being a gentleman isn't what it's cracked up to be, is it, old salt?" Then, to his men: "Three cheers and a tiger for Harvard Class of 1868! Sixty-eight forever!" A trio of "rahs" were followed by a guttural whoop before their oars swept through the water again. Marcus watched the perfect unison of the other team as the shell took the curve of the river ahead.

"Bob's right—those scrubs will see; we'll be the true pathfinders!" Edwin yelled, knocking water out from his ear.

"Oh, damn what I say, Eddy," Bob said. He shook out his hair as he floated back to their boat. "Come on, Mansfield, stop your gaping and fish us out!"

III

The Boston Police

A T WHAT REMAINED of one of the damaged wharves on Saturday, Sergeant Lemuel Carlton of the Boston Police paced along the cracked piers and the splintered docks. The fog had lifted by now, but it was still cloudy and colder than it should have been at this time of year. The best that could be said was it was a respite from the rain that had plagued the last wretched week in March.

"You!" he said to a patrolman who caught him by surprise. "About time you're back, man. What did the captain of the *Gladiator* say?"

"I've spoken to him, sir."

"I chose the past tense 'did' on the presumption of that very thing," Carlton noted in disgust.

"He testified that . . . well, the very same thing as the others, sir! The very same!"

"That so? He hadn't been on a spree—a bit cup-shot? He mustn't be ashamed to admit being a sot to the police," Carlton added, scratching his strong chin sagely.

"I questioned him thoroughly and he vowed he hadn't had a drop, and I didn't find any liquor upon his person or notice any in his rooms. Nor any of the others who were witnesses."

Carlton bowed his head and sat down on a barrel at the edge of the pier, staring at loose planks that were floating past him below. His head throbbed with the echoes of all the futile conversations since the morning with his patrolmen, unnerved sailors, angry shipowners, crying passengers. He dismissed his inferior to assist the rest of the men with the debris. The Harbor Police had encircled the wharf with their boats and were steering incoming vessels away, including a small fishing boat weaving in and out with a heavy-duty net, looting lost booty.

Boots thumped aggressively on the planking behind him, and he was rising to attention before he even turned.

"Chief Kurtz," he said, bowing. "I believe you will find we have the situation in hand."

"Indeed!" responded Kurtz with surprise, pulling at one end of his bushy mustache and inclining his head toward the destruction. "Tell me, Sergeant Carlton, what *is* this situation? What I see are two of the most important commercial wharves of our city in tatters."

"Three ships sunk, four others damaged or otherwise destroyed, with losses in excess of twenty-four thousand dollars. Fifteen individuals injured to varying degrees, mostly broken arms and legs, and burns, with loss of life avoided only by the great exertions of several experienced sailors."

"But how?" Kurtz demanded after Carlton finished the report. "How did this happen?"

"That is the very question," Carlton said, raising a single eyebrow, and clearing his throat assiduously.

"Hem! Haw! Go on!"

"Chief. I have spoken to several captains and navigators who were on the vessels involved and have instructed the patrolmen to interview as many others as we can locate. Each one, to a man, reports that their instruments failed—were deranged in their readings—all in the space of the same few minutes."

"How is it possible?"

"It is flagrantly not possible, sir! You need not believe me alone. The captain of the Harbor Police says that it is emphatically and categorically *not* possible for so many compasses and what-you-will to fail at once."

Kurtz stared ominously into the harbor. "Sabotage?"

"Chief," the sergeant began, then hesitated before going on. "Chief, all the instruments were on ships from different destinations with distinct schedules, some arriving, some departing. How it could be sabotage, well, I have wrangled with that question with the same success Joseph had with the angel."

"Then what, Sergeant Carlton? Necromancy? The devil? That's what some of the sailors are squawking about, and that means ships avoiding our ports, and tens of thousands of dollars lost. If the mayor and the legislature sink their teeth into this, it will touch off a volcano under my feet. What do you propose doing about that?"

"We shall remove the debris as best and as quickly as we can manage, so the city engineers can begin to rebuild."

Jaw clenched, Kurtz took off his hat and tossed it into the harbor. "There's one more piece of debris to fish out, Sergeant!"

"Very well, Chief," replied the officer obediently. "I will have my best man do it straightaway."

Kurtz rolled his eyes. "You can return my hat to me in my office when you know what caused those ships to lose their direction. Until then, I'd rather not see that thunderstruck phiz of yours back at the station house."

"But, Chief, perhaps the Harbor Police should lead this investigation."

"They swallow too much of our funds already, and they would crave any excuse to siphon off more. No. Over my dead body, Carlton. "

"Then perhaps I ought to consult with some of the professors at that new college in Back Bay. They are experts in all the new sciences, and if the usual reasons for accidents do not fit, perhaps they could advise us where to turn."

Kurtz pulled him away from the patrolmen who were milling around them. "Have you gone mad, Carlton?"

"Sir?"

"Don't rile me! The Institute of Technology? You know the reputation of that place. Their sciences are seen as practically pagan. Just speaking to them will draw fire against us. Try the harbormaster if you need more help! Try the city engineer!"

"I have! All baffled! We need to find someone capable of understanding how this could happen, or we shall not advance one whit!"

"The single place with the finest intellects in the nation sits just across the river. What about that?"

"Harvard."

"Yes! Go there and find *someone* smarter than you, and without delay! We are here to protect this city. I will not suffer another embarrassment like this!"

"Right away, Chief Kurtz. Chief, wait! You're still . . ." But there he went without a look back, stomping all the way to his waiting carriage, the chief of police of the city Carlton loved, hatless for all Boston to see.

IV

———

Circuits

A LMOST ANYWHERE MARCUS LOOKED as he stood outside the splendid
Boylston Street building was unused land of the Back Bay, or the
"new land," as it was known. Only a few years before it had been
marshland and was still so a few streets west, where rows of steam shovels fed by freight cars of gravel and sand continued the filling. Besides
the Institute, there were a few other places—including the asylum for
aged blacks and the Catholic academy for girls—that preferred distance
from the rest of the city. The area was a perfect setting for the improb-
able college.

Scholars should be surrounded by quiet, but President Rogers had
always said technological scholars should be surrounded by the progress of man. The Back Bay presented surroundings that were grandly
artificial, where the pupils would observe the way in which civil engineering could turn malodorous swamp—what had been a bubbling caldron of noxious filth poured out from the city, though they were too
young to have seen it at its worst—into a landscape of wide streets that
would alleviate the crowding of an old Boston, now flooded with so
many new residents from rural towns and foreign nations that one could
hardly move. It would be the latest example of modern architecture and
commercial and industrial progress—at least, that was the hope for the
still young, mostly still uninhabitable Back Bay.

"Come on already," Bob was saying, "at this rate, we'll be graduated
before we finish the preparations."

If you're to be graduated.

Marcus was carrying equipment outside with Bob. "Two steps behind you, Bob."

In the five days since, the Harvard stroke oar's taunt out on the Charles River had slowly wormed its way into Marcus Mansfield's thoughts with parasitic tenacity. On the one hand, a sort of childish superstition rose inside Marcus, without any particular legs to its logic, that he would not be graduated. Even after he had swapped the machine shop floor for the classrooms and laboratories of the Institute, he had feared deep down that a man like him had no right to be a college man and would, through the last-minute intervention of fate, be deprived of the title.

On the other hand, Marcus's more practical cause for concern was that he and the other members of '68 were to be the first to be graduated from the Institute of Technology, and until a thing had happened it could not rightly be proven that it could happen. They had been taught that from the first hour at Tech.

No doubt Bob Richards would have laughed away his worries, which was why Marcus did not bring them up with him as they finished preparing the equipment for the evening's public demonstration. Bob seemed to have been born with the ability to sleep off any problem in the way other men sleep off beer. But Marcus's thoughts swirled around and around the stroke oar's venomous jeer. When he should have been entering a stage of intense concentration on his studies as graduation crept closer (*If you're to be graduated*), he instead felt unmoored and a little wild—and for that he blamed the obnoxious Harvard men he'd likely never see again.

Only a handful of students gathered for the demonstration besides Marcus and Bob. This close to the end of term, most of the students raced home after five o'clock each evening to prepare for examinations and final papers. Marcus noticed Chauncy Hammond, Jr., gazing up at the cloudy sky. Hammie's jet-black hair was parted smartly, impervious to the breeze, but his bulbous forehead and gourdlike chin, inexpertly shaved, overshadowed his otherwise bland facial features, which seemed to have been left unfinished by their creator. A contender, along with good-hearted Edwin Hoyt, for First Scholar, Hammie generally floated along in his own rarefied world of figures and formulas. Standing near the front steps was that busybody Albert Hall, writing in a ledger held in the crook of his arm, maybe recording the names of students present (or, more likely, listing those not present, underlined by his pencil with spite), and next to Albert was Bryant Tilden, arms crossed petulantly across his tree-trunk chest.

Ellen Swallow was on her own at the outer fringe of the gathering. As the only female pupil at the Institute, Miss Swallow was taught separately from the others, so a sighting of her was rare. Her quick eyes darted around and caught his. He lifted his hand to his hat, but she simply looked the other way with a crimson bloom tainting her pale cheeks.

President Rogers was slowly approaching the podium at the front of the building. He was steadied on one arm by Darwin Fogg, the Institute janitor, and on the other by a petite chambermaid. She held on to her employer gingerly but with an unmistakable protectiveness. Marcus looked upon the condition of their college president sadly, remembering him in days of much better health.

Along the way, Rogers removed his eyeglasses from his vest and lost his grip on them; they bounced off his arm and, with one hand, the chambermaid caught them before they could hit the ground and returned them without waiting for any credit.

"Is she dark or blond under that cap?" Bob, sneaking up behind him, asked in a whisper.

"Who do you mean?"

"The pretty little nymph you're staring at as if her eyes were fully charged electromagnets—the Irish servant girl propping up Rogers. Never mind her. Have I told you this summer there will be dozens of balls thrown by good Boston society where you will make a fine prospect as a college graduate? Those ladies are so well bred they would rather be dead than not make an appearance at a public affair. Do not smooth your mustache like that—I cannot tell what expression you're wearing. Do you laugh or sneer at my plans?"

"Rogers is about to begin the demonstration. Do you have the circuit ready?"

"Sneer! No, wait. You do laugh!"

"Never at you, Bob."

"Ladies and gentlemen, welcome," President Rogers began when the clock reached eight. Despite his weakened condition, his voice easily cascaded through the gathering with authoritative calm. "The people of Massachusetts have always been a mechanical people and our age will see many wonders. At the Massachusetts Institute of Technology, it is our sincerest hope that our zeal for new invention is as infectious outside the college as inside our walls, where we endeavor to invigorate the observing and logical faculties of young minds, by asking each day: What limit of knowledge will man yet reach?" He stopped, put his paper down on the podium, and looked at the sky as he wiped his eyeglasses. "It *is* growing dark, isn't it? I'm embarrassed, I confess. I can hardly read my own jottings."

He nodded in their direction—that rugged face with the soft smile. Bob tapped a spring on a box. After about fifteen or twenty seconds, the lampposts lining Boylston Street flickered, then lit up simultaneously in a long procession of softly glowing orbs. At the pop of the lanterns, there was a collective gasp and a palpable excitement.

Rogers waited out the applause before he explained that Boston had five thousand streetlamps and spent over $42,000 each year on employing men to light them, not counting the wasted gas in the first lamps each night that had to be lighted earlier than necessary so the men could complete their rounds by nightfall. The Institute's invention, developed through the collective effort of students and faculty in four years of engineering studies, used wires connected through a circuit—a course that allowed the electricity to flow from one body to another, the professor said—from a box at each gaslight to a central location, where they could be activated at one time. Marcus opened the central box. Inside, a notched wheel powered by electricity was connected to a series of coils.

"This is what we call a 'circuit breaker,' " Rogers said. "When the spring is tapped, as Mr. Richards, one of our seniors, has shown us, it revolves around halfway, closing the valve for electricity, to turn off the wheel and extinguish the lamps—or 'break' the electric flow. When tapped once more, it revolves again, this time opening the valve and lighting our streets at night. Even as we gather right now, this system is being installed across the city."

People moved in for better views, marveling at the notion of machinery illuminating the streets all at once. The machine rattled as something hard struck it. It was a rock. A second one grazed Rogers's shoulder and another cracked the glass of the lantern above them, pitching them into darkness. Marcus felt the glass shards rain down on his hat and shoulder.

Three men emerged from a cluster of trees. Now they launched a volley of rotten tomatoes.

"Technology will bring God's wrath!" yelled a man dressed smartly in a crisp dark-blue Union army tunic, light-blue trousers, and kid-leather gloves. "Last month, a girl's scalp was torn off when her hair was caught in a factory machine she was operating in Lowell. Torn off! What was it that befell the ships at the docks last week? Ask them to explain that in their classrooms, if they dare!"

Marcus guided President Rogers away from the falling glass.

"I'll send for a policeman at once, President Rogers," said Albert excitedly. He had ducked behind a group of faculty members at the outbreak of the commotion.

"No, Mr. Hall," Rogers said. "Do not molest them. They're from the trade unions."

"Hall's right, President Rogers! It's a scrubby thing to do!" Bob protested. "Nothing burns me like anti-machine mania. This will make their own labors easier and safer."

"Mr. Richards," Rogers said calmly, "some lamplighters will lose their positions once our invention has been fully installed. Consider that before consulting your anger."

"Get inside the carriage. Please, Professor! Quickly!" the chambermaid urged him, leading him briskly to the street.

"Mr. Mansfield," Rogers said, beckoning to Marcus. "We do not want further trouble."

He followed Rogers's eyes and saw that Hammie was stomping toward the reformers.

Hammie had unleashed his wrath before Marcus could reach him. "Take your rocks and rioting elsewhere, you ruffians! All the scum of the trades with all their bluster won't frighten a Tech man." He turned to Marcus, who put himself between the magnate's son and the agitators. "Move away, will you, Mansfield? I have the situation in hand!"

"Hammie, let's mind our place."

"Don't tell me about my place! They shoot out windows, or put explosives in a foreman's desk from time to time at the locomotive works. But they are all brag, Mansfield. Especially Rapler here—he may act like a workingman but his true occupation is to collect fees from poor souls who know no better."

One of the other agitators lunged at Hammie, who stumbled and nearly fell over. Marcus steadied him, but Hammie pulled away from him, dizzy and humiliated.

"Hands off, Mansfield, I'll—Officer, Officer! Assault!" Hammie cried out to a policeman who was approaching from Berkeley Street. The policeman stopped but did nothing.

"You should know that officer's brother is in the bricklayers' union," explained Rapler, the uniformed man, who, now that he was not shouting, spoke with an impressively urbane tone. He was missing what would have been his two front teeth. "We've asked him here to ensure our safety from easily excitable young men like you."

"You have all had your say," Marcus said politely. "Look around. You see? People are leaving. Please follow their example."

Rapler studied him with interest. "What do *you* want? All of Boston's jobs lost to machines, perhaps."

"We want nothing at our Institute except to find the truth," said Marcus. "You might have heard President Rogers say that if you weren't throwing your rocks."

"And how powerful must you become through it, laddie? Has not man already overstepped his maker, if he does not know where his power ends?"

"It ends when mankind no longer needs the protections technology provides."

Rapler motioned to the men around him. "The men and women who join our cause are not anti-science. We simply see a science today set to run away with man. The machines you gentlemen—and one errant lady, as I understand it—at the Institute create will become so complicated that they will control us instead of our mastering them. Imagine a future when, with a single malfunction of your machines, man will live in the dark without memory of how to light a candle. He will be stranded without ability to transport himself with feet rather than steel rails. The machine is inanimate and heartless. Our unions respect the intelligence of man to act, to make decisions *only* man is capable of. Otherwise, we become merely tools of our tools. How will you protect us from that?" The speaker seemed satisfied when Marcus decided not to prolong the confrontation. "Fall in!"

Rapler locked arms with the other union men. They sang as they marched away.

> *Resolve by your native soil,*
> *Resolve by your fathers' graves,*
> *You will live by your honest toil,*
> *But never consent to be slaves!*

"At least they're gone," Bob said a few moments later. "And they couldn't stop us from demonstrating the circuit!" he crowed.

"But the people who came will remember only that they broke our lamp," Marcus said, "not that the lights went on."

Positively No Admittance

W HEN ONE ENTERED, one's senses came under attack. An amalgam of odors hung in the air, fresh fumes mixing with old ones that never dissipated. A film of dust clouded the eyes—not from a lack of tidiness (though the place was wonderfully untidy), but from the shut-in quarters and microscopic particles, some crystalline, others incandescent, floating in the air.

Touch a surface at one's peril; it was likely to be burning hot or morbidly cold without warning. Four furnaces made of clay, brick, and stone sat in different locations, evidence of each one's different purpose in the residue of its ash pan; tongs hung near each, ready to remove or adjust the smoldering contents.

A congealed substance had melted over one portion of the floor and now sparkled like gold. On the wall behind it, the bricks had been charred black from an accidental explosion in the not distant past. A table in the center of the main room stood within a glass enclosure; on it sat a copper box filled with sand. A pipe entered the box from a burner, and nearby were the glass crucibles, blowpipes, vessels, and other apparatus used to manipulate gases.

Gasometers, gauges, air pumps, and troughs of water and of galvanic fluid filled the rest of the chamber, their uses well beyond the comprehension of any visitor. Indeed, it seemed the whole world could be made, or remade, or undone in this room, with all these gangly and imposing tools, in a single day.

On a standing desk, a thick ledger was opened to a page near the middle that listed weights and measurements, seemingly the only volume a visitor might notice among the clutter of equipment along the tables, shelves, and cabinets. The endeavors under way here had not been published in a book, and never would be.

Of course, there would be no visitors. Nothing in this place was for public view. The hand that now neatly wrote in the ledger was suddenly stilled by temptation. That temptation? The nearby window, and specifically the delicious view beyond its thick shutters. The glass pane squared the harbor in the distance, where ships with cranes and machines continued repairs on the piers in the early dawn: Boston shaken by a hint of true disaster.

But even with almost a week passing, the meaning of that hint had not yet been comprehended by this sluggish city of intellectual giants. The sublime satisfaction at the sight of the crippled wharves was only a first step. This morning would bring true progress. The wet tip of the pen methodically added a fresh record in the ledger to mark the occasion.

Ba . . . 68-6 . . . 78–58

F . . . 18-7 . . . 21–42

BaF . . . 87 3 . . . 100 0

compound 17*a*

Baryta 87-47

Hypothet. anhydrous hydfluor. Acid 12 53

100 0

experiment . . . final

calculations . . . final

demonstration—imminent

A Good Morning

THE DAY THAT had brought Marcus the first inkling that he could ever aspire to college came a little more than four and a half years ago. He was working at the Hammond Locomotive Works when he noticed a stranger passing through. Six feet tall and upright, his weathered, noble face framed by long silver hair, he was a philosopher in a place with no philosophy. All of the machinists and apprentices bent diligently to their work while he inspected the floor.

"Who is that?" Marcus nudged Frank Brewer, the machinist posted with him on the drill bench.

"*Some*one," Frank answered, perfectly capturing the tension of the others on the floor. The whole length of Frank's body vibrated as he completed the revolution of the drill. He had bushy black hair and eyebrows and a face that was more manly than handsome. Although his limbs were sinewy, his tall, lean frame was so angular that he appeared to be just bones beneath clothing. While Marcus was in control of his machine, Frank in his skeletal way seemed almost to blend with the complex equipment he operated, its fleshy extension.

Even after their exhausting twelve-hour days at the machine shop, Frank would still find time to carve miniature sculptures in his boardinghouse bedroom—just as he had in the midst of infinitely harsher circumstances where he and Marcus had met. It was that patience and meticulous attention when no one else was watching, that, to Marcus, was Frank Brewer in a nutshell. His favorite piece of Frank's was a bronze statuette of the Headless Horseman from "The Legend of Sleepy Hollow." Once, he'd suggested Frank sculpt Ichabod Crane to match it. It was only later that Marcus discovered, to his dismay, that

Frank was teased for sharing the gawky features "loosely hung together" of the famous literary character.

As the elegant older man was crossing the shop floor, Marcus kept working. Maybe his intense concentration was what caught the eye of William Barton Rogers, who paused at their station. Outsiders usually appeared to be in visible pain with the deafening noise of the shop ringing in their ears, the sharp metallic clicks and buzzing of the giant machines. But not this man. More unexpected, after he introduced himself, he began talking about a college he was organizing.

"Would this school of yours be dreadful expensive?" Frank asked. "You say Institute of . . . ?"

"Technology, my son."

Frank mouthed the word back to himself with an intrigued smile, showing teeth that were small and round.

"We are developing plans for students to be able to work for the college, if necessary," continued the scientist.

"Well! I was not cursed with a fortune," Frank said, sucking his teeth. "Four years without an income surrounded by collegey aristocrat dolts and dandies wouldn't much help, would it, sir? Ha!"

Marcus laughed along with Frank.

The serene visitor turned next to Marcus. "What are you about, young fellow? Have you thought about college?"

Chauncy Hammond, Sr., the president of the locomotive works, joined them.

"Rest your hands for a moment, man," Hammond said to Marcus. "Mr. Mansfield is one of our best machine men on the floor, Professor Rogers. There is no problem his hands seem unable to solve. Boston is growing out of its skin, men; there is talk of the city swallowing Brookline and Cambridge into our borders after we finish chewing over Roxbury. There will be a great need for new machines and railroads to be built and the engineers to do it. You know, Mansfield, that my own Junior is going to attend the professor's institution as part of the first class."

Frank chanced a smirk at Marcus. Chauncy Hammond, Jr.—Hammie—would of course have a place. Earned or not.

Hammie had spent the previous summer as a draftsman at the locomotive works, and during that period had avoided the hard-pressed machinists. His air of aloofness and off-putting mannerisms—even when he smiled or laughed, he was unsocial—made him seem a relic of an older Boston. Hammie might as well have strutted about in a three-cornered hat and stockings.

"Don't mind my friend's *reticence,*" Frank said, the latter word spoken with the eager emphasis of one who read a page of Webster's each night. "His tongue takes a holiday sometimes. I don't s'pose he's more ashamed of being uneducated than the lot of us. He could be a foreman of one of the departments here—both of us will one day, I wager."

"I suppose I hadn't ever thought anything about college," Marcus finally answered for himself, shaking out the numbness from his right hand.

"*Would* you?" the visitor asked, his quick eyes scanning Marcus's hand before returning upward.

"Sir, I have only a common school education, and my family hasn't any money. Besides, I don't know any Latin." He looked across the bench to see if he had said the right thing. Frank shrugged: Facts were facts.

But Rogers flashed his unusual, magnetic smile. "Latin? Think nothing of such things, my son. The old system of education is passing. We are doing something very different. Something new. There are those who fear it, of course, among my colleagues. I need the right young men who will show them how wrong they are."

* * *

WITH THE FIRST LIGHT Friday morning Marcus resumed picking up broken glass and other debris from the field outside the Institute building. Under a light rain and dim sky, it was slow work to find the small, razor-sharp shards and avoid cutting himself.

The previous night, after the union agitators had scattered, a reporter who had come to witness the lighting demonstration accosted Rogers as he was being conducted up the steps into his carriage. "President Rogers, is it true what we have heard about the incident at the harbor? That such a strange phenomenon was no mere accident, and if not produced by wizard's work, must be the result of some kind of scientific manipulation?"

"Is that what the newspapers will print," asked Rogers warily.

"Already have today, sir."

A dark shadow passed over Rogers's face. "I understand no more about what happened than you do," he said, brushing off tomato remnants from his suit. "If you'll kindly pardon me."

The driver closed the door, sealing Rogers in and leaving the frustrated reporter below.

With the commotion subsided, Bob, flustered and frustrated, also left to return to his lodging house. Only Albert Hall remained with Marcus. Hall, his fat cheeks still flush from excitement, planted himself expectantly at Marcus's elbow. He hooked his thumbs in the armholes of his green-and-black-speckled vest, which was an imitation of a fashion that had been the very latest a year and a half ago.

"Hall, what do you want?"

"Aren't you going to clean this all up?" he replied impatiently. "It's your duty, you know, as a charity scholar."

"You're a charity scholar."

Albert blinked, tossed the cowlick from his forehead, and omitted a pitying sigh. His sigh was superfluous. Every syllable he spoke sounded like it was carried on an exhale. "Look here, Mansfield, for reasons I thought would be obvious to you by now, you're given tasks as part of your financial arrangement suited toward, shall we say, physical exertion. In contrast, it is my duty to see that the students at the Institute follow the rules and fulfill their individual responsibilities, pay their overdue bills and breakage fees and preserve perfect order in and around the building. Trust me, you don't want that degree of reliance on you. We may seem the same, you and me, Mansfield, because of our humble standings, but the difference between us is that I freely accept the restrictions on me without shame. Now, the rules in this case would dictate that you tidy up without any help from me."

"You're right. We aren't the same," Marcus said sarcastically, though his confidence had strained a little under Albert's words.

"Excellent." Albert smiled, shaking his hand and gathering his belongings. "I thought we'd understand each other sooner or later. Good night, Mansfield!"

But even with the benefit of the gaslight, the evening had grown too dark for Marcus to finish cleaning up, so he decided to take the train back to Newburyport. He returned to Boston on the earliest train.

As he crawled and crouched with the bag of glass, he heard the gravel crunching and looked up to find he was not alone. Bryant Tilden. He'd even prefer Albert to Tilden. Marcus pretended not to notice him.

"Bootlicking the professors again, Mr. Toady?" Tilden said, snapping his fingers as he spoke. He was short but muscular with a square chin.

"I'm not in the right spirits for sparring, Tilden."

When he first enrolled at the Institute, Marcus expected that his fellow college students would be sophisticated gentlemen who swore only in Latin. Exemplars of Boston manners and New England sobriety—or, as his friend Frank Brewer would put it, aristocrat dolts. That was exactly how they appeared the first day freshman year. But after a week or so, they seemed to change before his eyes into fast and silly boys who preferred sport and pranks over pretense. Looking back, he was relieved to abandon the mythological collegey of his imagination.

Still, Marcus could not help but marvel now that Tilden had lasted to their fourth year. When they were freshmen, he caught him writing out plane-trigonometry formulas on his shirt cuffs. Though Marcus had never said a word to Tilden or anyone else, Tilden never forgave him for knowing the shaky ground he walked on. Tilden prodded him so much when they were freshmen that one day Marcus took him by the collar. It was in the middle of a lecture, and Tilden's allies joined in, instantly locking the entire freshman class of twenty-five—the entire enrollment of the college, before ten gradually dropped out—in a melee. Rogers did not try to pry the young men apart, which would have been fruitless. Instead, he removed a gyroscope he had just bought for the Institute and set it in motion. The boys one by one stopped their fighting. Fixing neckties and tucking in shirt flaps, they passed around the awkwardly spinning object; it was the first time they had ever laid eyes on a device like it and, they suspected, the first time any college freshmen in the country ever had. Nobody was punished for the fight—it had not gotten very far, and it would have been messy to sort out. Marcus was lucky; the college could not cook their golden geese such as Tilden, whose father was a steel magnate, but as a charity scholar Marcus was there by the grace of the faculty. It was the first and last time he had let anger get the better of him as a Tech student.

There were still almost two hours before morning courses would begin. What in the land was Tilden doing? Maybe he came for extra study time, in a desperate attempt to pass all his courses.

"That lighting demonstration went a bit out of control last night," he mused.

Marcus started back toward the Institute building as though the matter were no concern to him. "You want to clean, Tilden?"

"Probably you're wondering why I'm here."

"Not really."

"Looked to my eyes like Rogers lost control over what was happening," Tilden went on, following at his heels. "Then ran away like a coward! That cross old devil must step down before we're seen to have a cripple for a president, and I've come to write a petition to that effect and circulate it around the college. He's going to die, and when he does the whole place will die with him."

Marcus felt his stomach clench. He tried his best to master his anger.

"Come now, Mansfield," Tilden went on. "You know the truth more than any of us. We will be the first graduates, the men of '68, who will represent the Institute to the rest of the country. Rogers is holding the Institute back from where it must go, but so are you. You never belonged here. You were one of the old goat's mistakes. You were never entitled to be here with the rest of us. You were an experiment, a shipwreck, a flummux, just like that wicked witch they've put in the freshman class."

Marcus stopped walking. He placed the bag of glass on the ground and buttoned up his coat. "Rainy morning. You should go inside."

"Don't twist the subject!" Tilden tapped his finger on the button just under Marcus's raggedy cravat. "Oh, Mansfield," he said, catching the fury in his eyes, "you'd like to strike me ever so much, wouldn't you? That would impress old Miss Swallow, wouldn't it? I hear she's religious, though—no use trying anything with her. I've thought about it, believe me, with her down there in her basement laboratory, alone."

"Keep a civil tongue in your head, Tilden."

Tilden snapped his finger and thumb together two inches from Marcus's face. He had the habit of snapping, indiscriminately, to express every kind of emotion or to signify emphasis. Sometimes, he snapped finger and thumb on both hands simultaneously, sometimes one, then the other. "Do you threaten me?" he asked Marcus.

"With fair warning."

"We both know that you can't do a thing to me, Mansfield. If you strike me while on college property, by strict rule you will be immediately hauled up before the faculty and shipped off. No excuses, no exceptions. A charity scholar walks on such a razor's edge I almost feel sorry for you. A man without a father to his name."

He might have said "a man without a farthing to his name." Either way, Marcus's fists clenched.

"Have you taken good notes this term on Professor Henck's lectures on survey, location, and construction, Tilden?"

"Now there's a course that's a soft snap," Tilden guffawed. "I use it as my nap hour. Why?"

"Because," Marcus said, gesturing with a flick of his chin, "the college property ends at the well."

Tilden turned to look and suddenly paled. He turned back in time to catch Marcus's fist full in the face. He flew flat on his back into a pool of mud.

Marcus's knuckles were stained with blood and his body pulsated with release.

Tilden blotted his bloody nose and glared at him as if he were a wild beast let out of his cage. "Scoundrel! Scrubby scoundrel! I'll serve you, Mansfield, you miserable insect! I see what you are now!"

"What is that?"

"You're not one of us."

"A factory boy. I know. I've heard it from you for four long years."

"That's not all, Mansfield! Your knot is not screwed on right. There are shadows in your eyes . . ." Tilden rolled onto his stomach, grabbed a big rock, and threw it with all his strength.

Marcus easily dodged the missile, then, when Tilden pushed himself up and tried to run, Marcus tripped him back down and this time pressed the heel of his boot onto Tilden's wrist and jammed his knee into his back. "You leave Miss Swallow alone. Do you hear me, Tilden? Do you?"

"Yes! Get off me! I will!"

"Good. One more thing: Bother Rogers at your peril."

"What's the old man to you, anyway?"

"He's the only person who never tried to tell me I was not entitled to something better. And if you dare make a move against him, I'll rip your guts out." He did not let his boot up until Tilden cried out his agreement. A second more and the wrist bone would have snapped against the stone beneath it.

"Thank you, Tilden. You have a good morning."

VII

Particles

COMMISSION STOCKBROKER JOSEPH CHESHIRE walked briskly through the narrow zigzag of streets. He carried the newspaper under one arm and his walking stick angled before him to push people out of his way. An early morning rain had become snow, which had quickly begun melting, but it still hobbled the pedestrians. Mr. Cheshire was not one to bow down to weather or people. On this April morning, as every morning, he displayed the same rugged determination that had first brought him from Cape Cod to Boston as a young bookkeeper setting out to make his fortune. None of his family or friends believed he could do it. They had underestimated him. Now that he had his fortune, people still underestimated what he might accomplish. It was some kind of a curse with Cheshire—his money inspired as little respect from the business-men of Boston as his dreams had on the Cape.

That was one theory to explain the curling snarl that permanently fixed itself under the shadow of the stockbroker's long, brushed-out mustache.

* * *

PINK CHEEKS BELOW FRIZZY AUBURN HAIR, Christine Lowe had already gone to the Continental Theatre, thence by crowded horsecar to the dressmaker's to leave a package for the theater manager, thence by foot here, to the crowded business-and-banking portion of the city, toward the telegraph office. The Old State House clock struck nine-thirty. She had been at the theater until late last night and was tired. So tired. How heavy were the rings under her green eyes by now? How would she make it through the day, and another night at the theater, before sleeping?

* * *

THEOPHILUS! THEOPHILUS! His name was called constantly, summoning him to one task or another. Among the crowded rooms of bank porters, most boys thirteen or fourteen like himself, he was known for being quick, reliable, attentive—the best. He was ever on the move, head swiveling, eyes surveying the floor, up on his toes, alert. *Theophilus!* Even his unusual name helped to single him out, unmistakable from all the others moving about the middle of the bank in the middle of the busiest business-and-banking portion of the busiest commercial metropolis in America. Only occasionally did he allow himself to dream—of far-off places he had never seen, such as San Francisco—his eyes growing distant, a slight smile on his lips. Then, *Theophilus!*

When he was younger, Theophilus would run circles around the city with two of his bosom friends, pale wisps of human beings, splattered with dirt and mud, tattered coats fluttering in the wind, hungry and bored and happy as princes. They used to like this region of the city best because everyone around them was in a hurry. When men were in a hurry, they dropped small things without noticing, coins included.

Even now that Theo was a respectable fourteen-year-old bank porter, when he walked along the streets his eyes would still duck and dash for lost coins or trinkets. Not that he could stoop and pick them up anymore; the risk would be too great that his employer would spot him, or a customer of the bank, and lower their opinion of his respectability, which was a thing still only a few months old, since the day he started his position.

Back in the olden days, Theo and his friends also liked to find the bank and insurance porters and messengers a few years their senior, crossing the streets on errands, and tease and provoke them until the tormented fellows, endeavoring so hard to remain sober and gentleman-like, broke down and chased them. But Theo's very favorite hobby, to tell the truth, had been quietly observing repairs. Something was always breaking on these busy, narrow streets—wheels came off coaches that were speeding heedlessly, horses had shoes that needed urgent fixing, people fell down from hurrying and required assistance to get on their way. There was no greater pleasure for a boy than watching something in the grand process of being fixed, be it human, animal, or thing, and hoping it would be a long entertainment. Theo had turned into one of those serious bank porters now, but he still gave in now and again to his curiosities to see the repairs around the city.

Just yesterday, it was a fireplug near the bank that needed repairing. The young porter had sidled up behind the laborer to investigate the purpose for this latest repair. These apparatuses, positioned near the gutters at every few street corners, were often broken by the firemen themselves during their tests, or when being attached to their hoses. During the winter weather, too, the frost had the effect of cracking the plugs, and they would be filled with a salt mixture to prevent that.

He was well acquainted with the master of fireplug repairs who was assigned to these streets, and because of this familiarity was usually offered a close view of the activity and sometimes the opportunity to touch the hydrant's internal equipment, which was hidden to the rest of the world. When the person kneeling on the ground turned around Thursday morning, though, Theo had started, for two reasons. First, it was not his familiar acquaintance. Second, the face that met him wore a decidedly unpleased expression at the sight of him. Could a bank director be disguised as a fireplug laborer for the purposes of proving Theo's interests were too juvenile for his place at the bank? Anything was possible, so he had turned to run, too quickly to notice that the usual hydrant tubes were being replaced by a series of alien nozzles and tubing that even a boy of fourteen would have known had no place inside a hydrant box.

* * *

TRUTH BE TOLD, Christine was not born an actress. She did not even think she was pretty. She was tall, her face was long, her nose little, her frizzy hair dull, and her arms and legs skinny. But she did not let this dampen her spirits. Other girls cultivated beauty. Christine was just happy to be onstage, playing opposite handsome actors. Take her current role. She was Miss Miggs in a production of Dickens's *Barnaby Rudge*. She was better suited for it than any one of the prettier gals in the company. People complimented her on her wit, and if Charles Dickens himself were to walk by he would no doubt recognize his literary creation.

In part, that was because she remained in her costume even now, a bright-pink gown meant to demand attention and look somewhat above a servant but below a mistress. It surely drew all eyes to her as she took the narrow stairs to the telegraph office on the second floor. "There!" She could almost apply one of her lines from the stage: "Now let's see whether you won't be glad to take some notice of me, mister!"

* * *

ALTHOUGH THE COMMERCIAL QUARTER housed some of Boston's great relics of the past, here the people lived only in the present. Boston had been called an "old new city" by one of the well-known literary scribblers of Beacon Hill, and nowhere was it truer. The crisscrossing of streets, the vortex of business in the heart of Boston, was an almost impenetrable labyrinth of brick. It swallowed strangers whole, physically and spiritually, in the confusion of telegraph rooms, banks, notaries, insurance offices, tailors, and constantly newer, taller buildings, reaching six stories into the sky. Joseph Cheshire knew every street by name and sight, and he recited them to himself as he approached: Washington . . . State . . . Court. . . . Long forgotten were the days when a much younger man had gotten miserably lost in this area of the city.

Clearing space in the busy stairwell with his walking stick in his usual fashion, Cheshire entered a large office building and carried himself up to the fourth floor, kicking the filthy slush from his boots along the way.

By his calculations, the higher the floor for his bank, the safer his money. Not that he trusted *any* bank. He distributed his fortune in multiple institutions, like Hansel leaving his trail of stones after learning the bread crumbs would be eaten. He knew that his caution and precise methodology should have won him any number of friends if even the greatest men of Boston were not his inferiors in the area of pure pluck.

He took off his damp beaver hat as he entered the bank but disdained the pegs on the wall, instead looking for—

"You there!"

"Yes, sir," said the boy, running over.

"Theo, isn't it?" asked Cheshire.

"Theophilus, but familiarly called Theo," confirmed Theophilus, beaming with pride.

"Well, just so. Don't expect me to remember. Must I be expected to remember the name of every lowly porter and shop boy in the city? Hold my hat and stick, will you, while I speak to your google-eyed ugly clerk over there about my business."

"Yes, sir! Goin' to be a foul day outside, sir. Read the news today, sir?"

"About the compasses?"

Theophilus bit his lip. His question had just been for the sake of conversation, since he hadn't read the news, but he replied, "Compasses! Compasses, sir!"

"Some mysterious mischief behind what happened at the harbor, the newspapermen now report. Tell you this: Shipping business has been at an awful standstill ever since."

Cheshire took a chair across from the old clerk and thrust onto the table a sheaf of documents regarding changes in his bank account. The clerk leaned forward, mopping his damp forehead with his handkerchief, and pushed up his small eyeglasses, which had slid down the bridge of his nose.

"I have business and I expect my business to be conducted immediately, Mr. Goodnow. You can adjust your glasses another time."

Foul day outside, foul day inside Front Merchants' Bank.

* * *

THERE WAS A LONG LINE of people at the telegraph office. How many of them wanted to wire about money, like Christine did?

Twelve dollars a week from the theater and two dollars for the odd sewing job was hardly enough to pay for her boarding, plus sundry expenses, even with a roommate. Her parents, who lived in Vermont, did not have money to spare, yet they had told her to wire if she ever needed help. Instead, she set aside every free dollar she could for them, and wired instructions to retrieve it at their bank. Though this increased her financial woes, she refused to entertain gentlemen in private outside the theater, the way some of the other actresses did.

The wait seemed endless. If only she weren't in such a silly costume, she could have gone to a better telegraph office at one of the elegant hotels like the Parker House, where Charles Dickens himself had dined.

Her feet were throbbing from the walking she'd done that morning, not to mention the hours onstage rehearsing last night, and she rested her weary body on the narrow windowsill. Across, she had a view inside the Front Merchants' Bank. Her eyes skipped to the street below. It teemed with activity, and yet, from her high vantage, she could hear nothing. It seemed a tableau, as if the Bostonians below were in dress rehearsals until the curtain would rise on their drama.

* * *

THEOPHILUS HAD WALKING STICK and hat ready even before the stock commission agent finished with the old clerk.

"Here you are, boy," said Mr. Cheshire, retrieving his belongings, and fulfilling his prediction that he would no longer remember Theophilus's name. He dropped a coin to the floor, then, after careful consideration, another.

"Thank you, sir, Mr. Cheshire," said the apprentice. He knew this man could be cross if business was not conducted in the proper way.

The clerk at the desk sighed heavily as he began to organize the stack of documents Joseph Cheshire had generated in his wake. His audible consternation seemed to please Mr. Cheshire, all his desires evidently met by leaving some of his life's sundry burdens behind for others.

"Good day, Goodnow!" he called cheerfully. "Good day, boy!"

Theophilus bowed as the stockbroker exited.

Whenever he bowed to a customer, he felt again the long path he had trodden since the days of being a school truant.

* * *

CHRISTINE HAD FALLEN into a deep sleep on the windowsill, her head pressed flat against the cool glass, her bonnet pushed askew. The telegraph clerk, who on some other day would have chastised loitering, was too busy.

Perhaps she dreamed. Or perhaps she was immersed in that species of daytime sleep that blocked mental visions and instead ushered in complete blankness.

It is difficult to guess whether she consciously felt how unnaturally warm and rough the glass of the window became on her skin. Whether she heard the startled gasps throughout the telegraph office.

* * *

"THEOPHILUS! LADDIE!"

In the Front Merchants' Bank, someone was calling urgently for the apprentice, but this time he did not respond.

He was mesmerized by the most ordinary of objects—the plate-glass window. He had never seen anything like it.

The glass was changing color, first yellow, then dulling into a shade of brown, then a surprising, exuberant pink. Then, as if continuing its playful game, the glass began to change still further. It was moving, dancing, as if the particles inside it were trying to come out.

It was melting. There was no unusual heat, no fire or flame in or outside the bank that could explain what was happening. The glass had simply come to a decision to melt, and the decision was unanimous, apparently, for every piece of glass up and down the street, in windows and spectacles and on clock faces, also started to melt.

Behind him, somebody fainted. Theophilus, jaw hanging in amazement, stretched out his hand.

* * *

JOSEPH CHESHIRE, walking stick outstretched, at first ignored the shrieks behind him. The donkey masses, he thought to himself. They *should* scream, just looking at themselves and their dress and the ways they carried themselves, the ungloved–donkey–hoi polloi. But there were more screams, and people ahead of him pointing up. Some pigs barreled under people's legs to get away, knocking two ladies to the ground.

The stockbroker followed the hysterical gestures and wide-eyed stares and almost screamed himself. Up and down the street, the windows were misting, turning strange colors, and melting. The air thickened with mysterious, transparent fumes.

At the corner, the glass face of the clock swallowed up the numbers.

"God help me!" Mr. Cheshire pleaded, dropping his cane and scampering into the heart of the pandemonium toward the bank. "My assets! Out of my way!" People ran over one another, shouted for help, tripped over their own overshoes and coats.

* * *

CHRISTINE'S HEAD SANK GENTLY into the glass window as it softened and transformed into . . . what? Part of the glass seemed to be escaping into the air as gas. The remainder was turning fluid and almost waterlike, wrapping itself around the frizzy head. Her eyes popped open and she opened her mouth but her voice was already muffled.

* * *

HE HAD TO DO IT. He just had to. He was always on guard to act like a man, as ol' Goodnow forever instructed him. But Theophilus was an adventurous lad by nature, and he had to. He thrust his hand right through the liquefying window as it hissed.

When it caught his wrist, embedding itself into his flesh, he screamed in pain.

Behind him the bank erupted into chaos, customers shrieking wildly as they fled. Goodnow, as he looked to see which way to run, felt his eyes sting and bellowed. The glass lenses in his eyeglasses sank into his eye sockets and left him flailing. The tumbler on his table similarly fizzled and lost its form, pooling into a puddle of liquid glass and sending boiling whiskey pouring over the side onto the floor.

* * *

JOSEPH CHESHIRE, connoisseur of control, master of all he encountered, was knocked to the ground before he reached the bank. At around the same time, what was once a piece of a window poured down through the air in discrete drops—perhaps from the very bank that held part of his fortune.

Inside the bank, a young porter's arm was still protruding from a crush of glass folded around it.

Across the street a large projectile tumbled hard from the sky and crashed through the wooden planks of a wagon. It was a girl, in a garish pink theater costume, entombed entirely—from top to bottom—in glass.

"Well, of course it's an honor," Albert answered, glancing at Marcus for support but not finding any. He tilted his chin into the palm of his hand, a frequent habit that tended to muffle his already drowsy voice. "Mr. Hammond has done so much as a patron for our college and for the development of technology."

"Technology! Is that what you think when you see this factory?"

"Of course. What else?"

"This is science—mere science, Hall," answered Hammie.

"Mere?" Marcus asked in spite of his determination to stay out of the exchange.

"Science is a railroad car, Mansfield. But technology is what you must do when you are in a railroad car about to collide with another."

"That's not really how I see what we do, Hammie," Marcus said.

"What do you think we do?"

He considered it. "I thought something about it after listening to Rapler at the demonstration."

"That rascal doesn't deserve to be listened to!" Hammie barked.

"Technology," Marcus continued, ignoring him, "is the dignity that man can achieve by bettering himself and his society."

"When a monk invented the first clock, it was believed Satan had given it to him. That day technology began and so did the hatred for it."

"Mr. Hammond!" Albert called out across the floor, leaving behind his classmates. "Mr. Hammond, if I may express our collective gratitude for this opportunity on behalf of the Class of 1868 . . ." His words were chopped up by the chugging of a machine.

Marcus found a chance to split from Hammie as they crossed through the sheet-iron shop to the three-story machine shop, where workers were assembling the locomotive engines. The dusty stone steps they climbed vibrated in time with the machinery. Marcus's hand, which had been throbbing all morning, now felt stiff, and he knew the fingers would soon begin to swell. In Bryant Tilden's face, he had also seen Will Blaikie's grin, belittling Tech and all of Marcus's friends, and all the people before him who smiled while telling him what he was not good enough to do. He doubted whether he should have done what he had out in the fields; it was only asking for trouble to be called down on his head. But the blockhead had deserved it.

VIII

Entombed

"THIRTY DAYS. Yes, thirty. That is the time from the start of constr[u]tion to the delivery of a locomotive as of—what is today? Tha[t] you—the tenth of April, 1868. When I built the 'Nahant,' my firs[t] took nearly three months to complete. Back when all of you were har[d] babes, there were so few locomotives they could have names; now t[h] need numbers. Now, this next building we will pass through is our n[ew] copper-and-sheet-iron shop, completed two years ago. The blast is f[ur]nished from the main engine of the machine shop. Watch where you [put] your hands as you walk, gentlemen! Danger abounds on a shop floo[r."]

The speech from Chauncy Hammond, Sr., was overflowing v[ith] pride. He was leading the visiting classes from the Institute of Te[ch]nology through the Hammond Locomotive Works. As they took tu[rns] examining the cooling cylinders, Marcus was one of two members of [the] inspecting party doing his best to hide his self-conscious discom[fort.] The other one was Chauncy Hammond, Jr., whose given name al[one] made him conspicuous.

"What a bore, isn't it!" Hammie muttered one of his usual refra[ins,] sidling next to him.

Marcus glanced warily at his unwelcome companion. Hammie [had] his hands buried deep in his pants pockets. Marcus withdrew his ha[nds] from his own pockets.

Then Albert Hall squeezed Marcus aside. "Hammie, I want to [say] what a true honor it is that your, shall we say, paterfamilias would i[nvite] us here."

Hammie made a short guttural noise that Albert interpreted [as a] question.

This was the part of the day he had dreaded since hearing of the plan to visit from one of the professors months earlier. While students such as Bob and Edwin spent their college vacations exploring mines and visiting machine plants in Paris and London, he had spent the three summers since freshman year at the locomotive works to fulfill his financial obligations to Hammond, who helped pay his expenses at the college. But he had been in the engineering office, in a different building, and the position had rarely brought him back to the machine shop floor, where the workmen endured poor ventilation and longer hours.

The men with the most extreme tasks were stripped down to the waist, revealing bulging arms and chests. Continuous eruptions in the furnaces, fueled by the unseen boilers, provided the giant machines and those rushing around them with a demonic glow. Under the gas lamps and in the reflections of the light and flames in cold steel, the machine press, with a thousand moving iron organisms spread across its length, came down mercilessly on its way to flatten the molten iron. If one watched the press long enough, as he had, it assumed a mindless but also human appearance. One could not help but imagine how the slightest skewed movement would crush the machines' master in a flash.

Yet it was difficult for the visitors to resist, angling for a better look at the riveting operation, and the foreman had to shout, "Stand back!" as flakes of fire shot forty feet into the air, then fell like raindrops that sizzled at the students' feet.

Some of the students fidgeted with excitement or worry as they neared each machine, though not Ellen Swallow, covered by a veil and in a long black dress. She remained steady and upright. With her feet obscured by her dress, she seemed to be floating through the grime and dust of the works. It reminded Marcus of the first time he saw her, early in the session. Their janitor, Darwin Fogg, had just been sickened from breathing in a mixture inside the chemistry laboratory and that area, not cleaned, was in no condition for safe use for the next class. As the seniors milled about at a loss, Ellen burst through, swept and organized the laboratory, and in the space of five minutes had it ready for class. Marcus had been amazed that she knew just how to treat the chemical spill even before reaching it, presumably from detecting the distinct odor.

The iron sheets were forged by massive steam hammers, thirty-five tons each, with sixty-five horsepower, controlled by an engine fed by an upright boiler and a master engineer. The hammers came down as though propelled by an ancient god to straighten his bolt of lightning. The steam hammer could complete the task of forging an iron sheet in four minutes with one man rather than twelve hours with a whole team. The operator demonstrated to the students the finely calibrated control he had over the degree of the machine's force by placing a handful of hickory nuts under a hammer and adjusting the engine so that twelve shells were cracked simultaneously while the nuts remained intact. Invited to do so, the students consumed the machine-opened nuts, with Albert shouting for each to take only one.

Now tireless drills were twisting down again. When the tour next paused, Frank Brewer, sleeves rolled up carefully over his long sooty arms, motioned Marcus over to their old workbench at one of the drills.

Frank held on to Marcus's right hand for a moment after they greeted each other, examining it. "How is it?" he asked with concern.

Marcus pulled his hand away. Before it was even back in his pocket, he was ashamed of his reaction. What right had he, of all people, to shrink from Frank's concern? He clapped his free hand on Frank's shoulder. "I'm well, thank you, my friend. I only wonder if it is my imagination that everyone is staring at me."

"Why should they?"

"Because my classmates know I used to work on this floor. And the machine men know I don't anymore."

Frank craned his head around to see for himself, raising an eyebrow as he scanned the faces of the collegians. He shrugged and looked back at his old friend. "Well, you'd do better not even thinking of it, Marcus. Don't you see? You've accomplished it!"

"I have?"

"Look," he said, extending his long neck toward Hammie. "Just like ol' Hammie over there, you made it to the end of four years at college." He couldn't keep the note of distaste out of his voice or his sparkling black eyes, as he looked upon his employer's son.

"He's an intelligent customer, Frank," Marcus said. "He is at the top of the class."

"So? He may have much, but only because it was shoveled into him by silver spoons. A machine more than a man, told what to do and how to do it from alpha to omega. Why, Hammond financed your institute before it even had a cornerstone laid down, didn't he? Hammie will never forgive the old man for that. All the while, you've done your part through your dreadful good brains and plain industry, *finem facere.*" This, Marcus knew, was one of the law terms that so impressed Frank when overheard during breakfasts from the law apprentices who shared his boardinghouse. "I know what hardships you've been through, and even if none of your other friends ever understand, we are bound together. Marcus, how I wish we'd seen each other oftener since the summer."

"I'm afraid we're tossed in every direction with graduation so near."

"Hallo, aren't the two fellows over there those friends of yours? Bob! Edward!" Bob turned and saluted, but remained with the rest of the student group. He was passing his pen through a stream of melted iron flowing from a furnace. Edwin, who would never think to respond to the name Edward, did not notice.

"Remember," Marcus explained, with a lighthearted laugh intended to brush off their unintended disregard, "seeing these machines in action is a fantastic experience to them, even the engineers."

Frank's expression turned more serious. "You know that I thought it was a mistake for you to leave here—I never hid that. I realize now I lacked the courage you showed when you left. It's put me in kind of a brown study of late, thinking of you finishing college so soon and me breaking my back over the same workbench. I just always assumed I would make a poor fist of being anything other than what I've been. But I cannot submit to belonging to Hammond forever. I believe, yes, I know I *am* ready, Marcus."

"Ready?"

Frank lifted his chin upward and rolled his grease-lined sleeves down over his arms, before continuing. "For a better life."

All of Marcus's anxiety vanished in a flash, and he couldn't stop smiling as he grabbed his friend's hand again. "That just takes the shine off of everything else, Frank! If I could have but one accomplishment at the

Institute, it would be to prove that other men like me deserve a place there. I know you would excel at Tech. Haven't I always told you? Why, I haven't a doubt."

Frank seemed to shrink inward a bit at the bold prediction. "I hope it's true!"

"Not a word about not being able to do it. You must come to Inspection Day this time, and I'll speak to President Rogers himself after our examinations are finished. You know, they aren't bad at all, really, Frank."

"Who?"

"The aristocrat dandies and dolts—collegies." Marcus grinned.

Frank abruptly turned his back to Marcus and moved off a bit, whispering into his shoulder, "Just keep walking."

Hammond was approaching, and Marcus understood. Frank would not want the owner of the works to see him taking too long away from the machine. The businessman was short but not slim, his expressions seemingly fixed by the deep creases around his eyes and mouth. He walked past the rest of the group, who were intently watching the manufacture of the pistons.

"Mr. Mansfield."

Marcus tried to hide his surprise at Hammond personally addressing him.

"Have you yet to come upon an invention that will make your first fortune?" Hammond asked brightly. He must have thought he was smiling, but it was a Boston business smile, which to anyone else looked like a sneer.

"Not yet, sir."

"Well, when you do, you just bring it to us and we'll manufacture it." Hammond nodded distractedly in the direction of Frank. "A loyal and determined young man, that Brewer, a man born to be part of a grand shop like this. And what an honor for me to have you and my own Junior return here in this fashion, soon to be graduated from the Institute. From what I hear at the meetings of the financial committee of the Institute, your President Rogers has been highly pleased with the progress of your studies."

"I am glad of it, and thank you for your assistance."

"Perhaps your natural pluck and humility can inspire Junior a little." The magnate made no effort to speak discreetly. Hammie, close enough to hear, glowered and turned his back on his father. "I understand you managed to remove the trade-union scum from the Institute's demonstration last night. You know what I think of those fools."

When Marcus was working in the machine shop, reformers infiltrated several departments and persuaded the foremen to demand a higher wage or stop working. Hammond was overwhelmed with orders and could not afford a minute of slowed work. Despite the shop supervisor's furious protests, Hammond called the agitators into his office, asked them to write out their demands, and granted everything without argument. "Today is their day," Hammond was heard saying after the agitators exited. "Tomorrow will be ours." As soon as the contracted orders had been met, Hammond discharged all the foremen.

"Actually, it was Hammie who confronted them at the demonstration," Marcus said to his former employer. "I merely assisted."

"Is that so?" Hammond appeared to enjoy the image of Hammie's bravery, but only for a moment. "Junior seems to find the world a very shallow place, and I fear wants to do nothing but beat the devil's tattoo on it. He must come to accept that one can no longer pass success down to the next generation with a few signatures on a piece of paper. Why, property that used to remain under the same family name for generations is no more fixed than an ocean wave, now that the fortunes of a magnate and a pauper can exchange overnight. Do you know what you will do after June?"

"Not yet."

"My advice? . . . Remember, no smoking around the machine, gentlemen!" Hammond called out. "Treat machines like they are your children, and they will obey. Returning to my advice, Mr. Mansfield, which I humor myself is good for something, it is to worry not what the other fellows do. When I built the first Hammond engine by modifying the usual design, I was called reckless. It took two months to find a railroad to purchase it, but after it was in place I could not meet the number of orders that flooded in. Last year we built five hundred locomotives! These machines on the floor, every year they grow more and more powerful. A race of giants, each one with the ability of a hundred men—a thousand—yet they ask for neither food nor shelter from us. And we all may profit from it, down to the lowest apprentice, if the almighty trade unions will not prevent it. Why, look at those poor souls who were hurt in Boston Harbor last week. I have been able to donate something toward their expenses from the profits allowed by these modern machines."

"That's generous, sir."

"Money is good, but it is not all about a man. You will have many successes and reversals, my boy, but remember it is your reaction to each of them that counts for your character."

"Mansfield!" Bob charged over to his side. "There you are. Apologies for interrupting, Mr. Hammond. Mansfield, you must come outside at once! Something has happened!"

* * *

LEADING MARCUS BY THE ARM down the steps of the locomotive works, Bob, in his usual fashion, began a long story that started somewhere in his childhood, when he first was taken to visit the business quarter of the city.

As Bob's meandering tale unspooled, Marcus overheard Albert Hall holding court with two of the sophomore architecture students with a more direct account. "People trampled. Quite terrible—quite unprecedented."

"What are you talking about, Hall? About what happened in the harbor?" Marcus asked.

"That's old news! Something happened in the financial quarter, just this morning. Conny heard all about it."

"That's what I'm trying to tell you," Bob insisted to Marcus.

"Who told you, Conny?" Marcus asked, walking up behind Whitney Conant and tapping his arm.

"The old organ grinder passed by while I was out here having my smoke and blabbed to me," responded Conant.

"What happened precisely, Conny?" Marcus asked the southern student. "They had another fire down there?"

"No, no, this was no fire, nothing so ordinary. Maurice said he didn't see it, but that he heard the windows of the buildings suddenly came alive. That the most common piece of glass in the area became a deadly weapon. Well," Conant added with a dry chuckle, probably realizing how his tale must have sounded when several classmates broke out into dismissive laughter, "you know these Papist organ grinders don't have the finest command of the English language, and dwell on their superstitions."

"Can we make it to State Street on the way back, before physics laboratory?" Bob asked Marcus. "It's almost one and a half o'clock now."

Marcus thought about it and agreed that they might.

"Wait, fellows, I wouldn't," Conant interjected. "You know what President Rogers always says about being seen to be associated with anything harmful to the welfare of Boston."

Conny was right. Every time there was the occasional incident inside the Institute, when an exploding chemical or some other loud boom was overheard by some outsider, the newspapers printed a column about a "dangerous accident." Then there had been the brief public outcry over Hammie's infamous idea for a Steam Man. Since then, the authorities at the Institute had never failed to remind the students that when it came to scientific investigations, quiet and smart was better than clever and loud.

"Perhaps it's not the wisest idea at that," Edwin stammered, then changed tactics when he saw Bob was unmoved. "Bob, you haven't even had your dinner."

"Eddy, didn't you hear Conny? The windows came alive!" Bob said with a chuckle. "Surely we cannot be deprived of seeing such a sight for ourselves, dinner or no dinner. I'm certain President Rogers would agree. No more old-womanish twaddle—we're off!" When Bob Richards led you by the shoulder, there was no resisting.

Bob, Marcus, and Edwin had no trouble finding the location of the incident. A mass of people crowded at the busy intersection of Court, Washington, and State streets. The police and two or three fire companies formed a barricade to keep people out. From the back of the crowd, they could hardly see a thing, a fact pointed out with satisfaction by Edwin. Unswayed, Bob kept pushing through the dense sea of onlookers, clearing a path as he went for Marcus and Edwin.

Marcus tried asking a few of the spectators whether anyone had been

52 | MATTHEW PEARL

injured, but they all seemed too busy trying to see over and around the nearest heads, tall hats, flowers, and bonnets to answer him.

"I 'ear there were some kind of thick fumes in the air and then hundreds hurt in the blink of one eye!" one woman finally said to him.

"First the harbor, now the very streets we walk on," shouted someone in the crowd.

At every turn, they were blocked from moving closer. Any available spot to stand was filled immediately, as if they were on the sideline of a parade. There were men, women, and children who were weeping, asking whether their relatives or friends who worked nearby were safe.

"We better go back," Edwin said. "This is all for naught, Bob, and a drearier scene I've never seen in Boston. We can't get close enough to even see!"

"Give a fellow a boost, will you, Mansfield," Bob said, jumping up to reach the railing of a balcony jutting out from one of the older three-story brick buildings. Marcus stooped and let Bob push up with his heels against his strong shoulders. Then Bob heaved Marcus up with him. Edwin waved away their offer to join them. A sharp, acrid smell like rotted eggs and oranges floated on the breeze.

Their vantage point revealed an immediate mystery. Almost every window in the buildings on both sides of the streets was missing.

"What in the devil could shatter all those windows?" Bob asked. "Some kind of earthquake?"

Marcus took off his hat for an unobstructed view. "You have your opera glass?" Bob fished it out of his coat pocket and handed it to him. "Look closer, Bob. They weren't shattered. The windows in the buildings and the carriages and all the glass everywhere on the street somehow has been . . . liquefied and . . . dissolved, erased. The glass didn't shatter—it disappeared."

"There's no sign of any fire or flame that could have melted them."

"Do you smell that? Some kind of acid or chemical is still in the air." Marcus paused, watching those who had been trampled in the panic and confusion as they were lifted from the ground or supported on the shoulders of rescuers.

Bob's face turned ashen gray. He took a few steps back and let Marcus stand in front of him on the balcony, watching a seemingly rigid object being lifted by two policemen out from the planks of a broken wagon. Marcus leaned forward as far as he dared and felt a quiver down his spine as he realized it was a woman, wrapped as though with another layer of skin in a weave of cracked glass. The college students exchanged glances but were speechless.

The dead girl's eyes remained wide open in her transparent tomb. It seemed, as they watched her lifted, that her stare implored them.

"Wait a minute. Wait a minute, Mansfield, give me back the glass." Bob muttered something to himself as he peered through the lens.

"What is it?"

"That girl—I think. Yes, I've seen her before. Heavens! Chrissy, I think she's called."

"How?"

"You know sometimes I find myself in the theater, and wander my way to the third circle of seats, where, well, the friendlier sort of actresses and other young swans congregate to make fast acquaintances and a few extra pennies, sometimes selling apples or pencils, sometimes keeping a visitor from a lonely evening."

"She was one of them?"

"I only knew her to give a greeting by name, but she seemed cheery enough company. Not pretty, really, something far better. Bless her! What kind of fate for a dewy-cheeked girl! What's happening?"

"What's wrong?"

Bob lowered the opera glass, then took a breath. "Nothing, Mansfield. I thought . . . My nerves are out of tune. I don't know—it was as though everything blurred together for a moment."

"Let me see that again." Bob handed Marcus the small binoculars. "There!" The top of one of the lenses had become discolored. "Whatever caused this, there's residue still in the air."

When Bob and Marcus had climbed down to the street, they found a change in the spectators. General curiosity and annoyance had been overtaken by quick boiling anger, fast turning the crowd into a mob.

"Stay back," Marcus said, holding Edwin's arm so he wouldn't be trampled. "Edwin, what do you make of this?" He passed him the opera glass.

Edwin studied the lens, bringing it close to his face, then looking through it from the other side. "Nothing, Marcus. I can make nothing of it! Our age has an engine but no engineer," he said, dropping into a whisper.

"What?"

"Emerson," explained Edwin, closing his eyes tightly. "In a lecture I heard, he said our age has an engine but no engineer. What if he's right, Marcus? What if it's all unraveling around us? The crowd will tear us apart."

"They don't want us, Edwin," Marcus said. "Look."

The mob was heading for the policemen who blocked the way to the devastation. People began to throw bricks and rocks and to light fires in the middle of the street.

"This is Sergeant Lemuel Carlton speaking," shouted a flustered man on horseback, who moved out in front with a speaking trumpet. "You must move away immediately, or my men will be forced to make arrests! You needn't be afraid. Boston is still as safe a place as any the world over!"

IX

The View from Number 18

THE FOLLOWING DAY, across the river, at Number 18, Stoughton Hall, William Blaikie sipped his tea, puckered his lips, then tapped on the table for the college waiter.

"I changed my mind," he said, handing off the cup. "I no longer wish any tea." As the waiter took the cup away, Blaikie glanced wearily around and said, "Ten. Is that all?"

"Many of the fellows are studying for examinations, Will," answered one of the other collegians present.

"Ten men? Are there so many wretched digs in this school that we cannot manage more at a meeting of the Christian Brethren?"

"Others are frightened about what happened in the city yesterday. Perhaps we should start the meeting for those who are here," suggested a soft-spoken junior.

Blaikie ignored this. "Ten men. No wonder a weakling from Tech could think he'd get the better of a Harvard man."

"What do you mean?"

"A Christian university like Harvard should be able to muster better class feeling than this, that's what. We are declining, I say, in moral and intellectual strength. Some of our own professors teach disgusting and degrading literature, putting alien languages on the tongues of decent young men. The honor of our school is in danger. That is why an ugly duckling like the Institute of Technology—the ugliest duckling ever seen—would have temerity enough to even put up a building in Boston and dare call it a college, when it is nothing more than a resort of weaklings, which should be duly subordinated."

"Blaikie, pardon me," said the junior, "but do you not think we should begin the meeting with our scheduled business?"

"Am I made of glass? Is my skin like water?" Blaikie asked dramatically. "I know you hope to be president of the society when I am graduated, but at the moment that title is mine. You do see me sitting here? Then you would not mind postponing your electioneering until after June. Too many cooks, you know. Pardon me if I happen to personally believe, with all my soul, that our commonwealth's colleges should turn out men—not machines."

"Pardon me once again, Blaikie," the junior replied, just as mildly. "I simply do not think it very Christian to speak poorly of another institution, however odd it might be, out of some personal spite."

Blaikie rose as if to strike him across the face. When the junior stared back at him, the society president took a long breath and said, "So let us begin, shall we, gentlemen? I would like to add to our agenda a motion that college studies do not afford an excuse for nonattendance of a meeting of the Christian Brethren. We shall also discuss a request from Professor Agassiz of the scientific department to assist in refuting, using Christian principles, the increasing support of Darwin's theories among certain so-called intellectuals in Boston. Finally, if time permits this morning, we will consider two other proposals—"

Blaikie stopped in midsentence, his gaze fixed past his flock and out the window. The Brethren rose to discover for themselves what had arrested their leader's attention. Down below in the college yard, the shiny buttons and blue uniform of a Boston policeman caught the sunlight. The representative of the law was marching through the middle of campus, followed by a stout man who had the self-important air of a typical politician and, in fact, was a politician, and another man whose bulky frame required him to slow his steps every few moments to draw a handkerchief across his brow, despite the chill in the air. The more knowledgeable among those watching from all four stories of Stoughton Hall, and from behind the handsome edifice of the library housing nearly one hundred thousand volumes, and from within the university's busy administrative offices, recognized the stout man as Representative Cyrus Hale of the Massachusetts state legislature. Some of the students who had had the misfortune of being dragged into the police station after a night of drinking in Boston's less gentle neighborhoods ruefully recognized Sergeant Carlton, the blue-garbed officer, as well as his superior, Chief of Police John Kurtz.

Dozens of curious watchers wished they could be invisible among the small party on their expedition and know what exciting business had brought them onto the university grounds.

Leaving behind the curious gazes, the three visitors followed a less traveled path to the street opposite Divinity Hall and into the Museum of Comparative Zoölogy building, where they inquired after its director and were pointed to the floor below. On every shelf of the cellar, huge glass jars displayed exotic fish, mollusks, and sea urchins afloat in yellow alcohol. The air smelled of some ancient sea.

"Professor?" called the politician, his inquiry echoing ahead through the chamber. "Professor Agassiz? It is Cyrus Hale here."

There was the sound of a crash. Among the barrels and jars, the powerful figure of Harvard's chief scientist came into view, puffing a cigar. He was shaking his head, sweeping his long chestnut-gray locks behind his coat collar. His neck and feet seemed too small to support his grand head and chest. He was scolding a young man who was collecting glass from the floor.

"But it slipped from my hands, Professor," the student insisted.

"Mr. Danner, you are completely uneducated! Some people perhaps now consider you a bright young man. But when you are fifty years old, if they ever speak of you at all, what they say will be: 'That Danner, oh, yes, I know him. He used to be a very bright young man!'" Agassiz turned and nodded at the Speaker of the House without any formal greeting and without acknowledging the two men from the Boston Police.

"Hush, hold this!" he said in his thick Germanic accent, handing Hale a dead grasshopper. "Danner knocked over the poor fellow's jar. In natural history, it is not enough for a student to know how to study specimens. You must know how to *handle* them. I cannot impart this. That is my dilemma. I must teach and yet give no information. I must, in short, to all intents and purposes, be as ignorant as that boy over there picking up glass shards. Hale, did you hear what happened?" he asked, his voice rising with excitement. "There was an arson fire at the stables of the racetrack last week. A dozen horses dead—at least, they say. What a pity."

"It is a terrible loss of property," Hale said, nodding.

"Horrible!" Agassiz exclaimed with emotion. "Poor noble animals! However," he said brightly, "for years I have wished to compare the skeletons of Thoroughbred horses to those of the usual kind. I have sent one of my assistants there."

"Why, he shall be tarred and feathered for asking such a thing only days after a fire," Hale said.

Agassiz threw up his large, expressive hands. "Science is not always a safe pursuit, Cyrus! I venture to bet my student shall not return without a skeleton, even if pursued the whole way by a mob of angry jockeys. Are these gentlemen here to talk with me?"

Hale nodded.

"Fine, fine. I shall take you upstairs, and I will try to make a guess of the subject along the way."

Climbing the stairs, as Agassiz sang the second half of an old French song, they passed through several rooms of young men bent over magnifying glasses as they sorted through plant specimens. Reaching his lecture room, Agassiz proudly showed them cases filled with specimens of insects and fossils. The police chief winced as he studied a hideous dead insect with fiery red eyes.

"Did you know there are more than ten thousand fly species living among us?" Agassiz advised, upon seeing the officer's interest. Finally he sat down after his guests had chosen their chairs. "My guess is you wish to speak of my proposal to fund an addition to the museum."

"This is something else, I'm afraid, my dear Agassiz," Hale said. "You have heard the tidings about the terrible incidents of late around Boston."

The light in Agassiz's bright eyes dimmed, his interest evaporating. "Of course—I suppose nobody has been immune from hearing of it."

"The scientific knowledge needed to comprehend what has transpired is vast, and beyond the police. Yesterday afternoon, after the event that came to pass in the business district, we voted to pass an emergency measure in the legislature to engage a consultant for the police department. Nobody, even the municipal experts, has been able to properly investigate what happened. We wish the consultant to be you. Will you do it, Professor?"

"Me? Are you not aware how occupied I am currently with the museum, Hale?"

Chief Kurtz broke in. "Sergeant Carlton has been leaving notes for you, Professor, over the last week, which he says you have not answered. These are matters of life and death, happening practically outside your window!"

"Do you not think what we do here is important, *is* life and death, even if it is not written about in the newspapers?" Agassiz demanded, his round face turning a dull crimson. "How sad for a naturalist to grow old. I see so much to be done that I can never complete. Look, look, look—in that glass case behind you. Yes. See what you can make of it. Those are Jurassic cephalopods. Soon we will outrun even the best museums of Europe."

"Professor, I speak of life right here in Boston yesterday, today, and tomorrow," Hale said firmly. "You have seen these? God save the commonwealth!"

He slid a pile of newspaper cuttings across the table.

TALES OF TERROR IN THE HARBOR AND STREETS
—MORE INJURED RECOVERED—
Women and Some Men Faint of Fright as Countless Windows Spontaneously Dissolve—Fears of Plot out of New York to Ruin Boston Commerce—Damage to Shipping, Brokerage &c.—Further Particulars of the State Street Catastrophe.
Is Technology a Threat to Our Peace?

APPARENT SCIENTIFIC EXPERIMENTS WREAK DESTRUCTION ACROSS BOSTON.
Amid fears of more to come, droves of citizens attempt to flee the city limits at the same time, one bridge collapsing from excessive weight and injuring three.

A TIME OF TERRIBLE DISASTER. SCIENTIFIC CURIOSITY MAY PROVE A CURSE IN BOSTON.
WHERE IS IT ALL ENDING?

"Scientific curiosity a curse?" Agassiz laughed derisively at the newspaper heading.

Hale continued, "Chief Kurtz has assigned Sergeant Carlton to assist you with your inquiries."

"At your service," said Carlton.

Agassiz, not trying to hide his anger, exploded from his chair and circled the lecture room.

"Professor," Hale said with a mollifying smile, "I understand you are enough occupied already following your fossil footprints and such. We all were occupied in other matters. Why, I must contend with another attempt from the blasted trade unions to pass a ten-hours bill. But we have entered the midst of a true crisis, the scale of which I cannot recall."

"Me! Why come to me?"

"Is there a single man in Boston with the same mastery of all branches and departments of science?" Hale asked.

Agassiz paused very briefly before continuing to pace, showing no sign of disagreeing with the sentiment. The stalemate went on.

"The alcohol you use to preserve your specimens. We passed that measure so that your museum would not have to pay the usual duties on alcohol. Remember that?" Hale's tone was less friendly now. "We handed you a check of ten thousand dollars even when our budget was severely strained during the war. Your latest proposals for expansion are expensive ones—seventy-five thousand dollars, at least."

"So that is true. I am afraid I must rely on the generosity of the state and my benefactors, Hale. I haven't had the time in my life to stop and make money! This museum shall be the pride of Boston and of the country when it is finished. The revelations that are dawning upon mankind from the study of nature cannot fail to bring His intelligent children nearer to their Creator. Someone must counter such places as the Institute of Technology, with its unbridled quest to expand the profits of industry using science!"

"You speak of money, Professor Agassiz," said Chief Kurtz, suddenly impassioned. "Boston is no longer the town it once was. It is a true city. Investors and foreign interests already are being driven away from State Street because the banks and the brokers cannot explain to them what happened yesterday. Between that and the merchants that already left the harbor, the whole city may spiral into a state of debt, leaving none of us unaffected."

"Right now your city and your country need your help with this," added Cryus Hale. "Immediately, in fact. Stand by me, Professor, and we will continue to stand by your pursuits."

"What is it all about, anyway?" Agassiz demanded, picking up the newspaper cuttings, then tossing them back on the table. "Why is it you presume these are some kind of deadly tricks?"

"Some believe it could be an unfriendly foreign concern trying to weaken us for invasion. Others are talking of sabotage by rival commercial centers, or temperance organizations attempting to shake industry against relaxing restrictions on liquor sales, while the spiritualists claim it must be the work of the dead who communicate with them. The truth is, no rational motivation can be discerned, Professor. As you can see in the papers, it is thought science itself has gone wild and unleashed itself into the very air we breathe. The only course we have to obtain the clues we need is a study of the scientific arts behind these events, for which we stand ill equipped." Kurtz added, as casually as possible, "Sergeant Carlton had mentioned at one point the idea of consulting the Institute of Technology for advice."

Agassiz stopped pacing. He returned to his chair and glared at the two policemen gravely.

"Of course," Kurtz continued, still nonchalant, "I explained the Institute has been seen as a questionable . . . institution."

"Questionable, to say the least, Chief! I accept no student to study under me here who cannot show evidence of good moral and Christian character. Over there they will teach atheist machinists and the sons of farmers alike. The knowledge of science in such individuals cannot fail to lead to quackery and dangerous social tendencies. Do you know why that institute is so uniquely dangerous, Chief—Kurtz, is it?"

Kurtz said he did not.

"Because William Rogers and his satellites are handing the lowest classes of society the most powerful weapon, with which they could set fire to the earth if they wished. Science. They hand over the keys for rebellion. If you wish to see how science begins to be unhinged, go there! Here, in my dominion, we shall never separate science from responsibility, or from its ultimate Creator. I'm afraid," Agassiz said by way of confession, "that it is because of me that William Rogers founded the Institute of Technology in the first instance. I will accept the blame entirely and all of its consequences."

A surprised silence filled up the room. "How is it your doing, Professor?" asked Carlton.

"Rogers applied for a position at Harvard when he arrived in Boston, but as he would not relinquish his personal beliefs in that scourge of science—I mean Darwin's monstrous ideas—I refused to consider him. We are all in danger from someone so wedded to his own fancies that he would twist all knowledge to make it suit some pet theory. I understand that Rogers even hired a dusky janitor who calls himself Darwin; I'm certain only because he liked the correlation! I also understand there is now a young woman in their building, as well, which will not fail to introduce feelings and interests foreign to the proper classroom."

"The world owes you a debt of gratitude for your combat against the despicable teaching that we are descended from monkeys," Hale proclaimed.

"At the moment, we wish only to understand the scientific mischief that has been happening around us," said Chief Kurtz impatiently.

"Wrong, Chief Kurtz," Hale said. "We need to understand it *through the correct and moral means.* Not since Professor Webster of the Medical College was found to be a murderer has the public trust in science found itself in such peril."

"Then I suppose you leave me with no choice but to restore it," Agassiz said, nodding purposefully. "Sergeant—I suppose, Mr. Kurtz, you could have assigned me a captain instead, but very well, and, Carlton, was it?—Sergeant Carlton, I wish to see all of the police reports at once, and in the very order that they were composed. Methods, gentlemen, in any scientific examination, as this is, may well determine the result. One must first learn to walk in life—I shall never take to the American fashion of doing up science running. It will be that tendency that shall hasten the day of judgment to William Rogers's little kingdom. Chief, how many men are at my disposal?"

"As many as you need to do as you see fit."

Agassiz crossed his arms over his chest as a smile eased across his face.

X

Resolved

ONDAY AFTERNOON, while the other students savored their afternoon meals or played football in the fields, Marcus Mansfield stood inside the door to the faculty room, his arms draped with coats from professors and committee members as they burst into the long meeting room, some passing him a nod or salute along with their outer garments. Albert Hall, meanwhile, finished carefully positioning pencils and paper at the last places at the long table.

In the small snatches of conversation he heard, Marcus was convinced the topics prevalent among the faculty were the same as those that had consumed the students. Since the hour their classmates heard about their visit to the business district, he had been bombarded with questions from them about it. He simply shook his head, not knowing whether he had the words to describe what they had seen. Bob, usually so garrulous, paled at the questioning. Strangely enough, it was Edwin, who had not wanted to go at all, who seemed almost compelled to repeat the details over and over again to anyone who inquired. Marcus still saw the images of the frightened mob when he closed his eyes, and tried to banish them from joining the mobs already inhabiting his nightmares, the suffering multitude crammed into a basement.

The professors were chattering and gesticulating to one another with grave excitement as they filled the room. Then there was silence as William Rogers entered. In addition to the monthly public demonstrations, Rogers still conducted most of the faculty meetings at the Institute, despite his weakened health. The rest of the sundry college business he conducted out of his home: students sent to him for admonishment; papers awaiting signatures that could be delivered to and picked up from his house; benefactors calling on him to receive his personal pleas for urgent donations to the Institute. Faculty representatives, usually Runkle, the professor of mathematics, would visit every few days and · deliver the latest intelligence about the college.

As he entered, he supported himself on the arm of the janitor, Darwin, who lowered the frail man slowly into the chair at the head of the table. Only once the president was seated did the shuffling of papers and chatter resume.

"Let us call our meeting to order, gentlemen," Rogers said after getting his breath back.

Marcus, hanging the last of the coats in the closet, withdrew to a hard, low stool. Albert's stool was in the corner opposite. Every few minutes at meetings, a professor would hold up a worn-down pencil point, or an empty inkstand, or a drained glass of water or brandy, and the closer of the two charity scholars would jump.

"Everyone is surely aware of the startling events that are a source of unprecedented terror for the city," the college president began. "Neither common sense nor ordinary experience has been able to suggest any answers to the general public. The question has naturally been raised by some present whether our Institute should not provide some service in the attempt to understand this mysterious chain of events."

"Inquiries must be done, indeed!" exclaimed Watson, professor of civil engineering, slapping the table with his palm.

"Absolutely so," said Professor Eliot, "but by the Boston Police, Professor Watson."

"We are an institution devoted to science and technology, the only one of its kind so fitted up in the nation," Watson retorted. "If these disasters are the results of a sort of scientific manipulation or perversion, Eliot, as they appear to be, we cannot fail to extend our services to aid in their analysis."

"It does seem rather shameful to sit on our hands, if there is something we might be able to accomplish," said Rogers.

"My dear Rogers, you know, more than any of us, that the Institute has from the very beginning been the subject of distrust and suspicion in the public," Eliot said. "Look what is apt to happen. Whenever there is an accident with a new machine in a factory, we are inundated with letters calling on us to cease our innovations and instruction, whether or not the machine had anything to do with us. The Luddite trade unions accuse us of trying to use technology to eliminate the laborers and starve their wives and children. Simply put, our college is the most conspicuous symbol of the new sciences in Boston, and thus we become the scapegoat for any panic about science."

"What course of action would you suggest, Professor Eliot?" asked Runkle with sincere curiosity.

"Simple. That we do nothing, Professor Runkle, in this or any circumstance, that could draw unwanted attention or criticism to our institution. In the meantime, let us have confidence that the police will resolve it."

Edward Tobey, a member of the Institute's finance committee, broke in. Tobey's gentle gray eyes were worried. "President Rogers, I must state my agreement with Professor Eliot on one point. Each time there is something unsavory or dangerous associated with science, and, even worse, associated in any degree with the Institute, it becomes more difficult to find sympathetic men to give money to replenish our funds. Truly, the throwing overboard of all rusty, old, worn-out college machinery— that is what has kept me going despite all this! I have asked one of our most generous donors, Mr. Hammond of the locomotive works, to join us today to advise us on our challenges. Here he is now."

"Gentlemen," Hammond said, entering and greeting everyone with a single nod in the brisk manner of a Boston businessman. Marcus sat up straight but the newcomer did not notice his former machine man in the corner. He took his seat and began. "My Junior was one of the first students here, but others without such strong ties might not be as immune to unpleasant criticism. I'll donate to the Institute as long as I have a penny in my pocketbook, President Rogers, you know that, but I shan't be able to fund the entire place by myself. I am not a member of the college government, but I should think you must find some way to bolster your treasury to prepare during this difficult time. Sell some of these clever inventions brewed up here. Why, I'd purchase one of your confounded engines right now—say the word."

"We might also consider naming our building after a benefactor who gives, well, a certain specified amount of money," Professor Storer added. "Or we can name the various classrooms in the same way. Harvard does it."

"The financial status of the Institute is a deep and troubling matter," Eliot added. "Indeed, it may be in the best interests of everyone to strictly limit the number of young men from charitable institutions and machine shops who are welcomed in next year. We depend on the student fees for our equipment, for our very livelihoods, and the charity scholars take away from that."

Marcus and Albert traded quick glances. Neither showed any outward emotion. After all, they were present only to offer assistance, not to listen to what was said, and certainly not to have opinions.

The faculty and committeemen talked and argued over one another.

"But pray remember, we are doing them no favors!" Eliot was responding to some statement of disagreement from across the table. "Conferring degrees on factory hands will not erase who they are—they will find out soon enough when they go out into the world to present themselves as gentlemen."

"If you are on the topic, Charles," someone said in a half whisper to Eliot, "we might well talk about the young woman, too. What place will a lady scientist find for herself in life?"

"Come, come," Rogers said, taking up his gavel for silence. He passed an apologetic glance over at Marcus and Albert, then looked over the rest of the group. "Please. Gentlemen. I thank you for the suggestions. First, this is the students' building—they come to learn, we come to teach, and that shall never be a thing to profit from by renaming it, or selling the work done here. As for the charity scholars, wealth, position, and birth must no longer monopolize college education. Certainly not at my institute. This first group of boys may be something of a picked-up lot. Each a Robinson Crusoe on his own island. But they will do credit to the degrees to which they aspire—you will see. As for Miss Swallow, she may appear too frail to take such difficult courses, but not once you look into her eyes. They are steadfast and they reveal a courageous woman. She will not fail.

"Boston is in the midst of a crisis, a time under assault. Pray let us concentrate right now on the matter directly before us. There must be some way the Institute can contribute."

"Mr. Hammond has announced he will pay the medical expenses of those injured in the disasters," Tobey said. "Because of his close association with the Institute we may also, I hope, be viewed with approval by the public."

"I also hope that is so," added Hammond.

"That strikes me as ideal," commented Eliot, with a grateful nod at Hammond. "We demonstrate concern—but indirectly and staying a safe distance away from the heart of the matter."

Watson laughed dismissively. "A rather small thing! No offense, my dear Mr. Hammond—I applaud your charity. But at least we should be offering the police department the use of our equipment and resources in conducting an investigation. If what has happened in Boston represents some experimental deployment of technology, why, the mastery, the command, of the darkest reaches of scientific and mechanical arts shown may exceed even the collective knowledge of this room."

"You exaggerate the matter, surely," Eliot insisted.

"Is there a man here who can say before God he sits here today unafraid of what has happened, and what may happen next?" Storer asked.

His words cast a pall over the meeting. Even Eliot could not volunteer.

Rogers had a far-off gleam in his eye. "I can recall when I had first proposed the formation of a school of technology, my presence was requested at a meeting of the state legislature," he said. "*The New York Times* had printed a column entitled 'American Science: Is There Such a Thing?' I knew then I could never stop until such a column would not be suitable to print. Even our name proved a rather bold and controversial choice. The word *technology* was then found in even fewer dictionaries than it is today. The Speaker, a Mr. Hale, suggested the indefinite descriptions of this institute were likely thin disguise for a house of ill repute, or some other sort of sordid operation that would turn Boston into another Paris. If it *were* a brothel, would not more than fifteen boys be in our first graduating class?"

Laughter swept the room, washing away some of the tension that had built up. All except Eliot, who studied his colleagues with disapproval.

Rogers continued, in complete control of the audience even with his occasional interrupting cough. "The lawmakers finally agreed to pass our charter, but only if we consented to a gratuitous insert they called the 'public peace and harmony' clause, stating that at no time would any individual affiliated with the Institute use expertise in science to harm a fellow citizen. If we were to take part in discovering the scientific causes of these incidents, we might finally show that the kind of science we teach here helps society. That our institution, that the new men under our care, filled with the fire of modern thought, however different they might appear from those at other colleges, and the technologies we promote and teach here, will protect, not threaten, the public good. I believe in my heart we shall be safe while we pursue this policy, and in danger as soon as we abandon it. Is it not our duty to give the victims solace, by at least providing an explanation? If I could but live to see it, I hope that we might make a small but important accomplishment: that our institution be understood rather than feared so that our students can step forward into the world outside and proudly call out a promise, 'We Are Technology.' "

The words swelled inside Marcus. Only when he saw Albert's stricken look did he realize that he had lost his inner compass as he listened to Rogers and had jumped to his feet. A few professors craned their necks to look over at him standing awkwardly in the corner. Fortunately, Professor Storer was holding his glass in a manner that suggested a request. Marcus grabbed the pitcher of water and filled it.

"If I could but live to see it," Rogers repeated, in softer tones, his eyes meeting Marcus's as the student perched back on the edge of his stool. For a moment, it seemed they were the only two present, and that they were testing each other.

"President Rogers, such noble sentiments are appreciated by every man here, to a person. But I only wonder if everyone has seen the late edition of the *Transcript*," Runkle said reluctantly. "I have it right here. It seems the legislature has assigned Louis Agassiz a position as consulting detective in this matter."

The gavel thumped again to quiet the outbursts.

"Agassiz!"

"How awful!"

"Humbugs!"

The gavel's echo traveled up to the high ceiling as the outrage continued.

"That Harvard fossil, with his pickled mollusks!" added Watson.

"Agassiz despises the Institute," Rogers whispered gravely. Louder, he said, "Professor Agassiz does not conceal his wish that I—and our college—will fail."

"Indeed," Runkle said, nodding. "I fear any involvement we attempt now, any assistance, however well-meaning, will be twisted by Agassiz. If we stepped forward and anything were to go wrong, the Institute would be harshly blamed."

"There is nothing new in that," said Eliot sadly, eager now to prove his points beyond a doubt. "Nothing new. When I was a student at Harvard, my very interest in chemistry made me an outcast, and later Agassiz refused to allow me to teach it there. The Institute is on the verge of leading the way to a new age of scientific acceptance among the public, and we cannot risk delaying that. Agassiz will listen to nothing we say, regardless. We must protect ourselves and the Institute, first and foremost!"

"Thank you, Professor Eliot. Let us put the matter to a vote," Rogers said, regaining his composure. "Those in favor of the Institute insulating itself from any scientific inquiries involving the recent disasters, indicate your vote now."

Eliot raised his hand high in the air before Rogers had completed his sentence. Professor Watson, his angular cheeks reddened, crossed his hands across his chest and wore an expression of stubborn resistance. One by one, hands around both sides of the table were brought up, some assertively, others bashfully, until all but a few of the men present were showing affirmative votes on the motion. Marcus looked on, dumbfounded, as Rogers gingerly lifted his own hand.

"The ayes have it, then," Eliot crowed. "Resoundingly." He looked around as though expecting gestures of congratulation.

"The Massachusetts Institute of Technology faculty, students, and employees will hereby refrain from any involvement in these matters, and the committee shall censure with forceful action any who shall defy this agreement," Runkle said, by way of dictating minutes of the meeting to the appointed secretary.

Marcus was crushed by the decision.

"Well? What are you going to do?" These words, hissed from the mouth of Albert Hall, broke his trance.

"What?"

"The hats and coats. What are you planning to do, wait for them to return themselves? The meeting is at an end." Albert shook his head. "No wonder Eliot speaks of eliminating the position of the charity scholar, with you as one example!"

* * *

THE INSTITUTE'S FRONT STEPS appeared imposing to the outsider. But it was a monumental place to Tech students—a central gathering place, a meeting point, an outdoor dining room, the public debate forum. Near the middle tread of dark granite, Edwin Hoyt had propped his notebook on top of his Bible and was making notes between bites of his afternoon meal. He had conceived a new hypothesis: Heat did not, as believed, emerge from the vibration of molecules. If he could work it out, the topic could form a crucial part of the senior dissertation he was finishing. The intense mental exercise, moreover, helped put the ruins of State Street out of his thoughts. He had probably spoken about it too openly to his classmates, but maybe the more people who knew what he saw Friday—the panicked mobs, the injured lifted into ambulances, the screams of worried family members—the less it would be his responsibility to carry around.

This afternoon was pleasant, if chilly, though the Tech senior preferred to eat on the steps even when a dark sky or a rumble of thunder counseled against it. It gave him a valid excuse to keep his hat on, anyway, over the patch of salt-and-pepper at the back of his head of tangled hair. The truth was, it would have lent him a dignified air if not for his awfully boyish face and frame. Nobody at school really noticed anymore, but the taunting by Will Blaikie on the river brought back memories of past torments when he had first started at Tech. Not from Marcus Mansfield—never Marcus, who had seemed to Edwin from the first to be more man than boy, not simply because he was a few years older—nor did he have to suffer any teasing from Bob, who was too bewitched by his own majestic curls to notice the flaw atop someone else's head.

After the initial hazing, Edwin had considered himself friends with almost everybody at Tech, and for that matter almost everybody else. He never imagined having an enemy, and yet he knew in a way that reflected the chief deficiency in his own character: He did not possess the bravery to proclaim his beliefs or challenge those of others.

If he did have an enemy—no, a rival—it would have to be Chauncy Hammond, Jr. Not personal, but strictly academic. The two were forever neck-and-neck for the top class rank of the '68 boys. The rivalry was more acute in the eyes of others than in the hearts of the contenders, though the whole college wondering who the first Top Scholar of Tech would be could not but alter them, especially with graduation approaching. Edwin's natural reticence was deeply jarred by knowing he was a subject of any gossip. This was the same young man who unconsciously left a little of every meal he ate so that he would not appear gluttonous.

Edwin's personal determination had been fired his first year at the Institute, the sophomore year for the Class of '68, when President Rogers had proposed that the students create scientific demonstrations out of proverbs or sayings. Edwin had worked with a team that put out a well-liked version of "too many irons in the fire." But Hammie, voluntarily toiling alone, filled a porcelain teapot with a third water, a teaspoon of chlorate of potash, three minuscule shavings of phosphorus, and a healthy quantity of sulfuric acid poured through a clay pipe to the bottom. A storm of hissing, popping, and explosions resulting inside made Hammie's "tempest in a teapot" the undisputed victor. As Edwin watched the accolades, his own aspirations grew—not only to be scientifically correct, but to achieve scientific imagination.

The tempest in the teapot turned out to be Hammie's peak, bringing him good will and popularity. A few months later, at another college-wide assembly of demonstrations, Hammie had grandly proclaimed he would usher in a new age and announced plans for building a "steam man." The steam-powered machine would be made of various metals in the shape of a man, with a complicated series of mechanisms that would allow the metal being to pull a carriage or complete other tasks with the strength of twelve horses. Even the technological mavens of the Institute, students and instructors alike, were confounded by Hammie's intricate scheme to invent an artificial worker and his insistence that such "men" (he used this term, despite loud objections and a silent shudder in Edwin's own soul) could ultimately not only save their human masters immense pain and labor, but also prevent future scourges of enslavement such as the one that had led the nation into war.

"Man is nothing without steam, nothing more than animals, anyway. Steam has given us the power of machines; now we must give machines the power of free force and movement. The iron men will be joined by iron oxen and iron horses to plow all arable land so no child will ever again starve and no man live in poverty. Carlyle says, our era, if we must give it a name, is not the Heroical but the Mechanical Age!" Hammie intoned portentously at the conclusion of his presentation, standing in front of his diagrams in the large hall. From that point on, Hammie was an oddity, at best, and would never regain a favorite, or even comfortable, status among his peers. When his idea was somehow discovered publicly, the Institute was written about in newspapers as far away as London, warning about their secret plans to diminish humankind with artificial beings, starting with the worry, of all things, that the ugly steam men would be put in hotels in the place of comely chambermaids. The steam man was held up in religious sermons to preach against the dangers of science, and used in magazine fiction to entertain juvenile readers.

If Edwin could work out his new theory about heat and molecule vibration, he thought he could beat Hammie by a hair—although he reminded himself that it did not matter one brass farthing who was at the head of the class. He was not at Tech to *win* anything or to prove himself to others, but to be a scientist. He had started his college career at Harvard, enrolling in the science curriculum overseen by the celebrated Professor Agassiz. When the bashful freshman quietly chafed about learning chemistry through memorization of theories from books, rather than in a laboratory, Agassiz scoffed and noted that Harvard was not a place of "practical education" and would not tolerate a desire for "industrial science." "You are totally uneducated, Mr. Haight! Yet you presume to question my methods?" When Edwin later expressed sympathy with theories held by Charles Darwin, and the idea that science, just like the species, would have to change and advance to survive, Agassiz asked him pointedly if he believed in God.

"Professor. I have carried a pocket Bible since I was twelve. But didn't God make the world a workshop for us to discover all His earthly machinery?" Edwin asked earnestly.

There was nothing personal in Agassiz's exclamations and outbursts—he would often forget a student's name or substitute one pupil's name for the other as he did with "Haight" for "Hoyt." Yet Edwin found himself, as some kind of punishment, locked in a room filled with turtle shells, with no teacher, where he was expected to classify the markings on each and, in doing so, recognize some higher truth. Edwin grew certain during that first year that what he sought existed only at the new Institute of Technology he had read about. Of course, Agassiz would be furious at the defection. He and Rogers had had six public debates on Darwinian evolution at the Society of Natural History several years before. Even those who sympathized with Agassiz's position admitted that Rogers won these contests. He had remained calm and collected, methodically presenting scientific fact, while Agassiz was quick with his temper and insults, thrown into an absolute fury when he was speaking and Rogers shook his head in silent disapproval. Patient and irresistibly tranquil, Rogers seemed almost to trick Agassiz into admitting several errors key to his whole argument. He used his own guns against him.

After being examined by President Rogers, Edwin was permitted to skip freshman status and left Harvard to be placed with the Technology Class of 1868.

The only part of the sublime Tech schedule Edwin dreaded as a sophomore was Military Drill Day, which the Institute was required to conduct for freshmen and sophomores as the price for receiving a federal grant for their plot of land. After the first session, Edwin nearly decided he had made a mistake leaving the comfortable Cambridge confines of Harvard. The dusty marching, made worse by the sandy wasteland surrounding the college, severely irritated his throat, nor could he keep pace with his faster classmates. Marcus Mansfield, whom Edwin had encountered briefly in the laboratory, had been exempt—having already been a volunteer for the army during the war—but he went outside and helped Edwin with the formations, earning the younger man's eternal gratitude.

"You know Greek and Latin," Marcus said casually one day as he coached him.

"How did you know?"

"Oh, Bob Richards. He said you two were in the same preparatory academy together before college."

"Yes, though I never thought he noticed me. Not that he was a snob, mind you! Only, I wasn't the most popular boy at our academy."

Though his countenance resisted reading, Edwin suspected Marcus was timid about what he really wanted to say.

"*Technology.* I've wondered about it—about the word," Marcus finally murmured.

Edwin didn't make Marcus say more. "*Techne* means 'art,' *logos* can be interpreted as 'sciences.' The science of the practical arts, you might say."

"Thank you, Mr. Hoyt."

"Edwin. Please call me Edwin. May I ask you something? They say you were on the machines."

"Who did?"

"Well, I think his name is Tilden. I gather he's a friend of yours."

Marcus smirked. "Only for a few minutes as freshmen."

"Will you tell me what it feels like to have the machine in your power?"

"Monotonous. Every year the machines improve, and there is less and less to think about in their operation. At first, it becomes a part of you, then you become a part of it."

Now, as Edwin grappled with his ideas on heat, something new was in the air at Tech. In the long corridors, talk turned to the future with the slightest prompting. So much would be finished. There would be no more convening at the start of a new year teasing friends about new styles of neckties and mustaches. No more summers volunteering for mining companies or in a naval yard, surveying caves and mountains, inspecting the construction of ironworks or paper mills. No more sitting on these hard steps. Soon—in two months—they would leave the Institute and begin life after college, what they had worked toward these last four years. A college term had never passed so swiftly. The members of Tech

'69, '70, and '71 looked on with special interest, envious of their positions but also thankful Edwin and the fourteen other '68 boys—*men,* perhaps, maybe *gentlemen,* daresay—would be the pioneers. The most daring experiments produced from the Institute so far: graduates.

Marcus carried out his tin of food. He sat down with a nod as Edwin made room next to him. He looked almost as distracted as Edwin was as they both stared out into the fields. Their company alone put each a little at ease without having to say a word—about the reluctant rivalry with Hammie, on Edwin's mind, or about whatever it was that made Marcus appear as if he had just seen a ghost.

"I suppose we should go secure our seats in Watson's class," Edwin said after a while, checking the time.

"It's begun," Marcus whispered.

Edwin was about to object, looking at his watch again, but then heard the footsteps approaching and looked up, nearly dropping the heirloom in his hand. A dozen, maybe fifteen, blue-garbed policemen were heading right toward their building in a double-quick march.

XI

Plymouth

WILLIAM ROGERS HAD CHANGED HIS LIFE, had shown himself the most original man Marcus had ever known, had built an institute that could be the pathway to the future for the whole country. Still, he was wrong this time, wrong to yield to Eliot and the others. *Rogers was wrong.* The words finally confronted Marcus as he rode back to Newburyport that evening. They were not easy words to come by, even contemplating them silently to himself, and he realized they had never before appeared in his thoughts.

No institution in existence had the resources Tech did to inquire into scientific causes. They were even preparing the first laboratory of physics in the country. Perhaps offering to help would indeed provoke criticism from those who distrusted any new sciences, but what if it did? Was it not worth it in order to identify the scientific means that had led to such unthinkable acts? Was that not their moral responsibility?

Now Agassiz had turned the police into his puppets, no doubt directing their visit to the Institute. The entire afternoon, uniformed men wandered up and down their halls, interrupting classes to ask professors what they were teaching, standing at the back of the laboratories as students tried to concentrate on their experiments, obstructing freshmen on the stairs and asking at random if they had learned anything "dangerous," "strange," or "suspicious" lately. Albert Hall shook in his boots as one patrolman leaned over his shoulder, poking confusedly at his test tubes and beakers.

"And what's this?"

"A blowpipe," Albert said meekly.

"A *what?*"

"It's an instrument that safely communicates gas into a mixture," Albert explained.

"What's in this one now?" another of the policemen said as he recklessly picked up a glass crucible at Hammie's station.

"Nothing much," Hammie said, with a lurking grin. "Sulfur and saltpeter. I've just mixed it."

"Well!" the policeman said, unimpressed.

"Here," Hammie said. "You may add this dash of carbon to it if you like."

"Perhaps that's not the best idea," Marcus said, swiping the vessel Hammie was reaching for from the shelf. Then he whispered aside to his classmate, "Are you mad, Hammie?"

"How?" Hammie replied defensively.

"Sulfur, saltpeter, carbon? You're about to have him manufacture gunpowder!"

He didn't deny it. "They deserve a little explosion," Hammie said, sulking.

Hammie aside, most of the students and professors tried to go about their business as though everything were normal. There was no indication the police would come back again the next day, but to Marcus the passivity of the faculty was unforgivable.

When he calmed down enough to open his notebook to study during the train ride back to Newburyport, a note slipped onto his lap. It was a sketch of the Charles River exquisite enough to have been rendered by a professional surveyor. At the bottom, in Bob's hand, it indicated to meet at seven the next morning. Marcus sighed—he did not know if he had much taste for rowing after their last time out and after all the serious news since. But before the train reached Newburyport, he had decided he would meet Bob, as requested. He had not talked about the faculty meeting with Edwin as they ate their dinners on the steps—Edwin appeared occupied enough, and Marcus still was contemplating the debate he had witnessed. But he would talk about it with Bob.

Though his personal circumstances could not have been more different from Marcus's, Bob had made Marcus feel as if he understood him from the first time they spoke. They had been freshmen, but more than that, since they were the first class and therefore the only students. They considered themselves princes, involved in the greatest overthrow of an old and worn-out system since the destruction of tea in 1773—in this case, the classical education they and their professors were kicking out the window.

In those weeks after the Institute opened in temporary space rented from the Mercantile Library while the construction of the building was under way, Marcus had habitually found an empty corner of the lecture room in which to sit alone and do his work during dinner. His stepfather hadn't been too far from the mark when he had predicted that, whatever Rogers promised to the contrary, nobody would want him at the college. "Factory boy! You there, factory boy!" This time the taunt was issued not in a sneaking whisper but in a booming, unapologetic voice. Still, Marcus wouldn't turn his head. A paper dart glided over him and landed rather gracefully between his boots. He picked it up and studied it. "Notice the lower corners are folded up to the middle—that provides far better flying velocity. My own design. My governess looked like a porcupine by the end of a lesson, with her hair filled with these—but then again the old girl looked like a porcupine without help." Marcus now faced a tall, handsome young man, with an air of brashness and familiarity in his wide smile, as though the two young men had known each other all their lives.

"Is that really what they've been calling you?" the stranger went on. "Factory boy? Is it intended to be insulting? Goodness! I'd as soon walk through fire as take that as an insult." Marcus asked the stranger why. "It means you'll be more of a machine man than any of us can learn to be from a classroom," the young man said blandly, stretching his hand out. "Mansfield, right? Bob Hallowell Richards, by the way. You are the one who took Tilden by the neck. He is jackassable. I've been wanting to do the same thing since we were five years old. They are afraid of you, old boy, only because you belong here. Fellows like me, on the other hand . . . How my father would toss and turn below the dirt of Mount Auburn to know I chose the Institute over Harvard. Here, have one. Not a smoker? Well, come anyway—you can finish my dinner while I have a puff before mechanical drawing."

"What makes you think I want your dinner?"

The truth was, he was living on about a dollar a week. He had to spend most of his small store of money on the books and papers he needed for classes, and food was the first thing he sacrificed, since his stepfather deemed his lodging enough charity.

"I know because I watch. That is what I do and have done since I was a boy, spying on the habits of the birds and animals, before long learning what every twitch and movement of the frog's eye meant. You take small bites from the same biscuit throughout the day."

"I'm not a frog," replied Marcus bitterly.

"Understood. You aren't letting me go alone, right?"

* * *

Now HE WAS FOLLOWING Bob Richards again. Marcus arrived back in Boston safely before the appointed hour and followed the map along the riverbank. He thought he was at the approximate meeting spot, but did not find Bob or Edwin or the shell and he was about to give up. Then a hand shot out of the bushes, pulling him down and in.

"Quiet! Stop breathing so loudly, won't you, Mansfield?" came a whisper from low in the thicket.

"What are you doing, Bob?" Marcus asked, then stopped when he heard a noise. "Why is he here?"

A few feet away, Hammie also crouched in the grass. Hammie's distinctive silhouette was easily identified even in the low light of dawn.

"Eddy wouldn't come and I needed a third hand for my operation," Bob answered. "Hammie was the perfect choice."

"I thought we were rowing!"

"Now, keep calm, Mansfield. Don't grow warm with me this morning. It's an important and, moreover, *just* cause."

"You know with graduation so close I cannot afford even a trifling breach of order, much less whatever it is you're planning with *him*. That lunatic nearly tried to blow up a policeman yesterday for sport!"

Bob motioned him to keep his voice quiet and looked over at Hammie, who was occupied sorting through a chemical case and did not seem to have heard.

"I told you to come out for your benefit alone," Bob insisted.

"Mine?" Marcus asked skeptically.

"I didn't want to deprive you of any pleasure, old boy. Does that surprise you, even after four years of bosom friendship? Don't worry—if we're caught, I'll tell them you and Hammie tried to stop me. You'll be heroes!"

"I don't want to be a hero," Marcus grumbled.

"Then just enjoy the scenery," Bob said, peering down at the river before turning back to Marcus. "Besides, if they find us and start a set-to, I'll need you. Eddy's too much of a dig—he would run away. You know his blasted philosophy in life is live and let live and wait for God to sort it all out. He's a noncontroversialist. Not you. I heard you finally used Tilden up; at least that is what the rumor-mongering freshmen say. I wish I could have been there. One thing, though. He can lie and tell them you struck him on college property, you know."

"I don't think he will. He'd have to admit he was licked, and he wouldn't do that, even if it meant my being shipped off."

"Lucky God gave you the fists of a prizefighter!"

He bowed his head. "I'm not proud of striking him. Well, maybe a little. I was mad as thunder, Bob."

"Say, what puts you in such a brown study this morning? That little social call yesterday from the men in blue?"

"There was a faculty meeting yesterday before the police came. Albert Hall and I were assigned to help there."

"So? You go to one almost every week, don't you?"

"The police can make nothing of the events of late. And yet, when it came up, the faculty voted not to do anything about it. Not to even try to help."

"Repeating myself: So?"

"Squirty Watson made some noise, but I think he rather enjoys disagreement, more than it being a matter of conviction. Bob, even Rogers voted to do nothing. Rogers! I have lost my respect for him."

Bob looked at him with genuine surprise. "Truly?"

"Yes."

"Think of it this way, Mansfield. Tech cannot afford to create a scene in Boston any more than you can afford to create a scene at Tech. Do you see?"

Marcus swallowed hard. "There must be something to do."

"What?"

He tossed his hand in the air. "I don't know. But even when we sit and do nothing, the police are still sent to bother us."

"What difference does it make?"

"It makes a difference because of the principle of the thing—those who embrace the new sciences, who experiment forthrightly and dare search for truth, will be seen as harboring secrets and dark intentions. Science explains so much, anything unexplained is pinned to it."

"There will be time to show them what we are really all about. Remember how close we are to graduation—they are right to protect our college until then. They are professors and not policemen."

"I suppose I was hoping you would convince me."

"Have I?"

Marcus thought about it, then smiled. "No."

"Mind and Hand! You have it in spades, by heavens! You never could watch the sun go up without trying to push it along. When we march out the college doors for the last time, I'm following you, Mansfield!"

"I haven't a clue what I'll do."

"No matter what, I'll be by your side."

"I'll still be a former factory hand, even with a diploma. I may have to go far away from here to be given a position."

"Wherever!"

"Say I'll go to Japan."

"I'll be there!"

"India?"

"Skipping through the poppy fields!"

"I don't think I'll go to those places."

"Just you wait, Mansfield! There's Cuba, too. We'll go to the ends of the earth, you and I!"

"Well, right now, I have to get to the Institute to study. The train from Newburyport was late last night, plus I hardly slept—my thoughts would not rest."

"Your thoughts, or your dreams?" Bob asked.

Marcus turned to Bob with a questioning look.

"I've seen it, you kicking and tossing in your bed," said Bob, "the times we've shared a room, or after you've fallen asleep on a train. Is it scenes from the war you see?"

"Your imagination is too vivid, Bob."

"Wait!" Bob grabbed his arm when Marcus began to rise. "Why not stay with me in my rooms at Mrs. Page's through the end of examinations?"

"I cannot afford to pay my share."

"Pay! What nonsense. You know I spend half the nights at Mother's, anyway."

"If you are certain . . . It would be an immense help for the busy season."

"It's settled, then. Be a good fellow and stay for the performance, though, won't you?"

Marcus reluctantly crouched back down as payment for Bob's generosity. "What is it he has there?" He pointed to the instruments Hammie was arranging.

"An element," Hammie interjected, as though he had been part of the conversation all along, "that would not be protected from explosion by remaining isolated in water, but prompted to one."

"Sodium," Marcus answered the riddle.

"Bravo, Mansfield."

"Pure as could be," Bob added, beaming. "I happened to have asked around, furtively, mind you, about Will Blaikie's practice schedule for his Harvard six. The worthless scamp is very protective of it, afraid that Oxford has secret agents here, I suppose. . . ." He held out his palm for silence and inclined his head to the water. "They're coming! Do you hear that? Hammie, old boy, get ready! No, that's not them," he said with disappointment. "Hold it, Hammie."

"Bob, you cannot seriously—" Marcus began.

"If we're to be graduated!" said Bob.

"What?" Marcus asked.

"Did you hear the squirtish little miser Blaikie say that out on the river? *If* we're to be graduated. As if the future of Tech were some kind of fairy tale. Wouldn't you like to fix his flint?"

Marcus tried to think of a good answer, but knew his silence gave him away.

"Then you will do it! Do you remember what that graceless scoundrel called me out on the river?"

"No," Marcus said.

"You lie, and I thank you. But he called me 'Plymouth.' When I was at Phillips Exeter, I was always at the foot of my class. Studying Latin and Greek was to me like hitting my head against a stone wall. When I asked *why* I should study them, I was told that was the way people like me were educated. But I was a misfit, and had no facility for learning dead languages. No matter how many tutors were thrown my way, I liked climbing around the floor of the forests and studying rocks, not books. One fine day, I was asked to tell the class where the pilgrims had landed, as we had been assigned to read about. I froze. 'On the shore, sir,' I finally replied. This brought down the house, as you might imagine, and I can still see Blaikie's grinning phiz right in front of me. He called me 'Plymouth' ever after to memorialize the moment. I did not know Eddy well back then, for he was an out-and-out dig, and I was well known as a bird, and digs and birds do not mix at Exeter. But he never called me that. I secretly loved that little fellow for that.

"My examination for admission at Harvard was even more distinguished. They asked me to translate the first three books of *The Iliad* on sight. How I stared at Felton's *Reader* until the old blind poet was my mortal enemy! Rejected by Harvard, even with the Richards name."

"Rejected," Marcus repeated, then stopped himself.

"I know, I know. I might tell people now and again I turned them down, but it's a cowardly lie. However brave dear Eddy might think me, he was the one to go to Harvard and decide Tech was the right place for him instead. To give up such a guarantee of position and respect in order to pursue a passion the world thinks is worthless—there is courage! I have always been the stupid one in my family, Mansfield, the dunce of every school, and since my father died it was assumed to be my brothers who would carry on the family success. My rambles in the woods and by the river, watching the habits of birds and animals, and studying the earth formations, these were my shameful delights.

"Because President Rogers's wife is my mother's cousin, Rogers had urged Mother to consider his new college for me. At Tech, well, finally

I found mathematics, languages, and history were nothing but a means to the end. I had always tried to study because I knew I ought to *want* to study, done only from love of Mother. Now I study because I cannot help it. The first days at Tech captured me body and soul. You see why I have to make Blaikie pay for running down Tech."

"What is the plan?"

"Hammie has done calculations on the water current, Mansfield. Don't worry—we know just when to drop—" He held one hand out again as the bandannaed Blaikie and his grunting oarsmen flowed into sight. He now looked down at a gold pocket watch, which lay next to an open notebook with a messy list of scrawled calculations in Hammie's oversize handwriting.

"Now!" he hissed and Hammie promptly used a modified slingshot to launch a solid mass into the middle of the river, then a second one, right by the Harvard shell. All three students on shore held their breath, Bob taking up his opera glass. He usually kept the device on him to spy on the Catholic girls' academy located a few lots down from the Institute building, and had replaced the one so peculiarly damaged on State Street.

At first, the Harvard shell rowed on in its usual grandeur. Then a blinding, fiery ball exploded out of the water like a rocket. Three of the rowers dropped their oars; one shrieked, and another yelled something about war breaking out. Blaikie shouted for order, but then another rapid pair of dull booms followed by explosions burst simultaneously on the other side of the shell, and on the first side, yet a new round of eruptions. The whole river seemed on fire. The shell tipped as half the boys tried to steer away from the fires and half tried to lean their bodies away. The team tumbled headfirst into the frigid waters below.

"Mind and Hand!" Bob bellowed. "Mind and Hand!" The words echoed up and down the river.

Blaikie pulled himself up to his chest onto the overturned boat, as his dazed crew flailed and coughed up water. The stroke oar scanned the river on all sides, but could see nobody and heard only the sounds of distant spasmodic laughter.

"Tech," he said, spitting out the word. He pounded his fist on the boat bottom. "Technology, I'll be satisfied, upon my word! I'll be satisfied, do you hear?" He was so overcome with fury his speech slurred, sending such a paroxysm of joy through Bob Richards and Marcus Mansfield that they could hardly take his next proclamation seriously:

"You've dug your grave now, Tech!"

XII

Temple Place

THE AIR OF MISCHIEF CLINGING TO THEM, the three seniors slipped quietly through the double doors leading into the chemistry laboratory. They were two minutes late for class by Bob's watch, three and a half by the tall clock in the polished oak case at the end of the corridor. They had left the river with ample time to spare, and had rid themselves of any sign of having spent the morning in the thistle and brush, but the horsecars had been delayed by a cow on the tracks, who was impervious to the shouts of the conductor. By the time the animal was dragged to another spot, they lost nearly ten minutes in their journey. By any reasonable clock, at least, they were well before the five-minute-late mark, a milestone that would come with a report to the faculty committee.

The other seniors were arranging their instruments at their tables. Marcus and his friends were pleased that Professor Eliot was writing instructions on the blackboard and had not yet begun the lesson. As they entered, Eliot's sharp eyes followed Marcus from behind his small wire eyeglasses.

"Mr. Mansfield."

Marcus and Bob had just taken an empty table near the back. Hammie was one table up.

"Sir," Marcus responded to the professor, rising.

Eliot exhaled through his nose. "Mr. Mansfield, wait in the corridor to speak to me privately."

"Sir?"

Bob and Hammie exchanged guilty glances. They had arrived late together. Yet only Marcus was to be punished. Hammie fidgeted with the cover of his notebook.

"Professor Eliot," Bob blurted out.

"You have something to say about the oxidation of red phosphorous, I presume, Mr. Richards?" Eliot responded impatiently. "Then sit back down."

"But, Professor—"

"Bob," Marcus warned him off.

"But, Mansfield, it's not fair!" he whispered.

"Mr. Richards, pray sit down!" Eliot rapped the table with his hand for silence. Impressively tall and slender, his youthful looks at thirty-five made him appear only slightly older than his pupils, an impression he tried to minimize with a set of long muttonchops. "You men have too much to accomplish to act as fools. Mr. Mansfield, you are here still?"

"Just leaving, sir," Marcus said, peeling off his apron.

"Good. Leave all that behind. Mr. Richards is obviously a devoted friend; he can collect your belongings for you. You may report directly to Temple Place to President Rogers. Immediately, Mr. Mansfield."

Marcus hesitated again, a bit stunned despite trying to take it stoically. As he took in his surroundings, everything seemed to come to a momentary stop. His eyes fell on the sign that read SMOKING IN THIS LABORATORY IS STRICTLY FORBIDDEN—with residue where students had repeatedly marked out SMOKING and painted in its place their revisions, SLEEPING, LAUGHING, FALLING IN LOVE. Beyond this, a shelf with extra burners and tubes, then a row of goggles for the protection of the eyes, which were rarely ever touched. Tilden grinned at Marcus under the thick bandage ornamenting his nose. Then there was Albert Hall, shaking his fat head with superior disapproval. Before Eliot could look back in his direction again, Marcus fled the laboratory.

He stopped on the stairs for a moment to compose himself, when he heard a deep but feminine voice. "You are in my way and I would be obliged if you moved."

Marcus turned around to face Ellen Swallow, standing over him on the landing, a test tube in her hand. She wore her large apron over a severe black cotton dress that appeared to be homemade, from a simple pattern. Her home-sewn dark clothing made her look like a farmer's widow instead of a twenty-five-year-old Boston woman.

"I am sorry, Miss Swallow."

"And I haven't any use for apologies either," she said, then scanned him head to foot, one long eyebrow sharply arched, followed by two blinks. "You have had a mishap in your chemical manipulations class."

Marcus stared at her for a moment before replying. "You heard?"

She tilted her head to the side in birdlike fashion. "You mistake me for someone with whom gossip is shared. I have heard nobody talk. But it is the hour for the seniors' chemical manipulation class, yet here you are, distinctly in my way, wearing a despondent air. Observe, record, collate, conclude: That is what we are taught to do with facts." She cleared her throat loudly. She was studying a transparent liquid in the test tube, tapping the glass, which caused a group of purple globules to rise and fall. "Whenever something goes wrong among the freshmen, I am reliably blamed and censured."

He detected a note of sympathy in her voice that he wished to return. "Freshman year can be trying indeed," Marcus responded. "If you should ever need assistance, please do not hesitate to find me."

"Sir, I haven't any use for assistance, either. If you insist on speaking with me in the future, I shall call for your reprimand from the faculty. I am not meant to mix more than necessary with men in our school, you know. Nor the boys. Good morning." Before he could reply, she was away and down the stairs.

It was a long walk across the Public Garden to the other side of the Boston Common and on to the president's house, but he went by foot instead of waiting for the busy horsecars. He could not bear to look into the faces of any other human beings at the moment. He craved only solitude.

He could not blame Bob. After all, Marcus had relished the stupid trick against the Harvard swells. Nor could he entertain too hard a grudge against Eliot, who perhaps had really believed Marcus had entered later than his companions. And what Eliot had said at the faculty meeting the day before about the bleak fates of a charity scholar haunted him, not out of anger but because he had thought the same things to himself so many times before.

* * *

HE WAS ADMITTED into the Rogers home by the same pretty chambermaid he had seen assisting Rogers at the public demonstration, but she showed no sign of recognition. As she led the way through the vestibule, he handed her his hat and his gray unfitted tweed overcoat with the increasingly shaggy fur collar, as though surrendering them were part of his punishment.

"I have been sent to see President Rogers," Marcus said to her sheepishly. "I am a student at Tech—the Institute."

"Wait here," she said, without looking up at him.

She disappeared up the stairs, leaving him standing awkwardly in the long vestibule, neatening the part in the middle of his hair. When it came to discipline, a student sent to Rogers for a private admonishment knew it would not be a scolding, but rather a conversation, one man to another. Because of this, by the end of the encounter, whatever the infraction, the student would have fervently vowed to himself never to disappoint his president again.

After what seemed to be an eternity, the petite girl returned and, still with eyes downcast, reported that Rogers would see him.

"Follow me, please." She could not have been much older than seventeen, and looked younger, but Marcus felt obliged by her commands.

As he mounted the first flight of stairs, he heard the bell ring at the door below. He glanced over his shoulder as a second servant admitted Professor Runkle and Edward Tobey into the vestibule. Runkle was carrying various documents and a handful of ledgers, which Marcus recognized from the faculty meetings as containing Institute business.

Marcus slowed his ascent.

"Miss?"

She had not noticed he had slowed down, or if she did, she did not care, and he had to catch up to her. "President Rogers may wish to see Professor Runkle first."

"If you please. My instructions were to bring you up, sir."

"What is your name, miss?"

"Beg your pardon!" she said with surprise.

"Pardon me," he said, chastened, worried he might have insulted her by asking.

"Aggie. I mean, Agnes," she said after another half flight of stairs. "No caller has ever asked me that."

"Why not? You know the callers' names."

"Yes," she said, considering the argument with some amazement. Now she faced him squarely. "I always do."

"Miss Agnes, can you tell me how he has been lately?"

She shook her head sadly. "Not very well, sir. Some days are better, but . . ." Her words trailed off. "He felt excited while taking breakfast, talking rapidly to Mrs. Rogers, and its ill effects came later—giddiness and a light head. He works too industriously for a man feeble of health. I heard from the upstairs girl he was up half the night at his desk among his papers. Mrs. Rogers says the doctors never will be able to diagnose his ailment, because only she knows what it is called."

"Is that so?"

"She says he suffers from 'Institute on the Brain.' "

Marcus replied with a knowing laugh.

"Is what you do there so consuming?" she ventured, appearing emboldened by his easy manner.

"In some way, I suppose it must be. There was a time when the distance between a discovery and putting an invention to practical use was centuries, but President Rogers says seedtime and harvest can now happen in a single season. I believe the next ten years will change all of our lives as much as the hundred years preceding. He recognizes that a new kind of education is needed in order to be prepared. I shall always see him in his prime of health."

"I have been in his employ only three months. When he grew worse, Mrs. Rogers hired more of us to assist around the house. I never saw him before that."

"Commanding and dignified. That was President Rogers, before he had to cease his teaching duties, showing us a theory of physics or describing the formation of a mountain. Picture him entering up the aisle of the lecture hall like this, miss." He passed her, taking two treads at a time, to demonstrate. "A strength of gait only a man who had crossed the Appalachian chain could possess."

"Imagine!" she said dreamily, dropping her guard further. "I'd die to see one of those classrooms in your building."

"At the sound of his voice, we would no longer be restless boys, but twenty or thirty future Rogerses. At the completion of every class, he would draw a free-hand circle on the blackboard without any tools to assist him, like this." He moved his finger in the air to show her. "The circle would be perfect, without fail. Then we would all erupt in applause."

"I have heard something, sir, about a young woman entering the Institute this year. Is it so?"

"Her name is Ellen Swallow. She is a freshman. A chemist."

"Then it's true! She has not been here to call on the professor. I am wild to know how she wears her hair. What color is it?"

"Black as night. Pinned up, I believe. Black bonnet, too, usually. She dresses, well, like a nun. But I shouldn't really talk about her."

"Why not?"

"I don't know. It's a rule—an unwritten sort. Tech does not want to start an outcry about a girl learning such advanced forms of science. We must be very wary of criticism. Her name is not even included with the rest of them in our college catalog. "

"How brave she must be inside that building full of young men. Do you know her well?"

"Hardly at all. But it is said she is a genius. Supposedly, she mastered an entire year of Squirty—sorry—Professor Watson's descriptive geometry class in three weeks."

"Well, I think you all must be geniuses at the Institute."

"I would hate to undeceive your ideas by trying to prove that."

"Since it would be wicked for someone to think so about themselves, you oughtn't. Is that what you called Professor Watson? *Squirty?*"

"Pardon me, miss. You see, the fellows started calling him that because of the energetic motion of his hands when squirting the chemical-wash bottle on the blackboard."

She looked down with a blank expression.

"It is one of those jokes peculiar to college that is funny even though the fellows don't really understand why."

"I see!" she exclaimed, grateful to be offered an explanation.

"He is the most teased of the faculty, maybe because of his dandyish dress. They fill his beaver hat with water, or pay the old Italian organ grinder who wanders the streets with his monkey to play at the window during class. Squirty hates organs and really hates monkeys."

She laughed playfully at the college gossip.

Marcus wished there were another flight of stairs, though he did not know whether the desire came from the reluctance to disappoint Rogers or the wish to continue his talk with this maid. All of a sudden, he also felt rotten blaming Rogers for his decision at the faculty meeting. He could not begin to imagine the struggles to keep the Institute going in the face of soaring expenses and hostile critics.

Agnes opened the double doors into the library, which stretched out into a long, spacious chamber, the combination of dim lighting and thick curtains casting its rich array of scientific relics and books in deep shadows. She leaned in closer to the nervous caller and whispered, "You will do good."

Marcus braced himself. "Thank you."

She closed the doors behind him. Rogers was sitting at his table by the window, leaning over a mountain of papers.

It was a long walk across the room. His head downcast, Marcus's eyes traced the intricate patterns of the plush carpet that sank under each step of his boots.

"President Rogers, I apologize for being sent here. I know how occupied you are, and that you are in need of no disruptions. I arrived late to chemical manipulations class this morning, and Professor Eliot asked that I see you."

Rogers said something low and unintelligible. Marcus considered apologizing one more time and then turning to leave the president in peace, until he realized with another step into the light that Rogers did not look right. He was leaning rigidly to one side of the chair, which his hand was gripping tightly, while only his eyes, glassy and distant, moved. Marcus could now make out the words he was repeating as he struggled to speak from one side of his mouth: "Help me, Mansfield."

* * *

"SEND FOR A DOCTOR! QUICKLY!" Marcus rushed from the stairwell back into the library. Rogers was now slumped farther to one side and slipping out of the chair. He caught him by the shoulders and eased him down onto the floor. The professor's head was jerking back and forth, moisture gathering at the side of his mouth.

"Help is on the way," Marcus reassured him.

Agnes came running through the door, clutching the sides of her dress to keep from tripping.

"Did you fetch a doctor?" he asked.

"Professor Runkle has gone for Dr. Putnam! Mrs. Rogers is out for at least another hour."

"We must lift him to the sofa."

"I don't think we should move him," said Agnes. "I will bring a pillow and a blanket."

As she did, he scanned the room for water. There was a glass where Rogers had been sitting and his eye fell for a moment onto the table.

A glance was all he needed to take it in. Diagrams of compasses. Cuttings from multiple Boston newspapers on the disasters, annotated minutely in almost every blank space in Rogers's increasingly shaky hand. Maps, hand-drawn, annotated with measurements and distances, of the harbor and the business district. Scraps of notebook paper covered in formulas, lists of questions, sketches.

There was thumping up and down the stairs and sounds of commotion through the house. Agnes returned clutching two pillows and a narrow wool blanket.

"Last time, the doctor made certain he got more air at once," she said. She nervously bent in and loosened her master's silk cravat with a gentle touch. His breathing was labored. His eyes were closed and he had fallen into a state of unconsciousness.

"I need something," Marcus said, searching around the table.

"What?"

"A bag, or a portfolio, something to carry all this in unseen—"

"What in heaven's name!" she exclaimed, appalled, as he began to bundle the materials on the table. "The professor is stricken and you are stealing his things!"

He leaned his head out the window. The view was wide—the Boston Common all the way to the Frog Pond, carriage-and-horse-lined Beacon

Street, the shimmering dome of the State House. Runkle and Tobey were running, leading a man holding a chamois-leather bag up the red-brick mall back toward the Rogers house.

He passed his hand over the table. "Agnes, Professor Runkle and Mr. Tobey must not see any of this."

"I don't understand you!"

Marcus held up a handful of the papers. "This is what President Rogers has been up all night working on. This is important to him—it is far bigger than any of us, bigger than the Institute." She continued to stare, unmoved. He took her hand. "Please, Aggie, you must believe me. They must not be found here."

"What will you do?" she demanded. Having jumped at the touch of his hand, she now pulled hers away.

"Keep all of it safe so he can resume his work once he recovers."

They both looked at the man on the floor with concern and some doubt at the prospect.

"Does it have to do with the disasters?"

"How did you know?" he asked.

Thumping along the stairs again. Marcus looked back out the window. There was no sight of Runkle, Tobey, or the doctor now.

"They're in the house!" he said, turning around, but Agnes was gone.

A moment later, she reappeared holding a red leather portfolio. He unclasped it and hastily swept the whole pile of papers into it. The doctor with the medical bag ran inside a moment later, followed by Runkle, Tobey, and more house servants. After a brief examination and a few whispers traded with Runkle, the doctor instructed the servants to help him bring Rogers to bed.

"Mr. Mansfield."

Marcus had taken a few steps back toward the door when Runkle called him.

"Sir?" He twisted his body slightly so the portfolio would not be as visible.

"Thank heavens you are here. Return to the Institute at once, and tell them President Rogers has suffered another attack of apoplexy.

What will we do without him . . . ? May Providence watch over our future!"

Marcus whispered to the maid on his way out of the room, "Thank you, Miss Agnes."

She gave the Tech student an imploring look he could not quite interpret, then joined the other servants at the side of their fallen master.

XIII

Man-field

W HEN MARCUS ARRIVED at Bob's rooms that night, he expected questions. After all, he had mostly avoided speaking to Bob—and all his friends and classmates—for the rest of the day after returning from Temple Place with the awful tidings.

"There he is! M-M! M-squared himself!" Bob shouted a little too raucously, a drunken hoarseness to his voice. "Where have you been half the night?"

"Just ambling by myself," Marcus said as he stored his coat in the closet. He had climbed the two flights up to Bob's rooms. The redbrick boardinghouse managed by Mrs. Page was situated in the center of the city, and with all the lights and activity on the streets he found it hard to keep a sense of the time. "It's President Rogers. I keep thinking of how dire things were when I left him this morning." He turned to face Bob and was caught by surprise. "I'm sorry."

"Why, that's downright morose, Mansfield, walking the night alone."

"Morose!" giggled the girl with long blond hair and a flaming bright dress sitting beside him on the sofa. "Highly morose! Morose Man-field!" She broke into a fit of laughter.

"I should walk awhile longer," said Marcus, giving his friend a small grin and reaching for his coat again.

"Have a drink with us!"

"Thank you, Bob, but I feel out of spirits."

"Exactly the fittest time to drink." He followed Marcus back to the front door.

"You'll excuse me, miss," said Marcus.

"Farewell, Man-field," she said, waving her handkerchief as if he were going to sea.

"You wouldn't believe this tigress," Bob said in a confidential voice. "I happened to start a conversation with her over at the theater, and was telling her about the Institute, which she simply didn't believe existed, and laboratories, which the poor ignorant girl had never heard of, and the lass, on top of it all, has never been to the Back Bay! I have been regaling her with stories of our freshman year. Remember the ancient bell?"

"She is lovely," Marcus said indifferently, slipping his coat back on and taking the portfolio.

"Wait!" Bob said, gazing at him suspiciously. "What is that you've been hugging to your vest all day?"

The leather felt hot to the touch. Maybe it was, from his gripping it so tightly from the time he returned to school until now. "What do you mean?"

"That portfolio."

"Merely some papers."

"A fine-grain leather. I've never seen you with it before today."

"So?" Marcus asked, forcing a chuckle at his friend's untimely curiosity.

"Come now, Mansfield! The rule for chumming in my rooms is that there are no mysteries from each other."

"You hate rules, Bob."

But before Marcus could make it to the door, Bob had snatched the portfolio from him, holding it up like a trophy, as his new acquaintance applauded from the sofa.

"W.B.R.," he read the initials carved into the silver clasp with increased interest. "Say, William Barton Rogers?"

"Give it to me, Bob!" The anger in Marcus's voice was sharp and uncharacteristic. He wrestled his friend to the floor until the portfolio tore open and the contents flew across the floor.

"Look what you did!"

"Sorry, Mansfield," Bob said contritely, bending over the mess. "I was just trying to cheer you up. I know how difficult today was."

"Sorry to grow warm," Marcus said promptly, trying to sound a conciliatory note as his secrets spread out across the floor. "I can pick this up. Please, tend to your guest."

But Bob was already on his hands and knees peeling the pieces of paper off the floor. As time went on, he moved more and more slowly to restore the papers to the pile Marcus was making. He looked over at Marcus, opened his mouth as if to speak, closed it without a sound, then rose to his feet and directed a beaming smile to the young woman. "My little dear, do you mind waiting in the next room for me for a moment while my friend and I have a bit of a discussion?"

When they were alone, Bob said in a searching whisper, "Mansfield, I'd rather be a chaplain than let you leave here without telling me what is really going on."

Marcus smoothed his mustache as he often did when reflecting over a difficulty. "This matter must be wholly between ourselves," he said finally.

"No doubt!" Bob was growing excited.

Marcus finished stacking the materials on the table. "When I found Rogers, he had been feverishly at work, analyzing the scientific details of the disasters. I think he was trying to find a method for resolving them before he collapsed. He had been at the task all night, according to the maid."

"You took these papers from his desk?"

"I didn't have time to think, and didn't know what else to do. Runkle and Mr. Tobey had entered the house directly behind me. They would have confiscated all of it if they found it first, by order of the resolution. Rogers may even have been censured by the faculty committee."

"You told me yourself that Rogers voted at the meeting that the Institute not become involved in any of this business. If he planned to inquire into the disasters, why did he not tell them he was going to?"

"What would the faculty have said?"

Bob thought about that and shrugged. "That group couldn't agree that the grass is green. Each professor thinks himself an emperor."

"I've been turning this over in my head. I believe he saw this as the only way. Even if the faculty could somehow be persuaded, even if they agreed to make the resources of the Institute available to assist in an investigation, the college would be in jeopardy from the forces already lined against it. Rogers knew that, and Agassiz proved it at once by send-ing the police in to give us a scare. But William Barton Rogers could not sit and do nothing while innocent people might still be in danger. It is not in his constitution. He could not stop himself from acting, and even if he were discovered, the college itself could be shielded from the worst of the criticism, because the vote of the entire faculty was on rec-ord against the involvement."

"So he had to keep this secret from everyone," Bob said, flipping through the newspaper cuttings and the pages of notes and drawings. "These may represent the scientific study of a lifetime, Mansfield." Then he crept across the room and opened the door to the bedroom. He motioned back with a pantomime indicating their visitor was asleep, and continued in a quieter voice. "What are you going to do?"

"I'm going to return these to him, hopefully tomorrow. Rogers put his faith in me the day he asked me to come to the Institute, and I owe him this."

"Are you protecting Rogers because you owe him loyalty? Or be-cause you agree with what he is trying to do?"

Marcus stiffened. "I know this is the right thing, Bob."

Bob grabbed his temples with his fingers as though he, or the room, had suddenly begun to spin on its axis. "Wait. Have to think for a mo-ment." He leaned on the arm of the rocking chair, then lowered himself into it. He frowned with a new concern. "What if, Mansfield . . . what will you do if he does not recover?"

Marcus looked away.

There had been a snowy day, midway through their junior year, when Rogers had walked in on Marcus and a few other Tech boys playing cards in the mathematics room during dinner period. Instead of order-ing them to stop the prohibited pastime, as most professors would have done, Rogers sat among them and without a preface began to tell them a tale of one of his geological expeditions when he was younger. His raft caught between two blocks of ice in a fast-moving stream, he had only a hatchet and thirty seconds before being taken by the current, all while being responsible for important soil and rock samples in his possession. The boys forgot about their game as they waited to hear the outcome of his adventure. One asked whether he feared for his life. Rogers looked at the young men seated around the table and answered that he had never doubted he would survive because he had a purpose.

In his mind's eye, Marcus could not help seeing Rogers not in his bed surrounded by doctors, but trapped in a deep valley of rocks.

"He *will* recover, Bob," Marcus said finally.

He craved someone to agree. But Bob had rocked himself into a deep sleep.

* * *

AT THE REAR ENTRANCE to 1 Temple Place, a young woman was stooped over, emptying buckets of filthy water into the nearby sewer grate, her arms stretched out so her body would not be splashed by the refuse.

"Miss Agnes!"

Startled, she dropped her bucket and looked around with eyes wide.

"Miss Agnes, I need to speak with you," whispered Marcus, stepping out from the shadow of the next house.

"Gracious! Are you—" she started to say.

"It's Marcus Mansfield, from the Institute," he reminded her.

"I was going to say, are you half mad? If I am seen by one of the other girls, what would they say of us? Walk behind me a few steps to that corner. Make haste, man."

She pointed and Marcus complied.

"Stop!" she called.

"What?"

"I changed my mind. I don't like you staring at the back my skirts. Walk in front of me."

"Yes, miss."

"What are you doing here?"

As they changed arrangements and then stopped at the end of the small lane of Temple Place, he noticed more than their last meeting the shiny chestnut hair showing from her bonnet, her bright blue eyes that she often squinted for a better view, and a nose dusted with brown freckles. Classical or elegant beauty didn't single her out—her features were not sculpted and her fair skin seemed to flush and drain easily—but there was an alluring expression to her face. She was stamped with the permanent look of having a private song on her lips.

"I must speak with President Rogers as soon as he is well enough, Miss Agnes. And I must do so privately. I'll need your help arranging it."

She studied him for a moment and saw he was serious before answering. "You are bold! Considering you have stolen the portfolio I handed you."

He held up the offending object. "Can you find a way to return it inside without anyone noticing?"

The chambermaid slipped the portfolio into the large front pocket of her apron. "I wasn't born in the woods to be scared of an owl, Mr. Mansfield."

"Miss Agnes, how did you know that President Rogers was working on analyzing the disasters before his collapse?"

She shrugged, but a proud smile played on her lips. "I am not blind or deaf, sir. He had asked me to bring practically every newspaper in the city published in the days following each catastrophe. He inquired after every one of the domestics about what we were seeing around the city. He sent us on errands, seemingly at random, near the business district and the harbor, then asked us for our observations without ever giving his reason. I daresay he seemed unsatisfied that we looked closely enough."

"He was trying to explore the city while he was barely able to leave the house," Marcus mused. "Is there any improvement since yesterday?"

She shook her head gravely. "He can speak again, but only with a struggle. I think he is hardly aware of what has happened."

"Do you think you can arrange for me to see him?"

"You are out of luck. Even if he were strong enough to stay awake long enough to converse with you, Mrs. Rogers would never allow it."

"How do you know?"

"Because she has forbidden all persons from the Institute from coming anywhere near him. She believes it is the anxiety of the Institute business and his mental work that has imperiled him, and the only way he will recover is to be away from it. She is taking him to his brother's house in Philadelphia later this morning to recuperate."

"The Institute needs him here!"

"And he needs to regain his health without someone from the Institute showing up at the door every few minutes with a new calamity," she countered.

"Are you going with them?"

She raised her eyebrows at the question, then shook her head. "The downstairs girls will stay behind to keep the house in order, though we will be liberated from our labors by two or three o'clock each day. I shall have to look to hire myself out temporarily a few hours a day somewhere else to make my expenses."

"But Philadelphia! It is urgent I find a way to see him before that, Miss Agnes."

"Blessed Mother! You know I could be dismissed for how I helped you?"

"Then why did you?"

She sighed at his persistence. "Was it your father who taught you about science?"

Marcus looked away. "Why do you ask that?"

"Not with any meaning," she said carefully at seeing his reaction. "I was only thinking of your question to me. You see, Mr. Mansfield, when I was a little girl, my father labored on the railroad. Back Bay was still a basin and it looked like a swamp to my innocent eyes. But I thought it the most wonderful place I had ever seen, because you could imagine anything you wanted being built on all that space, even a castle! When the big machines, the steam shovels, came to fill the land with gravel, he brought me to see them. There was that giant iron maw, picking a mouthful of gravel from the cargo cars and spitting it all out with the most perfect, terrible grace you could imagine. When it stopped, and was being hauled away, I tried to run after it and my father had to catch me. I cried for want of the big ugly machine and he was able to console me only by promising to return the next week—which we did, and almost every week after that."

Marcus laughed with her. "I remember running out of the house when I was only five years old and following the other boys of the town to a large house fire, where I stood examining the operation of the steam fire engine instead of watching the blaze like everyone else. I saw my father only a few times as a boy. I was alone much of the time and would have been idle but for my hands—my hands wanted to build things even as a boy, so I earned extra money by helping to fix sewing machines. There came a time, later in life, when it seemed to me that to use my hands could save my life. That is how it feels at Tech every day."

"Do you see the difference, Mr. Mansfield? Only a few years after the time of my story, when I was but nine or ten, I was no longer to watch the steam shovels or go anywhere near them. Now the machines were dangerous, dirty, and unladylike. When I hear the shovels now, I cannot help but pout like a little girl and dream."

"Your papa only wished to protect you."

"I suppose I helped you, Mr. Mansfield, because I wished I could have aided the professor with what he was doing. The portfolio feels light. You have kept the papers?"

Marcus nodded. "I removed them until I knew I could bring them to Rogers. But they are safe."

"Aggie dear?" a voice called from the direction of the Rogers house.

"Lilly!" Agnes whispered, throwing a glance over her shoulder. "Go on with you, quickly."

"Well, Aggie, what are you doing out here! And who is this?" She was a buxom kitchen girl whose white cap failed to contain her bright-red hair. She wore a similar uniform of white apron over black dress, though with more frills at the edges than Agnes's, and a big, flashy bow in the back. Catching up with them before Marcus could run off, she forced a greeting out of him.

"Marcus Mansfield, may I present to you my cousin Lilly Maguire."

"You," Lilly trilled on, staring at him for a long time before continuing. "*You* are one of the Technology boys, aren't you? I have seen you before calling on the professor. I always wonder what they must teach you young fellows about science! When Aggie and I were girls, the nuns taught us a little geology and mineralogy. She was a prize pupil. Do you study those?"

"We study all facets of science and industry. Each student chooses a specialty among practical chemistry, civil and topographical engineering, building and architecture, mechanical engineering, and experimental physics. Mechanical engineering is my field." He was so accustomed to being asked to explain the purpose of the Institute, he had begun to feel like the college catalog.

"How fanciful a place it is!"

"There will be others like it, I believe, someday, once Tech has the chance to show its success. In Ithaca, New York, they say there is a college of industrial science that they are attempting to organize."

"Tell us everything about a typical lesson, Marcus Mansfield, everything you can think of—do you hear? Tell!"

The kitchen girl peppered him with questions and he found himself describing their laboratories, the first in the country to put the apparatus into the students' hands. She lavished attention on his every word, though it was the stray look from the quieter Agnes that was thrilling to him. Finally, Lilly was called back to the kitchen door.

"They are gossiping about us right now," Agnes grumbled, her arms crossed over her chest with an air of annoyance. "There is something I wish to show you," she added, looking around again in case they were being overheard. She removed a folded piece of paper from her apron. It appeared to have been crumpled and then straightened again. "He was holding this piece of paper when he collapsed. It fell on the floor when he unclenched his hand, and I put it in my apron, not knowing if it might be important to you."

He hurriedly folded back the flaps. It was a rough sketch of the Institute seal. "He had this with him when he was working at his table?"

"Perhaps it was the closest thing to him, and he grabbed it as he suffered his attack."

"It is dated 1861," he said, examining it. "This must be one of the first drawings he did when designing the college seal, before the outbreak of the war delayed the opening of the Institute."

"Why do you think he brought it out now?"

"I think he was remembering, Miss Agnes. Remembering," he said again, more to himself, "when the Institute was still an idea in his head, what that idea was."

She seemed moved at his reaction to the little slip of paper. "Oh! Here comes Lilly again! I can hear her whistling a mile away. Meet me back again in half an hour. Will you?"

"Yes. Thank you."

"Go!"

At the appointed time of their reunion, Agnes skillfully managed to escort him inside and upstairs without being seen. She established the signal that all was clear, picking at the side of her apron as she stood on the rear stairs. He passed her and went into a chamber she had pointed out, closing the door behind him. From the floors below, he could hear an assortment of sounds from family members, domestics, and doctors making the preparations for taking the patient away. But in the mausoleumlike bedroom, where the heavy drapes were pulled closed, the crackling of the hearth was the only sound and movement. A pair of slippers waited at the foot of the bed. The earth itself seemed to have stopped moving beneath this room.

He forced his feet across the carpet to the bed, swallowing hard and searching for the strength to explain his audacious actions. There was a mosquito net boxing in the bed and the invalid, whose head was elevated on a pile of pillows.

"President Rogers. It's Marcus Mansfield. I am awfully sorry to come in like this, but I had to speak with you before your departure. Can you hear me?"

The older man's eyes slowly opened on him, motivating him to continue.

"President Rogers, I have kept the papers that were on your desk from being seen. I wish you to know I only did what it seemed to me you would want. You asked for me to help, and I hope I have."

Footfalls came closer—but they then moved off in a different direction.

"I mustn't stay," continued Marcus, hearing his voice crack. He had never seen a man whom he so respected, who had once exhibited such vitality, brought into such low condition. "Do you wish me to leave the papers, President Rogers? If you could nod, or make any movement to indicate your desire . . ."

There was a short motion of respiration from Rogers's chest, then his eyes closed again. There was no evidence of a response, no sign that he had really heard anything Marcus had said.

"Quickly!" Agnes's voice warned from outside in the corridor.

Before he could exit, the doctor entered with a purposeful march to the bed. "You," he addressed Marcus. "What are you doing in here?"

His surprised expression seemed to carry no recognition from the previous day, for which Marcus was grateful. But he still had to say something in response. He opened his mouth but was interrupted before he could speak.

"There you are," broke in another voice. It was Agnes, showing a frown in the doorway. "Boy, have you fetched those clean sponges yet to bring along in the carriage for the long drive? Go on, now."

"Yes, miss."

"And make haste for once," she added, with a sparkle of mischief in her eye.

Marcus bowed his head slightly to the doctor and hurried out of the room. After he waited a few minutes, Agnes met him by the servants' entrance in the back of the mansion.

"Well?"

He shook his head sadly. "It was as you said. I do not think he understood at all."

"I am sorry, Mr. Mansfield. What will you do now?"

"I do not know. I see now how fortunate it was that Professor Eliot sent me to him when he did, or I am certain Runkle and Tobey would have disposed of his materials altogether."

"Fortunate!" She turned on him with a questioning expression.

"What's wrong?"

"I believe you are confused, Mr. Mansfield."

"No, I do not think so."

"Indeed you are! It was Professor Rogers who sent a note to Professor Eliot asking that you come to him before class. I believe he was already feeling quite ill at the time. His hand was terribly unsteady as he wrote."

Marcus was stunned. "*He* asked me to come? Are you certain?"

"Quite! He even marked it 'urgent.' I handed the note to the messenger myself to be brought to the Institute. Rogers was waiting for you."

XIV

Mind and Hand

"THREE CHEERS FOR TECHNOLOGY CLASS OF 1868!" Bob called out. "Some class feeling for once, fellows, please?" he asked after a sputtering response.

The players were stripping down to thin cotton shirts with turned-down collars and narrow cream trousers, leather belts circling their waists.

It was afternoon break, and Bob was arranging the football game in the empty fields around the college building. Some Tech students preferred to lounge, doze, or continue studying inside, but with eight hours of sitting in classrooms and laboratories, six days a week, there were others who relished any chances for physical activity outdoors.

As the game got started, Marcus kept pace alongside Bob. "Bob, I've been trying all day to find a minute to speak to you alone."

"Over here!" Bob waved a teammate for the ball. "Rats. Are you blokes blind?"

"Bob, please!"

Bob ran past him. "We're in the middle of a game now, Mansfield! Can't it wait?"

"It's important."

"You were the one to disappear this morning. And I couldn't find that little tigress anywhere when I woke up on the chair. I hope Mrs. Page didn't catch her leaving. Do you hear that?"

"What?" said Marcus, keeping up as they crossed the field.

"There! I heard it again, the sounds of melting hearts," he said. "Shall we cause some trouble?"

"Could I prevent it if I said no?"

"No," Bob replied thoughtfully, "I suppose not!"

There was no mistaking the sounds from the Notre Dame Academy on Berkeley Street as they moved closer. The ball came to Marcus and he kicked it forward until he was close enough to propel it over the high fence that marked the boundary of the Catholic academy for young women.

During free hour at the academy the young ladies, age seventeen years old down to six, would be out in the gardens strolling and chatting in the sun. A sensible plan would have sent one or two men over the fence to retrieve a ball. Instead, a column of six, then seven, now eight, climbed in pursuit.

Bob started to follow, but Marcus held him back by the sleeve.

"What's the idea, Mansfield?" He tried to shake him off.

"Bob, listen to what I have to say. I went to see Rogers's maid this morning, the girl called Agnes. She said that Rogers had told Eliot to send me to Temple Place the morning he collapsed."

Bob stopped to consider this. "That would explain Eliot's hurry for you to go there, and his annoyance, since we walked in late to class. He was concerned with being reprimanded himself. But why would Rogers send for you just then?"

"I don't know. Judging from the fact that Rogers instructed Eliot to do it directly, and had those materials together on his desk, I think Rogers knew he was growing weaker again. Bob, I think he was going to ask for my help!"

"Why? Why you, I mean, Mansfield?"

"He noticed me during the faculty meeting. He knew I thought something should be done. He could read it in my eyes."

"Well, speak with him, then."

"He is in no condition, and Mrs. Rogers is taking him to Philadelphia now and will not permit any Institute business! If only I had reached Rogers a few minutes earlier. If only I had not been delayed by Miss Swallow, or by walking instead of taking the cars."

"A pity! All of it. Come on, no more time to waste." He started to run for the fence, but Marcus ran ahead and blocked him. "Mansfield, those lovelies are waiting for me," Bob protested, trying to shove him aside. "You know how they applaud when I stand on my head."

"You said last night that this could prove to be the scientific study of a lifetime."

Bob laughed. "You know it was the liquor speaking!"

"Well, you're sober enough now!" replied Marcus, his frustration rising. "If we can discover who and what caused these incidents, we demonstrate once and for all to the world that the kind of science the Institute teaches helps society, just as Rogers wanted. We can protect Boston *and* ensure the Institute's future at the same time."

Bob shook his head and became uncharacteristically serious. "There are adventures and there are adventures, Mansfield. There are experiments and there are experiments."

"Please, Bob. Look what's happening before your eyes. The city fears what we do here too much to ask the Institute for help. The Institute is too anxious about the public perception of us to volunteer it. So now we wait for Professor Agassiz, a man who is a brilliant practitioner of every type of tired science we seek to make obsolete, to stumble his way to a solution? Someone here has to do something. I'll need your help. Nobody knows Boston as well as you, not to mention metals and geology."

"You would put your entire future in jeopardy! Would you do that for Rogers? Maybe he did not want to ask you to do this at all. Maybe he planned to ask you to repaint his library."

"It matters not even if that is so. This is our institute. Not just President Rogers's and Professor Runkle's but mine, yours, Edwin's, even that foolscap Tilden's. We were here at the beginning, and we are here now. It's something that Frank said to me when we toured the machine shop. I am still here, Bob. Four years later, I'm about to be graduated. Nobody would have expected that."

"What would you have us do?"

"If I understand them correctly, Rogers's notes detail how the maintenance of compasses corrects for the alternations in magnetic value from the metals used in the construction of ships. I think I can get some metals right from the foundry at the locomotive works and we can use the new machines upstairs in the metallurgy room to separate them by their degrees of magnetism. We'll need to secure a variety of compasses to test. We could do this."

"Or we could fail. Have you thought of that yet? Fail the Institute, fail Boston," Bob said, his mind far away. "That actress, her glare, it lives in my head at all times, Mansfield, I see her everywhere I turn. I feel an awful guilt. I thought that girl last night would help me forget her, but she began to look more and more like her in my eyes. Don't even think of her name, I say to myself. See, you've forgotten already, because it's not your business! Then, I think: Chrissy. Hang the rest of the world, I say, but for once can't you even follow your own counsel? Now think, if I had tried to stop that, and could not, how much worse it would sting?"

"More people could die."

"Your knot is not screwed on right at the moment."

"That's what Tilden said to me."

"Mansfield, have you thought about what can happen if you're found out?" Bob pressed, suddenly agitated. "Why, I'd have to take Runkle's mathematics class again to be able to count the number of violations. Arranging unauthorized experiments, defying a college-wide resolution. Listen to me—I'm beginning to sound like Hall."

Bob's voice was clear and resonant, but it did not overtake the low, simple plea of desperation Marcus still heard in his ears: *Help me, Mansfield.*

"It is too big for you, for any of us." Bob kept trying. "You're talking about building castles in the air, but this is no college ruse!"

Then, his winsome smile restored, he ran backward toward the girls' school, waving for Marcus to follow. "Mansfield, enough of all this. We're seniors, we have our whole lives to be occupied but only a few minutes before the nuns call for reinforcements!"

Marcus took his time walking back to the Institute. He stood in the front hall looking up at the Institute seal. The emblem, a more refined version of Rogers's sketch, depicted a laborer in workclothes, with a hammer and anvil, along with a scholar in a gown, studying a book. Underneath the pair of men was the Institute motto. *Mens et Manus:* Mind and Hand. As a sophomore, he used to stop and stare at the freshly painted seal, proud that he was in a building with its own emblem. These days were so hurried, he could not remember the last time he even noticed it.

"Mens et Manus."

He thought he heard the hushed words echo up from the chatter of his classmates heading toward classes. He turned, but found no sign that his classmates were thinking of anything more than their latest adventures with the Notre Dame schoolgirls. Then he joined the student stampede into a laboratory, as though everything were as it had been before.

Book 2

PRACTICAL CHEMISTRY

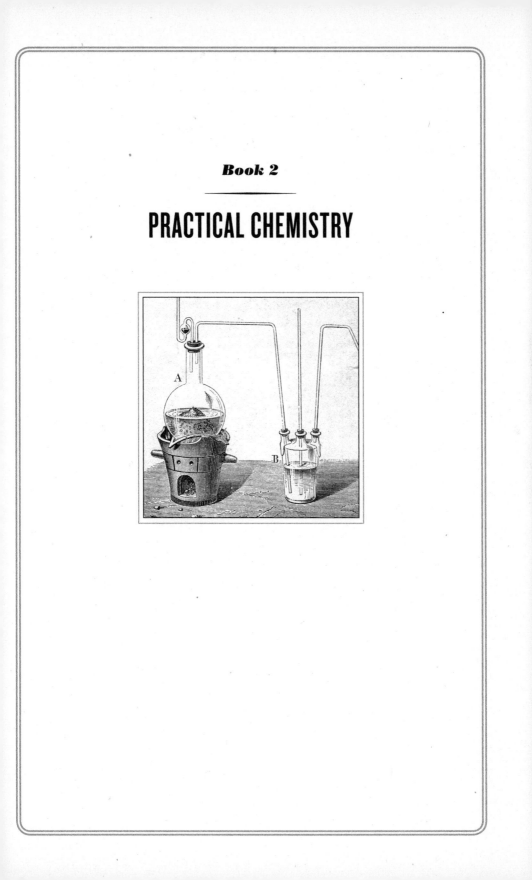

XV

The Police Chief of Smith Prison

Three hundred soldiers from the battlefield hospital are told the prison to which they are being taken is spacious and comfortable, and will be a great relief from their marching and fighting. But it is too dark to see much outside on the night of their arrival at Smith Prison that spring of 1862. The prison itself looks like it is inside a four-story brick building, and Marcus Mansfield's detachment is led into the basement.

Men take up every square inch of the hard floor. At night, you must remain still; if you turn over you will disturb the sleep of two dozen comrades; if your foot twitches it will kick another head, and brutal fights can begin. In claiming your place through means of a filthy haversack on the floor, you seek to be as far from the privies as possible.

The stench stays with Marcus, as it will always. It isn't only the smell of disease and filthy men; before the war, the building had been a tobacco warehouse. Every crevice and crack in the floor is covered in dried tobacco juice. Stale tobacco and its dust fills their mouths, eyes, and noses every waking and sleeping moment.

To make matters worse, the amount of space for each man—at most, five feet of sleeping room—is limited further by thirty large tobacco presses. When one of the friendlier guards is asked whether the presses could not be removed to free more space, the sentry shakes his head and says, "No, sir. When we defeat you damned Federals, all the warehouses and factories now used as prisons will be fully in operation again. It's a matter of time."

There are windows that could open to provide more ventilation, but Rebel guards are stationed outside with orders to shoot at any man standing at a window. Sometimes it becomes so bad that a prisoner will lean outside for a breath, knowing the risk. In the first three weeks, five men are shot dead that way, clean through their heads or necks. Twice the rifle ball misses the man at the window and hits another prisoner, injuring one and killing another.

Marcus makes the acquaintance of the prisoners whose haversacks are nearest. One of these is Frank Brewer, who is also an eighteen-year-old soldier from a Massachusetts town. Marcus pities the boy, who arrived frail and sick from battlefield injuries.

When a new detachment is brought into the basement, taking the place of some who have died, one of the men looks Frank over, taking in his dirty skin and his tattered clothes. Frank is naturally bony and angular, and now is even more so, like all of them, subsisting on the scanty rations. "Are you a foreigner?" the stranger asks, not yet understanding what a man becomes after months of confinement.

"I belong to Massachusetts, and am dreadful proud of it!" Frank says. "When I'm home again, I'll wrap myself in God's flag."

Marcus smiles at this display of passion on the part of feeble Frank. Marcus is naturally reticent, and almost speechless when under duress, but Frank, when prodded, is defiant and verbose, his eyes burning with conviction.

"You should know," Frank says, "that Chauncy Hammond will probably be investigating my whereabouts already. He has great influence and we should all be out soon."

But Frank is going to die. Sometimes he speaks very clearly on the topic, and he asks Marcus to tell his mother, sister, and niece in Springfield that he died a soldier. At other times, he seems to be living in a dream, talking of revenge on the Rebs who injured him, or weakly singing the battle songs they all happily had on their lips as they marched, new soldiers with only hazy thoughts of the trials to come.

We are coming, Father Abraham
Three hundred thousand more . . .

Frank reveals that his father had followed his own father before him as a lumber merchant in Chelsea, but after each sign of success began drinking more and inevitably failed his business, until there were no more chances from the bank or his creditors. Frank's mother prayed over her son's bed every night when he was asleep that he would not succumb to these same demons, and sometimes he would stay awake in order to listen, the fire of some vague determination burning in his young heart. Years later, when he heard of the great need for soldiers, he jumped, traveling from Springfield to Boston to answer an advertisement for a substitute for a young man whose father, a successful industrialist named Hammond, did not want him to serve. Frank is proud of this. It means he will have a position waiting for him at the industrialist's works, while many other uniformed men wonder anxiously what they will do when they return home, with the trades and industry changing so rapidly. It means, he believes, he is already a Boston man before having lived in Boston.

Marcus watches over him day and night, since a sick man is a target for thieves. He tells the ailing soldier about his own family, his own secrets and shame, hoping to keep his interest and will to live.

What Marcus tells him, which he has tried to hide from everyone he's ever met, is about his father. Like many wandering men of the day, Ezra Mansfield was a sailor, a mechanic, and a salesman by phases of the moon—and had lived with them in Newburyport for only a few years. Marcus says that although his mother told him he died at sea, he later heard his father had left and started a new family elsewhere. Marcus worked at seventeen at a small printing press on the machines, but the press, like many businesses in town, could not compete once the railroads had fully stretched out their iron arms and drawn employees into the city and their massive factories. He did not volunteer for the war to be a hero, nor to change the world, either, but did think it was the best thing a man could do. And it would get him away from Newburyport and his disgruntled stepfather.

Almost as wearying as the lack of rations and the physical conditions at Smith are the enforced idleness and crushing monotony, which alone might drive a man mad with self-loathing. The men occupy themselves by searching for and removing insects from hair and clothing, and talking and telling their stories, often of battles. A third release is the contemplation of escape. Plans and ideas are whispered from the very first minutes.

A New York man whom Marcus helped hide a pocketbook before the guards could confiscate it has the idea of tying his own toes together and posing as a dead man. He would be dragged to the dead house across the courtyard, from which he feels confident he could run into Richmond and from there be able to disguise himself until reaching Union lines.

He asks Marcus if he wants to try his grand dodge with him.

Marcus hesitates. "Why pick me?"

"You helped me. I stick with my friends, a lesson a young buck like you should take to heart. Come now . . . Mansfield, right? Don't you want to get home to your family?"

"You will get shot dead."

"Maybe. But would you rather die in here, breathing in the stench, or die trying?"

"Maybe there will be an exchange."

The New York man gives up. Marcus doesn't voice the real reason he wouldn't try the escape, because he feels the plotter would laugh. When roll call is given, if anyone is missing, rations are withdrawn for one or two days for everyone. The daily ration is just half a loaf of maggot-infested bread soaked in beans and water, with insects mixed in that have been inside the beans before boiling, and sometimes a beef bone. One missed ration, and several of the sicker men could die, including Frank, and others still might easily meet their death under questioning by the guards. The New York soldier, Marcus feels certain, is not evil, only indifferent. Anyone who could not help him might as well go to the devil. He is taken out that night with the dead bodies. His escape is discovered and the rations are cut, leading to two of the sicker men expiring before their eyes. Marcus never learns the escapee's fate.

Marcus is elected by the other prisoners to be part of the "police" force to prevent the theft of blankets and clothes, which are most sought after, and help provide for the men too sick to fight for themselves. This isn't an honor most of the men want, as it is correctly seen as a burden and a path to unpopularity, but people have noticed that Marcus gravitates toward the sick and weak anyway. After the former chief of police used his position to extort supplies from a group of prisoners, and abused his authority by whipping fellow prisoners with a cat-o'-nine-tails, Marcus reluctantly comes to accept the promotion.

There soon occurs a series of watch thefts, which cannot be reported to the guards, since the watches themselves are contraband. Marcus questions several men who have been there the longest about the physical intricacies of the warehouse and follows an assortment of clues to a cache of watches hidden in broken boards of the ceiling and also to evidence that reveals the culprit.

When the man is brought before Marcus, the others tell him that, as police chief, he must deliver a punishment. Marcus is given a razor, one of the few weapons in their dungeon. He hesitates. If he refuses to mete out punishment, another man might be made police chief and punish Marcus for his failure to act, or renew the depredations of Marcus's predecessor.

"Hold him down," he says. The man struggles, spits, and curses. Marcus shaves half his head and half of his beard and mustache. "You'll be remembered by anyone who sees you," he tells him. "It would be unwise to steal ever again."

The guards seldom enter; they, too, hate it here. The first time he sees the glaring eyes and red face of the comically short, stooped Rebel officer, he thinks there is a certain generosity and sadness reflected in his face. He cannot conceive the degree of hate he will later possess for this man. He wears a thick black beard and his eyes seem always in motion, rarely stopping long enough to make contact with those of another living being. Those on whom his gaze does come to rest soon regret it. When he speaks, his gestures are abrupt, choppy. Vicious. Marcus learns this is Captain Denzler, director of the prison. He comes after roll call whenever there is a missing man and takes one or more of the boys to question them.

"You will not be laughing soon," Denzler always says, though nobody is ever laughing. When those taken return, if they return, they are broken and silent.

Marcus hears from others that Denzler was an engineer in the field before suffering an injury to his leg.

He also likes to visit them with news of the war. He brings in Richmond newspapers and reads aloud, in his peculiar accent, of Rebel triumphs in battle. He also reads the reports of planned prisoner exchanges. Each report of an exchange results in the silent erasure from the prisoners' minds of a hundred daring plans of escape.

"*Do you hear of the latest disease on our floor?*" Frank Brewer asks Marcus.

"*Smallpox again?*"

"*Exchange on the brain, Marcus.*"

Those who have been there longest have learned to be skeptical of any promises of release. When the scheduled day comes, there is always an excuse or reason for postponement. When Negro soldiers begin to be captured, the Rebel government refuses to trade any of them for their own white soldiers. Soon, the prospect of exchange will vanish again and new ideas for escape will emerge, until Captain Denzler reads another new announcement—surer always than before—promising release.

When the first prisoners from the Negro regiments are brought to Smith, Denzler directs the other prisoners, "Make the damned niggers wait upon you. If they do not, lick them, or report them, and I will lick them."

Marcus knows, as chief of police, that he will have to protect the newcomers even if it puts him in danger. But while there are many among the prisoners who do not think Negroes have any place in the Federal army, no one follows Denzler's edict—out of contempt for Denzler, or maybe respect for any fellow captured in uniform, Negro or not.

Marcus and Frank are both known as good tinkerers, having been in companies that were shown how to rebuild bridges and railroads as they marched. They use the beef bones from rations to make rough spoons, buttons, and pocket knives for the men. Using his hands in this way for the first time since he put on the uniform of a soldier brings Marcus the wonderful and elusive feeling of accomplishment. When he works, he is alive and without doubt or guilt over his circumstances. Frank, whose health has gradually improved, makes pipes for his comrades, but Marcus can't stand the thought of anything associated with tobacco. It is not the pipes that attract attention, but the intricate carvings Frank creates on them, picturing landscapes from home, battle scenes, and various favorite dogs described by the boys. Even the guards notice these, and begin trading laurel root and extra rations for them so they can show the "Yankee fixin's" to their families back home.

It is Marcus's idea to begin taking parts out of the tobacco presses. The winter is upon them, and the sick suffer in the cold. They are given no heat. Marcus feels it his responsibility to rectify this. Frank helps him use the bolts and iron plates from the presses to build a fireplace that will not burn the floor. They can dismantle the device quickly when a guard approaches. It does not occur to them that they have started a sequence of events that will bring the full wrath of Captain Denzler down upon them.

XVI

Girl from the Galapagos

IT WAS LATE AT NIGHT when he climbed the rickety stairs to the second floor and parted the same Venetian screen he remembered well. For the most part that feeling of familiarity ended there. He had not been to this place for at least three years and it stood obstinately without change, including a hard-looking crowd that might have been the very same who'd gathered in 1865 to make toasts to the fallen president of the United States. There had been many nights when being in this beer hall was far preferable to struggling to sleep. Now it felt as though he stepped into another country, an unwelcome alien.

"Anything you wish? Beer?" asked a scantily dressed girl with a pretty English accent, who carried a tray of empty beer glasses.

"I'm waiting for someone," he said, offering her a smile as an apology. She moved on to other customers without a second glance.

"Not waiting for me, I suppose, laddie," a man's voice said at his shoulder.

Marcus's hand was grabbed and held tightly before he could reclaim it. The grabber smiled, showing off the gap in his front teeth.

"I do not believe we were formally presented at that crude lighting demonstration held by your institution Thursday last."

"My name is Mansfield. I know who you are. Roland Rapler. I've seen you gather your flock here before. I have my own affairs that bring me."

The man, garbed in full military dress, as he had been at the demonstration, looked him over intently. "I can feel in your hands you were not born to be a college student. You worked in a mill or a machine shop, I'd wager."

"I'd guess you could find out if you wished," Marcus said. "If you haven't already."

Rapler's smile was a confession. "The injury to your hand: Was it from the machines?"

"This? It was from meeting the face of a fellow a little too hard, actually."

"That species of violence," Rapler said coolly, "runs against my principles."

"Your principles include throwing rocks and destroying private property?"

The man was slow to lose his composure and quick to speechify, a mixture of polished eloquence and common vulgarisms. "We command attention, at the cost of manners, sometimes, yes. But you fire into the wrong flock, laddie. Invention after invention, and do you trust every one of your peers with their knowledge? The man who invented a weaving machine was strangled and drowned three hundred years ago because it was believed his creation would turn workingmen into beggars. We do not question the need for invention or try to stifle it. But when science finally runs away with man, it will surely blow up the whole world before it's done. Apprenticeship already has been replaced by machinery. My people want machines to aid our labor, aye, but every minute we spend around them hazards turning the balance, as we become more and more mechanical. When the machine unmans its user, science becomes suicide."

"When you stop the mind from inventing, you stop nature," Marcus countered.

Rapler delicately drew the kid-leather glove from his left hand. Underneath, where his thumb and first two fingers belonged, were stumps. He flexed the remaining two fingers and looked upon them with a mixture of longing and pride. "Who invented the shell that blew my fingers to bits, laddie?" Rapler did not lose his intent grin. "You see, Mr. Mansfield, I shan't work on a shop floor. But once I did, and now I can do all in my power to see that the people who do are protected. When I was recovering from my wounds I read all about history, the stories of great men and the first leaders. I wear this uniform because I am still in battle—for the men you see in this room, and their sisters in labor, across New England. Now all of Boston sees the terrific danger of science used without constraint. Where a few months ago, I would see a dozen chums at my gatherings, after these disasters I see a hundred, two hundred new faces."

Marcus had seen plenty of injuries both in war and on the machine floors. But he could not resist watching the last two fingers of the hand divide, come together, bend, and straighten. In surrendering to the sight, he had also surrendered their contest of wits to Rapler.

On the other side of the room, piano music came to a stop and was replaced by light applause.

"Marcus!"

Marcus turned and saw Frank Brewer coming through the screen. "Mr. Rapler, if you do not mind," Marcus said.

Rapler nodded farewell, replacing his glove before excusing himself. "Remember the march of improvement must somewhere come to a stop, laddie, before it tramples us. When it does, I wager you'll be on the right side."

"Sorry to be out of season, Marcus," said Frank, adjusting the bag that was slung over his shoulder.

"I wasn't waiting long," Marcus assured him, then looked over at Rapler. "Nor did I grow lonely."

"Mr. Brewer—a loyal machine man if ever there was!" Rapler sang out as a greeting.

"Loyal to Chauncy Hammond for employing me, not to some unionist dolt," Frank replied, more to Marcus than to the union leader. "Come along, Marcus."

They sat at a table in an empty section of the beer hall. The man in front of the piano was bowing left, right, and center.

"Were you able . . ." Marcus began, then changed his mind. "Frank, perhaps I shouldn't have asked for this. I would not place your position at the machine shop at risk."

"Marcus, as your friend, I order you to shut up." Under the table, he opened his bag and took out a smaller canvas bag that he pushed to Marcus's feet. "I did it as soon as I got your dreadful serious note. What do you need this for so urgently?"

He could remember being in the same beer hall the evening of his final day on the machine shop floor. Frank had seemed withdrawn and cool to him that night, and when he finally asked the matter, Frank pulled him into a corner. "You'll go to that place, that college of theirs, they'll chew on you and spit you back and it will show once and for all . . . well, perhaps we are meant to be machine men forever!" It was not clear which prospect troubled him most, that Marcus might be misled, or that their established standings in society would be confirmed.

"If that is the case, I will come back to the floor wiser for it," he had reassured Frank, though it was Marcus who needed someone to reassure him as he was about to cross the once-unimagined threshold into being a collegey.

Back at the same ill-lit chamber, only a few feet away from the spot of that conversation, he let an exhale escape at Frank's question about the favor his old friend had just done for him. "You probably wouldn't believe it if I explained, Frank."

"I see," Frank replied in a softer tone of voice. "I suppose I might not understand, anyway."

"Frank, it's not that!"

"No?" Frank brightened again.

"It's only that it's something I have to do on my own, that I am probably mad to even try. But I cannot see my way to not trying."

"Ain't it like a college student," marveled Frank, laughing with excitement as though he were his partner in the enterprise.

"How do you mean?"

"Intrigue and abstraction!"

"I suppose. For now, I can only thank you for helping, though I know that's not enough. One day soon, I vow I'll be able to explain it all."

"I'll be all ears." Frank smiled and changed the subject. "Can I show you something while we're hanging 'round the lower crust? Been working on some new statues."

"You should start selling them. Maybe have one placed in a museum."

"Some chance of that!" Frank said, laughing. "Imagine me being given the chance to be a famous sculptor! No, but I have a new one I thought you'd like to see," he said, barely suppressing a proud grin.

He removed a bronze statuette from his bag. It was of Ichabod Crane riding a horse in full flight, representing the moment from the Irving story when the schoolteacher flees for his life from the specter of the haunted horseman.

Marcus looked up at him in surprise.

"For years, I have been called Ichabod for my loose limbs and long neck." Marcus began to protest the point, but Frank spoke over him, still smiling cheerfully. "That's not me anymore, Marcus. You see? I have a plan now to change, with your inspiration."

"Mine?"

"That's not me, being under the thumb of someone else's judgment," he said wistfully, nodding to the statue, "and I want you to keep it in case I ever need a reminder once I take the plunge at Tech."

"What's that one?"

There was another head sticking out from Frank's bag. "Oh, this! I thought you might have a laugh about this one. Do you recognize him?" Frank removed the figure and held it up.

"Why, it's Hammie!" Marcus exclaimed after a moment of study. The miniature sculpture showed the unmistakable figure of Hammie in a soldier's uniform with one leg thrust forward, as if taking a step into battle. "In a soldier's dress."

"Imagine that. Mr. Hammond asked that I sculpt his family, and requested that I show Hammie in military garments, I suppose to placate the spoiled brat's giant ego, though he never came close to volunteering. But when your employer asks for a sculpture . . ." Frank's line of thought drifted away.

Marcus could tell how bothered Frank was by Hammond's directive. "Well, I thank you for the Ichabod Crane. I'll treasure it especially."

"Two beers!" Frank called out loudly to the girl. "You remember this fellow at the piano? He sings quite well—about girls left behind on the Galapagos Isle, that sort of balderdash. Stay. We'll play a game of cards, just you and me, ex parte, like during our dinners at the machine shop. Which game do you favor these days?"

Marcus shook his head. "I shouldn't, if I am to be prepared for class in the morning. There is one other thing, Frank. I wanted to apologize if I seemed cool toward you when I came into the machine shop."

His face coloring, Frank said, "No, I called attention to your bad hand in front of your friends, Marcus. I didn't think first—as usual. I'm to blame. Did Mr. Hammond say anything to you when he spoke to you after that? You don't think he heard me telling you I was ready for something better than working for him? After arriving late that day to the shop, I don't look to call down more of his ire, at least not until he finds out I'm through there."

"No, I don't think he heard," Marcus said, knowing his friend must have been severely troubled by the prospect for the last week. He didn't want to repeat Hammond's remark about Frank being born to be in a machine shop. "He mostly spoke about Hammie, actually."

"Hammie!" The return to that topic creased Frank's brow. "I think you should keep your guard around that fellow. Mr. Hammond is a strong man; he sees into the future everywhere he looks. But he sees not his own son. He is like a father to us at the shop, and we are his sons more than Hammie can ever be. That fellow . . . well, don't believe the mask, Marcus."

"Hammond might expect Hammie to be someone that is not possible for him, Frank."

"I suppose that is the way with fathers sometimes. Not mine, though. Ha! He always expected me to accomplish nothing, just like him. You are lucky, in a way, my friend. You could imagine yours however you wished, rather than having to answer to a man who could not understand you, even on the day he died."

"I suppose," Marcus answered quietly.

"I wanted to ask you about something but . . ." Frank waved his own comment away. "You'll think I'm stark-raving distracted. Just me and my phantasms."

"Tell me."

"Sometimes, Marcus, in the streets and crowds around Boston I look out and see . . . his face, savage, watching me, warning me. I convince myself he found me."

"He? You mean Denzler." Marcus said the name with a shudder. They never talked about Denzler or Smith Prison, not since the early weeks after returning, when Frank helped secure Marcus a place at the locomotive works. It was an unspoken pact to trust the future would be better than the past.

Frank looked down at the floor, which was covered in sawdust boot-prints. "Yes, Marcus. I mean Denzler." His voice broke on the word. "I see him at a distance, or think I do. My heart flies, I feel danger all around. I try to give chase, but he always vanishes before I reach him."

Denzler still occupied Marcus's nightmares sometimes, and so did the ghosts of their fellow prisoners who did not survive, or survived as shadows of themselves. But to speak about it aloud seemed to invite its control over his nights. "I heard he fled to Germany to escape any tri-als," Marcus said, as though repeating a newspaper report distant from his own life.

"I heard that, too. But what if it is not true? It sets my teeth on edge to think of him, even the possibility that he could walk among us. It makes a man want to do something more, while there's time enough. You know . . . I'm going to do it, Marcus!" he said with the excitement of a new idea.

"What do you mean?"

Frank scooped up the statue of Hammie, glared at it, then stood and tossed it into the open stove in the corner with a big laugh.

"Frank," Marcus said as his friend sat down again, smiling with satis-faction. "What did you just do? What about Hammond?"

"Boss Hammond!" Frank called mockingly. "Why, Marcus, I tell you, you've been an inspiration, and the Institute, too. I'm not going to be pinned down by him anymore and live my life in sackcloth."

Marcus was still beholden to Hammond, whose financial arrange-ment had allowed him to attend Tech, and Frank would need some similar arrangement even as a charity student. But he did not say that. Instead, he raised his glass to the notion of Frank's freedom.

"You will come to Inspection Day to see the Institute," Marcus said, urging him in a more practical direction.

"I count the hours, Marcus! Three cheers for the Institute!"

They finished their beers and Marcus stood up from the table. Even before he heard his name called, the unmistakable odor had reached him: a mixture of grease, soot, and sweat.

"Marcus Mansfield! You must have made a wrong turn."

Four young bucks from the Hammond Locomotive Works. Two of them he knew from the machine shop, and the other two he'd seen working in the wheel room and the pattern shop. The speaker, in the center of the group, was a man he remembered was called Sloucher George. He was known as a lovely singer around the works, but generally had a rough voice and crude manner.

"Why would some collegey show himself here?"

"Because he is drinking with me, George," Frank said, rising swiftly from the table. Frank, though his body was more sinewy than muscular, was tall enough to make most other men insecure.

"He doesn't belong here, Brewer," Sloucher George said, jabbing the air with his finger.

"Come. You know what's what. You forget he's one of us."

"I ain't forgetting," Sloucher George replied, hitting a table with his fist. "Maybe he was one of us once, when his throat was filled with iron dust. Or maybe you want to be what he is, Brewer? A collegey, with the airs of a false gentleman."

"What if I do at that?" replied Frank.

"He's no companion of yours, Brewer, nor any of ours."

"I was about to go," Marcus said. Sloucher George had probably wanted to start a row long before walking into the beer hall and seeing him. The truth was, the machinist's punch was said to be harder than a sledgehammer, and Marcus did not like the prospect of a set-to. "Good night, Frank."

George put his hand out to stop Marcus, then gestured with a grin to the bar. "Aren't you at least going to shout?"

"I haven't money, George," replied Marcus. "You'll have to buy your own beer."

"No money—is that right? You weren't paid to gawk at us with the other collegey scum visiting the machine shop Friday last? What's in there?" Sloucher George pulled at the handle of the bag Frank had handed Marcus. Marcus, alarmed, grabbed George's wrist and held on tightly.

"Let go of that," Marcus said.

"You better let my wrist free and let me see inside," George growled. "Whatever it is feels awful heavy."

Frank stepped to Marcus's side.

"This ain't your concern, Brewer! Step away!"

Frank snatched a glass from the tray of a waitress passing nearby and dashed the wine into George's face. "It's my concern now, Sloucher George," he said coolly, as the big man released the bag and wiped his eyes.

The other workmen gasped. Nobody ever called the brute by his nickname to his face. For mild Frank Brewer to have done it, in front of a crowd of peers, while dousing him with a glass of wine, was a shock. The silence that ensued seemed interminable, as a flush spread over George's big purple-stained cheeks, and perspiration formed a floating bridge over his brow. "Four beers!" he screeched to the waitress, suddenly intent on finding a table.

Marcus, awed and a bit startled by his friend's actions, whispered to him, "You should leave with me."

"Why?"

"He's a real whaler, Frank!"

Frank smiled, breathing heavily, but exhilarated. "You don't have to protect me here, Marcus! All his wrath comes out the little end of the horn. Sloucher George is a big man and he takes pride in his work, and that is the one way he can be injured: to hear that his habits at the machine are slow. Go on your way, Marcus. And Godspeed—for whatever it is you're doing. Remember, you are representing a thousand fellows like me who might one day be thought good enough to be collegies themselves."

"I never forget it," Marcus said.

* * *

MARCUS WENT BACK to Bob's rooms to pack up his belongings. He was hoping Bob might be sleeping at his mother's, or out for the night, so he could just write out a note explaining, but he was there.

"Mansfield, what are you doing?" Bob came out in his usual shabby silk dressing gown, chosen out of a wardrobe filled with newer ones, and carried a dumbbell.

"I thought I might have woken you."

"I was doing my lifting. What's this? You're leaving?"

"You are right that what I'm doing can call down trouble. If I go wrong and I'm staying with you, you might go overboard with me, Bob. I won't risk dragging you down."

Marcus expected Bob to argue, either that he should stay or that he should give up his whole folly, but he listlessly stretched his long limbs out on the sofa and watched with vague attention as Marcus collected his things. "If it must be this way," he said finally.

"It must," Marcus said, a little sad at the lack of protest.

"Oh, Mansfield, I have something for you before you go. There."

There was a bulging potato sack on the floor in the corner of the room Marcus had not noticed.

"What is that?"

"Have a look for yourself," Bob said nonchalantly.

"Not another soph stuffed inside, is it?" He walked around from the other side of the table and bent down. Loosening the strings, he found in the sack an assortment of compasses and navigational tools. Marcus rummaged through them. "Bob, I need all this for the experiments! But yesterday you said . . ." He looked up in astonishment.

"Oh, damn what I said, Mansfield! That was yesterday. I was in a fix."

"You were entirely sober."

"Yes, and now I'm a little liquored up and see everything clearly! If there is a time to build our own castles, this must surely be it."

Marcus tried to gauge his seriousness. "Do you mean it, Bob? You're willing to help?"

Bob was rubbing the palms of his hands together. "Of course. This is just the ticket. Yes, of course. Of course we must go onward! We'll show Blaikie and those Harvard scrubs what Tech is worth! It's decided. Put down your bags—you're not going anywhere. We rescue Boston and Tech . . . together!"

"Bob, remember our position. If we run into trouble, Rogers is in no position to help us now."

"You told me the Institute was yours, ours, Mansfield. Well, you're right. The Institute is mine, too. I was also there in the first golden days when it was but three dusty rented rooms, when there were nearly the same number of students as instructors. Every Richards in history has gone to Harvard, and I'll show them that what I'm doing is worth every bit of that stuff and more. You will need more pairs of eyes if you are not to be exposed. If droll old Albert Hall finds you out, or Squirty Watson or Eliot or any of the faculty members, it will be over in a flash. And there's Tilden, who would relish nothing more than to see you sacked from the college for violations, and don't forget that goblin Miss Swallow, who is everywhere and nowhere. I owe Rogers as much as you do for giving me my place at Tech. Your hand, Mansfield. Do you have a plan yet? Mansfield, your hand!"

The machine man and the scion of Beacon Hill grasped hands and shook heartily, their grips strong, their smiles equally fierce and determined. "The start of a plan," Marcus said. "By my count, the first step is to find out exactly how these two disasters were engineered, using Rogers's notes as a beginning. I thought I would use the storeroom in the basement of the Institute, since I have a key."

"First rate! But we'll need a better space to conduct our investigation properly, probably in one of the laboratories."

"Why would they permit us to use a laboratory?"

"I don't know yet. It will be an obstacle. But have no fear. Resourceful Bob Richards will find a way. Come, hand me that sack—we'll decide more on the drive there."

"Drive?"

"To Eddy's. We'll need Tech's best physicist on hand, of course!"

XVII

Underwater

CRAMMED INSIDE THE BASEMENT STOREROOM of the Institute, the three students arranged blocks of iron and a variety of compasses of different sizes around the shelves.

"Where did you get all this?" Edwin asked.

"I purchased the compasses from a warehouse near the Navy Yard," Bob said.

"Edwin, you remember the lectures on nautical navigation sophomore year?"

"Excellent lectures," Edwin answered Marcus, feeling himself gain some energy after being roused in the middle of the night and ushered into a carriage. "Yes, I remember. Bob, you wore one of those sailor's caps slouched over your face, to annoy the professor."

"Ha! Exactly right!" Bob recalled fondly. "Let us remember the earth is magnetic. Really you might say the earth is one giant magnet, and since magnetic poles of opposite charge attract each other, the north point of a compass needle is actually a south pole, since it is attracted by the north pole of the earth. Likewise, the south point of a compass needle is a north pole. Edwin, hold that bar of iron horizontally—east to west, I mean. Thank you. Now, Mansfield, place that compass at the very end of it."

They did as Bob directed.

"The needle is not disturbed at all," Edwin said.

"Edwin, try raising the far end of your bar one degree—right . . . there, stop," Marcus said.

"The south point of the needle is attracted!" Edwin declared.

"And if you lower that same end, just a little," Bob said, nodding to Edwin, who complied.

"Now the north point jumped," Edwin reported.

"At any angle with the compass needle, soft iron attracts each pole of the needle with almost equal force," Bob said.

Marcus nodded. "Shipbuilders take this carefully into account so that the proximity of a nautical compass to the ship's materials remains a neutral factor."

"There would be a magnetism, too, with the iron in the earth," Edwin added.

"Exactly. Watch this. You may wish to plug your ears." With Edwin taking Marcus's advice and Bob inclining his head as if to dare the noise to disturb a Richards eardrum, Marcus brought a sledgehammer down onto one of the bars of iron. Edwin stumbled backward. Upon the hammer's impact, the needles of all the compasses twitched.

"Wait another second," Marcus said, the noise ringing in their ears. "And another second . . . Now, Bob!"

Marcus tossed the bar of iron at Bob. He caught it, and all the needles of the compasses followed the bar. Bob swung the bar around like a baseball bat, the needles moving with it.

"Of course," Edwin declared after a moment's thought. "The hammering increases the level of magnetism that would, under normal circumstances, hardly register, after the compasses had been in the magnetic meridian. The iron's inductive magnetism now controls the *permanent* magnetism of the compasses."

"What I believe we will find in testing the different classes of iron Frank secured from the works," Marcus said, "is that the softer the iron, the greater degree of influence on the magnetism when it is hammered or disturbed."

At that point, Bob asked for the softest piece of iron fresh from the Hammond foundry. He stirred the basin until it became a small whirlpool, then dropped the iron into the water. When the iron hit the water's surface, the needles leaped into another frenzy.

"The waves," Edwin remarked. "If the iron is soft enough, the action of the waves on the solid will induce even greater magnetism. The waves were harnessed, as though by Neptune himself, to become tools of sabotage. Remarkable!"

Marcus put his hand on Edwin's shoulder and let it rest a moment before he spoke. "Edwin, you know you do have a choice."

"No, he doesn't!" Bob took his other shoulder with a hearty laugh.

"You do, Edwin," Marcus repeated. "Rogers had just begun this work before he collapsed and his notes are not more than a start. We have no allies in this. It will be no easy task. It is your choice whether to join in or not. What do you say?"

"Marcus," Edwin replied, stopping to take a deep breath, "I think we should be getting to the harbor to make a round of inspections at first light."

* * *

EDWIN HOYT LOOKED OUT at the cloud-covered sunrise. While the tide encroached against the piles, he marked the rhythm to himself and he shifted his glance to the islands along the entrance to the harbor, so singularly protected against invasion or attack. Not far from where he had paused were the wharves that had been decimated, two almost completely and one partially. Occasionally, wooden piers still floated by in fragments, clogging the channel. Two weeks after the event that overtook the harbor, the police were still removing wreckage from water and land and grappling for evidence.

Being a true Bostonian meant having a respect for the order of the world, for the position of the authorities and the citizens. This all-too-real experiment would be unlike any they had encountered. But the police had already sank in place, as soon as those ships went down in flames, hadn't they? As soon as they hitched themselves to Louis Agassiz.

"I have been thinking more about it," Edwin said when he caught up with his companions, who were now making their way through the eerie quiet of the wharf. "I still can't puzzle it out."

"What do you mean, Eddy?" asked Bob.

"Your experiments with the compasses in the storeroom are most impressive, Bob," Edwin continued. "But that was in a confined space. Look out there—look at the expanse of the damage. The amount of tonnage of iron needed to replicate the experiment out there, and in exactly the right position, without being seen by so many witnesses . . . I simply cannot imagine how it might be done!'"

"Well, walking around the harbor in circles isn't going to tell us enough to answer it," Marcus said. "We need to know more about what happened. More than what has been in the newspapers, but without speaking to the police."

"Ha! I'd venture to say the police do not know what we already do," Bob said brightly. "There is another force of men present from whom we will learn more. Look!"

Marcus and Edwin both looked up and down the harbor.

"I don't see anyone," said Edwin.

"Who do you mean, Bob?" asked Marcus.

"Rats!" Bob said.

"Rats? Are you serious?" Edwin asked.

"Of course," Marcus said with a smile. "The wharf rats."

Scattered around the harbor were the so-called wharf rats, impoverished old scavengers who haunted the piers looking for scraps of food or discarded cargo.

"I saw a few huddled in blankets, half asleep, as we entered the harbor," said Marcus, taking to the idea. "How would we know which ones to speak with?"

"Well, we'd want to find the ones who are most curious, watchful, who stay on their toes with one eye open at all times, even when asleep," Bob said. "I think I know how we can start. Wait for me."

Bob sauntered between several warehouses, then along a row of cotton bales, then across the quays. All the while, he was jingling the coins in his pocket until, ten minutes later, there sidled out with a lead-footed step a wobbly stranger who had been sitting, unseen, at the center of a circle of pungent fish barrels.

"I will give you some of these," Bob began even before turning around, holding the coins out in his open palm tauntingly, "if you answer a few questions."

"Say, that is a dirty trick," the man complained when Bob was facing him. The man's bright-red face was wholly unprotected from the elements by the fragments of his crushed velvet cap. "I'd rather pick an honest pocket. It's extortionate, that's what!"

"I'll make it worth your time, I vow it," said Bob. He whistled the signal for Marcus and Edwin, who soon caught up to them. Then Bob turned to face their new acquaintance again. "Tell us what you saw the morning of the disaster."

"Me! Why ask me, lad?"

"Simple." Marcus stepped forward. "Why make your home along these damaged wharves, instead of one that wasn't damaged, unless you did so before the catastrophe?"

"Foofaraw! Bull!" the old man proclaimed with irritation.

After some further prodding, the wharf rat confessed almost with pride that he had been there when it happened, that it was the most stupendous and terrible thing he ever saw, and that his moral sensibilities were too shocked even to try to salvage anything from the water for almost half an hour afterward. The chaos of ships crashing into piers and into one another had grown worse with every passing moment. He indicated for them the basic boundaries of the event, and told how he watched the marvelous vessel *Light of the East* as it was abandoned and saw its captain, whom he'd heard later was a man named Beal, save some steamship passengers who had been sucked under the water.

"Before it began, did you see anything or anyone suspicious, anything unusual or different around?" Marcus asked.

The old wharf rat considered Marcus, then shook his head no. "But since then, the whole harbor has been *different.*"

"How do you mean? Quieter?" Marcus proposed.

The wharf rat shook his gray head again. "Aye, but more than that. Sailors haven't shown up for their posts. The wharf masters say passengers with tickets for the steamships have stopped coming, too. The warehouses are empty of cargo to pilfer. Why, I've barely eaten, I haven't! I once had the makings of a gentleman, you know, when I was your age."

"Here, old fellow," Bob said, dropping the coins into the man's hand. "Buy yourself some chowder. Our united thanks for your help."

"From the area of the damage, then, it appears the event extended from here—the Custom House, and Central Wharf—to there," Edwin concluded as they left the wharf rat behind.

"That's Long Wharf," Bob said.

"Edwin is right," said Marcus. "The combination of soft iron and the motion of the waves would have to generate an area extending to those three or four wharves and out to sea, where the magnetism would have interfered with all navigational instruments in that region. How is it possible an amount of iron that large could be in position to do this without being seen?"

Edwin peered up and down the wharves with an unsettling sense of the true magnitude and difficulty of the task they had undertaken. Not only to discover what transpired, but to persuade others. They were trained in understanding events in scientific terms, not in convincing unscientific minds to do the same. "We need to find evidence."

"They've been removing the debris," Bob said. "The evidence won't be anywhere up here."

Edwin peered down doubtfully into the vast expanse of the harbor and listened to the sounds of the tide. As if speaking for the deep, mysterious currents, Bob put his arm around his friend's shoulder and pointed with his other hand. "Out there, Eddy. There's proof somewhere out there!"

"Now we merely have to walk underwater to find it!"

For once, Bob had no answer.

"Fellows, over here!"

Edwin and Bob followed Marcus, who was studying a circular tacked onto a telegraph pole.

"What is it, Mansfield?" Bob asked.

"What do we do with it, Marcus?" Edwin asked after he read it.

"Follow the directions," Marcus replied. "And begin to collect our answers."

A.B. SEAMEN WANTED.
Apply onboard schooner Convoy

———

—E. L. BEAL, CAPTAIN

* * *

WHARF RATS, like the ubiquitous rodent from which they received their name, moved from hole to hole for shelter. After eating his chowder at one of the dingy restaurants on the harbor, the red-faced wharf rat climbed into the fish house, where excess portions of the day's catch were stored, and where he'd often gone for shelter, especially these days, with the police swarming around. He was startled when his wrist was grabbed as he was stepping through the creaky doors.

"Honor bright, I've had enough of you!" he cried, thinking it was one of those collegies come back.

He turned to find himself in the grip of a fever dream, staring at a ghoulishly disfigured face that seemed to ripple and peel as he shrank back in horror. The hood that partially shaded it did nothing to obscure the fiery glare of its miserable owner, which burned above sunken, cadaverous cheeks and an unnatural, almost incandescent orange mustache. Behind the apparition was a taller fellow in a checkered waistcoat and bowler hat, with a stoic, sleepy demeanor that contrasted almost comically with his companion.

"I understand from some of your fellow worthless vagabonds that you're known to frequent Central Wharf picking up rags and other rubbish. I'd like you to tell me what you saw at the time of the disaster on the fourth of April."

"I just told 'em!" the wharf rat protested, then regretted it.

"Who? Who did you tell, you old fool?" demanded the hooded stranger, shaking him violently.

"Those nosy collegies a few hours ago—they looked like collegies, anyway. They were here asking about it, I vow it! I think they went toward Long Wharf. Ask around—they were putting their noses everywhere—if you don't believe me!"

The man in the hood nodded to his companion, who ran off. Then he turned back to the old man, demanding whatever information he could remember. He asked the same question posed by the collegies—whether there had been anything out of the ordinary that day.

More prepared than in his previous encounter, the wharf rat had begun to compose himself and smelled opportunity. "Well, there was something, now that I muse on the topic," he said slyly. "What will you give me for it, kind gent?"

Without warning, the nightmare erupted, slapping the older man across the face again and again until the wharf rat fell to his knees. His assailant rifled through a pile of discarded fish parts, grasped his victim's head by the hair, and thrust a fish bone down his throat.

"What I will give you in return," he said, breathing heavily, "is your pathetic life." The wharf rat choked and gasped for air until the bone was yanked from his mouth.

"There was a sailboat!" the vagrant answered between tears. "I saw it cast off, and then I noticed that it laid anchor in a strange place—well out from the piers. When the commotion began, I looked again, and I thought I saw it in the distance, sailing away, undisturbed."

"Did you see anyone on it? Do you remember anything about it? *Do you?*"

The wharf rat flinched and nodded, sputtering. "It was too dark . . . I didn't see who was at the helm . . . I remember the name. *Grace.* The boat was called the *Grace.* I saw it when a light passed over the boat. That was my poor loving mother's name, Grace, my dear mother, Grace, honor bright! That is why I remembered. That's what I saw, if I saw anything more than that, shoot me!"

XVIII

Enter the Technologists

"THAT'S SOMETHING YOU DON'T SEE every day, Mansfield."

During classes, Marcus would scribble notes combining formulas, then cross them out and start again, until he had to stop to cradle his aching hand and flex his tingling fingers in slow agony, trying his hardest not to allow the pain to bring with it memories of Smith Prison. This was how he was occupied before the start of the latest chemical manipulations session, when Hammie leaned over his shoulder.

"What is?" Marcus replied with unconcealed annoyance in his voice.

"Hall is usually the bore who can't stop writing everything down, not you." Hammie nodded in the direction of Albert Hall's table. Sure enough, Albert's hand was flying across the page, leaving behind a trail of immaculate writing, with pauses only to sharpen his pencil with a small knife blade, or to vanquish his long cowlick from his brow. "Hall there believes his notes will mark the beginning of a new epoch in polytechnical education, that they will someday be petted in a museum by scholars. I always thought you were like me, Mansfield."

"How so?" he asked, surprised and suspicious of the rush of words—and the sentiment—coming from the enigma that was Chauncy Hammond, Jr.

"That science runs through your blood, not through your pencil," he said with his off-center grin. "That you were born to know how things work, and make them work better. I make my class notes in the evening, as a test to my memory. Say, those don't look like formulas for today's demonstrations."

Marcus casually closed his notebook as Hammie examined it. "I was working on some ideas of my own. Going ahead of class."

Hammie nodded meditatively. "I've always done the same," he said approvingly, yawning at him before returning to his own table. Bob nodded to them both nonchalantly as he passed their stations on his way to the chemical cabinet. Professor Storer, benevolently making the rounds of the room as the students prepared their demonstrations, was helping Bryant Tilden measure out a chemical. Marcus's eyes then fell on the two small, tilting mirrors Albert kept on his table, which he had explained in the past would allow him to catch anyone trying to copy his notes. But Marcus wondered what reflections those mirrors could capture from the array of other glass objects and vessels in the room. Was it possible Albert could see *other* students' notes—could see Marcus's?

The catastrophe that had struck the State Street district presented an even more discouraging challenge to unravel than the harbor did. Marcus's notes dismissed theory after theory about which chemical compound would produce the results they had seen with their own eyes, and that witnesses described in whispers and in the newspapers, however little any of them understood it.

He opened his notebook again and found a scrap of paper lodged inside, written in a kind of cipher, but recognizable as Bob's hand, ordering a meeting in the stairway between the third and fourth floors during their study period. At the appointed time, Marcus found Edwin there, waiting with a look of suspense and his own note from Bob. Before either of them could say a word, Bob burst into the stairwell from the third floor. Moving between them, he looped his arms into theirs and led them up in a full gallop.

* * *

"Here!" Bob called. "Now we can hold our conferences in perfect peace and privacy."

"This is where you want us to meet, Bob?" Marcus asked. "The roof?"

"Only temporarily," Bob assured him, closing the door behind them. "Haven't yet found a better space with more privacy than the storeroom, but I vow I will, Mansfield. See here. When have I let either of you down? I was able to secure the most recent Boston map from City Hall during the break, and have marked off the area of the second incident, using our own observation and the clippings Rogers collected from the newspapers." Flattening the map on the stone balustrades that squared the roof, Bob pointed to his markings in the business district around State, Court, and Washington streets.

The wind was strong, but at least they could speak freely. Suspicious behavior was of course to be avoided in the building. They'd not be able to miss more than a few classes without opening themselves up to questions. For now, being eighty-five feet above the ground would provide the seclusion they needed. If they were to succeed in helping Rogers and the Institute, they would have to work invisibly. They would impose these rules and regulations on themselves, and even Bob, who normally chafed at restriction, could abide them, given the satisfying rebelliousness of their secret mission.

That would leave them only the early mornings, their afternoon dinner breaks, their brief study periods, and evenings. At least with Marcus rooming at Bob's boardinghouse, they could all be in close proximity of the city. Unlike New York or Chicago, once you were inside Boston, any point in the city was fairly convenient to any other. Meanwhile, they had to continue preparing for their examinations, with Marcus cramming Bob and Edwin for engineering, Bob helping Marcus and Edwin read up in geology and surveying, and Edwin lending Bob and Marcus his mastery in physics and chemistry.

Bob drew another imaginary line around one portion of the map with his finger. "The chemicals had to be released somewhere centrally positioned within this circumference."

"If we can re-create the chemical combination that was used—as we will with the technique that disrupted the compasses . . ." Edwin began.

"We hope," Marcus said.

"We hope, yes," Edwin agreed. "If we can somehow re-create the compound in a closed setting, then it would allow us to calculate how quickly and in what fashion it would have traveled through that area, permitting us to work backward to pinpoint its source."

"I want to go back to where it happened," Marcus said.

"Why?" Bob said with a shudder, then felt embarrassed at his reluctance. The ghost of Chrissy still lurked there, though he would not admit that out loud. "What I mean is, we were there already."

"But that was before beginning our investigation," answered Marcus. "Before we knew what to look for."

"Very well," Bob said. "First, we have other business. Eddy, you continue to draw up the engineering plans Mansfield has started for our salvage work at the harbor."

"I will do my best—I am more a physicist than a machine man, you know," Edwin said. "To a physicist, unchanging law is supreme, but to a machine man the law must be always changing."

"Flat nonsense! You are a man of all sciences," Bob replied. "Anyway, we have Mansfield, Tech's best mechanical engineer, to coach you. And if I am not the strongest geologist and metallurgist in the Class of '68— well, I think I must be, really."

"Hush. Look," Edwin said in a whisper. Down below, behind the building, Professor Eliot stood smoking a cigar, holding a long, narrow case, the kind lined on the inside with tin and used to transport chemicals or sensitive equipment. They crouched down and watched.

To their surprise, a horse and carriage drove up the path behind the Institute, on the northerly side, along Newbury Street. This was rare in the middle of the Back Bay, which was usually deserted this time of day.

Professor Eliot seemed to be expecting the encounter. He walked swiftly over, leaned in through the window, and returned inside the building empty-handed, throwing his cigar into the dirt.

"He must have put the case into the carriage," Bob said, as they knelt behind the protection of the balustrade. "Did he see us?"

"He will not hesitate to reprimand us if he did," Marcus whispered.

"We don't want Eliot's eyes trained on us any more than necessary."

"There is something else we don't want, Bob," Marcus commented. "When you went to City Hall to look for the map, some of the fellows noticed you were gone. They were asking about you."

"Am I that important and handsome?" Bob bellowed with his deep bass laugh, and tossed his head.

"You *are* always the one leading the sports in the dinner break," Marcus reminded him. "I'm afraid your popularity will work against us. How are we to go anywhere during school hours, if your absence is wondered at?"

Bob nodded, thinking this over. "I have a plan for that, too."

"What is it?"

"Don't rush so, Mansfield! I don't have one yet, exactly, but I mean to have one soon."

Their heads swiveled around as the door to the roof opened.

"Eliot! He saw us," Edwin gasped.

Before they could try to conceal themselves, Darwin Fogg appeared instead, lifting his hat to them.

"Well," Darwin said, "are you boys supposed to be up here?"

They each waited for one of the others to answer.

"No," Edwin said.

"And you're the smartest fellow in the college?" Bob whispered to Edwin.

"Well, neither am I. I should be cleaning out the supply closets at this hour, but"—Darwin removed a cigar from his pocket—"don't tell Albert Hall, will you? I like being the professor of dust and ashes here."

"We like you being here," Bob said.

"You know," Darwin mused as he took a puff and enjoyed the view out to the Charles, "other than not being able to smoke inside near your equipment, I've liked working in a college where students like you fellows aren't all well shaven and cold-blooded, but running around digging through mines and such when they're not in classrooms. It makes for true entertainment."

* * *

THE NEXT MORNING, Marcus and Edwin claimed their seats in Squirty Watson's mechanical engineering class. Deep shadows framed their red eyes, the residue of having stayed up half the night at Bob's boarding-house, reviewing lists of chemical compounds and drawing up engineering specifications, on top of spending most of their free time during the day on the roof of the Institute. Fortunately, the days had been clear and a little warmer, but also sunny enough that their skin was as tan as sailors'. Then came a day of strong winds in advance of a heavy rainstorm that blew so much dust from the empty lots of Back Bay that the roof was useless. They could hardly see their hands in front of their faces, much less their growing sheafs of notes and diagrams. When Marcus woke up that morning, Bob had already gone, and by the time he reached the Institute Bob hadn't yet appeared there. He looked over his shoulder and exchanged a worried glance with Edwin, who was compulsively checking his watch. He mouthed, "Where could he be?" just as Bob slipped in the door and hurried to a table. Watson appeared a moment later, as well dressed in the Parisian style and apologetic for his tardiness as usual.

"Greetings, gentlemen! Now class can begin," he said, as though someone were forever trying to teach class without him. "I have some very interesting things to show the class today. Oh, yes!" First was a lecture on the arrangement of machinery in mills for grinding. When Watson was at the blackboard, Marcus twisted his head to the side. Bob was waiting for his glance. He held up a shiny metal object just long enough for Marcus to see it. A key.

"A volunteer, if you please," the professor said. They had moved on to the construction of bridges. Albert Hall braced his arm high in the air, his round face plumped up with anticipation, but Watson stopped in front of Marcus instead. "Mr. Mansfield. You can do us the favor. Break this."

The professor handed him a pine strip twelve inches long and half an inch wide, and he broke it in half.

"Very good, Mr. Mansfield. You would make a fine backwoodsman. Now, come with me. Everyone, watch Mr. Mansfield and myself as we play seesaw."

On the far side of his desk, Watson had constructed an isosceles triangle, using three sturdy pine strips, with a wire rod extending from the apex down to the base. A long strip of board was rested on top of the makeshift structure, which did not look trustworthy enough to support the weight of a small dog. Watson stepped up on one end and directed Marcus to stand on the other. The seemingly frail triangle supported both bodies without a problem.

A murmur of satisfaction filled the room, ejecting the well-honed cynicism of college seniors.

"Eh! I don't want to see any expressions of surprise on your faces! That's better. You see, Mr. Mansfield may break almost any stick in those strong hands of his. But remember when you write your examinations next month what I've said all year—in construction of a bridge, look for the placement of stresses. It is never about what *appears* strong or weak on the outside, but where the pressure falls. You won't find this sort of demonstration at Harvard, by and by, with Agassiz and his pickled starfish. You can thank President Rogers for making demonstrations like this possible somewhere in America."

To Marcus, the grating sound of pencils scratching could not cover up the forlorn, troubled note in the professor's last comment. Everyone at Tech carried on as though Rogers were merely occupied in his office, and would be down any moment for his next lecture, his hand still on the tiller.

After class, the three conspirators hurried together down the hall. "What is the key?" asked Edwin.

"The answer," Bob said, smiling mysteriously.

He led them down to the basement, near the location of Ellen Swallow's private laboratory.

"Are we going to see Miss Swallow?" Marcus asked sarcastically. "It might be hard to believe, but unlike most of the belles in Boston, I'm not sure you can win her heart with a smile, Bob."

"I hope we are not going to be meeting at the Temple," said Edwin, looking worriedly at the entrance to the urinals located under the basement stairs.

Bob stopped at the next door down the corridor from Miss Swallow's laboratory. With a wide grin and a grand flourish, he unlocked it.

"Welcome to the metallurgical and blowpipe laboratory!" Bob announced, swinging the door open. "No," he said to his friends' bemused expressions, "it's not used very much. When the treasury ran out of money during the construction it was never fully completed. I didn't know it was even here."

Marcus looked around at the ill-lighted room. It had a gas furnace, a reverberatory furnace, three crucible furnaces, bean pots along the shelves, a screw press, a forge, some crude ore-dressing equipment made of galvanized iron, and storage bins for charcoal, wood, and anthracite. It was dusty and had a stale odor.

"How did you get the laboratory key?" asked Marcus.

"Inside first, fellows, then I'll tell you. Close the door behind you, Eddy," Bob said. When the door was shut, he explained. "Two years ago, someone reserved this laboratory for the use of a society of students called the Technologists. I suppose some poor fellow wanted to emulate Harvard with their Rumford Society, the Hasty Pudding Club, and of course the Med Fac."

"Med Fac . . . what's that?" Marcus asked.

"Med Fac stands for Medical Faculty," Edwin explained, "although it is actually Harvard students who call themselves that because they see their dark deeds as aiding the health of the students. It is the most secret of all Harvard's secret clubs and to be initiated one must perform an act that could result in expulsion or even arrest—stealing the tongue of the college bell, shaving off a freshman's mustache while he sleeps, or, if they wish to be an officer, blowing up part of a building."

"Were you part of it before you left?" Marcus asked.

"Heavens, no! My time at Harvard was spent locked inside Agassiz's dissection rooms. The Med Facs are notorious, and some say worship the devil."

Bob laughed at the thought. "I hope not, since my brothers were all members. Harvard has suppressed them out of existence, anyway," he added.

Marcus rolled his eyes, not as amused as Edwin and Bob by Harvard boys' childish games. "This Technologist group must be very secretive itself. I've never heard of them."

"That's because nobody ever joined the society," Bob explained gleefully.

"Some class feeling Tech has," Edwin said, frowning. "Same problem as usual—too many brilliant ideas and not enough men."

"Nobody joined—until now," Bob corrected himself. "There are currently three members in good standing."

"Robert Richards, Edwin Hoyt, and Marcus Mansfield," Marcus said with a smile.

"We're now signed up as the society's entire membership. Which means we have this laboratory reserved, with our own key, for all times it is not in use by a metallurgy class—and you know the metallurgical professor this term is Eliot, who is too vain to give up time away from his lecturing."

They shook hands all around and took their time admiring their headquarters.

XIX

Mecca

"**D**OWN BELOW, BOY**," said a sailor busy coiling a rope, anticipating the visitor's question.

Marcus nodded thanks and descended from the main deck into the cabin of the schooner, escaping the unpleasant mixture of rain and snow that had begun sometime during the morning. He hastily removed his hat when he reached what had the trimmings of a stateroom, where a man clearly in authority perched on a hard stool.

"Well, what do you want?" the officer snapped, turning his face only halfway.

"The bill posted, sir," Marcus said. "Advertising for able-bodied seamen."

"You can read, then, that's a first all day. I am Captain Beal. This is the *Convoy* you stand in now, and I expect my men to remember the name of the vessel they sail in. So you have a taste for the briny?" He was older and thinner than Marcus had pictured the hero described by the old wharf rat, and he looked like he had fought his way to Hell and back again. His eyes were dark and sunken as they passed over Marcus, and he sat with his hands folded inside his sleeves.

"I have not gone on a voyage as a sailor before. My father, sir, was a merchant ship captain, for a time."

"Where is he now?"

"I don't know." He would have said dead, but there was something about the captain's face that warned against any deceit. Not that it would have been a lie, exactly—his father may well be deceased. Almost all he remembered of him was the large chair he used to sit in, on which was carved a motto: *He that wavereth is like the wave of the sea driven with the wind and tossed; let not that man think that he shall receive any thing of the Lord.* When he was a small child, Marcus revered this object and liked to think that his father had carved the words himself, and so lived by them. The boy committed the words to memory and recited them to himself whenever he felt himself losing faith or confidence. Later, when his mother married again, he cursed his father's absence and had to admit to himself the motto said everything that the man probably was not. This man in front of him, this bronze-faced captain, could be my father, thought Marcus, if he were a few years younger.

"I was born in Newburyport, sir," continued Marcus, "around ships and water. I helped with many riggings in port, and I can splice a rope."

"You helped your father?"

"No, sir." He regretted having mentioned his family history at all as he saw the captain had taken hold of the topic hungrily and would not let go.

Beal nodded absently. "I suppose you're the brave one of your friends, then."

"Sir?"

"First, to lose your father to the water, in spirit or in body, you don't say—no matter—but to lose him, sure enough. Yet still to want to ship out with us. Second, it is the rare young man right now in Boston who is looking to be shipping out at all, and in a vessel under my command."

"Why, Captain?"

"You heard what happened here at the harbor, did you? Yes, I suppose you have, unless you've had your head buried in the sand. Everyone heard, everywhere around the world, because of the blasted telegraph. Messages sent from land to land across the water, like cannonballs that can't be seen. Imagine, what name would an Arab give to that sort of black magic? Now look at me. Look at me." When Marcus complied, Captain Beal slowly drew his hands from his sleeves. They were both wrapped in thick, red-streaked bandages. "That's what a sailor is, boy! From pulling out some unlucky souls whose steamship caught on fire, burned on every finger by the steam. A ship captain with no hands to use for months to come—and not enough men to be my arms and legs for me. One day, boy, we all drown of our dead weight."

"What of the crew of your old ship? The *Light of the East?*"

"You do read the newspapers. Aye, a rough set of fellows, as usual in a merchant ship. Most of them couldn't read the articles of shipping they signed. They could take gales and disease and even a sea monster—but this? It makes shipwreck of their faith. What superstitions they concocted—half of them will never step onto the boards of another ship again, and the other half I wouldn't want. A spooked seaman on deck is a man waiting for death."

"They say the instruments were manipulated," Marcus ventured. "In the newspapers," he added quickly.

"The newspapers," Beal repeated gruffly. He stood smiling, and awkwardly plucked an object from his table with his bandaged claw. He tossed it at Marcus, who caught it in midair. A pocket compass.

"Look at it," Beal said.

He cautiously obeyed.

"It was the one I saved from the wreck. The rest are with the bones of the *East* on the ocean floor. The damned police officer wanted this, but I've had that one since I was younger than you. What do you see when you look upon it?"

"I see it is working," the pupil answered quietly.

"Fourteen September, 1492. Do you know what happened on that date?"

"The voyage of Christopher Columbus."

"Nah, that date was almost the *ruin* of his voyage, that's what. It was the day Columbus, sailing westward, saw that the north point of his compass needle no longer indicated the polar star, and his men began to mutiny. In their fevered minds, if the compass could be wrong, they would never again be able to return to Spain. They had sailed off the map. Now Boston has been knocked off the map, too, and I don't know if it can ever be put back where it was."

Marcus studied the compass top to bottom.

"And if it could be explained?"

"By who?" the captain inquired skeptically. "You?"

He did not reply.

"If they understood it," the captain said. "Is that what you mean?

Why, they'd be more alarmed than ever. They do not understand the science; they *rely* on it. Do you see? That instrument you hold wasn't 'manipulated,' as you say, boy—it was the very air of Boston itself that was poisoned. A wise sailor shouldn't be frightened of shipping out—he should be frightened of staying here! I wouldn't go an inch past Castle Island if I ever return this way."

Marcus looked up with interest. "Castle Island. Is that where your vessel was when the instruments went wild?"

"Aye, just beyond it. I understand we were the final vessel to be pulled in by the devil's breath."

"All of the compasses were affected at once?"

The captain bored of the topic. "If you can fetch five other able men by the end of the week to ship out with you, you can increase your rate of pay. No Irish, 'course. Well, those are all the terms. But heaven as my witness, you won't be back."

"Pardon me, sir?"

Beal stared at him. "I don't know what you are, boy. You're not a sailor."

"I can learn," Marcus insisted, as though he really were planning to go to sea.

"Aye, you can *learn* to sail but you'll never be a sailor. True seamen won't sail next to a man who is not like them; they can smell the difference. You have milk and water running through your blood. You'd be thrown into Davy Jones's locker, you and your luggage, too." Beal laughed harshly at his joke.

Marcus stiffened as if readying a protest. He realized how intently he had been gripping the compass and that the captain had noticed.

"Tell me why you've really come, boy," growled Beal. "Speak, but speak advisedly! I wouldn't trust you or your father with the simplest rigging on board."

Marcus threw the compass down to the floor, smashing the glass case. Beal did not flinch, a silent grin fixing itself on his face, as though finally satisfied with his visitor.

"Maybe you could manage the sea, after all," said the captain. "If they allow it."

"If who allows it? Your crew?"

"No. Those demons who have you tied up in knots."

Marcus turned his back to him and hurried out without another word. He found himself walking and walking along the water's edge aimlessly, as if trying to escape the captain's stinging voice. He went through less familiar parts of the harbor, but he did not mind feeling lost while he mastered his emotions. Then through the heavy weather he spotted Agnes Turner.

Hailing her, she seemed as surprised as he had been.

"Mr. Mansfield, how unexpected," she said, tidying her dress and bonnet with a quick motion.

"I had some business for the Institute at the harbor—you, Miss Agnes?"

"With so few of us at the house at Temple Place, we have to share the errands. I must gather this list of things for Miss Maguire to cook for our supper. I suspect my cousin liked very much the idea I would smell of fish the rest of the day."

Marcus laughed.

"Have you found extra hours somewhere?" he asked.

She nodded. "A few evening hours here and there with a woman of society who needs some help getting around the city. It is something, at least, until things are normal again. We hear little more than rumors from Philadelphia, only that the professor remains in a worrisome state. Well, I suppose you must be on your way," she said firmly. "As I must be."

"As you please," Marcus said, bowing.

"I must admit," Agnes added quickly, "I do not usually come to the harbor, and may not have followed Lilly's instructions as well as I intended."

"Do you mean you are lost?"

Agnes looked around and gave him an embarrassed frown. "I might be."

"May I escort you?" he asked.

"Only until I know where I am, mind," she said, shaking her finger at him.

"That might be a while," he said, taking her arm and glancing at their surroundings.

"Why, do you know where we are, Mr. Mansfield?"

"Do I?"

"Do you?"

He gave a little shrug and they kept walking. Something remarkable had happened. He felt light and unworried, and the captain's harsh interrogation had vanished entirely from his thoughts after only a few minutes of the housemaid's company.

* * *

WITH EVERY SPARE MINUTE, they made use of their private laboratory, the single key passed among themselves until they were able to access the right equipment on the second floor to forge several extra sets. Little by little, they were mixing compounds and constructing equipment, with the next fellow who had a free interval doing the next step and leaving modified instructions for the one after him. Marcus was locking the laboratory after one of his turns when his eye was caught by a piece of paper tacked with laboratory pincers to a wooden beam in the corridor. He reached up and unfastened what turned out to be a crude drawing of a slender woman in peaked hat, tied to a broomstick, about to be lowered into a boiling caldron.

As he studied the caricature he took a step back against the wall. He heard a clicking sound, then the muffled ringing of a gong from somewhere in the basement before the door to Ellen Swallow's laboratory was yanked open.

"Aha! You! What do you want?" The mystery lady herself peered out at him, her marble-white face and long neck a stark contrast to the basement gloom. She was a year or two older than Marcus, and four or five years older than most of his fellow seniors at Tech, even though she was only a freshman. That made her life there even more difficult than it already was. Her eyes were dark and intense as she stared at him and added, "I do not know you."

"I am Marcus Mansfield, Miss Swallow. We spoke on the stairs . . ."

She clucked dismissively. "I know your name, Mr. Mansfield. That's not what I meant."

"I am sorry for disturbing you. I didn't realize you were there."

"Then you are even stupider than the others. I am *always* here. I cannot attend classes with the other freshmen, lest I offend or elope with a man. This is where they cage me between my private sessions with professors; and that is how I like it. Are you down here to spy on me?"

"Miss Swallow," he said, thinking he would show her the drawing he'd found and express his sympathy. Surely she was accustomed to vandals among students who did not want her there, and a cartoon depicting her burned alive was probably the least of it. He remembered his freshman year, the whispers of "factory boy" dogging him. He crumbled up the paper and stuffed it in his pocket. "I assure you that I'm not spying," he said, holding her steady gaze.

She blew out an impatient sigh. "At the moment, Mr. Mansfield, I do not have the time to be misanthropic. If you are looking to drive me away from Tech, I must proffer my own apology. I am here for a reason—and *will* stay. What are you doing in there?"

"Where?"

"The metallurgical and blowpipe laboratory. You are a civil-engineering student."

He hesitated, taken by surprise that the Institute's hermit knew so much about him. "We have a society. It is called the Technologists."

"How I should like to belong to a society! The Technologists," she repeated in singsong, still staring a hole through him. "What is it this society of yours does, exactly?"

He hadn't thought about how to answer that.

"It isn't philanthropic?"

"Oh, no. We are a . . ." He stalled.

"A *secret* society." The voice was Bob's, who was entering with a jaunty step from the dark stairwell.

"Tech has no secret societies, Mr. Richards," Ellen protested when he joined them.

"Until now it indeed was lacking in them," Bob said.

"How good for the Institute," she said dryly. "It is not very secret if I, of all forsaken people, know the identity of all its members."

"Ah, we are only but two representatives of its membership, Miss Swallow," said Bob.

"Then I suppose your other pet, Edwin Hoyt, is another."

Neither Bob nor Marcus answered, but both appeared nonplussed. "Eddy is the smartest fellow in this place. Smarter even than Hammie," Bob finally blustered.

"It seems very queer," she went on, her long arms locking tightly on to each other. "I am cut off from all earthly ties in this private laboratory, not permitted to attend classes up there with the other freshmen, instead shut up down here like a dangerous animal. I have kept in my corner and worked for myself because I believe God is using my hardships to prepare me for something. Yet by choice you isolate yourselves down here in a dark, unused room, under the farcical guise of some society. Why?"

From inside Ellen's laboratory a strange noise sounded, like a baby crying or babbling some new word. Marcus could not help but picture the caldron in the cartoon—the awful power of suggestion—and imagine an orphan baby, whose eyelashes and toenails she used in experiments. To make matters more enigmatic, a pungent, stale odor like mold drifted out from her chambers.

"What was that noise?" Bob asked, quick to turn the questioning away from them. He took a step toward her room.

"This is my *private* laboratory, Mr. Richards—it is my sanctuary, my mecca, from crude boys like you two." But her advantage on them had weakened. "My time is too precious to waste in chitchat and gossip," she said, turning her back to them.

"Go back to your mecca, then. And I mean Salem!" Bob called out as she closed and latched her door behind her, silencing the weird noises inside.

As they walked back upstairs together, Bob worried aloud. "If she has an inkling that we are doing something out of the way, the faculty will hear about it at railroad speed. She will give us up without a murmur."

"I agree. She is placed in a position where she might feel she should take any opportunity to please the faculty. It is best not to draw her attention." Marcus hesitated, but continued. "It sounds like you wish her to leave the school."

Bob shrugged. "If she does, I should hold the door open for her like a gentleman. I have too many things to do to worry much on it. You know, it sounds very much like you wish to defend her, or accuse me, Mansfield!"

"We just need no other set of eyes looking at us."

"I wonder that hers don't turn us to stone," Bob quipped.

"I have had a conversation or two with her. She is never dull."

"Dull, perhaps not. She read our faces like we were signboards. Up close, her looks are rather striking—I mean, as struck in the face with the fist of an ogre. Did you notice one of her eyes is larger than the other?"

"No."

"From too much time looking through her microscopes, I'd wager. And each finger is stained another color of the rainbow from the myriad vials of acids and chemicals she handles. It makes me glad to work with metals. Turn the page, Mansfield—we have much to accomplish."

Bob told Marcus his latest plan: With the dinner break about to begin, Edwin would stay behind in the laboratory to finish sketching their salvage equipment, while the two of them would go back to State Street.

"Come, then, on to the sports fields," Bob said.

"I thought we were going to the business district."

"We will do both. Bryant Tilden is going to help."

"Tilden? Are you cracked?"

"I promised you I'd find a way to leave without being noticed, didn't I?"

When they reached the fields, which had been dusted with snow overnight, those eleven who had come to play looked to Bob, as usual, for direction.

He announced, "This afternoon, men, let's play baseball!"

There were audible groans, and many turned away. In their occasional baseball games, Bob, naturally the pitcher, had never found more than five men, who then had to do double duty, running back and forth between sides in each play. It was not easy to build enthusiasm.

Tilden stepped forward, relishing the moment.

"What a scrubby choice of game, Richards. I say those who don't want to play this scrubby baseball go to the fields over there and play football with *me.*"

Bob nodded with satisfaction at Marcus as the athletes fell in behind

Tilden. Marcus tried to hide a grin under a forced cough, as he, Bob, and Edwin were left standing triumphantly by themselves.

As soon as Tilden and his cohorts were safely away, the three bolted—Edwin circling back to the rear entrance on Newbury behind the building, and Marcus and Bob racing each other through the streets to the horsecar station.

XX

A Study of State Street

S TATE STREET REMAINED IN DISARRAY though the businessmen, as Boston businessmen will do, tried to go about their endeavors as if everything around them were normal. Sheets and towels were draped over windows that were still missing their panes, and on street corners there were piles of lumber stacked high from furniture that had been broken in the crush of people trying to escape buildings. As had been the case near the harbor, much of the public stayed away out of fear or superstition or both. Workingmen, by contrast, were in great abundance, installing new windows and removing debris, a process that had been stymied by dismal weather.

"We are in the very shadow of the Boston Massacre itself in these streets, Mansfield. Right there in front of that door, a mob formed, shouting from all sides, 'Drive out the rascals!' " Though Marcus had been in Boston ever since he was taken out of Smith Prison during the war, Bob still took pride in pointing out the historical sights of the city, and while he meant well, it reminded Marcus that Boston did not run through his blood. "Though I know not whether strangers to our city wish to find such sights anymore—it is the smokestacks of the East Cambridge Glass Manufactory, not Bunker Hill's sublime granite finger, that the eyes of visitors search for in our skies these days. What is it you wanted to look for, anyway?"

"Something I was thinking might be of use to us there, at the Old State House," Marcus replied, gesturing toward the quaint brick façade of the building. "First we will need you to be measured for a suit."

"Mansfield, you are sounding dangerously like me. What do you have in mind?" As Bob accompanied Marcus up the steps he listened gamely to the plan.

The Old State House had stubbornly retained its maiden name long after it had traded its government function for a commercial one. The lower story was mostly lawyers' offices, and there were several tailors above. Marcus rang at the door of a tailor's office that faced the State Street side.

Marcus frowned when there was no answer. "Perhaps they have not returned to work yet since the incident."

"I have known a few Boston tailors in my life, Mansfield, and if I can say one thing about them it's that they would have their tape measures at hand as they are lowered into their caskets." Bob rang the bell again sharply, and this time the old tailor opened the door and greeted them with gusto, as if welcoming the first customers to a new shop. With the streets around this location so empty, business had no doubt slowed to a trickle.

The tailor was a slight, shriveled man who was probably easy to miss outside in the world but expansive and enthusiastic in the kingdom of his shop. "You must be Harvard boys," he guessed.

"As a matter of fact," said Bob, "proudly so. I need a suit made. Graduation events coming upon us, you know, balls and so on, and the Boston rule is you can never decline an invitation. Let's cut a splurge! The latest from Paris, if you please."

"Of course, dear boy!" the tailor replied, dropping an array of needles from inside his sleeve into the palm of his hand, as proudly as a cat showing its claws. "Come stand over here, if you please."

While the tailor cornered his customer by the mirror, Marcus stepped quietly into a back room under the eaves. From inside his coat, he pulled out a switchblade. He peered back into the other room, where Bob regaled the tailor with stories of some legendary Phillips Exeter football game. Marcus gestured to Bob with an upward moving hand. Bob saw his drift, pitching his voice louder.

The window under the eaves was partially opened. Marcus lifted it higher and stepped carefully out onto the ledge. His balance was precarious at first on the sloping shingled roof, but he managed to pull himself completely out and then up to the narrow, flat top. On an ordinary day, the sight of a man standing high on the Old State House would have attracted attention and speculation. He counted on the fact that the laborers spilling up and down the street making repairs in, around, and on top of buildings would sufficiently disguise his activity. Above him, at the height of the tower on the roof, the flags of each of the Boston newspapers rolled and unrolled in the breeze, staking their claims for public attention. It was a clear, chilly day. Below him, he was struck by the many distinct noises he could hear—snatches of conversation, the shouts of workmen, the racket of horses and wagons. But no music, he noticed. No piano playing from any windows, and certainly no organ grinders. These were not welcome among the strict commerce conducted here.

He put one foot in front of another across the center line of the roof until he reached the edge overlooking State Street. Crouching, he leaned over the gold-plated clock that had faithfully kept time for the inhabitants of this crucial quarter of the city—until the day time had ceased. That day, the glass of the clock had melted over its face, obscuring and locking down the hands.

Locking time, Marcus thought to himself. Lying flat on his stomach, he reached down and carved off portions of the discolored crust of glass bit by bit. He hoped Bob was keeping the tailor busy. If not, the next face he might see would be that of a Boston policeman.

Reaching down, he maneuvered his hand through the melted glass until he could feel the Roman numbers of the clock face and the clock's hands. He pulled his arm out and mopped his brow with his sleeve.

Retracing his steps over the roof and back through the window into the tailor's office, he found he had nothing to worry about—he could have crashed through the roof without the old man noticing. Bob had the tailor enthralled, and was now in the midst of rich gossip about the finer Boston Brahmin families.

When Bob saw Marcus had returned, he declared to the tailor that he had to call on a young, pretty, and eminently wealthy young woman and her family to continue a great love affair, the prospect of which the tailor approved heartily.

"Dear me!" the tailor said as they took their leave. "But you never said your name."

"Many apologies, my good fellow. I am William Blaikie, stroke oar and First Scholar of Harvard '68. You may add the charges for the suits on the Blaikie credit, of course. To borrow is human, to pay back, divine."

"Indeed, Master Blaikie!" said the tailor playfully. "And give my regards to the Lowells and the Abbotts at the next mask ball, will you please?"

"Suits?" Marcus asked when they were coming down the stairs.

"Three, for good measure," Bob said, nodding. "Only the most fashionable for Blaikie for his summer in Newport."

"I see you had no problem keeping the old fellow's attention."

"Did you know the word *respectable* is used in Boston more than anywhere else in the world, Mansfield? Once you know that, you know everything."

As they exited the building, there was a young boy who had been loitering on their way in, now slumped on the steps to one of the office buildings under repair.

"On with ya!" growled a workman, throwing a brick out a window. Scurrying away, the boy almost knocked into Bob.

"Whoa there, lad!" he said, grabbing the boy by the shoulder. "You shouldn't hang around while these repairs are made. It's hard company."

"What do you know, you blasted swell?" the boy demanded, pushing with both hands against Bob's strong chest. "I belong 'ere more than you, I bet!"

Bob chuckled and continued down the street.

Marcus motioned with one finger for Bob to wait.

"I thought we were in a hurry, Mansfield," Bob complained.

"If he believes he belongs here, this is probably not his first visit," Marcus said. "Did you notice his arm when he pushed you?"

Bob shrugged. "Lame. What of it?"

Marcus turned back to the boy and stretched his hand out. "What's your name, lad?"

"Theophilus," the boy said, spitting the word out. "Theo, for short," he said in a softer voice, belatedly accepting Marcus's waiting hand and giving it a light shake.

"Theo," Marcus repeated approvingly. He was studying him. "Theo, my name is Marcus."

"Come on, Mansfield, what could he know?" Bob urged.

"More than you, I'd wager, you hog in togs!" the boy rejoined, snapping his cap at him.

"Really? And how much would a lad like you possess to wager?" Bob replied.

"This is my good friend Bob," Marcus interrupted.

"Well, he has a mouth on 'im, bless 'im!"

"Hold on there, you little scamp!"

"He does at that, Theo." Marcus smiled. "What's wrong with your arm?"

The boy shrugged, a shadow passing over his haggard face. With a heavy sigh, he looked down at his right arm and began rotating his hand limply. There was a thick band of scars around it. His face contorted into a wince. "Some weeks back now. Wrist hurt bad," he murmured, holding back a sob.

Bob raised an eyebrow when the boy named the time of his injury. Marcus knelt down to Theo's level and put his hands gently on his shoulders. "Were you inside one of these buildings when that happened? This one?" he said of the edifice nearest where the boy had been loitering.

Theo nodded. "Best bank porter Front Merchants' has ever had. Then the glass . . . My hand got stuck in the window when the glass, because I . . ." He paused once more, his lips trying to pluck the right words. "I wanted to touch it. Can't use that hand much now, but the doctors say in a few months, maybe even just three . . . Not as bad as Mr. Goodnow, who can't see right much out of one eye anymore after his spectacles melted into it. Well, I'll be here to claim my position back soon as I'm strong again!"

"Do you remember anything different in those days before it happened?" Marcus asked.

"Different?" Theo asked.

Marcus looked to Bob for help. "Anyone unusual around these streets, for instance?" Bob inquired. "You greeted customers when they came to the bank?"

"Sure I did. Took their hats, that kind of thing," he said forlornly.

"Anyone who might have been witness to any unusual activity?"

"I 'member someone the day *before* it all happened—a workin'-man repairing the fireplugs—I saw him there that morning, then through the window later in the day at a different plug."

"If he was in the street that long, the workman might have seen something. Would you recognize that workman if you saw him again?" asked Bob.

"Nah. Didn't know 'im and didn't stop to look at 'im closely."

"Do you remember anything about him?"

"Nah."

"What about inside the bank? Did anyone leave an impression, or mention anything strange they had seen?" Marcus asked quickly, sensing the boy was growing bored of the interrogation.

"Not too much," Theo replied, shrugging his shoulders again but still warming to their attention. "Well, Mr. Cheshire, the stock merchant, he was there that mornin', and I remember he talked to me about the harbor. The compasses."

"The compasses?" Bob asked.

"Remember," Marcus said to Bob as he rose to his feet, "the compass manipulation had just been reported in the evening editions the night before State Street. I'm beginning to think the experimenter didn't want to step on his own shadow. He waited until the city had learned more about what happened at the harbor and was properly terrified about it, before he unleashed his second maneuver."

"'Course, he's dead now," mumbled Theo, oblivious to Marcus's theorizing.

"Who?" Marcus asked. Seeing the lad's reluctance to continue, he added, "We're friends now, aren't we, Theo? Who did you mean?"

"Mr. Cheshire! I 'eard he was trampled to death in the stampedin' to flee from here. He was as gentle and kind a man—well, not so gentle and not always kind, really, but a rich man, a friend of mine, I'd say, who oftentimes remembered me by name and always gave a coin or two when I served him well. And if a man as great as Mr. Cheshire can be killed, why, all State Street can die."

As Theo stifled a tear for the lost stockbroker, a man in a sackcloth suit wheeling a supply of bricks grabbed the boy by the back of the collar. "I told you to scram! I'll mix you in with the cement, you stay a minute longer!"

"Leave him alone," Marcus said, stepping between them.

But Theo slipped out of the man's grasp and dashed down the street.

"Wait! Theophilus!" But then Marcus was grabbed by the same man.

"I've seen you."

"Hands off," Marcus said.

The speaker, ruddy and powerful, had an oily mustache that could double for the bristles of a blacking brush. "Right—I knew I'd seen that phiz of yours before. At the lighting demonstration. You're one of the boys from that technology college."

It was one of Roland Rapler's unionists. Marcus wrested away his arm but made no reply.

"You must be mistaken, sir," Bob intervened. "We're just visiting Boston for the week from New York."

"Visiting this particular quarter, you are?" demanded the laborer with a taunting air. "You and your school can make all the machines you want, but when disaster happens, we're the ones to save the buildings, the harbors, the livelihoods of your fathers and brothers. You should be out to help us, not the machines."

"Good afternoon," Marcus said.

He and Bob hurried away. Behind them, the man cupped his mouth with his hands and shouted, "Take care of the little lassie helping you, collegey!"

"What did he say?" Marcus said, his face flushed red with anger as he wheeled around.

"Hush, Mansfield—remember what Hammie told you," Bob said, catching his arm. "They are all brag. Damned agitator doesn't even know who you are."

But Marcus started back toward the much larger man. Bob managed to restrain him before he could reach him.

"It was a threat, Bob. To Agnes. He must have seen me with her at the wharves."

"Take a deep breath now! All brag, right? Remember, they are adept at making people believe they know more than they do."

Marcus calmed down. Bob was right, of course. The man now returned to his work, muttering to himself.

"So, then," Bob said when Marcus had grown calmer, and they were on their way again. "So."

"What?" Marcus asked with pointed irritation.

"That Irish serving girl at Rogers's. You saw her at the harbor?"

"Yes. After I visited Beal, I happened upon her."

"Is she your 'lassie' now?"

"I would be lucky if I were to say yes. But no, she hardly knows me."

"She is a biddy. A housemaid!"

"She does what she must, Bob, so she and her family can eat."

"Take no offense! But you remember that young lady, a Miss Lydia Campbell, I introduced you to in the Public Garden a few months ago. She is not only a stunner; she and her sisters hail from one of the great families. I know you want to make your way in Boston, and a wife is what defines a man in the city. I saw her again recently and was talking you up to the sky."

"I didn't ask you to do that, Bob. Tell me, with all your generous advice, why don't you court one of the fair Miss Campbells, then?"

"I!" Bob asked, titling his head back thoughtfully. "I, you ask? You have ambition, Mansfield. Understand, I was born respectable, and must find my way from it somehow. That rare girl who can mesmerize me is out there."

"You have met her?"

"No, but I shall find her if I must kiss every pair of female lips in the kingdom of Boston to do so."

When they reached the next street, Marcus turned in to an alley, where he removed a city directory from the pocket of his coat.

"I'm sure as a gun no one is listening now. What were we looking for at the Old State House?" Bob asked.

"Fourteen minutes past ten," Marcus said. "The time on the clock above the building."

"And you didn't plunge to your death to find it. What does it tell us, though?"

"If my idea works, it tells us our first of many numbers. We have more places to go, Bob, and we'll need your best foot forward. Come, look this over with me."

If they had known about another pair of eyes watching them, through the lens of a powerful spyglass, they would not have lingered even in the shadows of the alley.

XXI

Natural History

OW HE EVER FOUND HIMSELF floundering like this, he could not say. Seven years as a policeman in the first and finest department in the country, two years and counting in the role of a sergeant. He considered his varied experiences quite valuable. Yet nothing from his past seemed to apply to what he now saw before his eyes.

The Museum of Comparative Zoölogy at Harvard had been transformed. It was another kind of museum now, a museum of unfathomable disasters, you might say. The disasters that had descended upon the people of Boston were in this building dissected into their parts by the natural scientist as though he had found an exotic crocodile or other beast. Each room had been turned to another small piece of the disaster—in three of the small chambers, innumerable shards of debris collected from the harbor had been methodically cleaned and given neatly written labels. Three other chambers were similarly dedicated to the souvenirs from the State Street catastrophe. To Sergeant Carlton's eyes, the objects so petted and coddled—ranging from lost shoes to a giant barnacle-encrusted anchor—seemed rather arbitrarily organized, and each one seemed to be viewed by the scientist as equally as important as the next. The portly naturalist himself had over the last week and a half spent more and more time closed away in his private office, watched over only by a row of human skulls, where he pored over antique maps, to the point where he hardly emerged at all to give Carlton any new intelligence.

A few days earlier, Carlton had called for him when something slithered across his boot. "Agassiz! Agassiz! Come quickly—there is a snake in here!"

"Dear me!" Agassiz cried, hurrying over. "But where are the other five?"

When he later pressed the naturalist for any answers to the problems they were studying, Agassiz deferred, explaining, "If I have more ability than some men, my dear sergeant, then my mistakes are more dangerous than theirs. I shall continue my investigation until I reach a degree of certainty."

Once he came out of his private study laughing with glee. The scientist always smelled of oil and fish. Carlton, hopeful for some real and heartening news, jumped up and asked him what happened.

"Do you know, Sergeant, the story of Chamisso's Chinaman?"

Carlton did not.

"He decides he is quite discontent with the braid hanging from the back of his head, so, trying to escape it, he turns left, then right, but finding it still behind him, he keeps on spinning, expecting it to get in front. Don't you see?"

"I still do not see the joke," Carlton said.

"It just occurred to me that the Chinaman is just like the Evolutionists, who say they can effect anything, if given enough time and repetition, and so continue to turn around in circles!"

For the last two days, the scientist had ceased giving Carlton any information altogether, leaving the policeman to ramble through the museum and wonder in the company of a Dodo bird skeleton how this had become his lot. Finally, the sergeant sent for Chief Kurtz, whom he now greeted at the street door.

Kurtz listened with a sympathetic ear. "But you see, Carlton, Agassiz keeps the legislature at bay, forces them to increase our funds, and to leave us alone!"

"No matter how eminent the professor may be, Chief, I do not see how his methods alone can resolve the matters at hand."

"Pray they can, Carlton."

"Sergeant! Sergeant!"

Agassiz's assistant was scrambling toward where the police officers stood on the front steps.

"Yes?" Kurtz answered for him.

"Come inside, please, gentlemen. The professor should like to have an urgent word with you."

"About time," Carlton said, nodding happily at Kurtz.

The two policemen were brought to Agassiz's office. The naturalist stood impatiently, as though he had been waiting for them all day. "Here you are, gentlemen!"

"Professor," said Kurtz, "the sergeant and I would most appreciate hearing where we stand."

"Have you made some progress, Professor?" asked Carlton.

"Of course I have!" Agassiz huffed. "I know precisely who is responsible for the disasters."

"The dastard will hang higher than Haman for it!" Kurtz declared. "God save the mark! Who is it?"

"Yes, who?" Carlton asked, his heart rising, and feeling for a moment he could embrace the science professor.

"Man!"

"Any particular one, Professor Agassiz?" Kurtz asked after a long pause.

"What I mean is, mankind, Chief Kurtz," Agassiz said. "Them—everyone—out there! I shall explain. Please, have a seat. I have been studying these ancient maps of the Massachusetts landmass." The creased, yellowing maps in question were hanging from the top of a blackboard. "What I believe has happened is there has been a shift, a movement, in the plates and fissures of the land encompassing Boston. This would be due, in all likelihood, to the unprecedented alteration and perversion of our prominent land forms by industry and government alike to accommodate the ravenous and growing population. Over time, I suggest, this has resulted in a shift in the geological character of our region."

"How in the deuce does that explain what happened?" Kurtz demanded.

"I approach the whole question, mind you, from a standpoint entirely different from any popular opinion, as I do every question where science comes into collision with popular belief. My supposition is that the magnetic qualities inherent in any landmass shifted, and at a crucial period of this shift, influenced the navigational instruments as observed in the harbor, and, in a similar fashion, an unknown combination of minerals and chemicals were forced to the surface somewhere in the vicinity of the business district, resulting in the strange and unforeseen effects on all glass substances within a temporary interval of time."

"Do you mean to say, Professor, that nobody is responsible for what occurred?" Carlton asked in disbelief. "How is it possible?"

"What is impossible is for man to harness the forces of science to create such spectacle and destruction. That sort of plan is the exclusive domain of the Divine Mind, carried out according to the laws that regulate the geographical distribution of both men and animals on this planet. No, I do not mean to say nobody is responsible. I mean to say, Sergeant, that Boston itself is responsible, and I mean to prove it!"

"You see," Kurtz turned to Carlton and muttered, "science smiles upon us and prepares our resolution!"

"Be skeptical for now, gentlemen. But remember every scientific truth goes through three stages. First, people say it conflicts with the Bible. Second, they say it has been discovered before. Last, they say they always believed it."

XXII

The Watchmakers' Apprentices

IF ONE SPOT ON THE MAP OF BOSTON, perhaps even on a globe of the world, had the highest proportion of men consulting their watches at any given moment, it might be Boston's financial quarter. It was natural, therefore, that watchmakers sprang up in these fertile grounds.

Marcus and Bob visited six different watchmakers within three streets of the site of the disaster over the next two days. They explained that they were learning the art of watch repair and wished to observe the sorts of problems exhibited in a sampling of watches. In this fashion, they convinced all but two watchmakers to show them their selections of watches awaiting repairs. One of the watchmakers nearly put them out on the street, until Bob spoke dreamily about the isochronal adjustment of the balance spring, inspiring the man to not only open his cabinet of watches, but to offer them a detailed demonstration of the balance spring operations. "I heard Eddy say something about that when he was fixing his watch in the study room once," Bob later explained to Marcus.

By the time they'd finished, they had collected the times frozen in melted glass on twenty-three watches and matched each one with the name of the owner cataloged by each of the watchmakers. Using the city directory, each name was then given an office address.

"There you have it," Bob said, holding out a list of times and locations. They had reunited with Edwin between classes in the Technologists' basement laboratory. "Because of our friend's clever brain, Eddy, we have the time minute by minute as the incident spread over State Street."

"Marcus, that is A-one work!" said Edwin.

Bob added, "I had the same thrill that Galileo had when, making his first telescope, he looked at Venus and found she was a crescent like a new moon, which was what his studies had told him she ought to be."

"Of course," Edwin mused, "people do not always wind their watches correctly, and there are always some so-called timepieces that never keep time properly, but I believe I have come up with the formula to leave room for errors so that we will be as close as possible."

"We need to mark these on a map," Marcus said.

"Our City Hall map is as recent a one as is made, but is already out of date in the details," said Bob.

"The mapmakers cannot keep pace with the changes in the city. Every time a new one is printed, ten new buildings have been constructed, a waterway has become a street, and a street a railroad."

"What about the Architecture Department?" Edwin proposed. "They have been building a perfect facsimile of the entire city all year, continually changing it as the city grows."

"Bravo, Eddy! But we are not allowed in," Bob said. The Architecture Department, the first one in the country, though seen as another branch of industrial and practical education by Rogers, constituted its own island in the Boylston Street building. The professor at its head, Mr. Ware, had not started training his students until the previous year, meaning it had only underclassmen enrolled. In part because of its rarefied subject matter, in part because of its late start, the department and its students jealously guarded its equipment and rooms from the rest of the students.

"I think there's a way, Bob," Marcus replied. "Gentlemen, meet me on the third floor in, say, fifteen."

When Bob and Edwin arrived at the architectural rooms at the time Marcus appointed, a fresh-faced younger student stood in the doorway.

"Well, come on in," he said, closing the door behind him. "This way, fellows, and walk fast."

Inside, Marcus was waiting for them. "French, how much time do we have?"

"Twenty-five minutes, Mr. Mansfield," answered the younger student. "The sophs are in freehand drawing and the freshes are sitting in geometry with Professor Runkle—who won't miss me one bit, with my marks."

"We'll see those rise, I vow to you. Thanks for the help, French. I'll signal you when we're finished."

"Who is the young cub?" asked Bob as they left French at a table by the entrance to the next room.

"That's Dan French—one of the freshmen I'm assigned to coach. Masterful draftsman, they say, but received a sixty-two in geometry and a sixteen in chemistry at midyear examinations."

"Will he keep quiet, Marcus?" Edwin whispered, after gasping in horror at French's marks.

"From what I know, he's a discreet fellow."

They passed a series of drafting tables and entered a long, narrow room dominated by a table that stretched almost the room's entire length. On it was displayed a scale model of metropolitan Boston that stopped them in their tracks.

"Welcome to Lilliput, fellows," Bob said. "I never gave those architecture scrubs enough credit."

"Remarkable," Edwin said, marveling at the model.

"French says they plan on presenting this to City Hall when it is finished as a symbol of the Institute's gratitude to Boston for granting our plot of land," Marcus explained.

"A miniature Boston, from a bird's-eye view," Edwin said, kneeling down for a better look. "It is genius. Even has the cannonball lodged in the wall of Brattle Street Church."

The model included each street, sidewalk, pier, and building of the city proper, carved out of wood with mathematical exactness and painstaking detail as to its relative size and position. It rested on a platform that represented the elevations and foundations of the city. It was as though a machine had condensed Boston into the space of a room. Bob and Edwin located the various houses and churches they had known since childhood. Marcus found the miniature of the Institute itself and studied its design.

He was most impressed by the sensation brought on by seeing Boston all at once. Living in the city, he found it impossible to ever capture it whole in his mind. Every direction gave to the eyes a new Boston. There were the shanties and tenements crowded with foreigners, the elegant groups of brick houses shielded by trees and sloping hills, the busy commercial districts immune to the concerns of any outsiders.

"Nothing at all is missing, down to the very fences and sheds," Edwin commented, still in awe.

"French says they call it 'Boston Junior.' But there is something missing," Marcus said.

"What?" Edwin asked, inspecting the model for its error.

"A hundred ninety thousand people. Remember, that's why we're doing all this."

"Of course," agreed Edwin, chastened.

"French said they built this to exact scale?" Bob asked.

"Yes," said Marcus. "Here is our list of timepieces as they were stopped, and the time of each."

"This could allow us to surmise the type of chemical compound released into the air, by creating a formula for its rate of distribution based on the model," Edwin said.

Edwin took measurements on the model as Marcus read out the locations and times.

"Are you finished in there?" Daniel French inquired with a knock at the door. "Five more minutes before they return."

Marcus called out their thanks.

"I think we have what we need. Here are my preliminary calculations on the rate of distribution," Edwin said, holding up a piece of paper.

"Already!" Bob exclaimed. "That's fantastic, Eddy." Then, to himself, he said, "Hold on. Look at fireplugs."

"What, Bob?" Edwin asked.

"Remember what that laddie Theo said, Mansfield, about the workman repairing the fireplugs on that street? Fireplugs get damaged from time to time, but the odds of multiple ones needing repair . . . it sounded odd to me at the time, but I didn't think more about it. Look at the neat arrangement of the fireplugs squaring the area of the disaster. What if the fireplugs were used to release the chemicals that caused the glass to melt?"

"We'll go back right away—" Marcus began.

"No point, the experimenter is too careful," Bob said. "Any evidence of it would have been removed by now, but if we can include the position of these fireplugs"—he pointed to the tiny models of the water hydrants—"in our calculations, our precision may be greatly increased."

Edwin already began doing this. "We can put it all together downstairs by testing some combinations of chemicals to see how quickly they spread," he said, as they quietly slipped out of the Architecture Department.

Back in their basement laboratory, Edwin prepared the series of chemical tests while Bob helped Marcus in designing trial experiments for their underwater equipment. Many hours later, darkness had fallen outside and each of the three had taken a turn lying on the rough brick floor to rest.

"Say, look at this," Bob, perching himself on a stool, whispered to Marcus while Edwin had his nap.

Marcus took the piece of notebook paper Bob was proffering. "What is it?"

"A list I found that Edwin made of important mathematic, scientific, and technological questions yet to be solved. Thirteen of them. It fell out of one of his books."

Marcus read it over. "Do you plan on resolving these in our leisure time?"

"I thought we could post the list on the wall of the laboratory, and each place our initial by one we would like to do before we enter the heavenly kingdom." Receiving no response from Marcus, he added, "It would help our rooms look more like a real society or club, you know."

"We are not a real society, Bob."

"Treason!"

Marcus laughed as he handed the sheet back. "Post it if you wish, if Edwin allows it."

"Allows it?" Bob protested.

"Allows it?" Edwin asked as he sat up, rubbing his eyes and stretching out a big yawn.

After enduring a lecture from Edwin on the morality of looking at a sleeping man's papers, Bob got his way and the list took its place on the laboratory wall.

Later, just as Marcus was taking his turn on the floor, closing his eyes with relief, he was jolted by the sound of shattered glass and Edwin shouting. Marcus pushed himself to his feet.

"What happened?" Bob asked, coughing.

"The tube slipped out of my hand—I almost had it!" Edwin said with frustration.

"Turn on the ventilating fan!" Marcus said.

The fan yanked the gas through its moving teeth, but was no match for the lingering fumes. The three boys covered their mouths with handkerchiefs and barreled into the hallway.

There, a trill of feminine laughter startled them. Ellen Swallow stood in the doorway of her laboratory. She was smiling, which for her almost counted as a fit of hysteria. She wore a dark outfit that looked like a gymnastics uniform, with a black apron over it, and her hair was wrapped in a series of intricate braids that could only be described as convoluted and would have been roundly condemned by any modern ladies' magazine.

"Yes?" Bob said to her, not certain how else to express his annoyance.

She threw her sharp nose in the air and remarked, "Sulfuric acid with . . . fluoride of sodium."

"Right," Edwin said, then looked at his friends. "Exactly right! But how did she know that?"

Ellen's steel-gray eyes turned deadly serious. "Because I know what you're doing, Mr. Hoyt," she warned. "And now it stops."

XXIII

Afire

NOT *AGAIN!* was what Ellen H. Swallow had thought some two weeks earlier, when, from her half window in the basement, she saw the mud-encrusted police boots climbing the steps into the Institute. She knew if the sort of anti-science frenzy she had already witnessed grew worse, the already financially tenuous Institute would be hanging by a thread.

It is left to you, Ellen Swallow! was the next thought that crossed her mind.

She would have to work in secret. There were so many suspicions of their institution that any sign of entanglement with mischief could grow out of control quickly. She could relate to this, because Ellen Henrietta Swallow *was* the Institute of Technology. She, too, could not make a single misstep.

The morning the harbor disaster had transpired, Ellen had been returning to Boston from Worcester, where she had visited her mother. From the window of her rattling train—she always sat by the window of any conveyance—the harbor appeared to be afire.

Not again! Not that her first career at college was curtailed by similar troubles, but her aims had been cut short nevertheless, just as her current ambitions could be if dark clouds collected over Boston and the Institute. She had entered Vassar shortly after the women's college opened. Ellen had never had formal schooling whatsoever before; her parents were so disappointed in all the town schools that they decided to teach her themselves. They did so faithfully, and what they didn't impart to her she studied on her own. When Vassar accepted her it was as a junior. It suited her to have two years at the women's college instead of four, since she had to pay her own tuition and expenses. Even on her winter holidays, when she visited home she helped in her father's store for extra money, during which time she organized the entire stock of inventory and did the bookkeeping. To her father's chagrin, she flatly refused to allow his customers to smoke in the shop on her watch.

"Why do you sell us tobacco if you don't expect us to smoke it?" asked a man smoking a pipe by the stove on a cold day, as Ellen ushered him out the door.

"I sold you molasses as well," offered Ellen, "but we don't expect you to stay here and cook it up."

She liked the other girls at Vassar well enough, though was surprised when she counted twenty-two of them who wore their hair flowing to their waists without any attempt at doing it up. It was as though they had not dressed. Their bonnets, which they claimed were the latest fashion from Paris, were so small you would need a microscope to find them.

The only genuine trouble in her two years at Vassar was that the college's administrators wouldn't let her study enough. They feared if a student broke down from overwork it could prove to the world that girls could not get a college degree without injuring their health, which ultimately, as alleged by some medical experts, would disrupt their menstruation and future childbearing. With a death by suicide and one by illness among the student population, limitations became even stricter. But persistent Ellen received special permission to rise earlier than the other girls, and she soon discovered that she could study for nine hours without interruption before getting a headache from reading too long.

During an elective course in science, Ellen and a small group of girls volunteered to analyze anything that came their way, from shoeblacking to baking powder. Her immersion in this endeavor, her fascination with it—her talent for it!—convinced Ellen to try chemistry as her life work. But after she was graduated from Vassar, everything seemed to stop short at one blank wall after another. Despite all her hard work, a degree from a women's college proved insufficient to secure her admission into her newly chosen profession. She was living in purgatory, fretting and fuming so much that she began to think she couldn't live much longer. She was thwarted and hedged in on every side, as though God wouldn't help her a bit and man was doing his best against her, and her own heart even turned traitor.

She felt like the prophet Baalam, obstructed everywhere by an angel he could not even see.

If she were to cut the new path she imagined, she now knew she would need to demonstrate her qualifications as a scientist by pioneering her way through a new type of scientific education, the one begun a few years before by the Institute of Technology.

It was her birthday, December 3, when she sat down to write a letter to the Institute. Less than two weeks later she received a note from President Rogers. "Can you come to Boston before many days and see me? I will say now that you will have any and all advantages that the Institute has to offer without charge of any kind. I congratulate you and every earnest woman upon the result." Ellen knew, even in her joy at the news, that her admission, however noteworthy, was but a single step. Without an income, she would hardly be able to afford to live in Boston, which even in the last two or three years had become more crowded with laborers, who had formerly lived in rural towns but now needed to find positions in industry. Then there was the fact that many landladies would not accept "lady college students," never having heard of the exotic species, despite Ellen's pointing out that, unlike her male brethren, she did not smoke or wear boots in bed; many others did not take on single women, or admitted only a limited number, so that their house would not be alleged to be a brothel. Ellen finally found an arrangement with a landlady named Mrs. Blodgett, whose daughter had been a classmate of Ellen's at Vassar. Mrs. Blodgett would provide food and board in return for Ellen cleaning, cooking, keeping peace among the servants, and organizing the boardinghouse ledgers, whenever she was not doing her studies for the Institute.

Ellen promised her father, who worried about her safety, that she would bring to Boston a pearl-handled revolver she had won in a shooting contest when she was fifteen. She purchased several cartridges for it and carried it in her coat pocket when she was walking in the city alone, especially at night; fortunately, she had not yet had an occasion to brandish it against any of the rapists he'd imagined populated the city.

When she read details about such terrible incidents in the newspapers, she assured herself that she could defend her sanctity. Although she was not adverse to experiencing romantic love and physical passion, should she ever encounter it, she was not afraid of going through life without that experience. But it did frighten her deeply to think of being deprived of her own choice in a matter of intimacy.

After only a few months at Tech, she was visiting her family in Worcester when word came that her father's right arm had been crushed in a railroad accident while he'd been helping a friend who worked for a shipping company. Holding back her own anguish, she helped restrain him on the bed while the doctor amputated his arm, which almost took away her reason entirely. In his suffering and delirium, his cries for the arm that was not there, he looked to no one else but his Nellie for the four days before he died. After that, she sometimes feared she would give up her place at the Institute before the spring was over. For months, she went back and forth between Worcester and Boston every day so her mother would not be alone, yet she still succeeded at her studies.

For what special mission was God preparing her? In this dark time, she learned that she had the will and power to control her mind, to a degree. She never could have lived through those sad months if she had for an instant allowed her thoughts to dwell on the terrible scenes of her father's death. She dreamed only once of him dying, one night after sitting on her sofa in Boston mending a dress and thinking of home. Now when such thoughts ever came to her mind she shut the door tightly against them and directed her attention elsewhere, taking a book to read or a pencil to plan something for her future. Her mental focus seemed very like a child to please—so easily was it diverted from morbid and uncontrolled things.

Calmness and self-reliance: Those were the most wonderful Christian graces.

Most of the other students at the Institute took their positions for granted, but not Ellen, not for a moment. They wasted their time during breaks playing football and baseball, but not Ellen, though she would sometimes watch them run around outside her basement window, half of her wishing she could join in their silly, manly contests, the more sensible half of her ready to compose a paste of chloride of lime to treat their grass stains.

Her own stains changed almost daily. Sometimes, the skin on her hands was tinted blue, sometimes brown, sometimes both. Her dresses often boasted holes from acids, some of which could even penetrate her oversize rubber apron.

When they saw her inside the Institute, some of the Tech students hissed or made smacking sounds to mimic kissing. Others took off their hats and stopped all conversation in favor of chilly politeness. Whether polite or unfriendly, they all stared, and she hated herself whenever she felt color rising to her cheeks as she imagined what they were thinking. She far preferred being ignored. When she had to walk through the Institute building, she would usually shield herself with a stack of books over her chest, and if she had no choice but to wait on a bench for a passing throng of students in order to reach the stairs or supply closet, she would busily knit and never look up from her needles and ball of yarn.

Ellen Swallow had never waited for any person, male or female, to do anything she could do herself. In the first weeks of her time at the Institute, the students were brought on an excursion to a gun manufacturer. She was not expected to go with the class, but she had appeared that morning in her finest dress, which was nevertheless still of the plain sort. The professor's assistant, who was escorting the class, quietly pointed out to her that it was not an appropriate setting for a member of the gentler sex because, firstly, it was a factory that produced guns, and secondly, some of the brawny men on the shop floor would be half naked and disgusting to the eyes of a woman. Ellen responded, firstly, that there were mills and factories across the country employing young women, and if they could work in factories surely she could visit one; secondly, that she was never disgusted by any labor; and, thirdly, that she would do her best not to distract the men.

The professor's assistant wouldn't budge. He was a young man who had graduated from Yale and resented having anything to do with Ellen, gave her either too little or too much work for her assignments as suited his mood, and, passing her in the hallways, often greeted her as "Mr. Swallow."

"As you are apt to call me Mr. Swallow, I'm afraid I must insist you treat me as one of the men from now on," she said, "and you will be glad to know that, like some men, I am not afraid of guns." That was the moment the assistant became the only person in Boston to whom Ellen showed her pearl-handled revolver. When she glided by the stunned scion of Yale to join the group, it was already back in its morocco case in her pocket. Later, he complained to the faculty committee about her presence on the excursion (though his humiliation prevented him from mentioning the revolver), and they issued a resolution that her face and neck be completely covered up on visits to factories.

She complied without an objection.

After the visit of the police to the Institute, Ellen approached the matter as she approached all curiosities: with a book in hand. She researched the history of nautical wrecks and disasters and found, much to her amazement, that what had occurred at the Boston Harbor seemed unprecedented. Still, there were clues to draw from the past. An extract she found from a newspaper from 1843, for example, reported on the wreck of the vessel *Reliance,* traveling from China to England: "During the last ten days, Mr. Kent and his associates, who purchased the wreck of the *Reliance,* near Boulogne, have been busily employed in their endeavors to bring the wreck to land; they have found a chronometer, several silver and plated dishes, and a large iron tank, 46 feet long by 8 feet deep, and 6 feet wide."

Exploring this further in several French nautical histories at the public library reading room, Ellen discovered that the iron tank mentioned in the extract had been placed approximately eighteen feet below the binnacle compass. She calculated that the tank would have exerted a magnetic pull equal to 2,208 cubic feet of malleable iron, and that whatever part of the tank was on the port side of the ship would attract the south point of the compass. The *Reliance* would have charted an east by south course by compass, yet at the time of its disaster was running through the channel west by north, eight or nine leagues off its reckoned course. Driven ashore, the ship was lost and 114 people drowned.

Using the information gleaned from this and a dozen other historical wrecks she could attribute to some presence of iron or other magnetically charged materials, Ellen arrived at a variety of calculations to estimate the amount and placement of iron that could cause damage on the scale of what happened at the Boston Harbor. There was this difference from the other wrecks: No amount of bad fortune could have led to the Boston disaster. No amount of luck or stupidity. Nor could luck have produced *this*, thought Ellen doggedly as she read about what had happened at State Street on April the tenth. She struggled to find a starting point for her research into this next incident, but kept thinking back to demonstrations of glassblowing techniques she had seen when she was ten. She read every word of material she could find on the subject. She felt certain the key to how something like a glass window was destroyed from the outside would be to find how it was made from the inside.

When she saw Mr. Mansfield, that mechanical Johnny Appleseed, in her sphere, *her* basement, she knew it was no coincidence. She knew, for she assiduously collected every scrap of information about the Institute, its staff, and its students, that he was a charity scholar and beholden to the professors, enough so to spy on her as an agent for those elements of the faculty who did not wish her to remain.

"We have a society. It is called the Technologists," he had mumbled unconvincingly.

He and his friends were a nuisance and a threat to her seclusion, and if she could see them shipped off for some violation, she would do so with a smile and a flick of her handkerchief. Then again, they could do the same, were they to discover her.

"A *secret* society," that dandified, charmless, and overly handsome swell Bob Richards had added.

Secret society! That was rich. Even the mere scents of chemicals that wafted into her laboratory from theirs revealed them to her. There were no secrets in nature or man that Ellen Swallow felt she would not discover, given proper time.

She had to laugh to think how clever they believed they were, but she had decided. Worrying about them was a distraction. Instead, she would put them under her thumb.

XXIV
___

Greetings, Fellows

"**D**O YOU MEAN TO TELL ME *she* has been conducting her own investigation, right under our noses?" Pacing Ellen's laboratory, a pink-faced
Bob Richards, arms crossed and eyes narrowed, addressed his fellow
Technologists as though the mistress of the laboratory were not standing serenely by them, in front of the compass needles and fresh chemical
solutions lined up neatly on her shelves.

"The reputation of the Institute *is* at stake," Ellen answered Bob
evenly. "The reputation of everyone who teaches and works with technological arts rests on resolving this matter quickly, Mr. Richards. Anyone would be blind not to see that."

"But how did you know what we were doing, Miss Swallow?" Marcus asked, curious rather than hostile.

"Without much difficulty at all, Mr. Mansfield. I have seen and heard
you bumping and stumbling around that laboratory down here. And
when neither you nor Mr. Richards could credibly explain the intent of
your 'society,' I easily surmised what you were engaged in, though likely
with far less success than I. As little as I relish a collaboration, your separate investigations must end now, I'm afraid, for I cannot have mistakes
on the part of you three place my own progress in jeopardy. A little more
hydrogen fluoride, gentlemen, and you would have killed us all."

"Now what makes a stringy little thing like her believe she can solve
such enigmas?" Bob demanded. "And a freshman!"

"What makes you think *you* can accomplish the same, Mr. Richards?
Because you are so overfilled with good looks and charm?"

"Flattery!" Bob cried out. "Ha! I'm afraid that will not work so easily
on me, young lady."

"I believe I am several years older than you, Mr. Richards. And I see no call to defend myself, particularly if you cannot turn and look at me squarely."

"There," Bob said, locking on her face for a moment. "It isn't easy, believe me!"

She did not take the bait. "I know I am seen by some at the Institute, yourselves included, I am certain, as a dangerous person. I proceed with caution at all times. Rest assured, analytical chemistry is very delicate work fitted more for ladies' nimble hands. When I was a child on my family's farm, my mother would not permit me to milk our cows, saying it would make my hands too large and unsightly for a woman. Well, I believe you and Mother would appreciate each other, Mr. Richards. You with the spotted hair: Mr. Hoyt."

Edwin, who was studying the size of his hands, looked up. "Yes."

"If I am not mistaken—and I'm not—the composition you tested earlier needs more dilution if you wish to engineer the sort of compound used on State Street. When you do something like this, Mr. Hoyt, you might as well do it to a nicety. Let us look together inside your laboratory for a moment."

The party moved in one awkward, distrustful block to the Technologists' laboratory next door, where Ellen stood on a stool to examine the window near the ceiling. The glass had turned brown with pink veining from exposure to the spilled gas solution, but it had not dissolved like the windows on State Street.

"Have any of you gentlemen studied glassblowing?" she asked.

"Yes," Bob boasted. "I've done it a little myself, and not too poorly."

"In that case, you'll know that oxide of manganese is used in most glass for windows to give it a white color, but that it absorbs chemicals when it is exposed. If the fluoride from sodium were not so hard to purify, Mr. Hoyt, it would be well suited for the purpose you intended here. If you mix a dilute acid with the double fluoride of barium, aluminum, or lead we should bring the compound closer to the gas that must have caused the dissolving of the silicates in the business quarter. The seemingly simple principle that energy is not destroyed leads to metamorphoses far more astonishing than any we read about in mythology as children."

"Of course," Edwin agreed, nodding enthusiastically after a moment of stunned silence. "We must try it as she suggests, straightaway!"

"Wait a moment, fellows," Bob said. "Just wait a moment! Let us take the counsel of cooler heads—my cooler head, at least. Do you suggest our helping *her*?"

"No. I suggest accepting her offer to help us," Edwin said. "She is a true chemist, Bob."

"We are working toward the same end, Bob," Marcus said gently. "It would not be efficient to continue separately—you must admit those grounds, at least."

"How can we trust her?"

"Because she cannot reveal what we are doing without our revealing her," Edwin pointed out.

"I'd wager she just wishes to govern what we're doing, to try to take charge of it all!" Bob declared.

Ellen raised an eyebrow and, without making a denial, turned her back to them as she surveyed their headquarters.

"Bob, please, be reasonable about this," Edwin said.

Bob looked from Marcus to Edwin and back again, expecting some sudden reversal.

"I won't allow it! Why, I would almost rather be a law student than to have a woman in our group!"

"So mysteriously God leads us, doesn't He, Mr. Richards? Worry not, I am not one of the feminist reformers. I believe men are here to stay, and we women might as well work with them, not against them."

"Shall we, then?" Edwin proposed, motioning Ellen toward the chemical supply shelf.

"Professor Swallow, if I may," Bob said, easing his charming smile into place for another tactic.

"Oh, you are speaking to me now, Mr. Richards?"

"You should know we men have been working until late at night at these tasks—without the least bit of rest to speak of."

She accepted his challenge with a small lift of her shoulder. "I was up all last night at my telescope once I finally got home. I found what I suspect are seven new star clusters and three new nebulae, before being up with the lark. My body does not need pampering."

"You have your own telescope?" he asked with surprise.

"I spent two years with the same clothes at Vassar in order to afford the best one, Mr. Richards. I knew it would make my spirits more contented than a dozen dresses would, and luckily I have enough in my head to balance what is wanting on my back."

Bob did not admit defeat, but the standstill quickly resolved itself into a routine of activity. Besides, now two laboratories were at their disposal, and Ellen's was far better equipped. They were careful, however, not to enter her laboratory during school hours. Ellen's progress, meanwhile, had been impressive. Through different calculations, she had come to the same preliminary conclusion as her new colleagues about the manipulation of the compasses, and her chemical work, combined with Edwin's, led them to a rapid narrowing of possibilities on the State Street matter.

Her laboratory was also filled with cabinets of mold and pieces of food, which explained some of the odd smells that emanated into the hallway, as well as vials of liquids, which Ellen said she was testing. She proudly showed them twenty-four samples of water she had collected from Mystic Pond. The food and water they consumed, she said, was a minefield of chemical problems and contamination, and yet was entirely overlooked by analysts. She pointed out a canister of cinnamon that she had analyzed under a microscope, only to find far more mahogany sawdust than cinnamon.

"The world moves and science with it," she said to Bob when he looked over the shelves of food supplies with a skeptical blankness. "Shall we not one day find a way to convert the millions of tons of carbon in our atmosphere to wholesome food? When I studied physiology as a girl of seven, there were two hundred and eight bones in the body. Now there are two hundred and thirty-eight."

"I've never counted myself, Professor Swallow," Bob grunted. His new appellation for her, which he used liberally, seemed to satisfy his rebellion against the collaboration for the moment. "I should not argue the point with you. The idea of making science out of food might not be very scientific but it is, well, awfully womanly."

"Tomorrow, if not today, the woman who is to be master of her house must be an engineer also. Mr. Mansfield," she added, snapping her head toward the other side of the room, "you do understand you have been permitted inside my laboratory only for the present and for this very particular purpose."

"Yes, Miss Swallow," answered Marcus.

"Good. Because you are *not* welcome here if you wish to examine my private belongings."

He had been looking over the wires of what appeared to be an alarm mechanism, presumably what had warned her of his presence outside her door the day he found the offensive caricature. "It is impressive. Is it of your own construction?"

"It is," Ellen said, allowing a little pride to enter her usually dispassionate tone. "Go ahead, then, you may look at it briefly."

"Two circuits operated by one galvanic battery," Marcus described it as he inspected it. "Arranged with electromagnets, so that any breaking of the circuit by coming into contact with the wire causes that signal wheel over your supply cabinet to turn—the interruption causing the alarm to sound. Most ingenious of all, the mechanism is arranged so that the length of the alarm will inform you exactly where the location of the break occurred. Miss Swallow, have you been very harassed of late?"

Ellen's look of quiet pride vanished at the question. "From the very instant I set foot on the grounds of the Institute."

"I mean whether there has been an escalation in the hazing recently."

She crossed her arms over her chest. "Why do you ask, Mr. Mansfield?"

"Do you know who is responsible?"

"Of course I do!"

"Tell me, and I can see to it that the faculty put an end to it."

"Child."

"What?" he asked.

"You really are a child."

Marcus frowned, puzzled and hurt.

She showed her irritation at having to explain with a loud sigh. "Mr. Mansfield, if I were to point out the perpetrator you refer to, and he is punished or shipped off, do you think I will then be more readily accepted by the others? No, indeed. I will stir up more hornets from the original nest. It is not a fear of me individually that prompts hazing as much as what my being here will mean in the future, for rapid change is always fungoid to those who do not wish it. People are curious to know what monstrosity is to arise from my ashes, aren't they? Tell all such interested individuals that my aim is only to make myself a true woman, one worthy of the name, and one who will unshrinkingly follow the path that God marks out—wherever it takes me. I should thank you to remember you have no call to intrude upon my life—we are not friends, and shall not be. When this is finished, you shall return to your separate existences, as far from me as possible."

"On that point," Bob interjected, "I am with the good professor wholeheartedly."

During the next afternoon study period, when Bob and Ellen were in her laboratory finishing disassembling equipment for transport, to be reassembled at the harbor, there was that sound again—like a crying baby.

"There it is! That noise! What else do you do here in your secret little laboratory, Professor Swallow?"

"What sound do you mean, Mr. Richards?" she asked Bob innocently.

The sound repeated itself, this time as a wild shriek.

"That's what!" Bob said, satisfied now that he was closer to exposing her true wickedness.

"You mean my baby."

Before Bob could question this, a slender black cat leaped from behind a cabinet onto the table directly in front of Bob, who shouted and jumped back.

"A cat? You keep a cat in here?"

"He is my baby," she replied forthrightly. "And the handsomest creature ever made by God. He has a voice like an angel."

"He is a common black cat. His cry is loud and disruptive. Why don't you leave him home?"

"Usually I would. There is a building being erected outside my boardinghouse window, and I do not like him to be near the dust particles during the day. Neither human nor animal should breathe in such foreign particles. Here, at least, I know exactly how each compound is made, and have the use of a ventilating fan. You may wish to know he enjoys to be scratched on the chin."

"Do you not realize that with a black cat you are liable to provoke those less mature boys who think you're a witch?"

"You mean boys such as yourself?"

"Less mature even!"

"Did you know, and it is a fact, that sailors' wives kept black cats to guarantee their husbands' safe return from sea? In fact, due to this superstition, they were constantly stolen."

"A common animal does not belong in a laboratory."

"In fact, the laboratory may be the greatest friend to dumb animals. As science advances, the lives of animals will improve as we depend less and less on their labor and no longer ignore their conditions in order to improve ours. You know, there is much to learn from animals if we are ever to be truly industrial creatures. The beaver is the finest builder of bridges and the silkworm a better weaver than any man or woman. God gave industry perfectly to the caterpillar while we must learn our arts. That is technology—our way to become closer to being like the animals. I worry the pioneer cankerworms are having a cold time of it this spring, by and by."

"Cankerworms? Thunder and lightning, woman! See to it that animal is not here long, or I shall throw him out on the street myself and let a sailor's wife find him."

"I suppose you have seen the latest news," she said, changing the subject, and gestured to the day's newspaper on the table.

"We have been somewhat occupied!"

"Do not get too lost in your experiments alone. You know the story of the fate of the great Archimedes, I assume."

"Obviously!" Bob said, but his hesitation gave away his ignorance on the subject.

"I shall tell it anyway," she said with a knowing look. "When the Romans took Syracuse, Marcellus ordered that the enemy's renowned engineer, inventor of the dreaded Archimedes' mirror, be spared. But when the soldiers found him, Archimedes was too busy writing geometrical formulas in the sand with a stick to answer to his name, and was run through by a sword."

"Well?" Bob asked impatiently.

"Well, Mr. Richards, the latest news is that Louis Agassiz at Harvard is organizing expeditions at several points around Boston to examine the sediment formations."

"Heavens! The sediment?"

"Excuse me. I have matters to attend to in the other room."

"She ought to look into Archimedes' mirror now and again," he grumbled as he picked up the newspaper and found the column. "Well. Fossilized Agassiz, just our luck to contend with you."

The cat, thinking he was addressed, curled on his side in front of Bob. When he was certain Ellen had gone back to the laboratory next door, Bob scratched the chin of the animal, who purred throatily.

* * *

MARCUS COULDN'T CONFESS to Bob how tickled he was to be collaborating with Ellen Swallow. He had heard all of the stories about her eccentric personality but also about the rare genius of her microscopic eye in chemical analysis. If he did not have to hide what they were doing from the rest of the world, Agnes Turner would be enthralled to hear all about Miss Swallow. If he was tempted to tell her, the threats from the unionist worker had knocked sense into him. It would not be safe to involve her more than she was.

Over the next three days he made sketches refining a few of the mechanisms for the rest of the equipment they would need to search for evidence at the harbor. Needing to make some tests in water, he announced he was going to walk to the river, but Bob stopped him and said he had a better idea. They exited the laboratory and crossed the hall to the other side of the basement, directly under the entrance hall, where they passed through the engines for the ventilating fans and the rows of excess charcoal and other supplies.

They reached two water tanks, fashioned with pipes and steam pumps, that supplied special faucets inside the building with salt water for use in experiments. Bob pointed out a third saltwater tank.

"Where does this one connect?" Marcus asked.

"Nowhere," Bob said, unscrewing the top. "I have been using it to experiment with an injector device for aerating water."

"You have? Does the faculty know?"

"Indeed. They approved it."

He waited to see if Bob was going to make a joke, but he was busy adeptly preparing the tank. "You never mentioned your aerating device before, Bob."

"Oh, I shouldn't want you fellows to have the wrong idea that I am a dig or a toady like you or Edwin. Come, are you ready to start?"

"Much appreciated," Marcus said, laughing.

They lowered into the water a lantern slightly larger than the usual kerosene lamp held by hand, with a tube extended upward from the cage. After testing the lamp at different depths in the tank to determine how long the flame would remain, and getting mostly satisfactory results, they paused to make modifications.

"Do not permit her to distract you, Mansfield, old boy."

Marcus looked up at him from the floor, where he was fastening a gauge, wondering how he knew Agnes was on his mind. Bob had pulled an unusually serious face. "Who?" he replied.

"Who do you think, Mansfield? Ellepedia. She seems to have a Napoleonic faith in her own star, which cannot fail to annoy."

"Yes, you're right. There is too much important work to do to invite distraction. Enough people have been hurt already by someone out there."

"When do you think we will be ready with the rest of the machinery?" Bob asked.

"A little more testing. Day after tomorrow, maybe. How well it will work, Bob, I cannot say."

"Did you notice that sometimes her eyes appear gray, and other times, blue, the color appearing and vanishing like a meteor in the sky? There is some trickery in it."

"You mean Miss Swallow?"

"Who else?"

"Intrigued?" Marcus ventured.

Bob balked. "Terrified. She is, doubtless, the very first girl I cannot understand."

"Fellows, there you are, come on!" Edwin had barely burst upon them and caught his breath before turning and dashing off again, his laboratory coat fluttering behind him. Marcus and Bob put aside what they were doing and followed him back to their laboratory and took places near the table, where Ellen stood in her apron.

"I won't break. You can come closer, gentlemen," Ellen said. "That's better. Ready? Class begins."

"You see, fellows, Miss Swallow and I have changed the compound using the formulas she had been preparing," Edwin said without taking a breath, "along with the rate of distribution shown by the Old State House clock and the watches you two found, and Bob's supposition about the fireplugs, which appears absolutely correct."

"Eddy," Bob urged, though Edwin couldn't possibly talk any faster.

"You see, by working backward using those formulas, and adjusting the dilution of the acid that is combined with a fluoride to the right level . . ."

Ellen released a small amount of their compound onto the corner of a pane of glass at the table. That part of the glass fizzled and dripped down as a liquid.

"In gas form, it would have the same effect," said Ellen, "on a much broader area against any silicates or glass—not just windows but eyeglasses, drinking glasses, watches. Of course, I suspect the experimenter is using an impure, adulterated compound that we will never reproduce exactly, but replicating its behavior and primary components should allow us to observe what happened with some exactitude."

"If we have hit upon the right chemical formula," Bob said.

"Then we are leagues closer to finding where it could have come from," Marcus said, finishing his thought.

Their mutual excitement was interrupted by a knock at the door to the laboratory.

"Busy!" Bob answered.

The knock repeated itself and the door swung open.

"I said 'busy'!" Bob bellowed.

"Greetings, fellows."

"Hammie," Bob said, utterly surprised. As he spoke, he moved in front of the demonstration table, blocking it from Hammie's view. "You have a key to this room?"

Marcus tensed.

"Why are you in the building so late, Hammie?" Edwin finally managed a less leading question.

"Come now, enough of this pretense. I know what you're all doing here," Hammie said somberly, taking a few leisurely steps inside. His hat was cocked over to one side and his face was unevenly shaved around the bends of his cheeks.

"And," he continued as they stared at him, "I don't like it, not at all."

"Listen, Hammie," Bob pleaded, but Marcus put out his hand, sensing this wasn't what it appeared.

"The Technologists!" Hammie cried in outrage. "How dare you!"

"What?" Bob asked.

"My father might think to disregard my pursuits, but I shall not allow my classmates to do the same. I won't! I saw the papers in the faculty offices. You registered yourselves as members of the Technologists and have been holding meetings. I *started* the Technologists Society when we were sophs. It's a plain fact of the bylaws that you can't have meetings without me!"

The others took the opportunity to breathe again.

"Hammie, I didn't realize that you started the Technologists," Bob said. "Why didn't anyone join back then?"

Hammie gazed at the ceiling, then began looking around the room. "Frankly, I couldn't find any members—that's just it. What a bore everyone around here is. I always wanted to have a secret society. Say, what is all this?"

"You mustn't tell anyone," Edwin blurted out.

"What, Hoyt?" Hammie asked, distracted by the variety of objects on the demonstration tables.

"You mustn't tell!" Edwin repeated, while Marcus and Bob both gave him surreptitious warning glances that went unseen.

"Yes, you mustn't say anything, Mr. Hammond," Ellen said evenly. "The college has asked us to develop new experiments for next year's curriculum, but it is confidential, lest any underclassmen gain an unfair advantage in the competition for Top Scholar."

"But you're a fresh yourself," Hammie pointed out.

"Not allowed in classes," Ellen said.

"Well, that is something," said Hammie. "What a stroke, to have four members of my society all at one fell swoop and a commissioned task from the faculty. But in all my born days, I would not have imagined a girl among the roster."

"It's something novel, Hammie," Marcus offered. Hammie was unpredictable. If he didn't accept Ellen, he might decide to take their usurpation of his club to the faculty. "That's right, isn't it, Bob?"

When he was not dismissing them, Hammie seemed to crave acceptance among his peers, and there was no one more popular than Bob to offer it up. Bob grimaced at his predicament. "Yes, yes. She's not nearly as bad as she looks," he murmured.

Hammie meditated on it, chewing at the side of his mouth. "Say, miss," he said, turning to Ellen and inspecting her from the front and the side, "when were you born? Exactly?"

She clenched her teeth firmly as though to say that the answer would have to be wrung forcibly from her lips. Marcus pleaded with his eyes for her to oblige. She finally said, faintly, December 3, 1842.

"And time of day, Miss Swallow?" She told him. "You are nine thousand, two hundred and eighty-three days old, not counting today, of course," Hammie said almost instantaneously. This seemed to calm his reservations and he interlocked his fingers in thought. He paced the line of students like a drill sergeant. "Having one of the weaker sex in a private society is a *novel* idea. You do wish to have a position, miss?"

Visibly cringing at the choice of gender terminology for her, Ellen, barely audible, assured him in her tamest voice, "I do, very much so, Mr. Hammond."

Hammie's eyes lingered on her a moment too long as he continued his examination of the troops. "Well, I suppose I shall have to revise our charter. The Technologists, as perhaps you know, are dedicated to protecting the status and reputation of the Institute. One other thing. The charter states quite directly that each new member must pronounce the oath of the society aloud, or be banished at once and nevermore enter this chamber."

"Oath?" Marcus asked.

Hammie stood up straight and said in a grave tone: " 'I always swear by Tech and always mean to.' " He waited.

The others looked at one another and then repeated the words half-heartedly.

"Remember, Hammie, a member of a secret society must never speak of it to *non*members," Bob cautioned. "It should be kept entirely among ourselves."

"My dear Richards," Hammie replied with his sloppy smile, "I despise most people: ninety-nine percent, to approximate. Of course I know the rules. You are addressing the president of the Technologists Society. Does someone have glasses and some wine, or perhaps cider?"

"There are these, Hammie," Edwin said, gesturing to some porcelain tubes used for experiments.

"Here you are," Bob said, removing a small black bottle from inside his coat pocket.

"That shall suffice." Hammie poured a little whiskey from the bottle into five tubes. They each raised one, following his lead. "Fellows, let us drink to the health of the Technologists, now and forever!" The four men swallowed the drinks down. Ellen poured hers down the sink as the new president of their society was occupied doing a sort of ecstatic war dance around the headquarters.

XXV

───

Four Pulls

T HEY HAD NEVER SEEN ANYTHING like Marcus's machine suit except in the etchings of fantastic tales written to excite the imaginations of children. Even Marcus took a step away to examine it as they unwrapped the blankets it was bundled in and began assembling the parts.

"It won't kill anyone, will it?" Bob asked of the invention.

"I can't help but think I'm here to put together Frankenstein's monster," remarked Ellen.

Edwin had turned noticeably pale.

"Don't mind them, Edwin," Marcus said to reassure him. "In any case, I'm the one who is going to be inside."

"Perhaps we should test it further before anyone wears it," Edwin said.

But they had already agreed it was time. Ellen had already translated all the details in the science journals that described similar equipment a German engineer had constructed several years before. True, the German design had led to two fatalities but they had modified the design over the last few days by using the water tank to test their own improvements. Not that the prospective diver didn't have his own fears. As was always the case with Marcus, he found it much easier to risk something himself rather than worry about a friend in danger.

"The suit is as ready as it will be," Marcus said, as he snapped a woolen cap over his head and ears. "Help me on with the breathing cap, will you, fellows?"

The four of them were out by the harbor islands on a sailboat Bob had borrowed, the day so far chilly but clear. Bob and Edwin lifted up the heavy brass helmet and lowered it onto Marcus's head. This was attached to air pumps and pipes on a leather and canvas suit that Marcus stepped into, which was also fastened by Ellen to a dive lantern. The "breathing cap," as they named the helmet, had three window slots in the front and sides, and a long hose at its top that connected on the other end to a steel cylinder, engineered and built by Bob and positioned on deck. On Ellen's suggestion, they had added a device on the helmet so that Marcus could change position more easily without losing his air. They had also prepared a second suit in case any lacerations or dents were found in the equipment as they prepared for the dive, but it all passed their inspection. Marcus's sleeves and collar were fastened with India rubber rings for further security.

"There, that's not too bad, is it?" Bob asked. "Does it feel heavy?"

"He's wearing two hundred pounds, with leaden clogs on his feet, Mr. Richards!" Ellen said. "It needs to be heavy enough to bring him to the seafloor."

"One other thing," Bob said. He held out a dagger, which he pulled out of its sheath. "In case you meet any sea serpents."

Marcus waved this away and tried to say something, which sounded like little more than a dull echo from inside his helmet. He pointed to the steel cylinder, as if to say: Concentrate on that.

"Four pulls on the air pipe, we bring you up," Edwin confirmed, also pantomiming the instruction.

Marcus nodded as much as the massive helmet permitted. Through the front eye-glass, he could see that his shadow on deck in the morning sun looked completely misshapen. And magnificent.

Bob steered the sailboat carefully in the open water. He had used Rogers's notes, a nautical map of the area, and the results from their experiments, as well as the interviews with the old wharf rat and Captain Beal, to estimate the most likely regions from which the interference had originated. Beal had revealed to Marcus that the *Light of the East*, at the first sign of trouble, had been at Castle Island, which had been the outermost boundary of the magnetic disruption. If Bob's calculations were correct, the origin was far enough out not to be conspicuous but strategically located near the primary channels for ships preparing to dock. It was early in the morning, and the nearest piers were still under repair, so nobody would be watching, or so at least they believed.

With the boat anchored, Marcus was lowered on a rope ladder into the water. He had to perform a tumbling motion with his body to break the surface because of the weight of his costume. Though he had been breathing through the tubes as soon as the helmet was on, it was a startling change that swept through him when he breathed underwater, encased from head to toe by the sea.

There was a thrill about looking ahead and to each side from his three glass eyes. A terrifying thrill. He bobbed down the undulating ladder deeper under the water.

Breathe deeply. Breathe hard. He remembered giving himself those instructions when he had felt he would not live another hour.

By the time he reached the bottom, it seemed a half hour had passed. With every step he took, the entire seabed seemed to sink a little beneath his boots. The ladder and air pipe followed him like a marionette leading his master. At certain moments, there was a tranquillity about it, the distance and freedom from the world. At other times, the strangeness seemed eerie and volatile.

His vision underwater gradually sharpened. There were many objects—silver spoons, some wine bottles made use of by clever sea life—that Marcus supposed had been deposited in the ocean in the course of the disaster, as well as fragments of wood from the wrecked ships. What he didn't see were any pieces of iron. In fact, that seemed the only material he wasn't finding among the assorted detritus of shipboard life and marine commerce. After one pause to return to the boat to monitor the equipment, with extra weights added to the suit so he could drop faster, Marcus returned to the search below, shifting it eastward.

But soon, exhaustion overruled excitement and novelty, particularly since the closest thing to any loose iron he found was a lone crowbar and some pieces of a cannon. Had whoever engineered the disaster found a way to remove the iron afterward? This would be unlikely, considering the depth and the amount of iron the students had calculated would be necessary. Or had Marcus been wrong about the cause from the beginning? He looked at the shadow of the boat following above and considered giving the signal to pull him up.

As he had been doing through the expedition, he picked up the instrument that they had fixed by a watch chain to the diving suit. It was one of their less heavy pocket compasses. For the first time the needle was moving in an unusual pattern. Marcus's heart skipped. He studied his surroundings and found a steamer trunk stuck in the seafloor. He had seen it a few minutes before and surmised it was another piece of lost cargo. It was locked. This did not signify anything of great import, as a trunk full of dresses might be fitted with the sturdiest lock known to mankind for a mere ferry ride.

Marcus returned to the crowbar; when he picked it up with both hands, the edges bent as readily as a twig. At first he thought himself a victim of an optical illusion occasioned by the glass prism of his helmet and the movements of the water. Or the air he was breathing, despite their intricate adjustments and Ellen's calculations, must be giving him too much oxygen and, temporarily, increased his strength. Then he blinked, finding the bar straight again, and realized it was far more troubling than a moment of superhuman force. The condensed air was affecting his brain. He knew he could not stay down longer. He took the crowbar and returned to the trunk, which he was able to snap open with the bar.

"This is it!" he said to himself, beginning to attach the buoys tied to his suit for the purpose of raising the cargo.

His breathing had quickened, and this, combined, no doubt, with the excessive levels of oxygen, brought on a sudden flush of dizziness. The corner of the seabed where he stood seemed to darken until it was all blackness. A drumming started in his ears. He realized that because he had stayed in one place too long, he was sinking into the muck. As he tried to pull himself out, the swarming scarlet fauna wrapped around his air tube. He froze. If he jerked his body, or even gave the signal on his lifeline to be hoisted, the tube would be broken, cutting off his air in an instant. He remained as still as possible, his heart racing, his arms resting around the steamer trunk. The fish grew braver around him and brushed his suit, and the fauna grew redder and became massive tentacles. Until he blinked, when the weeds returned to their actual size.

Breathe deeply. Breathe hard.

When he thought of dying, he thought of his friends and of Rogers. He had failed them and could not forgive himself.

Then a shadow fell over him. The fish scattered in an instant. A nervous tremor shot through him. If there were sharks passing through these waters, Marcus would have to swim in his heavy gear, and his air tubes would without a doubt be pulled out by the fauna. The shadow slowly resolved into an imposing figure, and a stream of light broke in from above. It was a reflection of the sun against a helmet on another diver, coming toward Marcus, arm raised, wielding a gold-handled dagger that also caught the light as it flashed toward him. Marcus felt himself on the verge of swooning.

With a few slashes of the dagger, the diver attacked the weeds immobilizing Marcus's breathing tube and freed him. And now Marcus could see the familiar Bob Richards grin through the helmet of the emergency suit they had built.

After taking a moment to recover himself, Marcus signaled his thanks. Bob was already studying the trunk. They attached a chain that they had run alongside the ladder in the event of a hoped-for discovery.

* * *

"THIS CANNOT BE IT!"

Marcus was relieved to be on dry land again, his equilibrium restored. With some labor, they brought the salvaged trunk of large iron pieces to Ellen's laboratory through the rear entrance of the building. As they had guessed, the iron had been hammered and dented to promote the highest degree of interference to the navigational equipment, but Edwin kept shaking his head.

"This cannot be it, I tell you," he repeated. "It's impossible."

"Look," said Bob. "The trunk wasn't entirely filled, so that as the motion of the heavy waves that morning was jostling it, and the pieces of iron collided, the natural magnetism would be amplified even more. And with the iron in the trunk, nothing was ever seen. The perfect submarine weapon. Fashionable, as well."

"Fashionable?" Ellen asked.

"The trunk, I mean," Bob said, "is a very topnotch build. Something you might find in the finest steamship class."

"Even placed in a precisely calculated position, there is no possibility this amount of iron could derange the compass readings in a radius encompassing the length of that entire channel," said Edwin.

"Mr. Hoyt is correct, I'm afraid," Ellen said, studying the trunk of iron from every angle. "This trunk cannot provide the explanation for the disaster, which means this may be an entirely coincidental discovery."

"We both searched the seabed thoroughly down there," Bob insisted. "There was nothing else to find!"

"Then we have found nothing," Edwin replied.

"Let us not make our conclusions yet," Marcus said. "It is too early to declare a failure."

Marcus suggested they push the trunk to the back of Ellen's laboratory until they had time to examine it more. Their general proceedings had changed somewhat now that the female pupil was a partner. Since her laboratory was generally sacrosanct, protected by the rules and equally by fear of her imagined witchcraft, they could safely hide important objects inside. They had installed a one-half-inch glass speaking tube that ran between the two laboratories so they could communicate without the risk of being seen entering her forbidden sanctuary during public hours, and also warn one another when others were present in the basement. They also had begun the work to extend the alarm mechanism from Ellen's laboratory to alert them of anyone attempting to enter their laboratory. Ellen, meanwhile, had posted a sheet of paper listing all their names under the heading SLANG, and decreed that any use of slang or religious blasphemy from then on would elicit a check mark by the offending name and a fine of one penny. Bob put himself in immediate debt by sighing, "Goodness!" at the whole idea.

"You will not get any pennies from me," Ellen had warned.

"I suspected as much," Bob said to Marcus and Edwin.

"When I was at Vassar, the girls were as full of slang as any boy I ever heard. Every sentence began with 'I vow!' until I could only dream of cotton in my ears and solitude."

"Well," Bob said, reaching into his pocket, "I will put half a dozen more in now as a deposit."

As for Hammie, he never thought of entering Ellen's private laboratory, and the objects of investigation were divvied between hers and that of the Technologists, so even his sharp mind wouldn't ever glimpse the bigger picture. They stocked their laboratory with assorted extra items they found stored in the Institute, to confuse the picture further. Hammie obviously relished appearing periodically at the metallurgy laboratory to "oversee" the proceedings of the society, but was incapable of feigning interest in what they were careful to present as mundane curricular development. Just as in the classroom, once Hammie understood what was being attempted, his brain devoured and dispensed with it all in one fluid sequence before his attention wandered to other pursuits. Still, he seemed to savor short stretches of being in the room, and the semblance of camaraderie he found there.

He alternated between being aloof and being curious, sometimes playful in his awkward fashion, though never exactly friendly. Except with Ellen. He followed at her heels like a puppy and watched every darting movement of her nimble hands at work, fascinated by her presence.

"Mr. Hammond!" she would gasp, with an exasperated glare.

"Your humble servant," he'd say, showing his awkward smile. "What a novel idea, to have a female mind in our society. What can I do?"

"Nothing at all! In fact, *you* can—" She stayed her tongue, feeling the scrutiny of the others.

He was their "president," and all eyes began to turn to Ellen to invent one task or another for him, since he would obey her alone. She proved resourceful at this.

Even Ellen was at a loss, though, early one evening when Hammie arrived as they were in the middle of a crucial refinement of the second round of their chemical compound tests.

Bob abruptly pulled Marcus aside. "Take him to the opera," he whispered as if this were a normal request.

"Is that a joke, Bob?"

"No! His favorite opera singer is performing."

"Why me?"

"Who else? I am tied up finishing a report on the working of an anthracite coal mine that shall be my doom if not handed over tomorrow, and Hammie and Edwin cannot be alone together, should the topic of First Scholar come up. I heard the odd fellow say earlier he didn't wish to go to the theater alone, and if it came to that he'd lounge here instead.

If Hammie stays here, Edwin and Professor Swallow cannot finish their analysis, and we must not put it off. We simply need to shake free of him for the evening."

It was true that all Hammie would say to Edwin was "Hoyt" and all Edwin would say to Hammie was "Hammie," as though anything else would involve a pugilistic contest over First Scholar.

"What if I find someone else to do it?" Marcus suggested. "A fresh?"

"He won't like the trick."

Then he tried, "I don't have clothes for an opera."

"Say, Hammie!" Bob was already calling out. "Hammie, come over here for a moment—we have splendid news!"

Marcus's fate had been sealed. At the Boston Theatre, he sat silently and uncomfortably in the Hammond box during the interminable wait for the performance to begin. How much there was to do, and yet he was here! Hammie, for his part, couldn't stop grinning, and ran on in one of the extended soliloquies that alternated with his inviolable sulkiness and that Marcus had come to realize signaled happiness.

"The air in Boston has always made a man instantly hypercritical of fine arts, you see, Mansfield. But it is not good opera etiquette to critique the performers until the very last act has been staged."

Marcus had no desire to critique anything but the outfit Bob lent him, a double-breasted tailcoat with sleeves tighter and less comfortable than any he had ever worn, and white gloves that matched his bow tie but made him feel he should not touch anything. Bob had also given him his opera glass. At least he could relieve his boredom a little by watching the impressive denizens of the Athens of America settle into their boxes—women with necks and wrists sparkling in diamonds and hair adorned with flowers and bows, and, so it appeared to Marcus, bird eggs, escorted by politely bored, pale gentlemen in tight, low-hanging waistcoats. He was chagrined to see Will Blaikie moving easily among the operagoers, in the possession of what appeared to be a maiden aunt or other relative. As he surveyed the theater, he met enough other raised opera glasses to glean with a pang the intention of the long prelude to the performance—an opportunity for the aristocracy of Boston to watch itself.

"It is not very full tonight," Marcus commented to Hammie, breaking his silent protest.

"Not very!" agreed a short, ancient man leaning over the rails in the box next to theirs. "Not very," he repeated, and this time snorted, "because half of our fine families believe Boston shall be wiped off the face of the earth at any moment, and the other half choose not to ever believe anything has changed from one day to the next, were a century to pass before their eyes."

Though he found some of the singing in Italian remarkable, Marcus could not concentrate on the performance, and found the tinsel costumes and heavily painted faces of the singers artificial, while the instruments seemed mostly to grunt out their notes. After one particular performer, who sounded no better to him than the others, was applauded and encored to the sky, Hammie explained that it was because she was a Boston lady. The highlight of the evening came after the opera, as the crowd poured into the vestibule and Marcus, eager to leave the place behind, found himself eye to eye with Lydia Campbell, Bob's friend, resplendent in an amber dress with wide puffings and a cashmere opera cape. Hammie had ventured into a corner to argue some fine points of opera with the old man from the adjacent box, whom he had evidently known for many years.

"Well, Mr. Mansfield!" Miss Campbell said, her eyes bright with an almost metallic flash. "I should scold you and your friend Mr. Richards for neglecting to pay me any visits since we met in the Garden. What was your opinion of the opera?" She looked very beautiful and golden, standing tall in her elegant dress and well-chosen jewels—not large, but obviously expensive—all of which served to emphasize her figure, form, and grace. Her hair was coiled high on her head and tucked under a small hat with delicate flowers around the rim.

"I do not like to critique an opera before the performance is ended," offered Marcus.

"But it has ended, my dear puppy."

"Not for me," Marcus said honestly. "The music still rings in my ears."

"Lovely notion! I know exactly what you mean."

Miss Campbell presented Marcus to several members of her family as "my personal scientist."

"Science!" one of her sisters cried. "Why, that is all anyone fears nowadays."

"Only for the moment, you goose," Miss Campbell insisted. "One day soon, every woman will need her own scientist just to understand the strange changes in the world."

One of her other relatives asked if Marcus had been born in Boston.

Miss Campbell smiled apologetically to Marcus for the question, revealing two satiny dimples, then pointed out to her relative, very seriously, while adjusting her bracelets: "Nobody is born in Boston anymore, dear!"

When Will Blaikie interrupted the conversation to greet the Campbells, he was impeccably polite to Marcus. It was as if Marcus had stepped inside an enchanted realm and, for a moment, he might have been convinced he lived in Beacon Hill and had his own footman and stable. He nearly forgot his eagerness to return to the gloomy laboratory, uplifted by the good cheer and a strange feeling that he had been attending this opera his whole life.

The spell was broken when he looked to the side and saw he was being watched by Agnes Turner. She and another young girl were following a plump older woman with bright orange hair crammed with jewels and wearing a loud flowing dress.

* * *

IN THE MORNING, Marcus and Bob arrived together at the Institute to find some unusual excitement in the basement.

"We caught him!" Edwin said in a near frenzy to his friends. "You should have seen it!"

"Edwin, slow down," Marcus said, trying to calm him.

"Who are you talking about, Eddy?" Bob asked.

"It's a freshman," Edwin replied, then stopped to take a breath.

"Miss Swallow . . ." Marcus began, turning to Ellen for more.

"In the storeroom, Mr. Mansfield," Ellen said.

Marcus and Bob opened the door to the storeroom, across from the

Technologists' laboratory, and found a student, sitting on the floor, his hands and feet tied with rope.

"Mr. Mansfield!" said the fellow with a pleading, guilty smile.

Marcus slammed the door closed again and shook his head with dismay at the situation.

"You did that to him?" Bob asked Edwin with surprise, pointing at the door.

"No," said Edwin.

"I did, Mr. Richards," Ellen said.

"What in the heavens for?" Bob demanded.

"He was trying to force the door open to the society's laboratory," Ellen explained. "I really must finish extending the alarm mechanism. I need a few feet more of cable."

"Alarm," Edwin echoed Ellen's word back, though the others were too distracted to notice the look of realization animating his face.

"You know the fellow in there, Mansfield?" Bob asked.

Marcus nodded. "Another fresh that I coached. A very promising engineer, actually."

Bob walked back to the storeroom door and opened it. "You. Fresh. What were you doing at that door?"

"Well, you see, sir, some of the architecture sophs were chasing me in the stairwell and I believe wished to lock me in the closet again, so I was looking for somewhere to hide that they wouldn't find—"

Bob shut the door again and turned to Marcus. "Mansfield, I think we ought to put a fright in him to make certain he doesn't come back here and arouse the curiosity in his friends."

"I doubt that's needed, Bob. Stand aside a moment." Marcus opened the door again and cut the freshman's wrists and ankles free.

"Oh, thank you, Mr. Mansfield! Thank you!"

"See here, Davis, let us not give anyone else an account about what happened here today," Marcus said, putting an arm around his shoulder. "I mean, about a woman having overmatched you."

The freshman gasped at the idea. "How embarrassing!" he lamented.

"Worry not," Marcus continued. "We shall keep the matter quiet, and keep to our own places in the building from now on."

"Yes, sir."

"If the architecture scrubs trouble you again, tell me and I shall deal with them."

"Thank you, Mr. Mansfield!"

Once the liberated student exited the basement, they were beckoned into Ellen's laboratory by Edwin, who was dragging out the large trunk found in the harbor. They had removed the iron pieces and analyzed each individually, placing them in categories by weight, condition, and magnetism.

"Marcus, give me your knife," Edwin said excitedly.

Marcus handed him the blade he had used to free the captive from his restraints. "What is it, Edwin?"

"Something Miss Swallow said—about her alarm system and its cables," Edwin replied, patting the inside of the trunk. "I think I have our answer."

"Eddy, we've already emptied the trunk of everything inside," Bob reminded him.

"No, Bob, I do not believe we did." Edwin paused as though he had found what he was looking for. He used the knife to cut through the leather lining. Underneath, a series of cables ran along the top and bottom of the trunk. He gave his cohorts a boyish smile as he waited for their reactions.

"Copper cables!" Marcus marveled, inspecting the remarkable discovery. "But why?"

"To transform the magnetism of the iron to an electromagnetic charge!" Ellen exclaimed.

"Exactly," said Edwin. "That would exponentially increase the range of effect from this amount of iron to derange the navigational tools!"

"That's remarkable," Bob said. "Only, the moment the trunk was no longer connected to some source of electricity, the electromagnetic charge would disappear."

Edwin went on. "Exactly why the experimenter must have had a battery aboard a ship, one that retained its charge for at least a number of hours, and sufficient cable to maintain the connection as the trunk was lowered into the water enough to create as large a radius of impact as we have observed."

"Is it possible, Professor?" Bob turned to Ellen.

Ellen considered it. "If the battery such as the one I use for my alarm contained enough cells with, say, platinum connected to zinc, in sufficient amounts of nitric and sulfuric acids, the charge could last even longer."

A gong tolled from Ellen's alarm mechanism. She looked through a glass lens that allowed her a sight of the corridor. "It's young Mr. Hammond. He is using his key in the society laboratory."

"I escaped him as quickly as I could after the opera last night," Marcus said. "He likely wants to talk more about it. Edwin, what a discovery! Keep studying the matter until the first class begins."

Despite the disruptions he caused, Hammie occasionally proved helpful as an extra hand. Given their restricted space, they had to frequently take tools and equipment out of the laboratory and store them elsewhere in the building, and often resorted to walking in a roundabout path outside the building to attract less attention, since the area around the Institute was always so quiet. Back Bay, with its long stretches of nothing, now assumed the aspect of a faraway desert.

During the half hour remaining before class, Marcus took Hammie along to help him move some supplies.

"Shall we discuss the state of our little society as we walk, Mansfield?" Hammie asked.

"I don't know what there is to discuss, really, Hammie," Marcus replied, trying to hide his excitement over Edwin's latest hypothesis.

Hammie seemed hurt by his indifferent response. "As president, I feel that it is my obligation to look after it—don't you believe so? As president, I must organize all the activities and address problems."

"If there are no problems, you need not expend your valuable energy," Marcus offered hopefully.

"Well, I suppose if the members are satisfied with my leadership."

"I am confident in that very thing," Marcus was quick to add.

"Do you believe the same of Miss Swallow?"

"What do you mean?"

"I mean, Mansfield, do you believe Miss Swallow is sufficiently pleased with my skills as leader? Is she sufficiently . . . fond of . . . my presence?"

Marcus paused and looked into Hammie's face, which flushed. "Hammie, what are you asking?"

"No, it isn't right," Hammie said firmly, and shook his head decisively. "Do not answer. One must not speak behind the back of a member in good standing. I shall inquire with them each individually on their degree of satisfaction."

As they approached the back entrance, hurrying at the signs of another rainstorm, a man hailed them from across the way. Marcus cursed the possibility that it was another one of the unionists who periodically installed themselves there to harass students and faculty.

The man started to come forward, but stopped at a slight distance, holding out his hand as a warning to keep their distance. He wore a wrist-length wool cape and wool hood, which immediately struck Marcus as odd—it had started raining only seconds before. When he took one more deliberate step forward, his face was partially revealed. A series of bright, circular scars ran across his cheeks and brow, which might have looked painted on had they not been so horrific. His skin was shriveled and appeared almost reptilian, as though it would soon be cast off. The bizarre effect was only worsened by a stringy mustache that presented itself in a glowing tint of orange.

"Marcus Mansfield," the stranger said.

Marcus was startled. "Who are you?" he asked.

The stranger ignored the question. "I understand you have been in some rather interesting quarters of the city—very volatile parts—lately, with some friends: Robert Hallowell Richards, blond and strutting like a peacock; Edwin Hoyt, thin as a rail, plumage sprinkled with premature gray; Ellen Swallow, a sharp-featured woman with manly pursuits."

Marcus felt as if the wind had been knocked out of him. He wished Hammie were not there. He would have to be circumspect in his presence.

"Who are you?" Marcus repeated as mildly as he could.

"Tell me what you know."

"I've asked twice for you to identify yourself, sir."

"I am the avenging angel and my tongue is my flaming sword."

Marcus gestured for Hammie to continue without him, but Hammie stood stalwartly by his side. "Sir," said Marcus, "I am not in the way of conversing in riddles. It sounds to me like you make veiled threats, and I wish to know why."

"Nothing veiled about it, boy. Will you tell me what you know? What did you find on that sailboat you took out in the islands?"

"What sailboat?" Hammie asked.

They had been followed. For how long? "I know nothing of what you speak about," replied Marcus cautiously, gesturing with a tilt of his head to the building. "I am only a college student, as you see."

"You are a factory urchin disguised in the respectable garments of a collegey!"

"What is this blockhead all about, Mansfield?" Hammie asked. "Do you want me to fetch Professor Runkle?"

"No," Marcus said, too forcefully. "It won't be necessary."

"If you have secrets to keep from me, then I shall make certain that whatever they are they will be ventilated for the public," the stranger warned. "Count on it."

Marcus stared back at the intruder questioningly.

"I shall reveal that you and your comrades have your noses in business that does not belong to you," the man continued. "Then you shall be *forced* to come clean."

"See here, I've had just enough of this bugbear," said Hammie, his voice rising.

"Do not come closer!" their antagonist growled, hiding his damaged face with his arm.

Hammie started toward the man, but Marcus restrained him, touched and annoyed by his foolish gallantry.

"I will have you, the first chance I get." As the stranger turned away, he squinted up at the Institute building with a flicker of interest, before stepping into the street, his arm raised. A span of beautiful black and white steeds harnessed to a handsome carriage clattered forward in response, their driver as nondescript as his master was garish. Without looking back again, the hooded visitor climbed in and was borne away.

"Tell me, Mansfield," Hammie said, "what exactly is going on?"

Book 3

GEOLOGY AND MINING

XXVI

Number Ten

1st. To find two numbers, either integral, fractional, or irrational, representing the exact relation between the diameter and the circumference of a circle.

2nd. To find a geometrical construction for a straight line equal to the circumference of a given circle; or, vice versa, to find geometrically the diameter of a circle the circumference of which will be exactly equal to a given straight line.

3rd. To prove theoretically and practically that there is loss of motion in the use of the crank when changing "to and fro" motion into rotation.

4th. To find a geometrical construction for the elucidation of the cube, using only rule and compass.

5th. To prove that the different colored rays of light are transmitted with different velocities.

6th. To use electricity in place of heat, with the same or greater economy, as a motive power, making use of any of the thus far known methods in its production.

7th. To make a flying machine in which the power of a man will lift the weight of a man as against the force of gravitation.

8th. To change base metals into gold or silver, or even iron into copper, or, in general, any simple metal into another.

9th. To find the composition of the ancient material of war recorded by myth as Greek fire and employed in the defense of Constantinople.

10th. To make a self-motive, or a machine of which the effect produced is great enough to produce the primary motive power—in short, perpetual motion.

11th. To produce one single mixture that will cure all diseases or prolong life with certainty.

12th. To make a perpetual galvanic battery in which neither zinc nor acid is consumed.

13th. To produce a formula for finding the primary numbers to any extent whatever.

The list was headed UNSOLVABLE PROBLEMS—W. EDWIN HOYT. Bob had posted it on the wall of their laboratory adjacent to Ellen's slang board, and had chosen number eight for himself. Edwin had selected number five, Ellen numbers six and, of course, eleven. As the rain continued, beating hollowly against the windows above, Marcus read each item in the list. There was a flash of light, then a growl of thunder from outside. He fancied number ten and wrote his initials by it as they waited for Bob to return for their latest conference.

Perhaps Hammie was embarrassed at losing his composure in their encounter with the hooded man earlier that day, or simply bored again, but he had not reappeared that afternoon, which gave the others the chance to speak openly at leisure. Marcus had deflected Hammie's questions, insisting he had never seen the stranger before, and emphasized mundane details of their curriculum-improvement project to steer him away.

"Inventors, discoverers, tinkerers, improvers, fellow Knights of the Test Tube—we have had not inconsiderable success on our charge to protect the people of Boston, thanks to all of you," Bob said upon his return in a mock-officiating voice. "To review: We have now found a chemical solution as close as possible to the one used in the business quarter, and tangible proof of how the harbor assault was perpetrated. I think Mr. Mansfield may have grown gills, he was down there so long among the sharks and mermaids."

Edwin laughed. Ellen did not, as it was not one of her habits, nor did Marcus.

"What's wrong, Mansfield? You're thoughtful," Bob said as he brushed the rainwater from his hat.

"I'm only considering what our next step will be," Marcus said. "The events on the harbor and in the business district were less than a week apart. If the experimenter is planning something more—and we must assume that—it is overdue." He was about to tell them about the stranger who had accosted him, but stopped himself.

"Science cannot always be done running, as Agassiz liked to tell me in my failed career as a Harvard freshman," Edwin said.

Ellen chimed in. "Well, I believe we are verily inching close to our goal, gentlemen, which is all we can practically do, but we have yet a significant mountain to climb ahead, and a zigzag path up."

"Oh?" replied Bob.

"What we have in our possession now would only appear to the public at large as theory, not unlike the hypothesis of the existence of atoms," Ellen stated. "To the naked eye, unprovable, like Mr. Hoyt's list. The city is indeed frightened not just about what has happened, but about what might happen next, as Mr. Mansfield says. We need to show how our evidence leads to a resolution and demonstrably improves the situation of Boston, in order to be heard."

Bob was about to make some objection when Edwin asked, "How do we do that, Miss Swallow?"

"By taking the next step, Mr. Hoyt," Ellen responded. "The barium compound used on the windows would be difficult to procure. That is what is troubling me. It had to be developed by the experimenter in private somewhere, using the proper equipment."

Marcus nodded enthusiastically. "Yes, I was thinking something similar. As part of my assistance to the Institute—I mean, to compensate for what would be my tuition—I am sent on various errands. The Institute on occasion purchases hard-to-find equipment from commercial chemists, or sells some that is no longer needed here to the same places. The majority of the private laboratories are in one area, near many of the factories and foundries. Though it is in the city, that district is like an island in itself—here." Marcus went over to the map of Boston and pointed to South Boston, near Dorchester Bay.

"I know that area well," said Ellen. "My boardinghouse is not far from there. When I applied for a position in a chemist's office, the addresses where I posted my letters were all in that region."

"*You* applied for positions in chemists' firms?" Bob asked.

Ellen nodded wearily before replying. "After I was graduated from Vassar studying chemistry, I knocked at doors that never opened. I had made up my mind to find a suitable opportunity in that field. But there was nothing for me until President Rogers answered my letter and invited me here without any charge of any kind, for I am a poor country girl. Many of the private chemists in that district told me they did not operate out of a lady's parlor, and that the laboratory was no place for fine silk dresses, while a few others said they might sympathize with the desire for female education, but would not be the one to provide it."

"Marcus, what did you have in mind?" Edwin asked.

"If one of us approaches those laboratories as though seeking a job, we might be able to strike up enough of a conversation to gather some information on any experiments using the specific compounds in question. That is a singular spot on the map of Boston, and I suspect the scientists watch one another closely."

"With so many private laboratories!" Edwin said. "It is a long shot."

"Do you have a better idea, Eddy?" Bob asked.

"I suppose not."

"Some of the laboratories are even in the private dwellings of the operators, without any signs posted," Ellen pointed out.

"It could take months, and yield nothing," persisted Edwin.

Bob nodded. "You're both right—it would be nearly impossible to know where to start. But I have another idea. If we can obtain a list of the most active purchasers of extra equipment and chemicals from the Institute, and can find any that have purchased contents that make up the barium-fluoride compound you two re-created, that might give us guidance. Of course, it would work only if the experimenter happened to have bought chemicals from the Institute's surplus."

"How would we get such a list?" asked Ellen.

"Those ledgers are kept at President Rogers's home on Temple Place so that they remain confidential," said Marcus.

"I know who would happily help us," said Bob. "Or, should I say, help Mansfield."

Marcus listened intently, then nearly leaped up. "Bob! I don't want her involved."

"Why not? She helped you before! No one will know."

Marcus leaned back. "She saw me with Miss Campbell at the opera. I do not think she was pleased by it."

"This will be your chance to make it up to her," Bob said.

"Assuming you can get the information, who would go to the laboratory district?" Ellen asked.

"Well, I have done those errands from time to time, so I would risk being recognized as coming from the Institute," Marcus said, backing down from the argument with Bob.

"I am afraid I would not be able to speak a single sentence of such a ruse without my teeth chattering, even to save my soul," admitted Edwin.

"That leaves me, I suppose," Bob said, sighing with pride and tossing back his luxurious hair.

"Or me," Ellen said.

Bob gave a suppressed chuckle. "You are going to go out there alone, Professor? You are only a woman."

"I do recall it. I have gone out onto the public streets several times before without getting hurt in the course of my lifetime, Mr. Richards."

"These are very dangerous times in Boston."

"For two years before I left for my studies, I visited the jail in Worcester as a missionary to the prisoners, Mr. Richards," she rejoined, rising to her feet for emphasis.

"But you yourself said those laboratories will not hire women," Marcus pointed out.

"True," Ellen said, softening her position. "Do you think you can manage yourself, Mr. Richards?"

"Do I?" he laughed.

"Still . . ." Marcus began.

"Mansfield? You don't think I can be an actor for an afternoon?"

"I know you could, Bob. But I have met some of the men in these private chemistry firms. They are distrustful by nature, and I daresay collegies in their minds are about as unpopular a lot as there is. They must be secretive to prevent their processes from being used by an enterprising neighbor, which could empty their bank accounts in a hurry. If there was some way to elicit more of their sympathies, we stand a better chance. I think Miss Swallow might be able to help in that regard."

"Well," said Bob impatiently, "do you have another bright idea or not, Mansfield?"

"I might," Marcus said, "but first I'll need to plan how to recruit Agnes's assistance to find the names we need."

"Then you will do it?" Bob asked.

"Just this once," Marcus said.

Ellen and Edwin resumed work arranging their chemicals, while Bob followed Marcus to the closet, where he was changing out of his laboratory clothes.

"You're not dressing for the visit to the workshops at the Navy Yard yet?" Bob asked. "We have another hour before we're to gather."

"I won't be going today, Bob," replied Marcus. "I think we have our chance right now. Can you invent some excuse for me?"

Bob reflected a moment, then nodded. "I have it!"

"I won't even ask. I'll need to hurry. But you can help me with a little engineering work before I go."

"Excellent. What equipment will we need?"

"Just a piece of paper and a pen."

Bob leaned in as Marcus slipped on his vest and said, "Something else is bothering you."

"What do you mean?"

"Four years I've known you, Mansfield—"

"I know, Bob," Marcus interrupted. He was still chasing down the disfigured man in his thoughts and deciding what was to be done. The hooded stranger would have been difficult to miss: Either someone was following them on his behalf, or his stealth was exceptional, or someone had provided him with just enough information for him to make it seem that they had been followed all along.

"There *is* something else, Bob . . ." Marcus said.

At that moment, his eyes landed on the speaking tubes they had installed, then traveled up to the ventilation fan. Could the privacy even inside their laboratory have been breached?

Marcus hesitated. If they *were* being followed, it was the best course to tell the others. But though he trusted their intelligence and scientific knowledge, knowing they were being watched on the streets would be an entirely different test for them. Edwin might be afraid to ever leave the building again; already accustomed to harassment, fearless Ellen might accuse every man who passed by her, calling suspicion down upon their group. As for Bob, the adventure of espionage might draw him off the track of their priorities. In this case, at least for the moment, it would be best for everyone if Marcus pursued this new challenge on his own. He had the germ of a plan in mind to learn more about the hooded man.

"Well, what is it?" Bob asked impatiently. "The opera?"

"The opera. Yes."

"You said you saw Miss Campbell."

Marcus shrugged.

"Don't play bluff with me, Marcus Mansfield. I take it that means she was a dazzling vision with the blush and bloom of her eighteen years."

"She is a very fair girl—you know that, Bob. Unfortunately, Will Blaikie was also there."

"Well, what did that rascal Blaikie do? I bet he didn't say a word."

"That's just it," Marcus said with surprise. "Nothing. I thought for certain he would attempt to start a set-to, or speak poorly of Tech to try to embarrass me. Instead, he shook my hand as though we were bosom friends!"

Bob laughed with satisfaction.

"But how did you know?" Marcus asked.

"Do you see, it is written in the unwritten rules of respectable Boston. If he became unpleasant in manner while you were joined, even temporarily, with Miss Campbell, he would remove himself from the world they inhabit and appear permanently stained in vulgarity to those he lives to please. Once you gain entrance into their orbit, you are free to live among them. This calls for congratulations."

"On what account?"

"Why, Marcus Mansfield, you've just made your appearance as a Boston gentleman, with all of the advantages and benefits that await you!"

Marcus paused to think about this, then clapped on his cap. "Well, I suppose it means Blaikie no longer sees everyone from Tech as his enemies."

"Wrong, Mansfield. I guarantee he is even more heated now than when we doused him in the river."

XXVII

Theo

"**T**HE ANSWER IS NO. Absolutely no! Haven't I told you enough times? Every day the same interruption . . ."

"But, sir," pressed the youngster. "Sir, I'm right well enough to do the work again now. I vow it!"

"Listen here, Leo. What kind of atrocity is it, anyway, to be named after a Pope?"

"Theo, sir!"

"Ah." The bank director frowned, his indignation momentarily suspended. "Lad, you've been loping outside our bank too long now, with that lame hand of yours."

"I've been trying to show you. It's healed so very much, sir, as good as new, even."

"Let me have a look."

Theo struggled to lift his right hand, as if each finger were tied to a tiny weight. His knuckles sank below his wrist and his fingertips trembled.

"Blast it!" the bank director called out, waving the spectacle of the limp hand away. "Move along, young lad. This is a place of business, not a home for cripples!"

"But, sir, if Mr. Goodnow were here, he would surely tell you—"

"Goodnow can't even see out of his left eye. Why, that Cyclops is more useless than even you! Boy, no one in Boston wants to be reminded of that day by having to see your crippled hand, or that sweaty pig Goodnow's bad eye. We've moved on already, and so should you! Keep your chin up!"

Theo was left alone in the middle of the bank that had once seemed almost to belong to him as much as it had to the bank director or to the swells, like poor Mr. Cheshire, who had money in the vaults. He wanted to cry but would not give the satisfaction to the bank porters, who stared at him ruthlessly from their stations, knowing that he had been better than the whole lot of them before his accident.

Now what would he do?

He skulked out of Front Merchants' Bank and down the stairs, lamenting the difficulty of his position, that at fourteen years old his career was finished. He had more pluck in him than to give up so easily, but for the moment he felt like the starfish he had once seen washed up on a beach, caught in the wrong wave and suffering. He had flung it back.

He'd show them how wrong they were! (There was that old pluck, but it was fleeting, and then lost again a moment later.) How much like an old man he felt, all of the sudden. He felt slow and dumb—useless, just as the director had declared. Only four o'clock now, but the black sky made it feel like nighttime on the street. The crowds jostled him, as though they, too, were filled with hated bank porters waiting for him to go away and make room for someone stronger. There was another sensation that dawned on him as well, an even more unpleasant one than being ignored: the sensation that someone was following him.

He accelerated his pace. He had nothing on him for anyone to steal, but he also couldn't defend himself from an attack by thieves, not with this hand, and that had made him see villains in thin air ready to take what little belonged to him. At least he still had his speed—he used it now—and his knowledge of the short, confusing streets that knotted the center of Boston together.

He rounded a corner and fled down a flight of old wooden steps. These led into a dark alley that would not be found on any city maps, because no one would wish to find it.

Once in the safety of the hidden alleyway, he realized how loudly his heart was thumping at his chest and tried to quiet it by taking a deep breath. This wouldn't do, this behavior. Not for a lad known for his brave and adventurous spirit.

"Blast it all!" he cried despondently to himself, then sat down on the bottom step and broke into tears.

When he had gathered himself and stood to go, a figure cloaked by the darkness appeared at the top stair. Theo jumped back into the alley. The figure took the next step down, and Theo stumbled back some more. Then the figure took another step, and so did Theo. The man was covered by a thick hood, and only when Theo ran out of space behind him in the alley could he make out the alarming face, lined in scars and dead tissue.

"Why, it's you!" Theo cried out in joy. "Flesh and blood! Mr. Cheshire, sir!"

There was no smile on the other face, though he did lower his hood. "You recognize me," he stated flatly.

"'Course, sir! Why, I always prided myself on recognizing anyone, anywhere, who ever patronized Front Merchants', and to greet them accordingly! But I 'eard you positively died!"

"Not yet. Theophilus, there is a little matter of business I'm here to discuss."

"Sir?" Theo asked, his fear renewed by the icy tone.

"Seems you've been using my name freely to some nosy interlopers."

"Interred lopers," Theo repeated confusedly. "Why, I told some collegies that you were a great stockbroker, and a great man—that's all."

"You see, I have a new task in life ahead of me now, boy."

"Might I be of help, sir? I can come with you. Why, I can find those collegies again, and pretend to be their friend for you. Find out everything they know." It was almost like being a bank porter again—almost.

Cheshire's eyes traveled over him in a leisurely sweep. "Was your hand injured that day in the bank?"

"Sir," Theo nodded. "But not too bad, I vow it! Why, it'll be back to normal and better in no time at all. Already on its way! Could be in a pugilist match, if I had to. Just trying to keep my chin up in the meantime."

With a swift and powerful grip, Cheshire clutched Theo's lame hand and squeezed. "Normal! Misshapen and disgusting, boy, that's what it is! We both are what we are—but I plan to do something about it. I am to have my proper revenge, and for that I must operate in the shadows."

"What are you doing, Mr. Cheshire?" Theo asked, his body trembling out of control as he cringed in pain. "But I only told them you were a great man!"

The man had removed a dagger from his coat. He now gripped Theo's other arm by the wrist and positioned the blade over it.

"Mr. Cheshire!" Theo cried.

"You're working with those collegies, aren't you? Trying to sabotage my work!"

"No!" wailed Theo, struggling to twist away from the knife.

"You've said enough, and you know too much! Let's see if you can learn the art of being quiet once you lose some fingers on your good hand! Then your friends will be next."

Theo screamed at the top of his lungs, but the sound of his terror was drowned out by the heartless roar of the city.

XXVIII

Steam at Rest

WALKING HAND IN HAND with her friends under a shared umbrella, Agnes Turner kept her eyes fixed on the paths of the Common, despite the fact that she knew he would still be occupied at the Institute. Though he had taken her hand but once, in the library at Temple Place at a time of such terrible crisis, and took her arm at the harbor, in the luxury of her private thoughts he had held her and kissed her again and again. She would look into his close-set, piercing green eyes. During these mental flights, she did not merely share that sentimental contact with Mr. Mansfield—with Marcus—she grew fearless and independent, a leader of her own free will and that of others, an exemplar of self-possession and competence, like him.

She had told not a single one of the other serving girls—not even her cousin Lilly, though it took all her self-discipline and strength not to when they shared their meals in the kitchen at the bottom of the Rogers house, the girls all chattering over one another. How it would have stopped the conversation cold! But it would have been a great risk. Lilly did gossip so much to anyone who would listen, and, besides that, Agnes could not help but wonder whether Lilly favored Mr. Mansfield for herself . . . But if Agnes put out of her mind all boys on whom Lilly had trained one flirtatious brown eye . . . Well, that was an uncharitable way to think of Lilly, who was decent enough, even if she bore the predominant passion of envy.

Agnes did tell one person her secret feelings: Josephine, her smallest sister, who was only ten and could not understand the affairs of a girl of seventeen. She had to tell *someone,* and Josephine was safe, and sworn to secrecy. "If you ever whisper it to another soul, I shall never talk to you again, dear Josie."

"Never, dear Aggie! You love him, don't you, Aggie?" Josephine asked later.

"A little girl, to ask a thing like that! I hardly know the man. You read too many novels," Agnes answered, sounding like one of the nuns at their church or Lilly. But then . . . "I think I *could* love him one day."

"How do you *know*?"

"Because, Josie, it does not feel I met him, but as though I know him by inspiration, like a song on the piano you have learned but need not even try to remember the next time you sit to play it. He has no one to fight his battle, no one like Papa he can trust. But he trusted me."

Do I have pride in thinking myself special above others? That was one of the questions the girls were directed to ask themselves in their religious instruction by the priest after mass on Sundays, and now Agnes thought about it in relation to her new friend. She did feel—could not help feeling—she deserved the attention of Marcus Mansfield more than Lilly or the beautiful rival at the opera. Did that make her prideful? She was not like the other girls, who would light up at any man they saw, even a new priest at church. The governesses and child nurses had more experience with romance than the maids or kitchen girls, though usually not much of it. From the very first time he spoke to her, even in brief conversation, Marcus demonstrated a sincere interest in her thoughts and concerns, not just in the shape of her lips or the fashion of her hair, and for that alone she could almost give her heart to him.

"What do you think about it, Aggie?" Lilly asked now.

"I'm sorry," Agnes answered.

"Weren't you listening to Mary? Why, your cheeks are bright red. Where is your head?" Lilly asked with suspicion as they continued walking together through the Common. "What do you think about buying some candy from that apple woman by the old tree before we must return for curfew?"

Agnes thought exactly nothing about the matter, but consented to the idea, which sent Lilly and Mary away on their mission.

As Agnes lagged behind, a piece of paper glided over her head, twirled in the air gracefully, flipped over, and landed right at her feet. It was no mere slip of paper, but a carefully constructed paper dart. Her heart beat quickly and, waiting until her friends were entirely occupied with selecting their candy, she unfolded it. There were no words, only a simple drawing of a deer. She looked around but could see no one familiar, and put the paper in her pocket.

"Aggie, do come here. Which candy do you want?"

She called out her answer. Confirming that her friends were still occupied, Agnes began to walk backward slowly. She felt a few drops of harder rain on her bonnet. Finally, she broke into a run, which was daring in itself considering the great length of her skirts, and was satisfied she had escaped the watch of either of her companions.

Turning toward the Tremont Street side of the Common, she passed the old cemetery and entered the deer park, where two of the braver animals came to the gate to nuzzle her. She knelt to pet their strong necks and ears, and told them how lovely they were. Then, the raindrops stopped just for Agnes and the two deer, and a shadow circled her. When she rose, she found herself standing inches away from Marcus Mansfield—his smell alerted her first. It was like the oil and smoke of a machine, clean and plain.

"How did you know where I would be?" she asked.

"You said you were only to be given work until three o'clock on the days the Rogers family was in Philadelphia. I watched until you left from the back door, but needed to speak with you alone. Did the other girls see where you went?" he asked.

"No, I don't think so." She was out of breath, not from running, she realized, but from seeing him. "No, definitely not. I find I can run better than I thought in this uniform, if motivated."

"Good, let us both run," he said. He held her hand.

"Mr. Mansfield! What are you doing?"

Marcus kept his umbrella over both of them. After passing into the Public Garden, they slowed to a brisk walk and crossed onto Boylston Street, one of the avenues that ran through the stark, but oddly beautiful, Back Bay.

"What does all this mean?" Agnes demanded, stopping short at the front steps of the Institute.

"You said you always wanted to see inside." He marched to the top of the steps.

"I cannot go!"

"Why?"

"Because I am not permitted! I am not a student here, for one thing!"

"But I am," Marcus said, climbing back down and taking both her hands in his as he coaxed her up. "Trust me. Do you?"

"Yes," she said quietly, fixing her stance. "But I wonder if I should, after seeing you at the opera."

"I had to accompany a friend," Marcus said sheepishly. "Hammie—I mean," he added.

"And the lovely lady? She would certainly turn the head of any college man."

"My head was already turned, Miss Agnes. As soon as I saw you there."

She gave a skeptical *hmm* as reply but allowed him to guide her up the steps.

"I wonder if that is not unwise," trilled a feminine voice, as a figure shielded by a black umbrella approached the front of the Institute.

"Lilly! What are you doing here?" Agnes asked, unable to mask her alarm.

"Miss Maguire," Marcus said, touching the brim of his cap.

Lilly walked past the front steps, then back again, studying the place like a surveyor and savoring the moment. "Mr. Mansfield, understand that maids in respectable homes in Boston are not to be seen with any men without an escort. If the Rogers family heard of it, well, I am certain there would be consequences. Aggie, when I noticed you were not behind us, I located you from a distance. Then I followed. I hope you appreciate the trouble I went to on your behalf, cousin."

"Of course, Lilly, thank you," said Agnes, despite an almost overwhelming urge to push Lilly into the mud. Still, Lilly was right, obviously; Agnes should not be there, especially not alone with a man.

"Well, since we are all here, are we to have a tour inside? How novel," Lilly said. "Lead the way, Mr. Mansfield, so I can return Miss Turner to Temple Place before our absence is reported."

Marcus glanced at Agnes for help, but what could she really say? She gave him an apologetic shrug and a shake of her head.

"Ladies, please," said Marcus cheerfully, hiding any annoyance he must have felt at the unwanted addition. They went past him through the front door. As they passed through the vestibule and lower hall and entered the stairwell, Agnes was both relieved and startled to find the building seemingly unoccupied.

"Where is everybody?" she asked.

"The whole college had an excursion to the Navy Yard."

"Even Miss Swallow?"

"I should not like to be the man who tells Miss Swallow she could not come on an excursion. She is with them. The building is entirely our domain for the next two hours, except perhaps for Mr. Fogg, the janitor, but he and I have a good understanding."

"Surely you'll be missed from the excursion, and reprimanded?"

"My friend Bob has a scheme to ensure my absence will not be noticed. Are you ladies tiring of the stairs?"

"Not in the least, mister," Lilly insisted, increasing her pace.

Upon reaching the second floor, they were taken through one of the chemical laboratories. Agnes felt more at ease with each step while Lilly's face grew tense, as if she were surrounded by monsters. Marcus cautioned the visitors not to touch anything, though Lilly seemed intent on picking up every glass jar and decanter and studying the mixtures, declaring them, by turns, queer or ugly. She acted as a child rather than chaperon. Her evaluations became more strident as Marcus and Agnes became increasingly engrossed in their own conversation.

When Marcus was showing Agnes how the properties of carbon in illuminating gas could be exhibited by a candle placed inside a glass cylinder that was equipped with a small chimney, his steady voice was interrupted by a piercing shriek.

"Why, Lilly, what is it?" Agnes asked.

Lilly was studying her reflection in a glass container that she then dropped and shattered. "Oh, Aggie, I'm . . . I'm . . . I'm a Negress!" she said, breaking into tears and throwing herself onto Agnes's chest.

After Agnes convinced her to move her hands, Lilly's face was revealed to be entirely black.

"Lilly, what happened?"

"I don't know! Why, he did it, to rid himself of me and be with you alone for improper purposes!" she cried.

Marcus walked along the shelf behind Lilly and, after examining it, picked up a glass decanter that had a loose cover.

"Miss Maguire," he said, "do you use pearl powder in your cosmetics?"

Lilly nodded through her tears.

"Pearl powder," he continued, "contains bismuth, and sulphuretted hydrogen turns the oxide of bismuth black. Did you put this decanter near your face?"

"I wanted to see what it smelled like," Lilly said. "Oxide of bismuth . . . why, you are some kind of wizard, Mansfield, and now I've been horribly disfigured! Turn me white again this instant! Get me a towel, some water!"

"I'm afraid that wouldn't help. Only time will undo the effects, Miss Maguire. By tomorrow morning—"

"The morning! Am I to spend the night as a darky until then?"

"Oh, Lilly, you'll be all right, I promise!" said Agnes, though in the back of her mind she could not help feeling a little pleased at her comeuppance.

Marcus pulled a rope to call for Darwin Fogg, who promised to bring the stricken girl home in the Institute's carriage. Free of their interloper, Agnes looked at Marcus and they both exploded in guilty laughter.

Marcus brought Agnes into a room with large arched windows on each wall and a marvelous variety of alien contraptions on tables and platforms. He explained that, when it was finished, this would be the first laboratory of physics in the entire country, and would raise experimental science to new heights.

"What is that?" she asked of a machine that had two large glass plates with brass poles coming out horizontally, all mounted on a wood base.

"It is an electrical machine," Marcus said. "A very good one, we think. When the handle is turned, the plates generate electricity against the rubber pieces, and the brass extensions become prime conductors. Oh, and come see this one."

He brought her over to the phonautograph machine he and Edwin had assembled and began to turn the handle, his pride evident. "You see, the trumpet on this end is a device that captures sounds, then there is a type of stylus that records a visual impression of every vibration on this membrane below—it can be a voice speaking, or someone singing, or the sounds of freshmen boots trying to leave a classroom at the same time the sophomores are trying to enter. Even the air."

"The air! What a fantastic idea. To capture the air."

"It is a dream," he said, "that this discovery might one day replace all forms of stenography and allow us a sort of photograph of sound to reproduce each person's particular tones."

"Imagine being able to register, say, the voice of Jenny Lind for our children's generation!"

A smile crept over his face. The words *our children,* and their un-intended connotation, hung over her. She bit her lip and wondered whether she should apologize, but he gallantly moved on without a fuss. "You know, Mr. Mansfield, I had heard your name before I ever met you."

"Had you?"

"Indeed. Soon after I began at my position, I overheard the professor speaking of you to a caller from New York who was asking about the students at the college. He said, 'Marcus Mansfield is Tech.' That you were one never expected to come this far, not expected to thrive, yet you were doing so."

"I only pray it is true. Thank you for telling me that. Here," said Marcus. He handed her a piece of thin, membranelike black paper with white lines that moved in curves across the length.

"What is it?"

"That is our conversation just now—you see, there are hundreds or even thousands of vibrations to every species of sound. Now, since you've spoken of wishing to see more of science, I thought we could have a demonstration on the electrical plate machine."

"Oh, please!"

Marcus showed her two figurines that he had brought, sculpted by Frank during their time in prison, of a young man and woman. He placed them on a metallic plate, with another plate suspended above them from the prime conductor of the electrical machine. When he turned the machine, the two figures were drawn upward to the plate above them, then toward each other, then back down, and up again, all while moving around each other in a dance.

"Why, the electricity is attracting them!"

"They actually become conductors," he corrected her. "Then when the electricity escapes, or is discharged, they return to their positions, but are attracted once again by the electric current. Now watch this . . ." he said, as he made an adjustment to the machine. When he turned the handle this time, the dancers moved in the opposite direction.

"You reversed their dance."

"Exactly. I reversed the current of electricity. It is the same principle in the telegraph; the operator controls the current depending on the direction the charge is to travel. In our demonstration, it causes our miniature gentleman and lady to revolve the other way."

"You invented a charming dance!"

"Far better than my own feet can manage, I assure you, Miss Agnes! If only we had music for the little dancers."

"No, we needn't any—this is marvelous! Can you show me something more of the machine?"

"Will you draw the curtains?"

Agnes hesitated, then, embracing their excursion and the delicious fact that this was no normal circumstance, did what would normally be forbidden. As she darkened the room, he modified the position of the dancing figures, and this time instructed her to turn the handle of the electrical machine. When she did, feeling the power of all science in her fingers, the dancers resumed, but this time in the dark, with luminous electric sparks passing between them.

After they watched the performance, he led her outside and they walked hand in hand through the dusty plains that, it was said, would one day be filled with the finest museums, hotels, and homes in Boston. Marcus brought her along to the freight cars, or "dirt cars," as they called them around Back Bay, that transported gravel day and night, and they looked at the same giant steam shovels that had so fascinated her as a child, though at the moment they were all at rest, like horses drinking water. The workmen would have to wait for the rain to pass.

"Do not tell your papa you were here," Marcus said laughingly.

"No!" Agnes said more seriously than she intended.

"I would not want him cross at you. I have arranged for a carriage to come that will bring you close enough to Temple Place that no time will be lost, as far as the other serving girls are concerned. Agnes, I must ask you something."

"Yes," Agnes said, her heart pounding.

"I need your help again with something important."

She realized this was a professional matter he was to discuss, and, despite a quiver of disappointment, took hold of herself. "Do go on, Mr. Mansfield."

Marcus explained that he wished to see a list of the individuals and companies supplied with a specific combination of chemicals over the last few months from the excess wares of the Institute, and that the ledgers were kept inside Temple Place.

"I would never ask if it were not a serious matter. This may allow us to carry out Rogers's work to its conclusion."

"Then you are not just sitting on your hands waiting. You are doing something!" she marveled. "I know where the ledgers are, but I will need your help trying to identify the markings in them."

"I will give you all the information you need."

"Have you found how those disasters happened?"

"I think we are getting closer. As for the reason anyone would commit such horrors, well, that judgment may reside with religion. The dark and light shades of the soul."

"Well, I have been giving confession since I was eight years old, so I do understand about *that*. It is something to know how many misdeeds you have already committed after living less than ten years. Anyway, Papa will not permit my sisters to hear about what has happened and has confiscated all the newspapers. Of course, at Temple Place all the maids talk about it."

"I can see why your father would not wish it to be a topic of conversation. This is the work of the devil. I think it has stopped," he added, putting out his hand, and then folding the umbrella.

"You ought to be awfully careful attributing to man the work of the devil."

"Why?"

"People say the same thing about Tech, don't they?"

"I suppose so," he said thoughtfully.

"Do they have requirement for chapel at Tech?"

"Our laboratories are our chapels," he answered.

"Really!"

"It is not a matter of not holding religious sentiment. My friend Edwin carries his Bible with him to read when we are not in class."

"What it must be like to go to college!"

"There are several girls' colleges, you know."

"I am at the age where I can try to be a child nurse for a year or two, if I am accepted. Then, I am to marry a good Catholic gentleman if I do not become a religious."

"A religious?"

"It means to enter the holy orders—to go to the convent and become a nun."

"You are far too pretty for that," Marcus said, very seriously.

"There are many pretty women among the nuns, only their hair is cut and hidden under skullcaps and veils, so you do not know."

"It seems it would be a shame to have so few choices."

She shrugged self-consciously. "I know I sound like a featherbrain, a housemaid asking about serious subjects."

"Did your cousin tell you that?"

"That is presumptuous, Mr. Mansfield," Agnes replied, shaking her head. "But the answer is yes, she did. I suppose you are not influenced by what your companions do and say."

"Too often," Marcus said quietly, "I'm certain."

"Lilly also says that there can be no such thing as a friendship between a man and a woman."

Marcus laughed. "Is Miss Maguire so accomplished a belle that she knows everything about men?"

"A man who does not wish to make romance has no use for a woman, she says."

"I see. Does she say anything about me?"

"Indeed. She says you are not a Catholic, and therefore you would never court or marry a girl like me because of the fear that your friends and family will shun you."

Bells rang in the distance.

"Miss Agnes." He parted the hair from her forehead. "Tell Miss Maguire I am not afraid."

XXIX

Third and E

I

F ONLY HE COULD STOP TIME, thought a frustrated Marcus the next evening. Just now it was against them in a mighty way. This was the second consecutive night that he was strolling the city in a roundabout manner, watching by gaslight for any signs of enemies on his track. He traded greetings with tradesmen and beggars, talking of nothing more important than what an outrage it was that the snow shovels were still out in May. He periodically stepped behind a wall or into a doorway, to use Bob's opera glass to examine the vicinity, in an attempt to recognize a face he might have seen the hour before or the evening prior after he parted from Agnes; and to see if those whom he had approached were questioned by any other night wanderer.

He liked to think that if Hammie had not been standing beside him when that strange false prophet had appeared at the Institute, he would have given chase and at least gained some basic information about him, but the visitor had so taken him by surprise it was hard to be sure how he would have reacted. Then there was Professor Runkle. Had he witnessed the confrontation unfolding below his window, which Marcus had afterward noticed was open? Marcus had walked past Runkle in the corridor several times since then, but the professor, who was busy tending to Rogers's duties as president pro tempore, didn't glance his way.

After a thorough examination of their chambers in the basement when the others were not present, Marcus had satisfied himself that the speaking tubes had not been redirected or tampered with, and that their conversations could not be overheard through the ventilation fans. That meant either they had a traitor in their midst or someone out there *was* watching them.

But with this second night of rambling through the city, he still found no sign of the hooded man or his carriage, or, as far as he could tell, his agents. There was also the stranger's threat to expose them. If the stranger reported the Technologists to the authorities at the Institute, it would mean expulsion. Worse still, if the stranger went to the newspapers and city authorities, it could mean the most serious kind of trouble for themselves and the entire Institute, not to mention leaving the citizens of Boston vulnerable to the experimenter, with the matter entirely in the hands of Louis Agassiz and an overmatched police department.

Marcus knew he had to find the scarred man before any of that could happen. But despite all the considerable determination he mustered, the menace remained at large. Finding the narrow, labyrinthine streets more and more desolate, Marcus started back for Mrs. Page's, taking a detour to Temple Place. He checked whether Agnes had deposited another note for him in the hidden spot at the garden fence. She had left a message earlier, detailing various complications in her quest to obtain the list of chemical purchasers, but she had described her ingenious solutions with a game optimism and promised the list would be ready by the next morning. Nothing new yet in their hiding spot.

As he was about to leave, he heard her voice call his name from one of the open windows. He did not see Agnes, but a few moments later she emerged from the servants' door, running right into his arms.

"Oh, I did it, Marcus!" she exclaimed.

"You did?"

She wore a flush of excitement and broke into a joyous laugh. "An opportune moment presented itself! Oh, it was delightful. Not even Lilly knows what I did. Do you see?"

Marcus, savoring her flowing handwriting as he read, folded the paper into his vest pocket and exhaled with relief. Now they could move forward again—with any luck, a step ahead of their scarred rival.

"You are a marvel, Miss Agnes."

"Aggie."

"Really?"

"I think so."

"Thank you, Aggie."

"Tell me, will this help very much?" She patted his vest pocket where he had stored the paper.

Her hand lingered and he put his over hers, then leaned forward and kissed her lips.

* * *

"WHAT DO YOU WANT?" asked the white-aproned, stocky chemist, his nostrils flaring as he held open the street door to a brick building on Third Street and the corner of E in the region of South Boston.

"Good morning, sir," said the handsome young man, who gracefully flipped away his bowler hat to free a crown of golden curls. "I am new to Boston and looking to settle in by finding something as an assistant in the chemical industry, however humble."

"I am not out to hire anyone," grumbled the chemist.

The visitor bit his knuckle in a show of vulnerability. "You see, I am in an awful spot. My wife is"—he hesitated—"with child. Sick."

"Pregnant or sick?"

"Well, both, to say the truth," the young man affirmed sadly. "See?"

They both looked over at the street corner, where a woman waited in a long dark dress, with a veil swept back over her tightly pinned and coiled hair.

"You see how pale and stringy she is? Almost like an apparition from another world."

"I suppose she is a somber enough thing," agreed the chemist as he studied the figure of Ellen. "Is that a mourning dress?"

"Yes! Mourning our future. She will continue to be quite distraught and treat me like a dead man until I find some worthwhile position. I beg you to consider it."

"You know something of the chemical arts?"

"I was the First Scholar in my science course as a boy."

The chemist rubbed his rough cheek with his hand. "You look like a good enough fellow. But I'm not hiring. Not unless you're bringing a new patent along with you that can make me money. Now, good day!"

The door closed swiftly and was bolted. A moment later, the window was shuttered.

"Just our luck," Bob said, his hands deep in his pockets as he returned to Ellen.

"I suppose having me here has not helped as much as Mr. Mansfield hoped," Ellen said somberly.

"Not yet." Bob held his agreement in check. "I see why you and Mansfield found these private chemists not the most sympathetic sort. I fear we shall have to resign our expedition in defeat."

"My father used to say, 'Where anyone else has been, there I can go.' It was not a bad working motto, but I like to think adventurous spirits do what has never been done before. *That* is a pioneer."

"Well," he said, impressed, "perhaps we should have you stand beside me at the door when we ring at the next place on the list. Look distraught."

"I am not above falling faint, Mr. Richards."

"A-one idea! Come along." Without thinking, he took her arm in his. He braced for her to pull away and perhaps even strike him across the face. But, to his pleasant surprise, she allowed him to escort her.

So far, they had been to nearly a dozen places, and already tried changing speeches and strategies several times. They consulted the list compiled by Agnes Turner that matched the names and addresses of purchasers to the multiple chemicals they'd identified.

"Goodness!" Bob gasped. "Turn to the east and walk slowly."

Ellen's sharp eyes darted ahead and landed on a tall beaver hat of a light pearl color and Parisian style, shading a full-bearded, sallow face. He held an umbrella by its throat and pumped it as he walked, as though leading an invisible parade of men behind him.

"Professor Watson," she said under her breath, then wheeled around and followed Bob's lead.

* * *

THE OTHER TECHNOLOGISTS were just as alarmed by the sighting when it was reported to them an hour later. Their minds oozed with the troubling possibilities: Could Professor Watson have learned about their activities and followed their delegates into South Boston, then acted nonchalant when Bob spotted him? Or could Squirty himself have been involved with one of the private laboratories, perhaps even—unknowingly or not—one employing the experimenter?

"It makes sense of the whole thing, you see," Bob said with a frenzy of thoughts on the subject.

"How so?" asked Marcus. "Watson was the only one at the faculty meeting who pushed to investigate the disasters."

"What if he did so in order to have control over what was found," Bob proposed. "This could knock everything into a cocked hat!"

But whatever conclusions were drawn in the next hours were undrawn when Bob approached Darwin Fogg late that day, at the close of classes, with a mysterious and tentative air.

"I wonder, my good Darwin, whether seeing a faculty member of the Institute out in South Boston, in that region filled with so many laboratories, would cause you any surprise."

"Oh," Darwin said with an easy chuckle that made light of Bob's wary approach, "you mean Professor Watson."

Bob could not conceal his amazement, but before he could say more, Darwin continued.

"Or Professor Storer," he mused, "or Professor Eliot, or Henck . . ."

Bob stopped him. "You've just listed half the faculty, Darwin. What do you mean by it?"

"That's because half the faculty members possess private laboratories in that district," Darwin said.

"I never knew that!"

"They don't shout about it, lest the affiliation appear, well, unseemly. President Rogers never liked it, but he did not prohibit it."

In addition to explaining Watson's presence there, it also explained what Eliot must have been doing when they saw him from the roof with his chemical case, sending materials along to South Boston without wanting attention.

"Remember," Darwin went on, seeming to interpret Bob's expression as one of moral disillusionment, "President Rogers and Professor Runkle must struggle to pay your instructors enough to live on. Private scientific endeavors at least help them supplement their wages, and allow them to continue to teach. You mustn't think too unkindly about them."

"I won't, Darwin. Thank you."

That put to rest most of their speculation about Squirty Watson. It also meant that Bob and Ellen would take more precautions to conceal themselves when they returned to South Boston the next morning, in case they encountered any other members of the faculty. Ellen kept her veil down and Bob wore a wide-collared greatcoat that made him look a size bigger, and a false mustache.

At the next five chemists' doors, they were met with no answer or else distrust and annoyance. They had almost been through Agnes's entire list and found no helpful clues. Soon they would have to return to the Institute again to be in time for Bob's first Saturday class and Ellen's private session with Henck, professor of civil and topographical engineering.

"Perhaps I am not convincing enough as an errant husband," Bob said. They crossed the street where the next building on the list was located.

She sighed with empathy. "Or I as the wife. No surprise. The gentleman has not yet made his appearance who can entice me away from my free and independent life with the chains of matrimony. No matter. The world will surely be peopled without my help. Perhaps my reluctance shows through."

He twirled the walking stick he had brought as part of his new costume. "I have no idea what a wife ought to be to me, to tell the truth, or what I ought to be to a wife, but I know that her aims in life should be along the lines that mine will follow, not some silly girl who will bat her eyelashes at a scientific coat. I know that."

"When I first arrived at Tech this October, one of the students had found the letter I carried in my belongings confirming my admission and crossed out the 'A.B.' where it listed the type of degree I would study for. They left it in my laboratory where I would find it, and wrote 'A.O.M.' instead. What do you suppose they meant?"

"I haven't a clue," he said after thinking it over.

"I consulted with President Rogers and we believe it must be 'An Old Maid.' "

"Didn't that set your teeth on edge?"

"My feathers were well oiled when I arrived, Mr. Richards. Criticism runs off. The more I make myself useful, the more allies I have. That is why I carry around needles, thread, pins, and scissors at most times. I do not scorn womanly duties, and each time I sew up a professor's papers to be more easily carried or tie up a sore finger or dust the table, there is a smaller chance of a fuss being raised about my presence."

"Well, I would have knocked them around for teasing you."

"And suppose someone were to suggest I ought to return to Salem?"

Bob chuckled at the statement before recognizing his own coinage. "That's different, Professor. That was before I knew you. And I was honest about what I thought! It would have crazed me to not know the underhanded tricksters."

"Serenity is not natural. It is a virtue. I know the world questions whether a girl can get a science degree without injuring her health. I intend to demonstrate that it is not only possible, but desirable—even if it takes me through the desert of old maidenhood. Mr. Richards?"

"Yes, Professor," he heard himself answer with amusement but also real deference.

"You recall when Mr. Hoyt initially experimented with the chemical compound when trying to arrive at the formula that would have caused the destruction on State Street. Do you remember the tint to the glass in your laboratory after his mixture escaped and discolored it?"

"I suppose."

"The perpetrator we are looking for probably went through several trials to arrive at the right compound, perhaps similar to our own."

"I suppose that would be natural, but what . . ." He paused when she wrested his walking stick from his hand and hoisted it upward. The tip was pointed to a small ventilating window on the third floor of another brick building a few doors down the street.

From where they stood, it appeared that a distinctive mixture of brown and pink spotted the window glass.

"Our day has come, Professor," he whispered. "You're one of us now. Stand beside me. Be prepared for anything."

"I am."

* * *

"MR. MANSFIELD!"

Nearing the Institute that morning, Marcus stopped at an unexpected sound: his name. He touched his hat upon seeing the speaker. "Why, Miss Agnes, Miss Lilly. I wish you ladies good morning. Miss Lilly, I am glad to see you looking recovered."

"Hmph!" Lilly replied.

The pleasant surprise of Agnes's appearance there was diminished by her companion, dressed in a stylish, heavy dark dress as though she were on her way to a funeral. She fixed him with a distinctly evil eye.

"I wouldn't expect to find you out here on a Saturday," Marcus said. "Aren't you at Temple Place this morning?"

Agnes tried to smile but instead dabbed tears from her eyes.

"What is it, Miss Agnes?"

"Oh, I've done something terrible!" Agnes said.

"What do you mean?"

"I told Papa . . ."

"What did you tell him?" He took her by the shoulders and held on tightly, but she broke down into tears again. He began to panic at her words. He reassured her that she would be all right, but she only shook her head in despair.

"She told her father she wished to study science at one of the Catholic academies." Lilly spoke the words as though they were in a courtroom and he the accused. "That she then wished to enter a women's college and study science and perhaps astronomy, as girls our age have begun to do in some parts of the country."

Agnes flushed in embarrassment, and nodded an admission to her part in the story.

"What happened? What did he say?"

"He was furious with her, naturally," Lilly continued, "and believes— quite rightly, I say—her new desire has come from being in the employment of Professor Rogers. He has forced Aggie to resign her place and move back with her family. You see, Mr. Mansfield, we serving girls are meant to be machines, with particular functions that cannot be disrupted without consequences."

"Miss Agnes," Marcus began, then guided her as far away from Lilly as he could manage. "Aggie," he said, "does this have something to do with the list you gave us?"

She nodded and composed herself to explain. "Investigating the ledgers for you, and poring over all the complicated details about the chemical supplies, gave me such a thrill. It made me wish more than ever to study something real, to learn science—true science, not minerals meant to keep little girls occupied until their manners can be 'finished' and they can learn to keep house for the rest of their bodily existences—and be *finished,* indeed! I was doing something, however small—doing something important—like you and your friends do. I was not a nothing anymore, not just a servant to someone else."

He took her by the shoulders again. "Agnes, did you *tell* your father?"

"What?"

"Did you tell him about me or the Institute or what we're doing?"

"What do you mean?"

"If he asks too many questions, if he discovers that you gave us information, it could put me *and* Rogers and, as a consequence, our entire college at grave risk. . . . You must obey him for now."

"Must I?" Her body stiffened and her lips quivered.

"For now, please, yes. Just satisfy him for now," he said. "You cannot understand what it means."

She wrenched violently away from him. "Is that what you worry about? When I am the one accused of being unwomanly and unreligious!"

"No. You misunderstand . . ."

Her voice broke with anger and sounded as though it belonged to another person entirely. "No, I don't, Mr. Mansfield. I thought you were a different man."

"Agnes!"

"Maybe I am prideful to think it, but what I do with my life matters as much as what you do with yours, Mr. Mansfield."

"What did I tell you?" Lilly made no effort to lower her voice as she led her visibly shaking cousin away. "I told you he was unworthy, from the very first moment I laid eyes on him. . . ."

* * *

"Now I know what you meant," Frank Brewer was saying fifteen minutes later as a rattled Marcus met him on the front steps of the Institute. "At the machine shop, I mean. About all eyes being only on you. Good morning, old friend. How I have waited for this, Marcus! I owe it all to you."

It was Inspection Day for sub-freshmen at the Institute. This was an opportunity for prospective candidates for admission to Tech to receive a tour of the Institute and learn about the admissions examinations and the courses. Marcus had sent a card to Frank's boardinghouse reminding him to attend, though after the events of the past month, staining the reputation of both science and technology, only a fraction of the expected sub-freshmen were present. Thirty or possibly forty had been anticipated; instead only twelve young men arrived.

Now that the day had come for Frank's visit, Marcus was consumed with worry from all sides. Waiting for Bob and Ellen's return from their expedition to the laboratory district, he worried that he had snarled them into his own mad obsession with saving the Institute and put them in danger. He worried that the self-declared "avenging angel" who had shown up at the Institute would return, exposing them to the public. As for Agnes . . . he was stricken to the core by how he spoiled their encounter. If her father asked enough questions of people—especially Lilly Maguire—Mr. Turner could be led back to Marcus and then complain to the Institute. Worse still, she now detested him, and with cause, after his shameful display in the face of her tears.

"When was it you knew it?" Frank asked Marcus, pulling him out of the crater of his thoughts.

"Frank?"

"When did you know this was the right place for you to be?" Frank's steps had started to slow down the farther along through the Institute they proceeded.

"There are some here who still would say it is *not*, Frank."

"That is how you know it is." Frank nodded vigorously at his own adage. "Right, that's some dreadful good common sense, Marcus. I can prove to them eventually I'm not too big for my breeches. I'm up to snuff, ain't I?"

Marcus put his arm around Frank's shoulders. "A pinch above it, my friend."

As Marcus led Frank through the different laboratories, he noticed out of the corner of his eye yet another cause for concern—Hammie, exiting Professor Runkle's study. Now, with Runkle serving as acting president in Rogers's absence, any student seen visiting his rooms was the object of immediate speculation. Hammie seemed unruffled, whatever the nature of the interview had been, and sailed along in the opposite direction, without noticing Marcus and Frank.

"There go three words that would make me stay well away from this place," Frank said, rolling his eyes in an exaggerated motion in Hammie's direction. "Chauncy Hammond, Jr."

"He will be graduated soon, anyway," Marcus reminded him.

"But there will always be Someone Someone, Jr., with the same airs about him. The airs that shout: 'I belong—you do not!' "

As Frank spoke, his posture straightened and his narrow chin rose. Marcus could not help recognizing the telltale signs: trying to mend threadbare duds into something like the newest fashion, a studied nonchalance meant to seem polished and enlightened, a change in physical bearing. Resenting "collegey" airs even while trying them on. Marcus had been through all of it himself as a freshman, and Frank's presence was an uncomfortable reminder and a challenge to where he found himself now. Had Marcus done what he had set out to do? Had he become a true collegey, even after four years, and if so, was he better or worse for it?

"I've found there is more to Hammie than I had expected."

"Don't be fooled, Marcus. He is cut from another cloth, and not one to envy."

The more he thought about Hammie in Runkle's study, the more it chilled Marcus's blood. Had Hammie observed more than they realized about the Technologists' true purpose? What could Hammie have been saying to Runkle behind that closed door? Perhaps Runkle was merely informing Hammie that he had earned the position of First Scholar over Edwin. Whatever the conversation had been, Marcus would have no choice but to question Hammie about it later. It would be a true test of Hammie, whether he would attempt to deny having met with the professor.

Entering the college's study room, Marcus and Frank were preemptively hushed by a table of students in the corner before they even said anything.

"Who are those scrubs?" Frank whispered.

"Tech's architecture students. They're the tyrants up here—the earth must stop revolving on its axis while they examine their drawings. You will learn, Frank, that the architecture students and engineering students do not live in harmony. At most colleges, the rivalry is freshes against sophs. But here at Tech it is the future architect who is on occasion delivered to his course in a potato sack by a budding engineer."

Marcus was keeping a close eye on every clock they passed throughout their tour, expecting Bob and Ellen to have returned. What could be delaying them? Had they found something? He hoped someone had not found them.

At that moment, Hammie brushed past them into the study room, half-singing, half-humming the stave of an opera, which he was conducting with great delicacy using a pencil. He joined a table of sophomores and juniors, mostly mining engineers and a few chemists.

"You gents have started without me?" Hammie asked, squeezing himself in. "Well, I see it's my turn."

"You always win, Hammie," complained a player from one of the younger classes.

"Hallo. Is this one of our sub-freshmen?" Albert Hall approached the pair in a dutiful whisper. "Albert Hall. Pleased to meet you."

"Hall, this is my friend Frank Brewer," Marcus said.

"Pleasure!" replied Frank.

"Mr. Brewer, it's one of my obligations as a charity scholar, nor is it an entirely unpleasant one, either, to welcome all prospective students to the Institute," Albert droned as he shook his hand with a formal stiffness, staring too intently at his face. "Pay no mind to any architects. You look familiar. I know—from our visit to the locomotive works."

"Frank and I were employed together before I came," said Marcus.

Albert stopped midshake and reclaimed his hand. "I'm sorry to hear it."

"Pardon, Mr. Hall?" Frank asked, his brow knotted.

"What I mean," Albert started again, licking his lips, "is that some in the faculty had been urging our dear Professor Runkle to decline any charity scholars in the future. Perhaps Mansfield already told you. They desire college fees more than they desire eager young men like Mansfield and myself."

"Rogers won't allow that," Marcus was quick to say.

"When you're ill of health, when you're under siege . . ." Albert closed his eyes as though in prayer, and his sentence melted away unfinished. "Well, when his health is restored, we shall see. If you'll excuse me, gentlemen. Please enjoy the day, Mr. Brewer, and do search me out if I can be of any further help. Try not to be late for the tour."

"You didn't tell me," Frank said to Marcus.

"Frank, it is only one faction. Really."

Marcus and Frank remained where they were, standing silently in front of Hammie's table. Hammie and his companions were playing a modified game of hazards. Since being seen with dice would risk their being admonished, instead they each mentally calculated the probability of how a hypothetical dice throw would turn up.

Hammie celebrated some invisible advancement of his score before noticing Marcus. "There you are, Mansfield," he called, ignoring the architecture students' renewed hisses, then looked Frank over. "Why, I've seen this fellow."

"I'm Frank Brewer, one of the machinists for your father's works." Neither offered the other his hand, and while all three preferred to ignore it, there was a palpable awkwardness to the encounter.

"I knew I had. Seen you." Hammie stared off across the room.

"You've seen him with me," Marcus said, keeping the exchange alive.

"Oh, yes, yes, I might have, indeed," Hammie said, a little friendlier. "Did you know I've just a while ago spoken privately with Uncle Johnny?"

That was Hammie's nickname for Professor Runkle. "Oh?" Marcus replied, trying to sound as casual as possible about it. So much for trapping him in a denial.

"Not by choice, believe me. What a bore Uncle Johnny is—if only President Rogers would return. He has the only real character and spark in this place."

"What was it he wanted to speak to you about?" Marcus pressed.

"It seems he heard something through his window of our conversation with that lunatic—you know, the scar-faced wild man, the one who looked like some kind of wicked prophet."

Marcus was thankful that, because they were in the study room,

Hammie was whispering and the other players at his table were too absorbed with their calculations to pay attention. "Hammie, what exactly did Runkle say?"

"He'd heard that lunatic accuse us of secretly examining the catastrophes around the city. You know the time I mean? Out in the fields? Brace yourself, Mansfield. Uncle Johnny wanted to know if there was some truth to the matter."

Marcus waited.

"Say, what do you think those blasted architecture boys would do if the legs of that table were to collapse as soon as they sat down next time?" Hammie speculated when the architects-to-be hushed them again. "I think my brain is going soft with so many ignoramuses around here."

Marcus and Frank each appeared shaken and worried as they stood in the shadows—the dark shadows thrown by Albert's assertion about Frank's diminished chances of attending Tech, and now Hammie's oblivious revelation about Runkle—both of them lost in thought and fear.

"Hammie," Marcus finally asked, "what did you say to Ru— Uncle Johnny?"

"I was honest. Told him it was all stuff and nonsense!" Hammie continued, laughing out of his nose with a honking noise. "Just like everything around here. More . . . blabber."

MARCUS FORCED HIMSELF to remain impassive in the face of the ominous news. At least Frank would be occupied for the next hour or so without him. To Marcus's surprise, Frank asked him if he could stay behind and join Hammie's group for another of their strange silent games, this time whist, in which plays were communicated by tapping under the table using the "dashes" and "dots" scheme of the telegraph operators. After that, he would be joining the half dozen other sub-freshmen on a tour of the building organized by Mrs. Stinson, the chemical laboratory assistant.

Marcus excused himself from the study room and repaired to the basement to rinse his face and regain his bearings. On his way, a freshman stopped him and told him what he expected and dreaded: Runkle wanted to see him at his earliest convenience. It was rich, really. Here he was, promoting a friend's candidacy to the Institute, when on the very same day the acting president was likely about to throw him out on his ear!

He took temporary refuge in an empty lecture hall, where he reflected on everything he had accomplished and enjoyed over the last four years, trying to decide how to defend himself. Even forty minutes later, as he stood in front of the door to Runkle's study, he still hesitated before knocking.

"Mr. Mansfield. Please. I've been expecting you." Runkle pointed to a hard wooden chair on the other side of his desk.

John Runkle had a Quaker calmness about him. He passed Marcus a sheet of paper. "Now, I shall have to ask you a question and I hope you shall not take offense. Did you draw this, Mr. Mansfield?"

On the paper was a caricature of Runkle fishing, using his lecture pointer as a rod and a basket of calculus problems as bait. Underwater, clutched around the basket, were true-to-life renditions of the students in the Class of '68.

"I didn't, sir," Marcus said, struck by the incongruity of studying a cartoon before the desk of the somber, brilliant mathematician.

"Shame," Runkle said, then sighed, accepting the paper back. "I just found it downstairs on the floor of the mathematics lecture room. Decent work, don't you think? I didn't know such a fine artist graced our halls. I'd like to compliment him one of these days. We could have another Thomas Nast in our midst."

"The likenesses are pretty well done," Marcus agreed.

"I'm afraid I've brought you here to discuss some other serious things today. You had a conversation in the yard—I could make out only fragments from my window, but it was, shall one say, suggestive talk indeed. This man seemed to believe you and some other students at Tech were engaged in an inquiry into the recent incidents that have besieged Boston." No emotion at all—disappointment or shock or regret or fury—could be read behind Runkle's regal beard and imposing eyeglasses.

To Marcus's surprise, Runkle paused there, steepling his fingers under his chin. Would this be a "civilized" version of Smith Prison, where Marcus would be expected to make a full, drawn-out confession in order to identify and punish all involved in a transgression? Or would the philosophy of Hammond Locomotive Works apply, where punishment for disobedience was meted out without delay to set an immediate example to all?

"Professor Runkle, I haven't the slightest idea who that man is," Marcus said, thankful to have something truthful to say while bracing himself to lie, if necessary, in order to protect his friends.

"Your friend Mr. Hammond junior didn't appear to know to what matters the stranger referred. As it seemed you were the one being directly addressed, I cannot help but wonder whether you possess some more knowledge. It would be most interesting to me if what the man said had merit."

That still wasn't a question. In the ensuing silence, Marcus must have looked to Runkle like the caricature of him and the other seniors—flailing about in the deep end, waiting for Runkle to throw in a line before he drowned. As they studied each other, Marcus could not help but think of Rogers, and suddenly he had a giant realization—this man, too, had devoted his life over the last four years to the Institute. He might be seeking their help, just as Rogers had.

"Professor," Marcus heard himself saying, "I have undertaken an inquiry to protect Boston. I believe I am close to a resolution."

He wanted to say more but his throat suddenly felt dry and hard. The professor's gaze was unbroken and serene as he interlocked his fingers again. Finally, he said, "I'm very sorry to hear this, Mr. Mansfield. However good your intentions, however much I might personally admire them, I am afraid this constitutes a very serious violation. I am going to ask you to write out in detail everything you've done and sign your name, so that I can present the matter to the faculty committee for immediate action. Your fate in relation to the Institute will be decided with a fair hand by them, I can promise you. As will any of your friends who assisted you. You must know we may have to inform the police department, as well."

Marcus's heart dropped and his head burned. The purpose of showing him the cartoon became clear at once: to see how readily he might give the name of a classmate, or at least speculate as to a guilty party's identity. "I understand, Professor Runkle. I will do as you ask in regards to myself. But I have done what I have done alone."

Runkle considered this for a moment, then said, "I shall have faith that what you say is honest, Mr. Mansfield."

"Professor, I urge you to reconsider, at least for now," Marcus said. "I am trying to save lives."

Runkle gave him a final look of pity. "I shall give you some paper, and leave you in peace," he murmured, as he stood and unlocked his desk drawer. As he pulled the drawer open, something from inside exploded. Marcus threw up his arms against the blast, falling backward to the floor as the room shook, glass shattered, and heavy smoke filled the air.

When he rose to his feet, he found the wall spotted with blood and Runkle nowhere in sight. Groping through the thick smoke, he heard a weak cry and discovered Runkle had been hurled backward from where he'd stood through the window, where he was barely hanging, face bleeding from the broken glass, on the outer windowsill by the tips of trembling fingers. Even as he reached him, the professor moaned and his grip began to relax.

"Hold on!" Marcus cried, coughing, as the smoke thickened. He leaned out the window and gripped Runkle's left wrist with both hands, heaving him upward, but he had no success at the awkward angle. As he continued to struggle to pull the professor up and in, he caught a brisk movement in the street. His eyes met those of the laborer with the bristle-brush mustache, Roland Rapler's man, who had threatened him on State Street.

"Help! Help me!" Marcus called out.

The laborer gaped at them for a moment, backed away slowly, then turned and ran off.

"No! Please!"

His right hand burned in agony as he pulled with all his reserve of strength.

Runkle's wrist was slipping through his grasp, and the older man lost consciousness just as Marcus managed a desperate grab for the back of his collar with his left hand. A few more seconds and he knew he, too, would be overcome by the smoke, leaving Runkle to plummet to his death. He tried once more for the collar, this time seizing it and managing in desperate increments to pull the professor inch by inch through the window, until he was finally back in the room. Marcus, coughing violently through the heavy smoke, labored into the adjoining private laboratory, where he laid Runkle on the floor and switched on the lever for the ventilating fan, which sucked in the smoke from the study.

"Mansfield," Runkle groaned, his eyelids flickering.

"Are you hurt badly, sir?"

"Thirsty," the professor said, coughing. Marcus broke open the professor's locked cabinet and made a brandy and water, which he held to his lips.

"Don't try to move. I'm going for a doctor."

The older man struggled to sit up. His voice was hoarse and uneven, but in its way commanding, a tone he had never heard from the mild mathematics professor before. "Mansfield, you mustn't tell anyone! It will be twisted into something—the Institute's doom will be written."

"You could have been killed! We both could have!"

Runkle shook his head, a gesture of frustration rather than dissension. Marcus thought the blast might have temporarily deprived the man of his hearing or his common sense. Runkle managed to communicate that he wanted Marcus to bring him to Darwin Fogg, who was to take him down the back stairs to a carriage and get him to the doctor as quietly as possible. Darwin should then make haste to repair the window, telling anyone who asked that there had been an accident with some chemicals stored in the professor's laboratory.

"Sir!"

"Do what I've asked," Runkle said. "Then find the truth."

"But you said—"

"You and . . . the Institute's only hope . . ." Runkle could not force out any more words and could not find the right order. He lost consciousness.

"Professor? Professor!"

Faculty and students had come running from throughout the Institute building at the sound of the explosion but had been kept at bay by the smoke. By the time Marcus carried Runkle from the laboratory into the hallway, the crowd included the squad of sub-freshmen being led through the building by Mrs. Stinson.

"Everyone get back! Quickly, as far away as you can!" Mrs. Stinson ordered her charges, herding them, as the smoke still climbed the walls.

"Can't you see Marcus needs help?" Frank said, dodging past his keeper and taking the injured professor gently from Marcus's arms. "Marcus, can you tell me what happened? Stay where you are—I've got the gent."

"Thank you," Marcus said with a groan. "You are up to snuff, Frank."

"A pinch above, I hope!" Frank said, with a reassuring nod. "Your old army friend just cleaned Hammie out at the whist table. If I can do that, I can see this through. Don't try to go farther, now, Marcus—I'm here."

"Get Runkle downstairs, into the fresh air," Marcus gasped, pointing Frank toward the back stairs.

"On my way."

Marcus's legs gave out and he sank to the floor, coughing. As he took a moment to catch his breath, Darwin appeared at his side. He did his best to explain Runkle's instructions, and sent the janitor to relieve Frank.

The urgency of Runkle's situation lessened for the moment, Marcus pushed himself to his feet and, refusing various offers of help, made his way to the main staircase and descended into the basement. From somewhere above in the cacophony of shouts, he heard Bob's anxious voice. "Where's Mansfield? Is he badly hurt?" But Marcus couldn't turn back. His body groaned with each step down, and he grew dizzier and dizzier. He went into the water closet, where he tidied himself up as best he could, still covered in ash and dust. As he prepared to exit, he saw Bryant Tilden entering the Temple.

"Say, old Mansfield, that you? I heard there was some kind of explosion upstairs. Don't say you've had your hands in the phosphorus supply," Tilden said with a satisfied grin. "Or maybe it's Ellen Swallow. Heard that crone took instruction from a conjurer before coming here."

Marcus had Tilden by the collar and his head under the running sink faucet before the other senior could even stop smirking.

"Was it one of your pranks, you scoundrel?" Marcus managed through clenched teeth. He could keep the blackguard's entire head under water if he wished. Tilden could try to protest or to beg, but Marcus felt nothing at the moment. Nothing but rage. Blind rage. Even his faint satisfaction at the fantasy of giving Tilden his due was sucked into a void. Blankness.

He blinked and let Tilden free after only a few seconds under the faucet.

"I don't know anything about it! I don't even know what happened, you madman!" Tilden shook himself away. "Well, Mansfield?" Tilden demanded, putting up his fists.

Marcus buried his face in his hands and rubbed his eyes with his palms. "What?"

"You have something to say to me, do you?" Tilden shook the light spray of water from his wiry hair, then raised one fist and snapped repeatedly, "Do you?"

"The architecture students," Marcus said faintly. "They deserve a good dodge or two before we're gone."

"True," Tilden said, tentatively, apparently glad enough to accept a détente and their change of topic. He gave a devilish nod.

"Imagine their table in the study room collapsing as soon as they'd touch it."

"Say, that's a damned fine one, Mansfield!" Tilden said, backing away and still eying him warily. "That's very good! I'm going to work on that. You're not as much a dig as you let on."

* * *

"DO YOU THINK Professor Runkle had told anybody?" Edwin asked. "Marcus?"

Marcus shook his head, bringing himself back to reality, to their laboratory, where they reunited after classes. "I don't believe so. He indicated that my confession would be brought to the faculty."

"But how did Professor Runkle discover what we've been doing in the first place?" Ellen asked pointedly.

Marcus hesitated, then took a breath. It was time to let the others know about the stranger.

"No matter how," Bob spoke first. "The point is he suspected it somehow, and, more important, was going to put a stop to our endeavors."

Marcus shook his head. "Not now."

"He will survive, won't he, Marcus?" Edwin asked with great concern.

"No one knows. According to Darwin, Runkle is home in bed under a doctor's care and has been insensible."

Bob added, "We'll also have no way of knowing with certainty whether Runkle confided in anyone else among the faculty."

"How could this happen inside our own building?" wondered Edwin. "Perhaps it really was an accident of some kind."

"Accident!" Bob gasped angrily. "Eddy, if you had been around in the days when Dr. Webster had his famous row with George Parkman, you would have been the only man in Boston to argue an *accident* had chopped a man's body into pieces and incinerated it."

"I like to think the best of humankind, Bob. Shouldn't I?"

"Time for that is passed, Eddy," said Bob.

"Some kind of mechanism was set to ignite when the drawer was opened—that's certain," Marcus said. "It had to be deliberate. I was able to retrieve a fragment of the drawer, so we can take the powder from the explosive, although I do not know that it is something distinctive." They examined the charred specimen briefly before Edwin carefully removed it to their storage closet for closer study later under Ellen's powerful microscopes.

"Mr. Mansfield, perhaps some salted water would help," Ellen said matter-of-factly.

He realized he had been clenching his right hand, and, looking down, he saw it was swollen and trembling. He nodded his thanks to her.

"Mansfield, I'd wager a pair of gloves this was the work of that block-head unionist you spied out the window," Bob said.

"It is not unlike the sorts of things that happened when they were agitating against the locomotive works," Marcus admitted.

"Do you really believe it was the unionists, Mr. Richards?" Ellen asked as she returned from the sink carrying a bucket. "I cannot help but think the explosion must be connected to the other disasters."

"It's of such a different nature," said Marcus. "Small and private, rather than public and gaudy."

"Why would the unionist run away when Mansfield saw him, if he weren't responsible?" Bob argued.

"Remember that the trade unions are as fragile in their acceptance by the public as our college, Mr. Richards," Ellen said. "The man may have feared that if he became involved—even by trying to help Professor Runkle—their organization would be associated with that act of violence."

"Ha! So he would let Runkle slip and fall to his death instead?" Bob said, chortling. "Unless . . ."

"What is it?" Ellen prompted.

Bob paced back and forth, then, with a dramatic turn, said to his friends, "What if Miss Swallow is right that the explosion is by the same experimenter as the rest of it? What if those union scoundrels are behind *all* of it—every last dastardly thing that has happened? It would serve to prove what they are always preaching. That technology and machines are nothing if not dangerous, and imperil society, and all that nonsense and whatnot, and make people turn to them instead of to science for answers?"

"We've found no evidence of them being involved," argued Ellen.

"Mansfield, you and I saw the same rascal workingman at State Street that you saw out of Runkle's window," Bob said. "You said so."

"Yes, we did see him. *Working.*"

"By your logic, the catastrophes would benefit Harvard just as much," Ellen pointed out to Bob. "They have tried to keep the Institute under a black cloud from the beginning. Do you think Agassiz culpable, too?"

Bob and Ellen started to argue their points over each other until Marcus interrupted. "Listen! Haven't we been taught for four years to allow evidence to lead us, step by step, to rational conclusions, not to jump to suppositions based on instinct, then trim the evidence to fit them? Isn't that how the Institute seeks to advance the scientific world?" He waited for a reluctant sign of agreement from Bob, followed by the acclamation of Ellen, who seemed humbled by the idea. "Let us keep following the same guidance here. When you see the face of evil, it does not always look how you'd expect. I believe the sooner we complete our answers to what happened at the harbor and State Street, the sooner we shall also know how this came to happen to Runkle. You say the discolored window you found in the laboratory district was on the third floor, right?"

Bob nodded excitedly. "Once we determined which room it was, we tried to go upstairs, but the superintendent would not allow us in without permission from a tenant. And no one inside answered our ringing."

"Could you see anything else from where you were?" Marcus asked.

"I tried calling up to the window, but some of the other chemists emerged from their rooms and demanded quiet. We asked who occupied the laboratory in question, but they only shut their windows. Professor Swallow felt we could not risk the police being called for, so we came here, just in time to hear the commotion outside Runkle's room and find out you had been inside."

"The chemists we met in that district are highly secretive," Ellen added. "They work only for profit, and each believes his latest invention will be the one to bring him vast fortune. The private laboratories are everything Rogers stands against, even if some on the faculty do hold their noses to participate from time to time. Technology used for greed."

"Because of the sharp eye of my pretender wife we have the location of the laboratory used to develop that chemical solution. We must capitalize on this, and do so quickly after what has happened to Runkle. I went to a cousin in the city government after our discovery and we examined records and found the name of a concern that had rented the laboratory—one Blaydon Chemical Company, a subsidiary of a defunct company. Professor, where is that slip of paper? Thank you. Yes, a subsidiary of one Kersley Works in England. But we could not find any names of any individuals associated with either entity. I've begged my cousin to search through further records. He agreed, though he is not optimistic he will find any," Bob said.

"Do you think the other chemists who saw you at the door will report you?" Marcus asked.

"Mr. Richards asked them if he could apply for a position, so they were irritated but had no cause to be suspicious," Ellen said. "Mr. Richards was very cool and collected all along."

"Thank you, Professor," Bob replied with an almost giddy smile.

"They're gone," said Edwin. He had just returned from their storage closet. "I've looked everywhere. Vanished!"

"What? What are you about, Eddy?" asked Bob.

"I was putting aside the fragment Marcus brought from the desk when I noticed! The machine suits from our diving expedition—both of them. They're missing from the closet."

"Impossible! Stand aside." After a thorough search of his own, Bob confirmed that the machine suits were not anywhere in either of the laboratories.

"It had to be someone inside the building who took them," said Ellen. "Maybe Professor Runkle, when he became aware of what we were doing, had them removed. Or Hammie—he has access to the laboratory and has no reason to think twice of borrowing materials from his own society. Or simply some juvenile classmate hatching a practical joke."

"I know who must have taken them," Marcus said. "On Wednesday, a stranger approached me outside the Institute while Hammie was help-ing me with equipment. A man with a disfigured face. He knew we were investigating the disasters. He knew who we were; he even knew our names. Runkle heard a part of the exchange from his study, which is the reason he called Hammie and then me into his study."

Bob frowned in confusion. "Wednesday? That was three days ago. You didn't tell us?"

Marcus shrugged. "I'm sorry. I was hoping I could address his threats without causing you concern, and I couldn't know if we were being lis-tened in upon."

"Remember, Mansfield, forewarned, forearmed," Bob said sternly, crossing his arms.

"One more thing out of our control," Ellen said nervously.

"He said he was the avenging angel, with his tongue as a flaming sword," Marcus continued.

"What does that mean?" asked Bob.

"In the Book of Genesis, God places a cherubim with a flaming sword that turns in every direction to the east of the garden of Eden, to prevent mankind from ever inhabiting it again," said Edwin. "How did he know about us, Marcus?"

"I wish I knew. He has been following us, or has some agent to do so. I have been trying to find out without success. He demanded that I tell him everything we have found, and if I did not comply he would expose us. He must have watched us go in and out of our laboratory, and found a time to sneak inside and take the machine suits as evidence against us. Now he might be planning to use the suits against us publicly in some fashion."

"Or as blackmail," Ellen said.

"We could be in grave danger either way!" Edwin declared. "We must see whether anything else is taken."

Bob laughed.

Ellen narrowed her eyes at him. "I've missed another one of your grand jokes, Mr. Richards."

"Don't you see?" Bob said, pacing the room again and growing more animated by the moment. "It's a test. All of it. A test of our skills, for God to toss all these problems at us at once. Like one of our final examinations at Tech. Think of what problems we have had to overcome. The intricacies of engineering, chemistry, physics we have had to master without any other pupils to pave our way. God has given Tech's first students the most strenuous test, and we will not shrink from the occasion. It is the ultimate graduating examination!"

"I'm only a freshman," Ellen said.

"Well, I'm ready for it. Anyone else?" Bob poured a serving from his small black bottle.

"I never take alcohol," said Ellen.

"I should have expected as much," Bob replied, but in a kinder tone than usual. "Our resolution must be incontrovertible, fellows, and we can take heart that after the explosion Runkle realized we are doing what we must. We must find the person who did all this and identify him as soon as possible, all with the certainty of Babbage's calculating machine."

"Or her," Ellen said.

"Her!" Bob repeated, with a derisive laugh. "No mind of the gentler sex could be so cunning and malicious as . . ." Ellen tossed him a smile. He changed course with barely a beat. "Say, I believe Professor Swallow's rooms aren't very far from the chemists' building."

Ellen nodded. "Not so far at all, really. Without fog, one should have a clear view of that building with my telescope from one side of my boardinghouse roof. In addition, I am rather expert at lipreading."

Bob smacked the palm of his hand on the table. "Good luck! Lipreading, eh? No wonder my bills for our slang ledger increase by the day. We go immediately to Miss Swallow's roof and watch. We'll find out how the cat jumps."

"I do not think Mrs. Blodgett will take to strange young men sneaking around," Ellen pointed out.

"I suppose not," Bob said. "Does she have rooms free?"

"Yes, two."

"Good. I will engage one, then, and that will give me freedom to roam. Cash will always triumph."

"You and Miss Swallow take turns watching tonight, since you're both familiar with the chemists' building. Keep at it until you find out who occupies that laboratory," Marcus said.

"I'd wager the experimenter must do his devious work there under cover of night," Bob said. "We will have him like a moth into a candle!"

"In the meantime," Marcus said, "I will write up a paper that could be easily understood even by a Boston newspaper editor about how the harbor disaster was engineered. Edwin, can you do the same for what happened at the business district?"

"Certainly, Marcus, but why not just lead the police to the laboratory Bob and Miss Swallow located?"

"With Agassiz directing the police chief and his men, given his bile for the Institute, the officials won't listen to any scientific theories from us. We will need to have all the particulars in place, complete with the name of the culprit, and ready for public consumption through the newspapers. Once the press is convinced, the pressure will mount and the police will be forced to act, with or without Agassiz. Any loose ends could be used to unravel the whole."

"What about your scar-faced friend?" Bob asked.

Marcus took his hat from the rack on the wall. "That is just the man I hope to meet tonight."

XXXI

Sleep

ANOTHER NOCTURNAL EXCURSION FAILED to flush out the spy. This time, Marcus decided to visit the area around State Street, considering its apparent importance to the hooded man and his possible agents—but once again, various stratagems yielded nothing of interest. After all the dramatic events of the day, Marcus was not certain what he would have done had he really found the phantom. If they could only finish their enterprise before the stranger made good on his threats to disrupt it, all would be free and clear. It was entirely possible, too, that their adversary had fallen ill—his physical state seemed tenuous, at best—or had become otherwise diverted. Or perhaps he had been all brag from the beginning.

That night, after stopping first at Edwin's and picking up his written study of the causes of the State Street disaster—which was meticulous and brilliant—Marcus reached Bob's rooms. Bob must have still been at Ellen's boardinghouse. Marcus began composing his own paper about the harbor disaster. He had begun at the oak table, but now he climbed into his bed in the alcove. The few possessions and suits of clothes he had brought from Newburyport were stored in a small closet Bob had cleared for him. He leaned his notebook against the head of the cast-iron bedstead so he could rest a little while he wrote. His eyelids drooped, and he was drifting off, so he plunged his face in the washbasin and started once more. With the discovery of the location of the private laboratory, they were so near the end, so tantalizingly close, he could not allow himself to sleep. Not now! They had to finish, to protect Boston, to restore the standing of the Institute, and to win back Agnes's faith.

. . . magnetism induced by hammering, rolling &c. against the soft iron . . .

When his eyes fluttered, he saw the Avenging Angel, the purple facial burns pulsating and flowing with pus. The face followed Marcus, chasing him, then, with the addition of a dark bushy beard, transformed itself into the hated Captain Denzler. He had not been entirely honest when Frank asked if he ever saw Denzler's face in Boston: He saw it in his mind's eye more often than he cared to admit.

He did not know which disturbed him more, his nightmares that included those villains or the haunting images of the hurt and injured, of Captain Beal's trembling hands, of poor Chrissy, the girl in the glass. The boy Theo, waiting to heal, sobbing for himself and for the stockbroker, now dead, who used to drop him a shiny, cold coin. Something stopped Marcus in this line of thought. He had not noticed reports of any additional fatalities from the State Street catastrophe in the weeks since. In fact, among the scores of injuries, the actress had been the only reported fatality that day.

He picked up Edwin's report again, which had a lengthy addendum of news clippings. He confirmed that there were no other deaths reported in the dozens of columns—and the newspapers would have hungrily reported the details if they had discovered another one, just as they had done with Chrissy's. Then his eye fell on an entry buried in a list of particulars from one of the cuttings he had not seen before. "Mr. Cheshire, commission agent of Boston"—wasn't "Cheshire" the name Theo had mentioned?—"feared to have life-threatening injuries from severe burns, released by his doctors."

Burns. Released, yet little Theo, standing his loyal watch, had seen nothing of him on State Street. Thinking about the identity of the hooded man, it made perfect sense he would be a victim of the tragedy, filled with thoughts of revenge (*I am the avenging angel*), and flush with capital to finance his mission.

"Iron," Marcus said to himself, picking up his pen again and shaking off the distraction. Finding Cheshire, who might as easily have been a suffering victim trembling in bed rather than their hooded threat, would have to wait. Right now, they needed to convince the press of their findings. The explosion in Runkle's study had made that plain. Nearby, he had some of the pieces of iron and copper cables from the trunk, and a few partial compasses and magnets they had used during their experiments.

Staying awake is the least you can do for Rogers, he reminded himself, thinking that if he moved from the bed back to the table he'd probably do better, but not bothering to follow his own advice, since it would require standing. The joints and fingers of his rheumatic hand throbbed in agony, just as it had once sent pangs of desperation through him in the machine shop, when he could not stop the drill without risking being discharged by the foreman.

Then he made the mistake of falling into a shallow sleep.

"That's the room." The words floated in from the hallway.

The door crashed open, kicked hard from outside. He bolted upright. The candle had gone out and he could only faintly see the four men in black masks and cloaks charging in. He struck one on the side of the head with his elbow, but before he could turn, there was an arm hooking on to his neck from behind and a rag stuffed down his mouth; someone tied his hands behind him with rope and a sack was thrown over his head.

"The fellow fights hard," said one of them. "He deserves to rest." A blunt object stung the back of Marcus's head.

* * *

Rap-rap rap-rap.

Ellen leaned her ear against the door. "Clear?" she whispered.

Again, two pairs of distinct raps.

She unlatched the door to allow Bob to slip inside and then she closed it behind him.

"I wouldn't give the 'clear' signal, dear Professor, if it weren't clear."

"Mrs. Blodgett moves with a silent step through the house. You must be careful, or she will throw you right out the window," said Ellen. She had never had a man with her in her room before and enjoyed a spotless reputation among her fellow boarders, as well as in the eyes of Blodgett and her family. Ellen had coached Bob in his application for a room, telling him exactly what to say when confronted with the quintessential three-word question of Boston landladies, each one pronounced with the moral force of a hell-fire sermon: "Who are you?" Ellen's guidance secured Bob a room, as she had known it would, but that would not erase Mrs. Blodgett's suspicions of a young single man, which were only surpassed by those she harbored for young single women, and approximately equal to those held close to her breast about a student of science.

Ellen knew she must seem quite nervous to Bob as they stood together in the room—and that annoyed her at the bottom of her soul. She abruptly turned her face from him. "The telescope is there, Mr. Richards—but it is heavy."

"It is good for our sakes I have used dumbbells every evening for three years," Bob said, as he looked around and then paused, an expression of surprise on his face.

"What? Out with it," Ellen said impatiently.

"It is remarkable! Your room."

She had never considered the room special, but smiled at his appreciation for something other than her scientific expertise.

"I like everything in apple-pie order. Those are all my plants, you see. I have carved out the center of this dining table and lined it with zinc to better provide them with water."

At one window ivy emerged from a basket and wound its way up along the frame. An array of roses and silver-leaf geraniums were budding and spreading, while festooned clematis brightened the rest of the small parlor. Displayed above was a contraption made of two sheets of pasteboard and a pole.

"That is a barometer of my own simple construction," Ellen said before he could ask about it. "It is but a sample of the instruments, used correctly, that will allow science to predict the weather."

"Predictive weather! Another of your eccentric sciences." He continued to survey the room.

"If it should aid the practice of farmers, then indeed it is. What is it you're so interested in here, Mr. Richards?"

"Your rooms are not what I expected."

"Did you think I lived in a cave?"

"Something like that, perhaps. Or perhaps I imagined your laboratory at the Institute as your home."

"Mr. Fogg laughs on the nights I'm there later than he and says I am a spook. He said it is a darky term for a ghost spirit that wanders through the night." Ellen was chagrined to find herself speaking at an even quicker tempo than usual.

Baby trotted out to greet him. "Greetings, old fellow—any new experiments today?" Bob asked, petting him above the tail. The feline gave his distinct mew.

"Well," Ellen said, wanting a little measure of revenge for his assumptions about her, "I expect a rich boy like you to come from a mansion in the acropolis of Beacon Hill, with your doting family."

"Pinckney Street, only with doting mother."

"This is all I have, Mr. Richards, and I am content with it. I believe I—and Mr. Mansfield—are what Bostonians like to call their country cousins. I take no offense at the notion. This is the Athens of America, the brains of our continent, and I intend to make it my home for the rest of my days."

"Nellie!"

"What did you say?" Ellen asked, gasping.

Bob had found a drawing on the wall that was signed "With gratitude, to Nellie."

"When I was at Vassar, in order to earn my pin money, I served as a coach to some of the girls who had mathematical difficulties. I had to submit to being hugged and kissed and thanked in return, I'm afraid." She added, "I do not know why that is even on the wall. I suppose I cannot afford fine art."

"That is all good, but it is written here that this is a gift to Nellie! Is that what you are called?"

"By friends, yes, Mr. Richards." Even as she said it, she wished she had not. She meant only to be firm, direct, admirably unblinking, but not harsh. She no longer desired to control her fellow Technologists but would not be thrown off her guard. Bob appeared stung for a moment, though he quickly repaired his expression by unfurling his easy, charming smile. "We—you and I—are rather peers," she added.

"Peers," Bob repeated gamely. "Will you not call me Bob, then? You say you wish to be treated like the other Tech boys; therefore I suggest you act as they do more often."

She thought about this and shook her head. "Robert will do."

"Closer, I suppose. Would you do it again?"

"Say your name?"

"Coach girls to be up in science and mathematics."

Ellen considered. "I do wish I could teach women of science like myself at the Institute who will then educate the world in ways men cannot. Women can reason—they must. They desire to vote, but first must prove they deserve it."

"You mean to have such ladies put their microscopes into my blueberry pie and my drinking glass."

"I look at anything that interests me. Once I see it under the microscope it will interest me for certain. I have of late, before our present study became so pressing, been analyzing the appearance of ergot in rye and wheat."

"That's Dutch to me, Professor."

"Ergot is a disease occasioned by the presence of a fungus that needs far more study," she explained, "as does its constitutional effects on any that consume it. Science must learn how to keep the body in good condition to do the bidding of the spirit. Do you know how few persons there are who can properly analyze the chemistry of babies' food used to substitute for mothers' milk?"

"Well, I suppose you are set to bring many improvements to the Institute, with your vegetable chemistry and whatnot!"

"Make no mistake, I have a debt to Professor Rogers greater than any other person's at our school. He has given me a chance to do what no woman ever did. To be the first woman to enter the Institute of Technology, to enter *any* scientific school, and to do it by myself alone. Unaided." She felt she owed this senior, however bullheaded he might be, an explanation for her serious demeanor.

"Well, I promise not to aid you in any fashion after this is finished," Bob said, his tone a bit colder.

"Thank you for that," she rejoined with equal coolness.

"Shall we?"

He stared at her, putting his hands out. She realized she was standing right in front of the telescope. She smoothed her dress and stepped to one side. Bob Richards was concerned with saving lives and saving the Institute, as she was, and could not care a whit what she had to say about herself. She felt silly for having momentarily imagined she had in any way injured such a handsome boy's feelings. He who, when his beautiful hair grew out, looked like a statue of one of the ancient Greek gods. Until he cut it again and then looked like an ancient Roman god. How pathetic that she wished him to show feelings for her.

"Please be careful with it!" she called out as he moved the instrument from its corner near the window. "It is very dear to me."

XXXII

Wake

T HE ROUGH RIDE—the sack over his head must once have held rotten eggs; three times he thought he might pass out—pulled out of a carriage by his legs, shoved into the mud, yanked to his feet . . . turned around in a circle half a dozen times . . . dragged up one flight of stairs, then another, another. A series of locks unlatching. It was all darkness and noises and pangs of anguish for Marcus, his hands tied and his teeth clenching the gag so hard that if they clenched harder he might have shredded it and choked.

Maneuvered into a chair, he still felt his arm held by one of his captors.

> *A cow and a calf.*
> *An ox and a half.*
> *A church and a steeple.*
> *And all the good people . . .*

The rusty, high-pitched singing came from somewhere behind him, in the far corner of the room.

"We have him, sir." It was announced close enough to Marcus that he could smell the speaker's brandy-laced breath.

"Give the worm sight," said a gravelly, artificial voice.

The blinder was pulled off and the gag removed. Marcus's eyes opened wide and darted around in search of the scarred man as he coughed in the air and adjusted to his surroundings. He would not make any attempt to resist. Yet. Not until he knew where he was and whether any of his friends were in danger. The scarred villain and his accomplices had gone to much trouble to disorient him. They didn't want him to know his location, which he hoped meant they did not plan on killing him.

It was a large chamber, illuminated only by candles. He flinched as he examined the walls and ceilings. Vivid murals of grotesque, outlandish tortures and cruelty covered all surfaces in which demons and beasts of no identifiable species tore limbs and flesh of naked humans into pieces. *I am the avenging angel and my tongue is my flaming sword:* The warning of the scarred man ran through his mind. On a table in front of him, next to a monster crimson-leather Bible, a set of sterling silver surgical tools glimmered ominously under the candlelight, the sharp blades and tips level with his face and pointing at him.

He closed his eyes and half-expected all of it to have dissolved away into a nightmare when he opened them again.

A lifelike statue of the devil, its fangs bloody and horns rising up from its three faces, was seated in a high throne on the other side of the table. Only when the devil faces leaned forward and peered at Marcus through the smoky light, he realized it was no statue. The men who had kidnapped him from the boardinghouse drew off their plain black masks to reveal other grotesque heads beneath—a wart-infested demon, a witch, a rotting skull covered in leeches, and a dragon. He could now see the black costumes beneath were academic robes. At the doors behind them stood two large guards dressed entirely in flesh-colored tights.

"This isn't him!" the devil shouted. The beasts huddled together and seemed to be engaged in some debate. "He was in his room . . ." one of them whispered.

Marcus began to understand. The masked men had been looking for Bob. Imagining Bob beaten and tied up made him even angrier and, for the moment, grateful it had been him taken. What would they want with Bob? He felt the same blind rage he'd had with Tilden, and he knew he had to drive it down enough to get his bearings. *But if I could get hold of one of those silver scalpels, God help me . . .* While they were distracted, he craned his head and looked around again.

In the far corner, a young man no more than seventeen years old stood on his head singing the Mother Goose nursery songs that had greeted Marcus's ears on his arrival. Another young man crawled on the floor with a donkey's collarbone fixed around his neck. Marcus also saw a display of mustaches with names and years below them. He remembered Edwin talking about the Harvard secret society—Med Fac, he remembered Edwin called it—shaving off freshmen mustaches as rites of initiation. He'd explained it was jokingly called the Medical Faculty because they claimed their dark deeds created a healthier college for the students. Med Fac!

* * *

BOB RICHARDS WAS AT THE END of his patience. He had been pacing the roof of Mrs. Blodgett's boardinghouse, running his hand roughly through his hair, at intervals peering through the telescope at the entrance to the chemists' building, then at the discolored window to look for any sign of a lamp being lit, then back.

Marcus and Edwin were likely already finished writing their reports about their discoveries for the press and here he was, waiting for the same blasted event he'd been waiting for since late that afternoon. A Richards couldn't possibly remain this passive this long.

When Ellen came to relieve him again fifteen minutes later, he shook his head.

"Nothing! No sight of anything at that d—" He checked his tongue. "That wretched laboratory, and I'm tired."

Ellen nodded sympathetically. "Take some rest while I watch the building for a while. I was thinking, Mr. Richards, if there are any vacancies in the laboratory building, say above or adjacent to the laboratory we have identified, given time we might drill a passageway—"

"Do you have a gun?" Bob interrupted.

"What?"

"A gun," he repeated.

"I *heard* you."

"Is there a gun in the house?"

"I . . ." She hesitated. "Mrs. Blodgett keeps one. I have seen the ammunition in the storage closet."

Bob's strides became longer as he headed toward the stairs.

"Where are you going?" Ellen demanded, following at his heels. "Are you going to steal her gun?"

"Keep at the telescope, Professor. I refuse to stand around with my hands in my pockets, and we don't have the time for it. I'm going to find out who the experimenter really is."

* * *

THE ONLY SOUL Bob had seen around the chemists' building that night as he watched through the telescope was the superintendent, who appeared to keep his lodgings on the first floor. He had seen the portly man lumbering in and out earlier that night, once all the offices and laboratories had emptied, and had earlier followed his steps through the telescope lens to the grog shop and back.

Bob rang the bell at the street door and waited, listening to the man stumble and curse as he lit the lamp inside his lodging and found his way into the front vestibule. He undid three separate locking mechanisms and then flattened his wide face against a grate in the door, asking Bob's business.

"I know you," the superintendent said, thinking it over sullenly.

"Yes," Bob said, nodding. He'd hoped he'd remember. "I was here this morning, applying for a position with . . . my lovely wife."

"Lovely!" the superintendent laughed.

"Lovely," Bob repeated, dead serious. "She might seem a homely thing at first, I know. But in the right light—chemical light from a burning magnesium wire, for example—her little face looks almost healthy and downright beautiful, her lips not full, maybe, but soft and sure. That she'd think me a fool for saying so only speaks to her good sense and fine sarcasm."

The superintendent was trying to straighten the folds in his vest before realizing the buttons were matched with the wrong holes. "Well? What do you want, boy? You were the one ringing and ringing this morning, weren't you? Well, there's certainly nobody here this hour. Say, didn't you have a mustache?"

"Shaved . . . for my new position. You see, sir, later in the afternoon, after I spoke to you, I was hired by one of the chemists on the third floor. You know the one, on the southern side of the floor?"

The superintendent waved this away. "No difference to me. They don't say good night or good morning to me, and I don't need to know which one is which."

Bob frowned at the lack of hoped-for information. This would have to be the hard way. He reached his hand into his coat. "Well, I thought I'd celebrate the new position with some of the fellows, just for an hour or two. You know? A real celebration?" Bob held up a half-filled bottle of wine by the neck, and pulled a second one from the other side of his coat.

"Good bottles." The superintendent couldn't help noticing, his eyes big and following the swinging object.

"I was supposed to go into the laboratory this evening and finish some work so it would be ready in the morning. How time flies with a bottle, sir! And here's another one to spare!"

"Well, boy, bad luck for you. Anyway, I haven't the keys to any of the chemists' private laboratories."

"Oh, I have that," Bob said, showing him a heavy iron key. "I shall have to sacrifice the spirits. Or else I'll be too tempted and lose my position the very first day. My little wife will have my head on a platter! I promise to be quiet!"

"You oughtn't pour out two good bottles of wine, boy!" the superintendent chastised him as Bob started draining the first bottle into the gutter.

"No?"

The building's guardian suggested that Bob instead deposit the wine with him while he made haste upstairs to do his work. This was heartily agreed to, with the superintendent opening the next door and disappearing into his rooms with the gifts.

On reaching the third floor, Bob put away the key to his boarding-house and removed the gunpowder he had taken from Mrs. Blodgett's closet. The door Bob stopped at had an even larger sign of caution

POSITIVELY NO ADMITTANCE

than the other private laboratories he'd seen. He carefully poured the powder into the key hole and lit a match, plugging it into the small opening, and backing away as a dull explosion shook the inside of the door. No admittance? Not according to Bob. He'd hoped the superintendent was too busy draining the rest of the wine to hear, or too lazy to climb the stairs at this hour. In a building of private chemistry laboratories, the man was likely deaf to all manner of detonations.

Bob pried open the damaged door with ease, felt for a lamp and turned the flame. The black smoke and dust from the explosion made the laboratory too dense for several minutes—the longest three minutes of his life. Finally, it dissipated enough for him to look around at the gloomy vaulted chamber, which was suffused with even more than the usual laboratory odors of gas and vapor.

Bob sucked in his breath at what met his eyes. "I'll be damned!" he cried. "God save us!"

XXXIII

Satano Duce

"WHERE IS HE?" Edwin asked as Bob turned up the lamp. They were both entering Bob's rooms at Mrs. Page's.

"Mansfield? Where are you hiding?" Bob called out. After he had taken a quick visual inventory at the private laboratory, Bob had reported his remarkable discovery to Ellen, leaving her to keep watch for any sign of the experimenter from Mrs. Blodgett's roof. Then he fetched Edwin to come with him back to Mrs. Page's, in order to rouse Marcus. Now the two classmates stood in puzzlement over Marcus's empty, rumpled bed. Both men's eyes fell on the general disarray and on pieces of broken glass next to Marcus's bed.

Edwin put his nose into the air. "Someone's lit a fire here." He picked up the iron poker from near the hearth. "The tip is still hot, Bob."

"Look at that," Bob said, pointing to the wall.

A Latin phrase had been burned into the wall above the fireplace: *Nil desperandum, Satano duce.*

"It's a perversion of an ode of Horace's. 'No need to despair,' " Edwin translated, " 'with Satan as your leader.' "

"I know those words! I mean I've seen them before. Med Fac. Eddy, that's the motto of Med Fac. They must have taken Mansfield!"

"Here's another one!" Edwin said, discovering a second inscription behind the bed, this one composed in chalk. *"De mortuis nil nisi bonum,"* Edwin read aloud, then: " 'You can get nothing from dead men but their bones.' But the college had suppressed their society a few years ago, Bob!"

"It seems not so effectively."

THE TECHNOLOGISTS | 281

"Why would they snatch Marcus?"

Bob drummed his fingers on the table, biting his lip white as he thought about it. "They wanted me, Eddy. I mean, why else would they come to my rooms? They wouldn't know he would be here. We've got to find Mansfield."

"That's impossible. Nobody knows where they meet, not even other Harvard men."

"Edwin," Bob said, "I know just what to do to find them!" But in his eyes there was an unfamiliar gleam of fear and self-doubt.

* * *

BOB RANG THE BELL three times and when there was no answer sat on the doorstep, counting to a minute. As he readied to pull the rope again, the door creaked from inside. A half-closed eye regarded him through the gap.

"Is the master of the house home?" Bob asked.

"Do you know the time?" Phillip Richards pushed aside the servant and threw open the door. "You'll wake up the children."

"Phillip, I'm awfully sorry, really, but—" Bob began.

"No, you're not sorry, but I suppose you never cared about other people's comfort," interrupted his older brother, pulling his Japanese-patterned dressing gown tighter around his waist. "Come in and *try* to be quiet."

The paler, plusher incarnation of Bob, twenty-six years old going on forty-five, led him inside. Bob tried to step lightly to follow the hushed example of his brother's slippered feet. They walked through the cold, elegant house until reaching the study, where Phillip closed the door behind them. He halfheartedly offered a cigar.

"I need your help, Phillip. I haven't time for any pleasantries."

"Thank heavens for that, little brother." Phillip followed this with an impatient sigh. "Now, what in the deuce—"

"I need to learn the meeting location of the Med Facs."

Phillip snickered, lighting his own cigar and sitting back in his chair with a little more enjoyment playing on his face. "Oh, Robert. Are you serious?" He waited a moment before continuing, as if expecting Bob to laugh and reveal the joke. "Robert! You still haven't grown up at all, have you?"

Against his will, Bob's hands fidgeted. "Please, Phillip, this time, only this time, you really must listen to what I say."

Phillip shook his head. "The Med Fac was disbanded a few years ago. Apparently, there was some incident, supposedly someone was injured, and Harvard was wrongly led to believe the society presented a danger to the students. I thought you would have heard that."

"And I'd bet a fifty-dollar overcoat that you know full well it was never disbanded—not really."

Phillip laughed smugly, paying attention to the disposal of his cigar ashes away from the fine surface of his oak desk. "Not my concern. I'm a lawyer of some importance now, Robert, if you weren't aware, not a collegey."

"Once Med Fac, always Med Fac," Bob said. "Isn't that what they say? Please, Phillip."

"Tell me, why would you deem this important enough to barge in here like an invading army?"

"A friend of mine is in trouble," Bob said simply, his tone and posture softening. He had to make Phillip understand this wasn't about any resentment against him or Harvard. "My friend Mansfield."

"I'm sorry for it, brother," Phillip said genuinely. "I am. But even if I could recall the last time I was there, and even if the Med Fac truly survives, they change meeting places every few years."

"I'll take the chance—just tell me, and I'll leave you to sleep," Bob pleaded. "You remember this, Phillip? I'm pleased that you've kept it all these years. May I?" Bob picked up a stone from a shelf of keepsakes and trinkets. He cradled it in his palm. "We found it together, across the river from the cove, that summer we spent in England."

"I remember," Phillip said curtly. "Don't know why I still keep it, to be honest."

"We thought the shells encrusted in it made it look like an owl's head, and we were so proud of it. Do you remember that same summer we found the larvae of the galii caterpillar? We tried to guide one through the pupa to the moth stage, but never succeeded," he said sadly. "Anyway, Mother liked this stone enough that she allowed us to put it in the mineral cabinet when we returned home. You must remember that!"

Phillip stood and fixed himself a drink, making no offer to his kin. "No."

"Truly?" Bob asked, surprised.

"I mean my answer to your request is no. I took an oath to honor my society," Phillip said.

"Then Med Fac does survive."

"That's an oath of a gentleman, Robert. Perhaps that wouldn't mean anything to you and your institute, or men like Mansfield."

"What's your meaning, Phillip?"

"Come! He's the machine man, isn't he? I heard you've tried to plant the grotesque seeds in dear Lydia Campbell's mind that he could make a match with her."

"What of it?" Bob demanded.

"He's beneath her station! Her family would absolutely revolt."

"She can think for herself about her choices without her family's dictates, Phillip. Some of us do."

"For the life of me, I cannot comprehend what you are doing with people like that, at that place."

" 'That place'? If you refer to my college, to the Institute—"

"Yes, yes. That scientific school."

"The Institute of Technology. Go ahead, call it by its name. You speak dismissively, but it is important as anything else to me."

"And just like anything else, you'll forget all about it when something new comes in on the breeze to make your fancy wander."

"This is different. I've changed."

"Since when?"

"Now. Since now! What it's done for me, what in the last month I realized I will do to protect it, that's changed me greatly," he said, his voice strong but cracking with emotion.

"Has it, indeed? Well, if it ever were accepted by the public, that would be the end of your patience for it. It would be on to the next infatuation that could annoy your family and roil our society. Yes, I confess it, we collected rocks as boys. Boys! We played with toy wagons, as well. But you are a man now, Robert, or should be. Time to leave all that behind. In fact, take that rock with you. Bury it."

"Phillip, you *will* give me the name of the place before I leave here!"

"No! You can throw as many tantrums as you like, Robert, but I shall not betray my fellows. Damn it, little brother. You should be at Harvard. You should have taken your rightful place behind the rest of us. *You* should be Med Fac. You've insulted the whole family, forfeiting our reputation. I only pray my disapproval of you is known by all those acquainted with us."

Bob now spoke more softly, his words catching up with the raw feelings. "Mother supports my pursuits."

"Ha! 'Be to his virtues ever kind, be to his faults a little blind.' Mother's silly motto, not mine. Your faults have been coddled long enough, as far as I'm concerned." Phillip returned to his chair and clutched his temple. "How I will ever go to sleep with this headache now . . . ? Little brother, kindly show yourself out."

Bob pulled his arm back and launched the stone across the room. It whirred just over Phillip's head and shattered a vase above the fireplace.

"You are mad!" Phillip cried, having thrown himself to the floor, his arms shielding the top of his head. "Are you trying to injure me? You think that will make me accede to you?"

"Not at all. As much as I'd like to knock your teeth in right now, Phillip, you are my blood and I cannot. But I will start smashing everything in this room, until your sons come running to see, and you will have to explain to those trusting, well-reared bright-eyed little boys that the uncle who shares their blood is a madman. I will then keep smashing every last object in your house until the neighbors come knocking at the door and see your own brother Bob has become unhinged and, worse even, disturbed their sleeping. What do I care about it? I'm a Technology man, after all, with no future to speak of. But I'd wager you'll not step foot on Pinckney Street for at least a month without burning in humiliation."

"Ha! Nice try, Bob!" Phillip boomed, reminding Bob of his own big voice, though there was a tremor in his brother's that failed to convince.

Detecting it, Bob knew he'd won. He picked up the stone again and turned his gaze to a shelf filled with awards.

"No!" yelled his brother, holding both hands out. "Wait! Let us only talk calmly and resolve this. Calmly, brother!"

"Calmly. But quickly," Bob added, scooping up Phillip's drink from the desk. He gulped it down and the burn coated his throat.

XXXIV

The Police Chief of Smith Prison (Sequel)

HERE THEY WERE, perhaps mere hours away from identifying the per-petrator of the most mysterious chain of disasters in Boston history, and Marcus was caught in the middle of a petty schoolboy vendetta for Bob's sodium trick at the river! He almost laughed, thinking of his days as a prisoner during wartime, now at the mercy of these bored swells, somewhere in a comfortable college room made intentionally dismal. Though bound, though alone, he found himself feeling much more in control of the situation, with a key advantage over his captors: knowledge.

One of the beasts walked up behind him and began pulling out single strands of his hair, one by one, counting to twenty-seven.

At the end of the count, Marcus said, "Which one of you is Will Blai-kie? The stroke oar of Harvard. The president of the Christian Breth-ren."

All of the beast masks turned to Marcus when he said it. But it was only the man behind the devil mask itself who seemed to flinch.

"Greetings, Blaikie," Marcus said, bowing his head a little.

The three-faced devil stood and pointed with his jewel-encrusted scepter. "You are charged with chumming cozily with an enemy of the godly society of the Med Fac. Do you confess?"

Marcus did not reply.

"Do you confess?"

"I confess nothing to you."

The devil's hand made a slight flick. The dragon carried a sack to the center of the room and emptied it onto the floor.

"These are material possessions captured from your trivial existence," said the devil, waving his hand over the spilled pile of objects. "We will destroy them one by one until you confess."

Responding to his leader's signal, the dragon stomped on the pile. With a sledgehammer, he smashed Frank's Ichabod Crane statuette into two. Then he grabbed the notebook pages Marcus had been compiling—his and Edwin's report on the disasters, as well as Rogers's stack of notes and research. These were thrown straight into the fireplace, which flashed as it turned them into ashes.

Marcus stirred a little in his seat but said nothing. "You're too stupid to know what you've just done," he said.

"Now tell me, who made the first advances between the two of you, Robert Richards or you? No? More!"

Marcus stared at the decapitated head of the Ichabod Crane, the face that really did look like Frank himself, which he had humbled himself to carve as a gift for Marcus, as an offering to a better future.

"I will come back. I will find all of you. Fair warning."

Marcus's words were followed by guffaws of laughter and cries of "Burn the rebel! Squash the Tech worm! Punish him! He has blasphemed His Majesty!" The cries seemed to come from every corner of the chamber. The beastly masks rendered the sounds of the chorus muffled and as otherworldly as the grotesque disguises.

"Read the punishment, brother!" the devil screamed.

The witch took a step forward, waving its hands ceremoniously. "Whoever shall speak evil against the Medical Faculty of Harvard University shall receive the punishment of air, fire, water, or earth."

"Let the punishment of water be inflicted," the leader hissed. "Execute the law, brothers. I command it be so!"

Two of the beasts seized Marcus. He began to fight, shouting, writhing, and trying to kick. With the help of three more captors they forced him into a large box. The lid was closed and he felt the container being carried across the room. From the mutterings of the beasts changing positions, he surmised that the coffin was being lifted and then pushed out an open window. Suddenly, he and the coffin were in a vertical position. *What sort of lunatics are Harvard fellows?*

The coffin dropped down little by little and he could hear the cranking of a windlass.

They are lowering me out the window, he thought, with partial relief that he would be away from their grim chamber. Then he heard a splash and felt water on his feet and around his ankles. Inch by inch the coffin was lowered, water slipping through the narrow slots in the wood, now up to his knees. Marcus felt the first stirrings of panic. The ropes cut into his wrists as he strained against them.

"That's enough. Pull him up!" he heard from above.

"No!"

"The rope isn't strong enough, Your Majesty! Pull him up!"

"No, brother!" the voice commanded again. "He profaned the society! An accursed Technology boy, of all people! I warned them. He will find us, he says? Dowse him good!"

* * *

THE WATER IN THE COFFIN reached Marcus's waist. *They can't afford to let someone die, no matter what demented game they are playing. Can they?* He considered Blaikie's volatility, the rage Bob predicted had brewed in Blaikie upon seeing Marcus at the opera, the humiliating discovery that his comrades had seized the wrong man. *I should have given him their silly confession and dealt with them later,* Marcus thought, vexed at his inability to pretend and for having surrendered to his anger instead. *There are matters more important to settle than this, an entire city to protect!* But nothing Marcus could have said would have prevented this, no ascendancy to the title of gentleman could have stopped the stroke oar's vendetta. Blaikie was taking too much pleasure in his power. Anyway, it was too late for obliging them, and as for himself, the only thing he wanted more than to be freed from this box was to feel his hands around Blaikie's throat. Everything else mattered less: Boston, Tech, his friends, even Agnes.

His eyes closed as he concentrated on quelling his emotions. They'd want him to scream, they'd be listening for it—then they'd probably pull him back up briefly, then dowse him again or go on to the next torment. Screaming might divert them, but it would not liberate him.

Down into a dark tunnel of memory, he escaped.

* * *

In the barren courtyard of the prison, the August heat burns the back of his head and neck. His right hand was caught in a twisted position during the night and now throbs with an unfamiliar pulse that sounds in every molecule of his body. The young man is locked into the standing stocks, an infamous device of Captain Denzler's making. Holes for the neck, arms, and legs are fixed by movable bars. The punished cannot move in the slightest, can do nothing but bleed in the sun and scream. The man suffering and starving there, that summer in 1862, is Marcus Mansfield. Breathe deeply, breathe hard, breathe quickly. One of the other prisoners told him that, saying if he practiced, he could render himself entirely motionless for almost four minutes at a time so the guards would not bother him, because if he struggled they would strike him.

It had started with the fireplace he and Frank had labored on months earlier, using the tobacco press bolts, in order to warm the sickest and weakest of the prisoners during the winter.

"Those sick men may live now because of you," a prisoner from Illinois had said to Marcus one morning, with a strange tone of bitterness.

On the man's forehead a T *imprinted in needles and India ink marked him as a thief, a mark made by other prisoners here or perhaps those in another, earlier prison camp. Marcus nodded and turned away.*

Then T *had grabbed his arm. "I want you to do something for me now, Mr. Police Chief. You are a clever mechanic. And so is your skinny friend. What is his name? You do have a tongue in your head, boy?"*

"My friend's name is none of your concern, and neither am I."

"You will both help me."

"I don't know you." Marcus pulled away.

"But you will know, Chief. Or I will tell the secesh guards what you've been doing."

Marcus knew that if the thief informed the guards of their invention, the sick men who were using the fireplace would be punished, and the device removed. In their condition they would be unlikely to survive.

T's *assignment was challenging. He wanted a drill made from the machine parts, and it wasn't difficult to guess why.*

"Everyone must be able to escape," Frank had said after the plan, and the extortion, was explained to him. *"That is our condition."*

"We are in the basement," replied T forcefully. *"Any day, we could be moved onto a higher floor, and shall lose our only chance at freedom. You provide a drill that works, then we can build a tunnel big enough for two men side by side to stand up. Every man on this floor well enough to stand can make it to Union lines."*

"And what of the sick ones?" Marcus had asked.

T had shrugged. *"Either way they die."*

"We carry them," Frank had insisted, purple with offense. *"We carry them out, too, or we will not help you."*

"Empty the whole prison, if you wish," T had countered. *"It's no concern of mine. But I will walk through the tunnel first, and I won't be looking back for dead men!"*

Using saws that they'd fashioned from sheet iron out of the raw materials of the tobacco presses and then hardened with heat, Marcus and Frank engineered the requested drill from case knives, needles, and bars. By placing weight on a bar, the drill would revolve down, while raising the bar would make the drill return to its starting place. After several trials over the course of four months, they had made five drills and began the tunneling. The remarkable inventions were used only for a week before another prisoner, in return for a single plug of tobacco, reported to the guard having seen Marcus Mansfield and Frank Brewer taking parts from the presses.

Twenty-four hours in the standing stocks having passed, Marcus is removed from the contraption. Unable to stand without support, his entire body quivers and he crumples to the burning sand. The first thing he does when he has the strength is to turn his head to see if his scorched neck is still usable. He can hardly feel that his right hand is still there, until it wakes with a pain that floods his insides.

Ten or fifteen other men are being kept in the courtyard in various forms of punishment under the watch of guards. Marcus looks around for Frank but does not see him. Surrounding the yard is a ditch, with a berm of dirt on the other side known as the "dead line." Any prisoner who crosses or steps on the dead line is shot without warning.

Captain Denzler steps over three prostrate men on his way to Marcus. He has a comb and is using it to groom his bushy, rough beard into some order.

"Yank," Denzler says, "you seem smarter than most of your kind. You wish to say what it was you were making with the parts you took from the tobacco presses?"

"We made spoons and some toothpicks," Marcus says, surprised he can even speak.

"You know I am an engineer myself? Did you know? Do you like this invention?" He lifts his hand to the standing stocks and rubs it as if it were his pet. "I think it an ingenious design and I shall make a point to register it with the Confederate patent office. I have examined the scavenged presses myself, and I think you have been making more than spoons and toothpicks. Do you want to go back into the stocks?"

"No, sir."

"What do you think I will do with you?"

They have not found the drills, which means they have not found the other men who had become involved with their plan of escape. Marcus wants to ask where Frank is, but does not want to put him at greater risk by revealing that they are not only co-conspirators but also friends.

When he remains silent, Denzler laughs. "You know you have the eyes of a minister I once knew back home? Yes, exactly his eyes." He presses the thick steel toe of his boot down on Marcus's throbbing hand. Marcus emits an inhuman scream. "You may be able to use your carving hand again—one day. Who knows?"

Denzler digs the toe into Marcus's hand, grinding it into the dirt as he screams again. At last, Denzler turns away, instructing the guards to keep him outside in the yard for four days, with half rations only every other day. "Between you and the skinny one, whoever speaks first has a chance to live. The other will be killed," Denzler says over his shoulder. "You will talk to me."

Marcus is surprised at first not to be placed back in the standing stocks. He thinks they have forgotten. After a while, he regains enough freedom of movement in his neck to take in the whole yard. There he finally sees Frank, bucked, with his hands tied in front of his knees. Marcus can see other prisoners bound to balls and chains or in other devices of torture built by Denzler. Later, maybe much later, he sees a group of well-dressed Southern merchants, so they seem to his eyes, touring through to look at the Yankee prisoners.

Then he realizes what Denzler has done by releasing him from the stocks. His punishment was not reduced. He has given him the tantalizing choice of suicide on the dead line, to literally die by inches. He tries to lift his arm to signal a guard; he will tell Denzler everything, at least about his part in the affair, on the condition that Frank is protected, though deep down he knows that might be impossible. Whatever he does, he may not be able to prevent Frank from dying. The poison of these thoughts sends a wave of exhaustion through him and he is soon in a deep slumber. He is awakened when dragged to his feet by two guards. His eyes open on the blank expression of Captain Denzler.

"I will tell you," Marcus is about to try to say, but doesn't have the chance.

"Get him out of here," Denzler says.

"Where are you taking me?" He looks around and sees that Frank is no longer in the same place in the yard. His blood runs cold.

"You are going back inside the prison," Denzler says, as if this were a gift. "Your friend has ended this."

Then Frank has talked? Impossible!

After being tossed back into the basement, he crawls from prisoner to prisoner until he finds one who heard something about Frank.

"They say some Southern businessmen came here and your friend over-heard one speaking of the troubles in their factories with so many of the workers away in the war. He shouted out that he would work for one of them—a shoemaker, I think—on the condition that you were both freed from further punishment. The guards began beating him, but the shoe-maker, laughing at the spectacle as if it were Punch and Judy, put a stop to it and agreed to Frank's conditions."

Marcus tries not to believe it, but does not have the strength to investigate further. He sleeps for what seems three days straight. The next time Denzler is in the basement, he stops at Marcus's haversack and shakes him awake. "If it had been my choice," he says, "I would have left you both in the courtyard to die. But those were important merchants, and they must be pleased. No fear. I will still have my satisfaction, one way or another."

"Frank," Marcus whispers to himself. *It was true. He has turned himself into the one thing worse than being a prisoner: a slave.*

"It is just like a Yankee worm," Denzler says.

"What?"

"To barter for his life like a Jew, instead of dying like a man. My lame leg might keep me out of the field, but I could destroy you Yankees with my brain, if only I am ever given the chance."

* * *

"Tempest in a teapot?" Bob whispered, kneeling down on the rooftop of the Harvard building, bracing himself against the strong wind.

"Yes, Richards. You will see soon enough," Hammie said, grinning widely.

"You're certain?" Bob asked.

"Yes!" Hammie nodded impatiently. In his lap was an iron container that looked like a skillet, and inside that several tin bottles he was removing from their paper wrappings. "I devised it with my own hands, Richards. It will work, upon the word of a Technologist! Anyway, it worked for the Constantines. Now this—this is what we should be doing more of with our little society, curse your blasted curriculum."

After leaving the boardinghouse, Bob had sent Edwin to fetch Hammie at his family home on Beacon Hill while Bob was at Phillip's, a few streets over. Hammie was told only that they wanted to play another grand dodge on some Harvard fellows, but he relished the interruption. Once they reached the college yard, they secured a ladder from a maintenance shed, climbed it to the top of one Harvard building, pulling it up after them, and then used it as an unsteady bridge to the next roof, where they now were crouched. Had they lowered their lantern on the far side of the roof they would have seen a wooden coffin dangling below.

"Did you say Constantines?" Edwin asked Hammie. "Do you mean to tell us that you've made Greek fire in those bottles?"

"I do, Hoyt."

"What are you two gabbing on about?" Bob asked.

"It's on my list of impossible inventions and discoveries, Bob. Like Archimedes' mirror, it's an ancient weapon nobody has ever been able to decipher the formula for! It is said that an angel communicated the composition for Greek fire to the first Constantine, to be used as an overpowering weapon against their foreign enemies, but threatened heavenly vengeance were they ever to reveal its secrets."

"The angels did not count on Chauncy Hammond, Jr.," Bob said lightly, to smooth the hint of jealousy in Edwin's voice.

Edwin squatted closer to Bob and whispered to him as Hammie continued his preparations. "I don't know, Bob. For Hammie, it's just another grand dodge. But Marcus might be down there. We must think of his safety first."

"We have to try something," Bob said, his usual confidence noticeably lacking. "I have heard stories—more than one over the years—about persons supposedly snatched by the Med Fac having a way of disappearing, sometimes for weeks, sometimes . . . well, nothing was ever proven, but it's why they were suppressed in the first place. We must not fail to act."

"I hope your brother told you the truth," Edwin said gravely.

"I am confident he did; he didn't have much choice. But he could still be wrong about the building. The society moves their meetings to a new location every three or four years, so we can only hope this is still it. Hammie, are you ready? I can hardly bear the suspense."

They moved over to the chimney. Bob held the first tin bottle over the opening and nodded to Hammie, who leaned in with a match and lit the fuse. Bob let go, listening to the bottle rattling against the chimney walls on its way down.

"Let us pray for Mansfield," he said, bowing his head.

"Amen," Hammie said, then added, dreamily, "How Miss Swallow's waxy gray eyes would sparkle at my achievement!"

"Pardon me?" Bob looked at him in astonishment just as the roof began to shake.

* * *

A FEW MOMENTS EARLIER, inside the chambers of Med Fac, the dragon and the skull together cranked the handle of the windlass. The strained rope suspended from the window began to fray.

"That's enough!" said the skull. "It's too much weight on the rope. Pull the coffin back up!"

"I said dowse him more!"

"It's enough!" the skull protested vehemently. "It's not even the fellow you wanted, Will!"

The devil rounded on him. "Use a real name in these quarters again, rebel, and you're next inside that box!"

"Try it, Blaikie!"

A noise in the wall interrupted them, a terrific banging, growing louder by the second. Then a wave of bright orange liquid fire burst from the fireplace, washing across the entire length of the chamber, and licking the windows and walls before retracting like a jack-in-the-box. Clouds of white smoke billowed in its wake. They tore off their masks and fell to the floor coughing, the dragon and the skull relinquishing their hold on the windlass, which spun wildly.

"What in damnation was that?" one of the men asked a few seconds later as the shocked members of the society began to recover.

"The fellow," stammered a skinny junior with uneven teeth, who was formerly the skull. "We've just drowned him!" He leaned out the window, where the coffin had dropped into the basin.

"By Jesus," gasped Blaikie, "get down there right off!"

They plunged en masse out of the room and down the stairs. By the time they reached the water, only the loosely coiled rope was to be seen. They seized it, hauled the coffin out, tore off its cover, and carried the drooping, drenched body of their victim onto the grass near the water pump.

"He's dead!"

"Untie him, quickly!"

They frantically loosened the rope around Marcus's wrists and ankles.

"I told you we oughtn't have kept him down there so long," the junior shouted hysterically. He pulled and pushed. Another began slapping Marcus's face and murmuring frantically in his ear.

Blaikie said, panting, "Why doesn't he come to? Is he breathing?" He sounded as if on the verge of tears. "Come to, man! Don't die! You scoundrel, you runt, you bloodsucking Technology drone!"

"Will!" the junior cried. "Are you cracked in the head? That won't help!"

"What should I do?" Blaikie, his face bloodless, asked contritely.

"Hush, and pray."

XXXV

A Hundred Tech Boys

M ARCUS LIFTED ONE EYE OPEN. He let out the long breath he'd been holding.

"You're alive!" the young man leaning closest to him cried out with hysterical relief.

Marcus reached his arm up in a single smooth motion, grasped the handle of the water pump above the student's shoulder, and smashed it down onto his head, eliciting a loud crack and moan.

He pushed himself to his feet and wheeled around, dripping wet, to face the five remaining startled Med Facs. "You've abandoned your masks. You can be sure I will not forget your faces. Now I know who you are and where to find you. Harvard isn't a place you can hide in very well, is it?"

There were five of them, five Harvard men, five Med Facs, and Marcus was just one Tech. But they did not seem to know how to react without their usual weapons: fear, anonymity, rumor, and, most of all, legend. They stood exposed in the middle of the college yard. It took a moment to sink in that the secret society that the Harvard authorities had failed to identify and stop for forty years had just been exposed by a single outsider.

"Oh?" said Blaikie, pushing forward. "Oh? We'll see what you remember when we're finished with you."

"I will fight all of you if you wish it. But I will also enjoy watching you run away. I give you the choice," Marcus said, smiling and raising his fists.

Blaikie scowled and took a step closer, but paused as two of his followers scrambled away. Two others remained.

"That suits me," Marcus said.

As they started toward him, a ladder clattered over the side of the building and three figures half-climbed, half-slid down into their midst.

"Mansfield! Are you all right? You are wet through. Are you hurt?" asked Bob. Edwin and Hammie were close behind him. Bob glowered at Blaikie and his two comrades.

"You wretches," Blaikie snarled. "How dare you challenge us on our own yard? A hundred Tech boys couldn't match us . . . if there ever were a hundred in existence. You're all pathetic."

"Indeed?" Bob asked. "Is that what you think, Blaikie?"

"Indeed! Look at yourselves! Posing as collegies at an institution that four years ago was nothing but mud in a marsh, and a year from now likely will be mud again. Do you realize what we do here? The burden we bear for the traditions and moral principles of all our forebears? We are as strong and as weathered as the elms you see around us. You insult all of it!"

"Don't you see yet, Blaikie? You can't win for once," Bob said.

"Really? Watch me, Plymouth. I fight my own battles. I'll lick all of you—mark that, old salt."

"We'll see—" Marcus started, but was interrupted by a war whoop as the president of the Technologists hurled himself into Blaikie, driving him to the ground. The rowing captain managed to toss Hammie over, pinning him down, even as Marcus had Hammie by the back of the collar, hauling him off from the fight.

"Let go, Mansfield!" Hammie cried.

"Mansfield," Bob shouted, trying to pry Marcus away as a chorus of whistles erupted around them. "We have to run! Now!"

"The college watchmen!" Blaikie gasped at the sounds of the whistles, then tumbled over his friends to get away.

The Tech boys would be in just as much peril as the Med Facs if they were caught and turned over.

"Run!" Marcus yelled, a watchman appearing right at their heels. Bob and Hammie went one way through the yard, Marcus and Edwin the other. "Come on!" Marcus said, glancing over his shoulder just as Edwin crashed to the ground, shoved from behind by the watchman.

"Marcus!" Edwin cried.

Marcus reversed course and tackled the man, who tumbled back the other way with a curse. Marcus pulled Edwin up and they ran on together, with a few yards' lead on their pursuer.

"I'll lure him away from you."

"No, Marcus! Please don't leave me!" Edwin cried, struggling to keep his footing.

"Get into the woods and stay low until you can get out. Meet back at Bob's boardinghouse."

Marcus gave Edwin a boost as they scaled the college gate. Once on the other side, the two fugitives divided up, charging headlong into the thick, gloomy woods that draped them with welcome darkness.

XXXVI

Power

THE DREAMS HAD NOT STOPPED. Always, back on State Street, fighting his way through the unruly crowds as they began to pull and push one another. He turned around and around, taking in a kaleidoscope of fear, and however much he willed his feet in the dream to run, he felt himself pausing, as if commanded by fate, then knocked to the ground in the whirlwind of people.

There was the garish pink girl in glass, falling. There was the boy's hand thrust through the melting window, fingers clutched into a seared fist. Horror after horror, some remembered, some imagined from the newspaper accounts he pored over endlessly.

In the dream he would stir from his swoon, as he had on the last day of his life as he had known it, watching the gauzy remains of a window float leisurely down, down over him, feeling its fiery tendrils settle into his scalp, his hair burned through, flowing over his ear, peppering the pores of his face. He pulled three people down to the ground as he dove for the nearest fireplug and opened the valve, expecting a torrent of water, but as though it were a cruel joke, nothing came out.

He was up, he was running for the horse trough, scattering more people in his path, groping for the valve until he released its merciful flow over his face and head.

Always at that moment he'd wake up again, and his fingers would find the craters of his face, and Joseph Cheshire would scream as loudly as his weary lungs would allow.

His fine life gone forever, he could no longer look in a mirror and know himself. It was *not* him, not Joseph Cheshire the stockbroker; it was an artificial monster who looked back at him, a monster who had to be covered in a hood just to appear in public without frightening people. The Pinkerton detective he'd hired, Camp, had found the identity of the collegians who had been seen around the damaged wharves, as reported by the old wharf rat, and then again near the wrecked region of State Street by the union man who had accepted Camp's bribes for information.

"What is it they're doing?" Cheshire had asked the detective after he made his report.

"I cannot say for certain. Perhaps merely making schoolboy adventures out of observing these foul deeds," Camp had replied.

"What is this college they attend?"

"It's not yet been there for four years. It's scientific, you know, as they say, polytechnic," Camp explained without confidence that he could. "They learn mechanics and chemistry and practical arts. It is housed in an immense building over in the new land, the Back Bay, too large for the number of students enrolled. It's said by most the place cannot survive. They're worthless to you, I say."

"You don't have the power to say that—I do."

Camp nodded slowly at this and took a puff from his dwindling cigar. "As long as you pay my fees, Mr. Cheshire. I am a professional, you know."

"Well, I do pay, so you continue to do as I command." Cheshire's hot temper flared up even faster and more frequently since the day he had lost his face.

Camp touched his bowler hat and grinned. "Yes, sir, Mr. Cheshire."

After confronting Marcus Mansfield, Cheshire was even more certain those miserable students knew something. He would see to it they were forced to reveal whatever it was. In the meantime, he had been pursuing another piece of information from the wharf rat, tracing every sailboat and yacht named *Grace* registered to all ports around Boston. Unfortunately, it was not an uncommon choice for a name.

He'd come tantalizingly close one recent evening, he believed, when he'd climbed aboard one *Grace* where he'd found it docked, and felt the boat rocking in the water. He raced to the other side, in time to see a fleeing figure jumping from one boat to the next. Cheshire had no chance to catch him. When he sent Camp to watch the boat, it was gone.

But Cheshire felt sure he was drawing nearer to his quarry. He would discover who mauled his face with chemicals and destroyed his life, and would tear apart anyone in his way. Indeed, it was all he lived for now. Simple vengeance. Feed the monster. More lines from the Bible he had been forced to memorize as a child returned to him each day, sometimes jumbled or mixed with words from his own dreams.

> *God is a righteous Judge; and in strength he is angry against the wicked every day.*
> *The patient man is better than the valiant, and he that rules his spirit than he that taketh cities.*
> *It is written, Judgment is mine, I will repay.*
> *I am the avenging angel and my tongue is my flaming sword.*

Those responsible would suffer as much as and more than he'd suffered.

He applied the ammonia solution to his face ten times a day, at first, then five times a day. As he dyed his mustache, which had been bleached ghostly white, he prayed those long hours for satisfaction against his unknown enemies. His life's chief mission.

Cheshire always had a plan in reserve; this was no exception. If the newspapermen failed to act, he had another way in mind. Camp had reported Marcus Mansfield walking arm in arm at the harbor with a serving girl named Agnes. As a domestic, she would be an easy target to capture, and then he could force the Tech boy to give answers in return for her life. She was a pretty maid, Camp had told him. This plan, indeed, could promise an even greater personal satisfaction for the stockbroker.

He was ready for the day. His first stop would be the office of the *Boston Telegraph,* where he would leave a detailed description of what those Institute of Technology boys had been doing. There would be an investigation, and everything they had discovered would be revealed. Technology fools! He'd use that information, along with Simon Camp's help, to track down and destroy his real prey.

He walked down his front steps, wearing the hood he had grown accustomed to using as a cover for the painful half-healed scars on his face. Though others grumbled about the heavy rains that had fallen this spring, he welcomed them, for the dark clouds masked his hideous looks and protected his scars from the sun. He carried his dagger with him, having a vague sense as he stalked his enemies that they might be stalking him. That instinct grew sharper as he proceeded at this hour, and he kept his hand on the handle of his dagger inside his coat, alert for any sign of danger.

"Cheshire."

The call reached his damaged ears in an echo; it could have come from some distance or from close proximity. He unsheathed his dagger and swung around. Let them try to catch him off guard.

"Cheshire, here!"

He looked up and was nearly blinded by the flash of metal from what appeared to be a military uniform in the window opposite. Decoration Day was coming, and more uniforms, some battered and others fresh, could be seen up and down Boston being aired out. He squinted and realized that he was looking right at a rifle pointed at him.

"Technology lives!" came the cry, as the blast of the rifle sounded.

In a reflex, Cheshire's eyes closed and he felt faint, as he had that day on State Street. But then he realized he had been untouched. Opening his eyes, reality rushed in on him. The shot had flown behind him, hitting a gas main. Cheshire gripped his dagger and grinned at his good fortune: He was looking squarely at his enemy's face, and would now have his chance for revenge. Then he heard a hiss, hypnotic and loud. He realized he was standing over a sewer. He tried to jump away, but it was too late. From below the grate, a geyser of flames swirled up and over him, enclosing him entirely in its white-hot vortex.

_____

XXXVII

Dirty

THE SUN SHOWED ITSELF that morning, though a flock of clouds was drifting in. When the bell sounded for Sunday services in the Harvard chapel, the young men appearing around the campus yard rubbed their eyes and yawned with great spiritual emphasis. One of those strolling along the middle walk of the yard was more exhausted than the rest. Yes, some of the Harvard seniors might have been jollifying late into the night in their rooms; certainly a few of the freshes had been much occupied, systematically breaking the windows of the most hated sophs. But this particular collegian had been in Norton's Woods right outside the college yard for half the night, in hiding, covered in bugs and inspected now and then by the frogs.

Once Edwin had crossed into the woods and separated from Marcus, he'd tripped over a large tree root and fallen into the dirt. He'd only scratched his knees a little, but he felt safer pressed against the earth. The watchman's heavy footsteps and shrill whistles eventually gave way to eerie silence. He knew Marcus would have eluded the pursuer to meet up with Bob back in Boston, where they would be expecting Edwin to come, too. Nothing ever seemed to diminish Marcus's inner calm and composure, least of all the threat of danger to himself. But Edwin had felt paralyzed at the notion of making an attempt to show himself in the streets, imagining a barricade of policemen lurking there for him. His forte was chess, not cards; so he would patiently wait for the right move. He did not have the physical strength to run all night, and was hesitant to navigate much deeper into the thick woods all around Harvard's gates. Besides, if the watchmen were still looking for them, they would be smart to be posted on the edge of the woods. No, the safest way out was through the college yard itself. He had known the prayer bell would ring in just a few hours, and the yard would be overrun with students. He could walk straight through to the gates. He would blend in. So he had remained on his mattress of pine cones and soil with the bugs.

His clothing wasn't quite as neat as he'd like, even after brushing off the pine needles and shaking loose the dirt on his vest and coat. But not every Harvard boy was a dandy, and he could see at a glance suits nearly as crumpled and wrinkled as his own at this hour. He found a place behind a group of four or five such fellows sluggishly flowing toward the chapel.

As they neared their destination, the path clogged up with students, slowing Edwin's advance toward the gates, where he would be clear to exit. Two college watchmen appeared at the edge of the crowd. Were they looking for Edwin, or just ensuring that students fulfilled the college rules by finding their way to the chapel before the second bell?

"You," said one of the watchmen.

Edwin, swallowing hard, slowly turned around to face him. "Yes, sir?"

"Where is your Bible?"

He looked around dumbly.

"We've had too many fellows sleeping in chapel," continued the official, "instead of reading their Bible."

"Forgot," he managed to say in response. "I'll retrieve it. Thank you."

"Quickly, boy!"

Edwin steered his steps away from the chapel toward the gates. Keeping his head down so he would not appear too eager, he nearly walked headlong into a man rushing along an intersecting path.

"Fool! Watch yourself!"

"Pardon," he said, then stopped in a fit of surprise. "Professor!"

Standing before him, clutching his long, narrow case, was the slender figure of the Institute's chemistry instructor, Charles Eliot. It would have been difficult to say which Technology man, professor or student, showed more discomfort at the encounter.

Eliot composed himself and gazed down disapprovingly over his wire-rim eyeglasses. "What are you doing here, Mr. Hoyt?"

Edwin had the same question about Professor Eliot being on the

Harvard campus on a Sunday morning, though of course he said nothing about that. In fact, he said nothing at all, and lowered his eyes again. "I should be on my way back into Boston," he offered finally, although clearly waiting for the professor's permission.

Eliot's expression softened and he offered a tight-lipped smile. "Actually, I believe I know very well why you're here, Mr. Hoyt."

"You do?"

"I know there are some who believe the Institute is deficient in not having a chapel where our students would be required to pray. As a student at your age, I cherished going to the chapel here. Did you know I was stroke oar of the top Harvard boat in my day?"

As Edwin considered how to respond, the second bell rang and Eliot lurched forward as a freshman crashed into him from behind. "Sorry, sir," came the hurried excuse, as the wayward fresh propelled himself on toward the chapel, leaving Eliot's case thrown open on the ground. Inside were not glass tubes, as Edwin had assumed, but papers, which were now scattered.

Edwin sprang to retrieve them, happy for a chance to be useful.

"No," Eliot said forcefully. "Not necessary, Mr. Hoyt."

But Edwin already had a dozen pages in hand, peeled from the dewy grass. One was headed "Report on the Projected Annexation by Harvard University of the Massachusetts Institute of Technology."

Edwin read the heading twice, and quickly took in as much as he could of the rest of the contents. "This cannot be true," he murmured. "Professor Eliot, thank heavens you came here. You managed to persuade them to stop this—please say you did!" But when he met Eliot's gaze, he knew he had misunderstood.

"Mr. Hoyt, this is administrative business and none of your concern."

"Professor, if Harvard is trying to annex Tech—"

"*I* am proposing they do just that, Mr. Hoyt," Eliot said, tucking the papers under his arm. "Perhaps you cannot understand from the vantage point of a student. President Rogers remains in a grave state of health and the dear man will not long serve as our president, I'm afraid. I intend to offer myself for that position, and in doing so do what is right for the future of the Institute."

"To lose our independence?"

"To survive. The Institute was an extraordinary experiment, but it cannot go on without financial strength and the support of Boston's finest families. By uniting with Harvard, we will achieve that, and be able to carry on the important path that President Rogers has only begun."

"That can't be the only way."

Eliot gave him a hard stare but then smiled again. "I cannot expect you to understand, as I say, but you will. One day. How old are you, Mr. Hoyt?" The professor reasserted his commanding tone.

"Twenty-two, sir," came the automatic answer.

Eliot nodded. He was the sort of man who enunciated every syllable as though for the edification of his listener. "When I was your age, Mr. Hoyt, we had no place like the Institute. Nothing. Harvard did not give me my knowledge of science, but it did grant me the mental and moral strength I needed to teach myself the practical skills of science. President Rogers is a brave, even a remarkable man of our epoch. But far better than devotion to an idealized person is devotion to a personified ideal."

"I suppose," said Edwin, trying his best to make sense of it.

"There are reasons nobody at the Institute knows about my communications with the Harvard Corporation, Mr. Hoyt. I suggest to you it is preferable if they do not."

He wondered how Marcus or Bob would answer that icy suggestion. Before he could think what he was doing, Edwin exclaimed, "Shame on you, Professor!" To his own surprise, he did not want to take the words back even when he realized what he had just done.

"Pardon me, Hoyt?" Eliot snapped.

"Shame on you, for trying to sacrifice all that the Institute means," Edwin went on without hesitation. "The Institute gives a home to all those who can find nowhere else that supports their passions. To take its independence away, you take all that away, too."

Eliot's expression hardened into a threatening gaze. "It seems you have missed chapel. I wonder now, by the looks of your suit, if something more has transpired, that you, too, would prefer not to have to explain to the faculty committee. I heard something about a commotion last night in this very yard. Perhaps *everything* that has happened here this morning should remain private. I'd hate to think any students from Tech were involved, particularly one who is vying for rank of First Scholar. Really, I always thought better of you, Mr. Hoyt."

"Say, fellow! You are late to chapel." It was the watchman who had ordered him to retrieve his Bible. He strode over and took Edwin by the arm.

"If you please," Eliot said, "this young gentleman is assisting me with some private college business. Isn't that correct, Mr. Hoyt?"

Edwin nodded mechanically and the watchman withdrew. With a pointed look at his pupil, Professor Eliot, too, walked away.

After a last look around to make sure he was free, Edwin ran through the gates and mapped in his mind the fastest route to South Boston.

XXXVIII

Tempest in a Teapot!

I T FELT AS THOUGH he had been driving around in circles for hours before Bob's coach returned to his room at Mrs. Page's. There, he found Marcus waiting. He embraced his friend for a long moment before saying, "I was certain the college watchman nabbed you, Mansfield!"

"It was close."

"I was riding through Cambridge looking everywhere for you. You're not hurt, are you? Is Eddy with you?"

"No," answered Marcus. "We just made it into Norton's Woods by the skin of our teeth and divided up. He might have been afraid to come out if he thought the watchmen still were on the hunt."

"I still have the driver outside. While you were with those scoundrels, I've found something out at the experimenter's laboratory. We must get back there immediately."

"What about Edwin? And Miss Swallow?" Marcus asked.

"Eddy knows where to find us. We were about to go last night when we came here first and realized you had been taken. I already sent a message to Mrs. Blodgett's; our better half—better fourth, I should say—should be on her way to South Boston. We haven't a minute to lose."

Marcus appeared preoccupied. "Bob, the Med Fac destroyed the papers we composed for the press. We have little to use to convince them."

Bob pushed Marcus out the door. "It's far more dire than you know. I'll explain on our way!"

He described it all as they rode through the quiet streets of Boston that Sunday morning, relaying in detail how after he blasted off the lock at the private laboratory he found evidence of experiments related to the compass manipulation, including a battery designed almost exactly as

Ellen predicted, and the compounds they had theorized were behind the chemical assault.

"Everything we've searched for!"

"But that was only the beginning. There was a demonstration table near the center of the room, enclosed by a kind of protective glass. On it, a supply of chloride of lime, some that had clearly been heated and dissolved in water in a wooden vessel. Next to that, a glass ball that contained a solid I could not identify."

"None of those items would have been involved in preparing the disasters," Marcus said after considering the inventory.

"Exactly, Mansfield."

"Then the experimenter is planning something new."

"Something to happen soon, I fear," answered Bob, "an event even more destructive, and something bald old Agassiz couldn't recognize if he sat in it! If we go to the police now, under his influence they won't permit us to do what we must to stop what might be coming. I daresay we might clear our consciences but we'll leave a bull's-eye over Boston."

"Then what do we do, if we can't go to the police or the press?" Marcus asked, though Bob suspected Marcus could guess the answer.

"We must return to the villain's laboratory and find out what those new experiments are pointing toward. And fast. We cannot stop until we know."

Bob knew the task as he had stated it might be impossible. It reminded him of an assignment they had been given as sophomores. Professor Storer would pass out boxes of "unknowns," unlabeled glass tubes, and they had to gather clues to identify which chemicals were in each tube. The Technologists had succeeded in determining the causes of two disasters, yet now their challenge was about to be inverted. They were staring at the cause, and needed to predict the intended effect—and failure could mean another disaster and lives lost.

"What if the experimenter returns while we're inside?" Marcus asked.

"Then we'll have him, Mansfield!"

"Or he us."

Bob ignored this. "Did you find any trace of the scarred man before you were taken, Mansfield?"

"In a way," Marcus said. "I found in one of the newspaper cuttings a

THE TECHNOLOGISTS | 311

brief description of a man burned in the State Street disaster, one Joseph Cheshire, who was spoken about by that lad Theo as having been killed. But I was in a stupor of sleep when I made the connection, and wonder now what it amounts to. Bob, we are getting close, aren't we?"

"Follow my lead," Bob said as the carriage closed in on the chemists' building. "The superintendent is a jolly fellow, and I have a certain understanding with him."

Ellen, her face covered in a veil, was waiting in front and seemed relieved by their arrival. Bob rang the bell for the superintendent, but even after he'd tried three times, no one came.

"Come on! Answer!" Bob said, pulling and pushing on the door in frustration before feeling it give way. "Look! It's open."

"Take heed, Mr. Richards," Ellen cautioned him.

This was their chance, and, more to the point, Bob's. He had been bold enough to enter the laboratory in the first place, without help. Now he could finish what he started and prove Phillip wrong about him. Bob led them inside the front chambers, the usual station of the superintendent.

"Well, he appears to have enjoyed my gifts," Bob said, noticing empty wine bottles on a windowsill. "Greetings! Friend, are you on duty?" he called out, but there was no response. "Anyone home?" He checked the inner door that led from the vestibule into the rest of the building, then turned to the others. "What luck," he said, stifling a laugh. "This one is unlocked, too. He must have gone looking for more drink, and have been too cup-shot to remember to lock up."

"What are you doing, Bob?" Marcus asked, grasping his arm, much to Bob's irritation.

"I'm going back up to the laboratory, of course! Come on, Mansfield, let go of me. We don't have time for a discussion."

"I don't like this," Marcus said quietly. "The doors that are usually locked are unlatched. There may be someone else in the building."

"On a Sunday morning!" Bob argued. "Who could be here?"

"You know who, Bob," Marcus said grimly. "We must remain cautious."

Someone called from outside the superintendent's window.

"It's Edwin," said Marcus.

Bob changed tactic, laying an encouraging hand on Marcus's shoulder. "You're right, of course, Mansfield. Bring Edwin up and we'll all discuss this."

Marcus ushered Edwin inside, after peering outside the door for any sign of their being watched or followed.

"Did you see anyone out there?"

"No, Marcus, the street was deserted," replied Edwin.

"Quickly, close the door."

"I have much to tell everyone," Edwin said excitedly when he entered. "Professor Eliot was . . ." he began. Then, surveying the empty chambers, he stopped and asked, "How did you manage to get in here? Where's the superintendent?"

"Bob found the door unlocked," explained Marcus. "But we must take care in going any farther until we know *why*."

"Where *is* Bob?" Edwin asked.

Marcus and Ellen both looked around as the inner door at the other end of the vestibule was swinging closed. They heard footsteps hammering up the stairs.

"Blast it, Bob!" Marcus cried, then over his shoulder to Ellen and Edwin, "Stay here—keep watch for anyone trying to enter the building." He rushed away, leaving Ellen and Edwin standing together in the vestibule.

* * *

"WELL, MISS SWALLOW," Edwin began again, as the footsteps faded above, "*you* simply won't believe your ears when I tell you. It's about Professor Eliot . . ." But when he turned around, anticipating the inevitable surprise on her face, he found that Ellen was already on the far side of the room, examining the vestibule and the superintendent's chamber.

"There are still traces of a woman's housekeeping in these quarters," she said, passing a finger along the perimeter of the wall. "These rooms were once neater, though, I grant, probably not for some time. Poor man must have been abandoned by a wife, or sister, leading him into the vice of drink." She continued her investigation, pushing against another door.

"What are you doing?" In the absence of Bob and Marcus, he felt vaguely that he should order, or at least request strongly, that she stop and heed Marcus's command.

"I'm going to look in the basement."

"Marcus said to stay right here."

"Please remind me, Mr. Hoyt, who elected Mr. Mansfield general of our little squadron?"

Edwin scratched at his neck, no longer so keen to direct her. "Well, why go downstairs?"

"The superintendent may well know more about what has been happening in that laboratory than he has told Mr. Richards. From Mr. Richards's description, the gentleman may be too intoxicated to even remember what he knows, but he may have kept some sort of records for the building somewhere down there. Coming?"

Marcus *had* told them to stay in the vestibule and watch for anyone possibly trying to enter the building. On the other hand, as a responsible gentleman Edwin should be at Ellen's side and ensure her safety. Maybe if he counted to three Marcus and Bob would return.

"One . . . two . . .

"Good-bye, Mr. Hoyt," she said as she started downstairs.

Her swift exit put his own feet into motion. "I'll escort you, Miss Swallow," he said. He followed her down a winding narrow wooden staircase into the dark, poorly ventilated basement. There was a layer of dirty straw on the rocky ground and buckets filled with water at various points. The dismal, rustic compartment seemed like a cave, with its dark-red walls and a single, dimly burning lamp. It was an oozy mass of shadows, to which their own were added.

"I see the superintendent continues his habits down here, too, perhaps when he feels too many disapproving eyes on him up above," Ellen said with a frown, picking up one of the bottles littering the ground and releasing a few last drops from it.

There was a noise, like an inhale. The damp air made Edwin wheeze, and he had to force his words out. "Did you hear something? Breathing?"

Ellen stopped in her tracks, gasping. "Mr. Hoyt!"

Under two small windows that were covered by wooden shutters, by the sole lamp, a large shape slumped in the shadows. They moved closer one step at a time until they could see the face of the corpulent keeper of the building, his mouth hanging slack, his eyes closed.

Ellen smoothed her dress and dropped onto her knees, inspecting the moist folds of the man's chin and neck, then his hand. "No pulse." She moved closer to his lips, where there was a frothy residue faintly visible in the flickering light. "This man was poisoned."

"What? How do you know?"

"Mr. Hoyt, for the last eight months I've studied the composition of the most deadly poisoning agents known to humanity."

"But that is not in the curriculum of the—"

"It is in my own curriculum!"

"From his position, it looks like he was dragged down here," he whispered, determined to contribute despite the dread creeping up his spine. "If he's been dead, who was just breathing?"

She examined his collar and shirt. Then she opened her nostrils and took in the odor. Cringing, she pried open his lips and pulled out his tongue between two of her fingers.

"What in heaven are you doing with his tongue, Miss Swallow?"

"The membrane around the mouth is white and softened. But I need better light and some more delicate equipment in order to determine when and how this was done." She rose to her feet. "Hold on a minute, Mr. Hoyt. If I am right—and I am right—that this man has been a victim of foul play, we must warn them!"

Edwin tried to clear his mind. He was grateful that she was here, and thankful she did not hesitate to decide their next move.

"You noticed it yourself, Mr. Hoyt," she went on. "It appears he was dragged, probably from his chambers upstairs. Whoever did it left all the doors upstairs unlocked but rolled the body down here—not wanting his dead body to frighten away a visitor from coming inside and continuing up. Someone was expected to enter. *We* were expected."

His face paled. "It's a trap, Miss Swallow." Taking a step backward to try to steady himself, he lifted his face to gaze at the upper wall. There was a large arch that extended up and had been filled in with brick. "There!" he cried out.

Wires were hanging out of the archway, plugged into squares of some kind of clay.

Then the noise again, rising up and dissipating as though from some remote horizon. "You heard that?"

"Breathing," she whispered back, nodding. "I heard someone breathing, Mr. Hoyt."

* * *

THREE STORIES ABOVE THEM, Bob was stretching his finger in the keyhole of the door under the sign that read POSITIVELY NO ADMITTANCE. Bob smiled when Marcus caught up with him. "I arranged the lock plate to hide the effects of the gunpowder," he explained calmly, "and to open when I pressed it to one side. You could call me an engineer at this rate."

"Bob! Why was the street door unlocked?"

"A riddle, Mansfield? We need to study what I saw inside this laboratory to know what will happen next; otherwise it's all for nothing! More people will be hurt!"

"Professor Runkle was nearly killed in an explosion. It might have been the same scientist behind the disasters, and if it is, if the experimenter knows you found this, that laboratory could be loaded with explosives, ready to blow us to the sky when you open that door. Or the experimenter might be waiting to ambush us."

Bob had contemplated these possibilities, but thinking about them only bolstered his confidence. "No. No, I don't think so, Mansfield. You see, this door is just how I left it. I am certain. Nobody's been back here. This might—"

"You don't know that nobody's been in here since then, Bob!"

Bob hesitated. The easiest thing to do would be to step away. "This could well be our last chance, Mansfield. Our last chance to find what we need."

"Let us bring Edwin and Miss Swallow out of this building and to safety, and then decide what to do next."

Bob bit down hard on his lower lip. "It's easy for you to say that."

"What do you mean?"

"Telling me to wait!" He heard his voice shake, and that produced an odd flood of honesty. "I've waited my whole life to do something real, to act like a man. I will not shrink when my time comes—not again."

"Bob, wait!"

He pressed his finger into the lock plate, causing the door to pop open.

Marcus slowly joined him in the threshold to the laboratory. They both stood stock-still. The laboratory space appeared just as Bob had first seen it, and the enigmatic experiment inside the glass enclosure at the central table did not seem to have been touched since he had rushed out to find the others the night before. There were no explosives in sight, no wires, no phantom assassins lying in wait.

"There," Bob said, exhaling too loudly. "You see? It's all right, Mansfield, just like I said. You get the others up here and let us get to work immediately analyzing all of this."

Marcus tried to hold him back from entering, but Bob shook him off and took a big step inside, then froze again.

"Wait a minute," Bob said, his heart dropping. "That standing desk by the window—when I was here, there was a large ledger, lined with gold leaf, leaning on top of it. I'm certain of it. Now it's gone."

Click.

"Mansfield, did you hear that?" Bob asked, hoping to God he hadn't.

* * *

SECONDS EARLIER, Ellen and Edwin had climbed back to the first floor from the basement.

"The archways bricked-up down below . . ." Edwin was speaking in urgent bursts.

"What about them, Mr. Hoyt?" asked Ellen.

"I think this building must have originally been one of the barracks built during the Revolution to protect Boston in case of invasion of the harbor." Upon seeing her questioning expression, he added, "My father builds military forts; I have studied every variation of their design since I was a child. Those arches extend all the way to the top, and if those are damaged by explosives—if those wires extend all the way up—the whole place will come down on our heads, floor upon floor!"

As they reached the vestibule, the iron door leading to the staircase emitted a loud *click*—the same one heard above by their friends—before either Edwin or Ellen could reach the handle. They pushed and pulled but the door separating them from the rest of the building wouldn't budge.

"No use," Ellen said. "Some kind of locking mechanism."

"We have to tell them it's a trap!"

Ellen searched the desk and drawers in the chambers, while Edwin rapped his fists and kicked against the door.

"Are there any keys?" Edwin asked.

"Not that I see—maybe in the superintendent's pockets?"

"We don't have time to go back down there."

"Here, Mr. Hoyt! This might be our best chance."

He rushed over to her side. She had found a large knot of a half dozen speaking tubes, each tube half an inch in diameter, protruding from the wall.

"They must be arranged to communicate with the different parts of the building," he said.

"We could use this to warn them. But there are over a dozen of them, and they aren't labeled as they should be. I don't know which—"

"Try them! Try them all!" Edwin said, panic rising.

*   *   *

"YOU HEARD THAT?" Bob repeated as they stood in the third-floor laboratory.

"A clicking noise," Marcus responded, his eyes sweeping across the laboratory.

Bob held his breath, closed his eyes for a long moment, then puffed out an exhale. "Nothing happened. Nothing happened to us, did it?"

"No."

"We're safe," Bob said. "It was probably just old Eddy tripping over something."

They were both stunned when the voice of Ellen Swallow popped into the air. "You must get out! Quickly!"

"What the devil?" Marcus asked.

"There, the speaking tube."

At the wall where the tube emerged, Marcus spoke into the cupped opening. "Miss Swallow? Are you all right?" he said, then put the end to his ear.

"The superintendent is down below, Marcus! Poisoned!" It was Edwin's voice now. "The door—"

Another sound from the knot of tubes, the sound of someone breathing, interrupted them and they fell silent.

"Is that you, Edwin?" Marcus asked.

"It's not us," Edwin's voice replied.

Then a voice—a hoarse whisper, maybe a muffled laugh—slithered out from the end of the flexible tube: "Very sorry. *Positively* no admittance, gentlemen . . . and lady. Technology lives!"

Marcus and Bob traded terrified glances. A moment later, the stove in the corner of the laboratory began to vibrate. This was followed by a series of ominous cracking noises. Piece by piece, the floor bulged; cracks strained into holes. The wood and brick groaned; the west wall swayed.

"Thunder and lightning, Mansfield," Bob gasped. "Run, run for your life!"

The floor of the laboratory sagged, sucking the tables, cabinets, and machinery into a hole, as the ceiling split and the walls gaped open.

Tumbling down the stairs to the first floor, they stopped at the inner door to the vestibule.

"Ellen! Eddy! Open up!" Bob called out.

The walls rumbled, then growled.

"Something is jamming the door frame!" Marcus cried.

They could hear their friends pounding from the other side of the door to try to free them.

Bob pressed his mouth against the cold surface of the unyielding door that divided them. "Nellie, can you hear me?"

"Yes!" her voice was faint from the other side of the thick barrier.

"Take Eddy and run away as fast as you can!"

"Do not presume to order me, Robert!" her voice cried from the other side.

"Damn all stubborn women!" He pounded hard with his fist. "Eddy, you drag her out of here if you have to! Do you hear me? Eddy!"

"No!" shouted back Edwin. "We're not leaving you here! We will live or die together, by the will of God!"

Book 4

MECHANICAL ENGINEERING

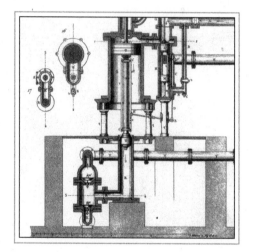

XXXIX

Two Documents

Document: From Phonographic Minutes of Police Interview Between Sergeant Lemuel Carlton and Assistant Fire Engineer Salisbury

CARLTON: You were present at the fire alarm this morning in South Boston, in the chemical laboratory building located at ———?

SALISBURY: That is correct, sir. We received notice of the alarm through our telegraph system. I joined my company riding with our engine to the scene. Our station house was the closest in proximity to that fire, and our engine arrived before any other company.

CARLTON: Do you believe the collapse of the building was the result of scientific activity inside?

SALISBURY: Sir, I would not be able to say. It was in ruins at the time.

CARLTON: Please describe what you saw.

SALISBURY: That a rather ancient brick building had collapsed at that location, sir. It was in ruins, as I say.

CARLTON: Were any persons inside the building at the time?

SALISBURY: We did not believe so, sir, although the rubble will have to be cleared to know for certain. As it was a Sunday morning, and a commercial building, we knew it would be unlikely. If there had been anyone inside, there would be no survivors. That I know.

CARLTON: Were there any witnesses present to view the incident?

SALISBURY: There were several persons who had heard the boom, and rushed toward the sound, some of whom proceeded to spread the alarm.

CARLTON: Anyone else?

SALISBURY: Along the way, directly across the street from the building, I noticed what appeared to be a man running strong toward the building.

CARLTON: A man running *toward* the collapsed building, you said?

SALISBURY: That is correct.

CARLTON: Please.

SALISBURY: Yes, he was running toward the building, and two other young men tackled him to the ground, as though to subdue or capture him.

CARLTON: Could you describe the appearances of any of these persons?

SALISBURY: The air was thick with smoke. I could not see the individuals very clearly.

CARLTON: But you could determine they were young?

SALISBURY: I know not why. I suppose by the way they ran. Yes, it seemed so.

CARLTON: What did the two young men do, having tackled the first one?

SALISBURY: I cannot say. By that time we had situated our engine nearest to a fireplug, and the smoke had mostly moved in another direction with the wind. I did not see them again.

CARLTON: They were gone?

SALISBURY: Yes.

CARLTON: The three of them?

SALISBURY: That is correct.

Document: From W. Edwin Hoyt's Holy Bible

God speed our journey, eternal book! Hours ago it seemed that my journey on the rough path of life would be brought to a singular and violent end. Inside the building housing the laboratory of Boston's unknown Experimenter, M. and B. were shut up like chickens in a coop, trapped behind a door of iron that had been bolted shut by some contraption unseen by us. Miss S. and myself futilely endeavored in every possible fashion to dislodge it from the other side. Good-hearted B. urged us repeatedly to flee from the other side of the barrier, but Miss S. boldly refused and I could not give the idea a second thought. However cautious nature made me, I could never abandon a friend. I told him this in no uncertain terms.

A second later M.'s voice clearly called out from the other side of the door: "Above!"

We looked, and I saw what he must have seen: The ceiling above was bowing and, in doing so, began to dislodge the door from its locked position. Oh, my dear Bible! We had only a few seconds to act.

"Ready?" M. asked from the other side.

"Ready!" Miss S. and myself answered in one voice.

"Now!" rejoined M.

The ceiling began buckling, M. and B. pushed from their side, we pulled from ours, and though I could see nothing I felt with a fluttering heart a thrill as the door gave way with a shudder.

A blur of dust and smoke came after that. We could only touch and guess our way out from the vestibule—a combination of memory, instinct, and luck. I felt myself hurried out the door by one of my companions and I ran across the street as fast as I could manage, even as bricks and other projectiles landed around me. Even now as I write this surrounded by the sweet tranquillity of plants and flowers, I can hardly say in detail how it all happened, or how long it lasted, or how it ended the way it did. The upper floors of the building pancaked into the lower ones, with a crash so complete it turned the world around us utterly quiet. In the distance, some seconds (minutes?) later I could hear shouts from strangers calling for help, and then the tolling of church bells with the same objective.

I could not see inches in front of me, but could hear every crumbling brick and rock fall and could hear my friends rustling nearby. B.'s groan emerged first, calling out for each of us to ask whether we were there and safe.

Then M. said, "We must leave before we are seen."

I know not what came over me amid such chaos, but something moved me almost to tears. "A building," said I, "a building perhaps a hundred years old collapsed, nearly crushing us underneath! We are likely the only witnesses. We cannot just go off and hide, M.!"

M. must have known immediately how perturbed I became over his idea. "Listen," he said, grabbing me by both shoulders, which he had never done before in three years of friendship. "If the police learn that students from the Institute were inside that laboratory building—and no one else in sight—they will conclude that we caused this through some kind of misuse of science, accidental or otherwise. If we're put in a prison cell over this, we can scream and shout all we wish, but how will we stop what is about to come next, E.? Make no mistake," he said, addressing himself to the whole group now, "the evidence that B. discovered inside that laboratory was intentionally destroyed. Now we still are left in a position unable to prove a thing."

B. was seething, distraught. I could hear it in his breathing and his trembling limbs next to me. "That was *all* intentional—it was a trap and I pulled us into it. We heard his voice inside there!"

"The speaking tube could have been connected to anywhere," I insisted. "Speaking tubes can work from hundreds of feet distance."

"No, I think he was watching us," Miss S. said. "He could be watching us still. . . ."

In the swirling dust, I could see M. suddenly latch his fingers on his own forehead. Mortality creeps onto us at such different times, and I can only imagine for M. how this time it differed from times past. But he now had B. by the shoulders in the same brotherly fashion he had taken me, and said, "You saved me. Another moment and—"

"What?" B. interrupted.

"I fell," M. said. "Before I could reach the door to the street, I fell and you pulled me up and out."

B. said he had done no such thing, that he could hardly see what was happening.

"But I made certain you all got out, then I fell. After that, I was pulled to my feet," insisted M., with an air of confusion, "but I couldn't see. E.? Miss S.? One of you pulled me to safety."

There was silence as we each waited for another to accept the credit; then more silence, as realization dawned on us.

B. suddenly wheeled around 180 degrees, then back again. "Him! Where are you, you lunatic?"

"B., no!" I cried.

"You think science is the art of destruction—is that what you are about?" he went on, picking up a brick from the ground and swinging wildly at the dust. "Come out and I'll show you destruction courtesy of Bob Richards!"

He ran back toward the building and hurled the brick. Thank heavens that foolish act did not harm any innocent, but sent the projectile into the vacuum of the just-created rubble!

We implored him to be calm and M. and myself fell on top of him and dragged him out of sight as he continued to scream in the same hysterical fashion. Luckily, over the din of the bells and the clattering of approaching fire engines, B.'s revealing words were almost entirely drowned out. A dozen or so onlookers had come running after the collapse to help . . . and to gape.

(Here B. approaches the table to stay my hand, but I *must* write, or I shall not know how to go on.)

Yes, we did run from the scene of this disaster before we could speak to the authorities. I know that to flee was wrong, but at the very same time I knew M. *was* right. We may yet be Boston's last hope, and had we reported the events to the police just now our endeavors to help would be made impossible.

I was frightened outside the ruins of that building, but I was not afraid. I have learned through this enterprise that science makes no place for cowardice. As long as I can protect my friends, and my city, I know I, too, shall be protected from harm. This, I know now, must be my purpose: I must keep the Technologists together, for if we are split apart the city will follow. Yet I cannot escape the feeling, dear Bible, that the deeper we become engulfed by these atrocities, the harder it is to know what actions are right. The scientific arts represent the mind of God better than any other human endeavor. Yet, we are chasing one who is vicious and without conscience, and as we stay at his heels, I live in a tremble that we will all be darkened by the shadow of the devil.

XL

Gatehouse

T HE GATEHOUSE opposite the dam had been called a model of security by a national magazine, fireproof and exceptionally well protected. With its hammered granite exterior and floors, and metal roof, and granite floors, the building was designed to preclude interference with the gates and conduit below. But the lake itself was three and a half miles long. It could not *all* be protected.

Around dusk that Sunday, the intruder entered the water from a secluded area toward the northern portion of the glittering lake. A beast, a creature, a waterlogged Frankenstein's monster: That's how the figure would have appeared to a watcher along the shore of the Cochituate, encased in a suit from which tubes sprouted like tentacles, its face concealed within a bulbous, windowed helmet. But there were no watchers as the thing lumbered into the shallows, moved deeper and deeper, and then submerged itself.

Down, down, down, through the pure, untouched waters channeled for all the needs of the city of Boston. Since its last use, the suit had been modified with a self-sustaining air supply, and now featured a specially designed air reservoir with a regulator valve at the shoulder. The suit's initial engineering had been skillful, clever. Its modifications reflected superior skills—genius, in fact. Now it could go deeper, for a longer period of time, independent of assistance from above. That proved an important point to the wearer. If all had to be done alone, without the help once promised and afforded him, so be it.

Soon enough beneath the gatehouse, the aquatic Frankenstein barely paused before fastening a mine to the cast-iron gates that allowed water to flow freely through the conduit, into the aqueduct, in order to fill the main that traveled into Boston. He turned the crank four times to charge the device.

Retreating to a safe distance to wait for the muted, glorious explosion, the saboteur patted with a gloved hand the vials protected inside the pocket of the suit. Boston would be reeling again soon enough. Almost as satisfying as thinking about this was to imagine how the destruction would all look through the astonished eyes of Marcus Mansfield.

XLI

May 17, 1868

E LLEN LEANED OVER HER STOVE TOP, bringing a spoonful of hot liquid to her lips and puckering. When she looked up from stirring some more, she saw Bob approaching Edwin's place at her table. He was nervous and distracted, and she worried he might tease Edwin, to repair his own ego after having lost control of his emotions at the site of the collapsed building.

"Put that away, Eddy," Bob said, mildly enough, after watching his friend's relentless fit of writing. "Isn't that sacrilege and whatnot?"

"I haven't anything else to write on," Edwin answered quietly, softly stroking his pocket Bible, the front leaves of which had now been filled with his microscopic print. "Every piece of paper in Miss Swallow's room is filled with equations and formulas. Besides, it seems an appropriate place for a diary, somehow."

"It is as appropriate as anywhere else after a day like this," she said, causing Bob to return to pacing around her living room. "But you *both* should be resting, gentlemen. The soup is almost done." They had retreated here because it was the closest of all their lodgings, but perhaps also because this was where they could be cared for best. She had not expected to take a motherly role toward the upperclassmen when all this started, but how could she not in her own boardinghouse, after such experiences together?

She removed a rag soaking in a dish of warm water and soap and walked over to Edwin's chair. "Let us see how it is," she said. He finished the sentence he was writing and closed his Bible as she pressed the rag with a gentle motion over a bump on his temple and began blowing softly on it.

"He looks better," Bob insisted, getting between them hastily and inspecting his friend's head, then patting his hair. "All better, see? Professor, but have you noticed this gash in my knee?"

Ellen gave Edwin a few more moments of care, then turned her attention to Bob. Fortunately, all their cuts and abrasions appeared to be minor. "Have a seat, Mr. Richards. We'll have a look."

Bob found a chair and rolled his trousers up over his knee.

"Thank you," she whispered.

"For what, Professor?" Bob asked.

"For asking me to leave when you and Mr. Mansfield were locked inside the stairwell. I believe you were concerned about me."

"We need you," Bob replied wholeheartedly. Then he quickly added, "You are a true chemist, and that is most useful."

"There," she said, judging the injury harmless.

"Why?" he said, falling back into his distracted state and turning to Marcus, who was sitting across from Edwin at the dining table with the cut-out center square that was filled with plants. "Why should the experimenter save Mansfield when he fell, Professor? He nearly turned all of us into dust!"

"The experimenter wants us to witness the power he has over us," Ellen surmised.

"The power to allow us to live," Marcus added, "or to finish us. He wants us to know one thing above all else—that he is better than us."

"Every fiber in my being still wants to tell the police we were present, and what happened," said Edwin.

"I know," Marcus said apologetically, holding out a glass of water to him. "Thank you for being patient, Edwin."

"Mr. Hoyt," Ellen said, "when you first arrived at the laboratory building, you said there was something about Professor Eliot you needed to tell us."

Edwin nodded, gulping down the glass of water before he explained what had happened that morning at Harvard, which now seemed a year ago.

"You're certain Professor Eliot was proposing to Harvard that the Institute be annexed, Edwin?" Marcus asked.

"When I questioned it, his eyes flashed with fire like a furnace and he implied strongly that if I informed President Rogers about it, he would make inquiries about how we were involved in what happened on the Harvard grounds."

"So no matter what we do, the Institute might be chewed up," Ellen said, "and then spat out."

"That is a worry for a later time," Bob said grimly. "At the moment, not only has the evidence of the experimenter's crimes been destroyed but so have our clues as to his next exercise in mayhem!"

"No, they haven't," said Ellen enigmatically. "Not entirely, at least. We have saved the most important clue we could."

"Why, my dear Professor, did you see the ruins of that building? Fortunately it is Sunday, or dozens of people would have been crushed flat, but there is decidedly nothing left to salvage, not with the most sophisticated equipment we might conjure."

"I believe Miss Swallow means something else by the most important clue, Bob," said Marcus. *"You."*

"Precisely," Ellen added.

* * *

"ME?" Bob laughed dismissively. "What are you two driving at?"

Marcus nodded. "You saw the demonstration table in the experimenter's sanctuary last night. You viewed it up close."

"Indeed, for hardly a full minute before I left to tell all of you! And I am no chemist."

"Come, Bob, Miss Swallow is right. You must at least try to remember!" Edwin said.

"If I remembered anything more, don't you think I'd have told you?" Bob roared. "Foofaraw and bull, all of this talk! I won't hear another word."

"Very well," agreed Marcus, disappointed. "Let us think of something better to try, then."

"I will!" Bob promised.

Ellen began dishing out bowls. Beef with noodles as thin as sewing needles, the soup's aroma seemed to soothe the mood in the room. "I think the time has come to tell Hammie," she commented as she passed around the bowls. "Tell him everything that has happened, omitting no detail."

"Hammie?" Bob and Edwin asked at the same time, both clearly opposed. Marcus looked at her with curiosity but did not make an objection.

"That's right. Hammie," Ellen repeated blandly. "He helped rescue Mr. Mansfield at Harvard, didn't he? And he is, after all, among the brightest intellects in the Institute."

"Hold on, Professor," Bob said, suddenly full of energy, "between Hammie and Eddy here, I'd take Eddy any day!"

"I hold nothing against Hammie and would never belittle his particular gifts, Bob," Edwin said diplomatically. "It's only the impression of a competition I reject. Well, in all events, perhaps Miss Swallow is correct, that we could use more help."

"This is not a contest, after all," Ellen remarked.

"No, no, I suppose it is not," Bob said, "but I don't care for the tone Hammie too often takes with you."

"With me?" she asked, sounding surprised, though not changing her expression.

"It's too . . . familiar. He doesn't know the first thing about addressing a woman properly, probably never has in his life, and I shouldn't like him around you more. He stares his eyes out at you. I shouldn't like to see that at all."

"I don't know what you mean. I'm merely suggesting—"

"You know," he interrupted, "perhaps I can recall more about that laboratory. I'll try, at least. It's worthwhile."

"Excellent idea," Ellen said, smiling, and allowing the other topic to vanish. "Close your eyes, Mr. Richards—the dark opens up new windows and vistas of our minds."

"*Mens et Manus,*" Edwin said encouragingly. "Mind and Hand, Bob. I know you can do it."

Eyes closed tightly, Bob stretched himself out and extended his long legs across the sofa arm. Ellen's cat took a liking to the position and made himself a comfortable nest in the folds of Bob's vest.

"Now, think back. Cast everything else out of your thoughts except the laboratory. What was it you saw in there?"

"Well, Professor, there was a quantity of chloride of lime there, as I said. Some must have been heated—there were remnants in a tray over a burner—and dissolved in a wooden bowl next to it, I believe. And there was a glass ball with a liquid inside. But I've already told you all that, haven't I? You see, I've said everything!"

"Did you touch it? The glass ball."

"I think—yes, I believe I did."

"Was it cold or hot?"

"Cold, I believe. Cold." Then, thinking about it: "Very cold."

"There was a substance inside the glass?"

Bob squeezed his eyelids together more tightly. His eyes underneath seemed to move, as though roving the laboratory as he spoke. "There was a chemical cloud of some kind; it appeared as if . . . frozen."

"What equipment was closest to it?"

"I don't know. I don't!"

"Envision the space around the glass ball."

"A platinum crucible and . . . some glass vials. A sieve! A blow-pipe . . . another Bunsen burner."

Ellen exchanged satisfied glances with Marcus and Edwin. "A platinum crucible, you say?"

"Yes," answered Bob.

After another half hour, Ellen had coaxed intricate details from Bob's memory, with Marcus supplementing the information from his own short time inside the laboratory, while Edwin wrote every word down in his Bible. When Bob, exhausted body and soul by the exercise, insisted he had dredged up every possible detail, Ellen excused herself to the next room and reappeared wearing dark gloves and an apron of India rubber and carrying a box of vials.

"You store chemical supplies here, Miss Swallow?" Marcus asked.

"Naturally. I cannot always be at the Institute, you know, Mr. Mansfield." She sent Edwin to a nearby pharmacist for certain items on their list that she did not possess in her miniature store. As soon as he returned, they began to trace backward the steps the experimenter had likely taken.

Bob took up the newspaper Edwin had brought back from his excursion.

"Mansfield?" he said, gasping. "The man who browbeat you and Hammie—what did you say you believed his name might be?"

"Cheshire, I think. But it was only a flight of fancy. At least, until we have time to investigate. Why?"

Bob rolled up the newspaper and tossed it to him.

A GHASTLY DEATH

UNSUSPECTING MAN BURNT TO DEATH
FROM SEWER EXPLOSION

An unfortunate accident in Boston Sunday took the life of Joseph Cheshire, respectable commission stockbroker, born in Cape Cod. It appears that Mr. Cheshire was walking along when the explosion occurred from a sewer below, immediately enveloping him in a sheet of flame, then spreading rapidly below along the sewer for some distance. A surgeon arrived on the scene but gave up hope for the victim, who died minutes later. Mr. Cheshire, in addition to being known in the world of business, recently exhibited great bravery and Christian perseverance as a victim of the catastrophe in State Street, which left permanent and revolting chemical injuries to his face, head, and hands. The Sewer Department is in pursuit of clues, but there is little doubt the explosion was occasioned from an escape of gas from a faulty main in the street communicating with the sewer.

XLII

Farewell, Boston

SIMON CAMP HAD BEEN A MINOR OPERATIVE on missions for the Pinkerton agency long enough to know when there was going to be serious trouble. Long enough to know when to stand his ground and fight, or, at times like this, when to flee and not look back.

This was not the first time he'd had to get out of Boston in a hurry, and as soon as he'd read in the newspaper of his client Cheshire's death, he knew the sands had run out. He did not feel much of an emotional qualm about the man's demise. After all, the deformed stockbroker was rather a miserable pissant, whose chief quality of any value was being rich. But he *was* rich, and he had thrown plenty of money in Camp's direction. Camp now regretted telling Cheshire about the boy with the lame arm whom one of his informants heard speaking of the stockbroker, and he had not asked or really wanted to know what it was Cheshire did about it, but he had seen the fury in Cheshire's eyes as he listened to Camp's report. Cheshire's murder—if that's what it was, but what else could an exploding sewer be in the jaded mind of a private detective?—was a shame. He did not like Cheshire, could not like him no matter what he was paid, but Cheshire was a true speculator, and Camp had always fancied himself a type of speculator—not in money and investments, but in people.

Simon Camp was a professional, through and through. He took cases to the end, and would not run away from one. But, he thought, as he packed his valise and laid aside his train ticket, this case was over. Prematurely, but still it had ended the moment Joseph Cheshire was burnt to a crisp. Cheshire was his client, Boston was not.

Certainly, Boston remained in great danger, and that was another shame. Joseph Cheshire's madness for revenge and his fiery end had convinced Camp not only that there was a lunatic scientist somewhere in Boston, but that the perpetrator would stop at nothing to carry his plan for the city—whatever it was—through to its unnatural conclusion. In that, Camp almost admired the unknown monster, though he liked Boston well enough and preferred not to see it destroyed. Camp indirectly had been witness to the most gruesome murders in Boston history, nearly three years before, and now? What word would one of those dandified bookmen he once trailed use for this chain of events? Anyway, Boston's security was a matter for the police department, and Camp didn't care a brass farthing what police ever did. Or, as he said in polite society, or to other detectives, he did not *meddle* with police affairs. He was a professional Pinkerton man, and had a much more lucrative opportunity up his sleeve that he was now free to pursue, whether Allan Pinkerton liked it or not, and that was that.

He did give a passing thought to those colleges the stockbroker had ordered him to follow and gather information on. Marcus Mansfield and the fellows he ran with knew something, and whatever they knew put them in danger, but also gave Boston a chance.

Just not a chance that Camp was willing to bet on.

"Your bill was paid in advance, Mr. Melnotte," said the hotel clerk at the Parker House, addressing him by the alias he had used upon arrival. Camp had insisted on staying at the nicest hotel at Cheshire's expense—the hotel where no less than Charles Dickens had slept on his visit to Boston. "We hope your stay in Boston was pleasant."

"It's been a fly in my teacup, actually. Thanks, fellow." He looked around at the shining marble elegance and felt a pang of regret for this proud city, which always seemed to think it could sail through any circumstance unscathed.

Farewell, Boston. Not a moment too soon.

XLIII

Pathfinders

"THAT'S HIM!" Marcus said of the etching printed alongside the column about Joseph Cheshire.

"Could it really be an accident?" Edwin asked.

"I doubt it," Marcus replied. "But the evidence to prove otherwise is gone—just like the laboratory."

"Well, one fewer problem to worry about, with Cheshire out of the way," Bob said sardonically.

"Assuming, Mr. Richards, that Mr. Cheshire didn't tell anybody about us already, before he was under the sod," Ellen pointed out.

Edwin shook his head at his friends in disbelief. "You are talking of a man's life! Why would someone kill him?" he asked, looking up at Marcus.

"Perhaps he was threatening other people besides us," he replied, shrugging.

"I'd have hanged him like a dog if he tried to stop us," Bob said. "Not literally a dog, Professor."

"Cheshire had been monitoring our whereabouts, our actions," said Marcus, freshly troubled. "If the experimenter knows that the boy told us about him, he might try to harm him, too. We must find the boy and make certain he is safe."

"Who?"

"Theo," Marcus said.

"What? Oh, the little fellow with the hand, you mean," said Bob indifferently.

"He helped us and now he could be in danger. We involved him. He's hardly more than a child, Bob."

"Right now, we have other fish to fry," Bob reminded him. "Don't we?"

"Of course, but—"

"Why, Professor Swallow," Bob interrupted, transfixed by something he saw in Ellen's face, "what is the matter?"

True to form, her concentration had remained fixed. A gleam of possibility was in her eyes. "What if the mixture of chemicals there was not placed in cold water?"

"But that was how Bob found them," Edwin said.

She shook her head. "Mr. Hoyt, you misunderstand what I mean. The water was cold, after what may have been *several days*, when Mr. Richards came upon it."

Edwin stared at her for a long moment. "Yes . . . I see it. . . . *It* might have *turned* the water cold!"

"Cold, or, more likely, frozen," Ellen said, nodding as she thought it through. "Mr. Richards saw what was likely several pounds of chloride of lime that appeared to have been heated before being placed through a sieve and powdered. We now believe, from what he recounted, there was residue of salt, too, and mercury. When combined, this mixture introduced into water *could* freeze it."

"If we have sufficient raw materials, we can find out if it works," Marcus said.

"We ought to move our inquiries to the Institute," Ellen said. "I fear Mrs. Blodgett will have an ear at the door by now, seeing us all come in. Plus, we shall need more materials than we can obtain here."

"Already preparing," Edwin said, wrapping up some of what they needed. Meanwhile, Bob went down to the street to hire a carriage to carry them all to Back Bay.

Once they arrived at the Institute basement, they arranged the necessary equipment. Using a burner, they proceeded to heat chloride of lime. It gradually formed a porous mass, after which they ran it through a sieve. In a wooden vessel, salt was added and then a glass ball of mercury was inserted with a pair of tongs.

"Look!" Edwin said.

The mercury in the glass ball gradually froze solid.

"Now, Mr. Mansfield! The water!" Ellen said.

He poured in a container of water. Bob then delicately positioned a thermometer into the mixture. The thermometer dropped down ten, twenty, thirty, forty, then another sixty degrees. The water froze before their eyes, clutching the thermometer in ice.

"Incredible! This must be it! It must be the purpose of this experiment!" Bob cried.

Edwin threw back his head and laughed wildly. "We've found it!" Then his expression retreated into its normal state of caution. "What did we find, exactly?"

"An answer, but only to half our question. Now we must discover its use," Marcus said.

"Yes. We must ask ourselves: What destruction could this create?" proposed Ellen.

"We'd have to consider every use of water in Boston," Bob said, "and how such an experiment could derange its normal function."

"We must think like a madman, you mean," Edwin said, swallowing hard.

Evening trudged into night, Sunday slipped into the early morning hours of Monday. They had written theories on a chalkboard and crossed them out one by one; they took their turns napping on the bench in the corner of the laboratory. Edwin practically collapsed there during his turn, while the others were preparing the blast furnace to attempt an experiment using iron pieces similar to those noticed near the demonstration table in the private laboratory. Ellen said she did not need to rest, though on several occasions her eyes closed for a few seconds at a time while she was sitting, with her perfect posture, at the microscope. As soon as her eyes opened again, her hands deftly continued her examination right where they'd left off.

With so much to do, Marcus had no expectation of sleeping, either, when his turn came for the bench. But when he looked at the clock again he found almost an hour and twenty minutes had passed, and he couldn't quite bring himself to resume his work. The next time he peeled his eyes open, someone swayed above him, shaking him and shouting. His mind returned to the fields in Baton Rouge, the wounded screaming in desperation or writhing in final moments of life. A blurry array of shapes and colors swam into view around the laboratory: his friends, all prostrate around the room. Senseless. They had been attacked while he slept.

* * *

THE FIRST FACE THAT HE COULD IDENTIFY among the attackers was that of Albert Hall. The cowlick hanging down on the forehead, the thin, perpetually open lips now saying something Marcus could not hear. He tried to reach out and strike that chubby pink face but could not manage to raise his hand. He fought as he felt himself lifted under his arms and half-dragged, half-pushed out into the hallway, followed almost immediately by a stumbling, groggy Bob. A few moments later, clear vision and sense returned, and Marcus, understanding, hurried back into the laboratory and helped Albert and Darwin Fogg drag Edwin and Ellen into the hall, while Bob crawled on the floor to the furnace and put out the burning irons.

"You all right, Mr. Marcus?" Darwin asked when they were back in the safety of the hallway.

"I think so, Darwin," Marcus said, holding on to his throbbing head.

"Carbon gas!" Bob said, bringing water to Edwin, who was gasping. "We were all poisoned by it. There was some loose brickwork on the furnace that we hadn't noticed, and it must have been releasing fumes."

They activated the ventilation fan and convened in Ellen's laboratory while the air cleared.

"Thank you for your help, Hall," Bob said.

"I come early to review the student account ledgers, and look what I find. What were you doing in there?" Albert demanded. "What *exactly* are you doing down here?"

"We have permission to use the laboratory, Hall," Marcus said. "You can confirm that with the faculty office."

"Oh, I will do so! But she is meant to be in her own laboratory only, isn't she?" he asked of Ellen.

"For classes, yes, Mr. Hall," Ellen, wiping her cheeks with a handkerchief, answered with proper deference. "Yet I am permitted to assist other students when necessary."

"I'll have to confirm that, too," Albert said with suspicion. "Something strange—well, I could have been killed trying to rescue all of you, you know."

Darwin continued to tend to the students until he was assured they were well, which they were, except for slight headaches.

"That will set us back," Bob said when both Darwin and Albert had exited.

"We've run out of time," said Marcus.

"What do you mean?" asked Edwin, who was still coughing and struggling for his voice.

"Think of it, Edwin," Marcus said. "The experimenter has had his freezing mechanism completed for at least a day and a half, maybe longer. Bob found it Saturday night, and he and Miss Swallow hadn't seen anyone enter the experimenter's laboratory for hours before that!"

"Then why wait?" Edwin asked. "Why would the wretch not just use it yesterday or the day before?" Then, prayerfully, "Perhaps it isn't intended for any harmful use."

"We must not relent!" Bob exclaimed.

"Enough, Bob. We almost just died in there!" Marcus shouted over him. "If Darwin and Hall hadn't happened to be passing—"

"That was bad luck," Bob interrupted, nodding his head.

"Or some kind of sabotage," Marcus said.

"Why, that furnace probably hasn't been started more than two or three times since the building was put up, and probably hadn't been completed when their funds ran low. You know half the basement was left unfinished. We cannot stop when we're so close!" Bob exclaimed.

"Cheshire."

"What?" Bob replied.

"Joseph Cheshire," Marcus went on in a louder voice. "He was conducting some sort of investigation into the events—we know that. Perhaps he was coming closer—he discovered that *we* were investigating, in any event, and may have known much more than that. Professor Runkle knew we were investigating. One man, Cheshire, is dead, the other, Runkle, may yet succumb from the attempt on his life. This isn't a schoolyard game—if it ever seemed like it was, it's not anymore. None of us is safe, not in our homes, not here, not in the streets. The experimenter knew that someone had been to his laboratory and destroyed the building—now he may work faster to execute his plans."

"Then what exactly do you suggest?" Bob asked.

"We cannot wait, and there is nothing left of the private laboratory or its superintendent to give us any further intelligence. We must bring everything we know to the police, and pray for the best."

"We will not get past Agassiz's hatred of the Institute!" Bob cried. "This is the police chief in you talking, Mansfield, not the Technologist."

"We've done everything so far as a group," Edwin said, getting in between them. "You vote for one, you vote for the ticket. We must keep it that way, above all else. Let us decide together." He waited until the others nodded their agreement. "Very well. All those in favor of what Marcus proposes, say, 'Aye.' Shall we yield our efforts to the police?"

"Nay!"

"One vote nay," Edwin said, acknowledging Bob's selection with a businesslike air. "Marcus, I believe we know what you wish, as well."

"Aye," Marcus said calmly, and with no pleasure.

"So one vote against, one vote for. Miss Swallow?"

"Miss Swallow, Eddy," Bob urged. "I know this isn't an easy decision. Think of all those people who have told you that a school of technology was a waste of your time. This is the chance to prove ourselves, to show the world once and for all why we're here!"

Bob directed an imploring glance at Ellen. Her expression was downcast, and she closed her eyes as she said, "I'm afraid Mr. Mansfield is right, Mr. Richards. Without examining additional clues, there are an infinite number of variations as to the use of that experiment. This is why I have always wished I were triplets! There simply isn't *time.*"

"You are an 'aye,' then?" Edwin asked.

"Aye," she answered.

" 'Where anyone else has not gone, there I will go.' Wasn't that your motto, Professor? Where did it fly to when I needed it?" Bob said bitterly, then turned to Edwin before she could answer. "If we tell the police now, our hands will be tied going forward! Eddy, I beg you! Make the right choice!"

Edwin shook his head. "I cannot find a choice, Bob. Let us gather the evidence we have, all of our materials and whatever papers the Med Fac did not burn. I vote 'aye,' also."

Bob threw up his hands. "Very well. Vote the ticket. I shall not resist."

Marcus stood from his stool and turned to the others. "I wonder if you can speak to the police without me. I have a friend—someone important to me—whose trust I have sacrificed. I wish to try to recover it."

"I think that is wise, Mr. Mansfield," Ellen said.

They agreed to return to their respective lodgings to recover their energy for a few hours, then Bob, Ellen, and Edwin would go to the central police station while Marcus attended to his personal business. The next time they all came together they would reunite as collegians, just like any of the others at the Institute.

"Wait—before we leave." Edwin removed his pocket Bible, and placed it on the table. "Let us pray together that we are doing the right thing for Boston, my friends. Let nothing be done through strife or vain glory, but in humility of mind let each esteem others better than himself."

They each repeated Edwin's prayer, said amen, then contemplated silently; though no one said anything further, they prayed for the safety of strangers across the city; but each also pictured one or two faces in particular.

XLIV

The Jaws of Hell

WHEN IT WAS ALL OVER, the faint perfume of white roses remained with him. As soon as the group divided, he had left a note for Agnes at her father's house, and then he had gone to the Public Garden. There he circled the pond, went up and down the brick walks, along the flower beds and between monuments and fountains, looking everywhere he could in the twenty-four-acre park.

Tired, he sat down on the edge of a fountain near a bed of milk-white roses. Two children, a boy and a girl, maybe brother and sister though they looked nothing alike, reveling in the light rain, waded up to their ankles in the fountain, laughing and kicking water at each other to see who splashed higher. He heard bells toll in the distance. If she were coming, she'd be here by now. He wished he could slow the clock or stop it altogether, before all hope of her appearing had vanished, as it inevitably would in a few minutes. He had lost her forever; she had retreated into her closed-off world where he was not welcome.

This hour would also mark another ending. Bob, Edwin, and Ellen would be starting on their way to the police station house without him, in order to hand over all records of their efforts. *Failed efforts.*

The city will be safer once we share our knowledge with the police, he thought, nearly convincing himself. *The police, Agassiz, they'll put a stop to all of it once they see what we've found.*

He thought about beautiful Agnes going to confession since she was a little girl. There must have been something uplifting about being obliged to leave behind your mistakes and wash them away in holy tears.

If he could, what would he say to her? He would say to her, "Miss Turner, I'm here to ask for forgiveness. My hat might have been on too tight, because you helped us, and I only thought of myself." That part about the hat sounded a bit like Bob might say it, and he smiled at the turn of phrase, repeating it aloud to try it out. That was one way he knew he and Bob and Edwin and Ellen had grown close: They had begun to unthinkingly use one another's distinctive phrases.

"I am very pleased to hear that."

Marcus looked up. And there was Agnes, sheltered from the scattered showers by a bright, parti-colored parasol. No longer in her servant's costume, she wore a light dress of yellow trimmed with pink.

"Miss Turner! You got my note."

Agnes looked away for a moment, watching the children and laughing at their happy antics. Her smile remained as she sat down next to Marcus. "I did get your note. Luckily my sister Josie found it before Lucy, who is a do-gooder through and through and would have brought it right to Papa. I did debate with myself whether I would come. I will offer a bargain, if you please. I will tell you when you are obliged to call me 'Miss Turner' again," she said primly, "and until then you will not do it."

"Agreed. Have you found another position?"

"Not yet. Papa wants me to enter the convent, and if he found us here together, you know he would want you to enter the catacomb under our church."

"Aggie." He took one of her hands in his. "When you came to me after what happened with your father, I acted as a proper collegey gentleman, but not like a man. I treated you as an outsider, when you had proven yourself a keystone to what we were doing from the very moment Rogers collapsed. You were a Technologist all along."

"Though I don't know what it means, you are sweet to say it," she said, offering him her other hand.

"When we did not find what we needed, even after we redoubled our efforts, last night, in the middle of the night, I could only think of this—I must wait until Monday, when your papa would be at work again, to look into the blue of your eyes. I begin to think I know myself best when you are looking at me."

She smiled and leaned in to him for a kiss. Just then, water splashed over them.

"Well, look at that!" she laughed, standing up and rounding on the triumphant children. "Imps!" She splashed them back.

Marcus stood up to shake himself dry, also laughing, but stopped suddenly. With the shadow of Agnes's disfavor lifted, his flimsy delusion about the police also dissolved. Edwin's voice sounded in his mind: *Why wait? Why would the wretch not just use it yesterday or the day before?*

"Because the casualties would be greater on a workday than on the Sabbath," Marcus answered under his breath. "The experimenter seeks the greatest spectacle and injury." He spun around. "It's Monday. It's Monday morning. All of Boston is stepping foot into the streets now."

"What did you say about Monday?"

In the garden and Charles Street beyond, Boston was coming alive, embarking on its day—businessmen striding to their offices from the horsecar platform, women moving along more daintily, covered from the weather by bonnets and parasols, children and dogs running wherever they pleased amid the growing crush of horses, carriages, and carts. He leaned one hand on a streetlight, one of those now linked to the Institute's electric circuit-breaker system.

Who were they, really? Just a handful of students styling themselves Technologists, grandly thinking they could rescue their college and defend Boston against an invisible enemy. Knowledge of scientific arts did not give them the power of clairvoyance. Yet, if there was a chance they were right . . . Torn, Marcus gave the lamppost a swift kick as Agnes, her eyes now wide with concern, took his arm.

There was a rumbling noise before the ground trembled beneath them. It was as though the earth held in its laughter. Then, a low hissing. It all came together in his mind now, the secret experiment, the frozen mercury, Monday morning. . . .

As sophomores, they had made a study in metallurgy about metals expanding unequally. One of the basic causes of such an expansion was a contrast in temperatures—which could be caused most quickly by the introduction of cold water to a hot metal.

The first things to start in the commercial metropolis of Boston on a Monday morning would be the boilers in the mills, the foundries, all the places of industry that had arisen across the city in the last twenty years.

"Boilers!" he cried.

If the feed water were too cold, with the steam heat pumping in at the same time, the metal would expand at different rates in different parts. Every apparatus in that condition could explode.

Right underneath where they stood in the Public Garden and Commons were the main water pumps connected throughout the city—the danger, once introduced into the pipes from the reservoirs, would be on its way, rumbling past them.

"Out with it, Marcus!" she demanded.

"I have to warn them," Marcus said. "Frank . . . Mr. Hammond . . . the locomotive works. Everyone, everywhere. I have to get to them." He took her by the shoulders. "Stay here, Aggie, in the garden, away from the buildings, do you understand?"

"No, I don't!"

"Forget the garden, actually. Find the middle of the Common—stay along the center mall, as far from the streets and buildings as you can. You'll be safe! I'll find you when it's over!"

"What's happening, Marcus? Where are you going?"

"Remember, stay in the middle," he said, guiding her quickly onto the lawn. "It's not too late for me to do something."

* * *

"**DID YOU WITNESS** the incidents when they occurred?"

"Well, not exactly," said Edwin.

"Do you know who perpetrated the incidents? This . . . 'experimenter,' as you say."

"No, not by name. As to being witnesses, we did visit State Street after we heard what had happened. And we saw the laboratory building in South Boston collapse up close—why, we were almost crushed by it," Edwin pointed out. He was sitting across the desk from a patrolman in the public area of the police station. Bob tapped his fingers against the wall and his foot against the floor. He was standing behind his friend, bursting with impatience.

The patrolman gave a long-winded sigh. "Tell me again why you are here?"

"Because we know more than you do," Bob said. "The whole city is in danger, and you sit on your hands!"

"We have the finest experts studying these strange phenomena, I assure you—"

"Ha! Agassiz and his shell collectors? You're not listening!" Bob interrupted. "There must be some relative of mine in a superior position to you somewhere here."

"Bob, please," Edwin admonished him, then turned back to the irritated patrolman. "Sir, if I may—"

"What profession did you say you were in?" the patrolman said, screwing his face into a skeptical expression.

"We're only college students."

"College students!"

"Yes, but you see, we've made a thorough study, and—"

"College students!" the patrolman interrupted Edwin. "Do you see all those people you pushed past on your way to my desk?" He indicated the churning mass of people who crowded the central police station. "Each one is here to try to tell us that they saw a mysterious man practicing black magic that caused all the ships to lose their way in the harbor, or that all the engines and machines have come alive and are in rebellion against us. Every day more fairy tales. Now, the two of you come in here acting as if you possess some vital secret, waving about schoolboy essays you wrote on the subject as if this were one of your classrooms—"

"Two of us?" Edwin asked. He and Bob turned around.

"I can't count, is that it?" the patrolman said.

"Where's the professor, Eddy?" Bob said.

"She was standing behind you," Edwin said.

"Next, please!" the patrolman called to two women with heavily feathered hats addressing each other in hushed tones.

Bob looked on in disgust before turning away. "Professor!" he called. "There she is." She was standing at the threshold to the station house.

"Miss Swallow, they simply won't listen to a word we say," Edwin said as they joined her. "Perhaps you can convince them."

"I heard something," she said to them, staring out into the street. "Like an explosion."

"Well, it could have been anything," Bob said.

Then, an alarm bell sounded at one of the electromagnetic telegraph stands inside the station, a call from another station in the city. The dial spun around and around to indicate a numerical signal of distress. Ellen, Bob, and Edwin all turned to look at one another as they listened. Then another telegraph stand brought word from another station, and another, another, another, another, and another.

* * *

MARCUS CROSSED IN AND OUT of traffic until he reached the walkway to a brass foundry. He shouted as he ran through the door: "Shut off the feeds to your boiler room, get everyone out! Shut off the machines! Shut everything off!"

Those close enough to hear him over the din of the machines looked as though a madman had burst into their midst. Marcus's heart sank. He knew, because he had been them once, what he must have looked like in their eyes—a fancy collegey who had no place there, probably playing some dodge on them. But he pushed forward, still shouting, until a burly workman blocked him, spinning him around by the shoulders.

"Listen, please," he sputtered, as the man picked him up by the collar and thrust him toward the entrance, shoving him out into the road and shouting for Marcus to tell the unionists they wouldn't shut their machines down and lose wages.

Marcus picked himself up and hurried toward a mill several hundred yards away. He shouted at everyone he saw along the way to get clear of the building.

An enormous roar stopped him in his tracks. He watched as in a nightmare while a fragment of a gigantic boiler tore through the wall of the main building of the mill and flew at least a hundred feet into the air. The second and third floors were blown in, and the mangled remnants of the boiler were propelled into the side of a wooden building across the street. Shouts of terror from the workers trapped inside filled the air as the mill building and the wooden structure simultaneously collapsed. Behind him, a wall folded in at the foundry from which he had just departed and its steam whistle howled.

He was too late.

Marcus covered his face with his arm as debris shot everywhere and he was thrown backward by the force. He felt as if the whole city were spinning around him. He wanted to stop and help ease the screams, but he had to keep going. He had to save Frank; if nothing else, he would move heaven and earth to do that.

With his arms and legs pumping madly, the ground seemed to rise up to meet each stride. Yet he felt he was standing completely still, with Boston flowing past him, catastrophe after catastrophe unfolding casually around him as scores of boilers burst. Each time, the ground shook like an earthquake. The giant chimney of the sugar refinery shot into the air, showering its bricks down. Windows of surrounding houses were shattered by the debris. Marcus ducked and swerved as debris and timber dropped from the sky and shot through the air from all sides. Three or four times he was knocked down and pulled himself up again.

At a hat factory, a section of the boiler crashed through the boiler house, taking out most of that wall. Victims were screaming for help from inside the rubble. Another section of the boiler had shot through the chimney, sending the shattered metal parts, along with bricks and hats, flying two hundred feet into the air. A group of street urchins ran in circles, catching the hats or collecting them where they fell. Marcus had to jump over the ten-foot-long warped piece of another boiler that had been thrown more than a hundred yards from the rubber manufactory.

Another object was blown through the air as a second boiler exploded out of the hat factory. As it was propelled over a five-story building, Marcus gasped to see the projectile was a man, who landed across the street, his brains scattered over the wall and roof of a house. The body was burned black by the steam shot from the boiler. Another workman, his head and arms scalded, ran along the street screaming for help. At the nail factory and iron works, employees dove out the windows as the fragments of boilers exploded through the walls of the building. An arsenal of nails pierced the air, just missing Marcus. Fire bells, whistles, screams of agony, and raw shouts for help joined the chaos.

At last, Harrison Avenue. A wall had already been blown through the Hammond Locomotive Works, with workingmen scrambling everywhere for safety. Marcus charged in and up the stairs to the machine shop, calling for Frank.

Near his old workbench, a figure was sprawled flat on the ground, covered in a thick layer of blood from head to toe. Marcus saw again an image of a devil breaking Frank's Ichabod Crane into pieces. He threw himself on the floor next to his fallen friend.

"Marcus?" the prostrate man groaned. "What are you doing here?"

"You're alive!" Amazed, Marcus felt blood dripping onto the back of his neck. He looked up and saw the body of a worker, no older than eighteen, who had been thrown and impaled on top of one of the taller machines. The blood saturating his friend was not Frank's. He seized Frank and dragged him to his feet, wiping blood from his head with his sleeve.

"All right," Frank said wearily, hanging on Marcus's shoulder. "I think I'm all right, Marcus! I think—I was thrown against the wall. How did you get in here? What is all this?"

"I'm so sorry I couldn't tell you before."

"You know what's happened here?"

"Yes, but I can't explain right now. It looks like your leg twisted around pretty badly. Can you stand on your own?"

"I think so." He cried in pain as Marcus pulled him up.

On the mezzanine above them, a prone Chauncy Hammond was being lifted by two of the bigger men and the supervisor, who was bleeding from one of his ears. Hammond came to consciousness with a start, struggling against his men. "What happened? My property! I built this! I won't let it be ruined! Scoundrel! Let me go!"

Damaged ceiling rafters started to crumble.

"Well, I guess it's a good thing I am ready to move on from the old machine shop to be a Tech man, isn't it, Marcus?" Frank joked weakly as he surveyed the wreckage and blown-out windows. "There might not be much of it left."

"You must get away from here, Frank. Get onto clear ground. The rest of the boilers could blow to pieces at any moment. Tell as many of the others as you can."

"What about you?"

"I'm going to try to shut them down, then warn more places."

"More . . . ? What in the devil is . . ." Frank looked around at the chaos. "Do it, Marcus. Go now! I'll manage." Putting on his soldierly face, Frank doggedly limped into the shop, holding on to the nearest machines for support, ordering the other workers to run to the exit.

* * *

HE HAD BEEN TOO LATE to stop anything, even with his voice now shredded from shouting. The frigid water had made its way through the system and exploded nearly every working boiler being operated in the city that morning. Now the world shrank for Marcus to the whereabouts and well-being of his friends. He had to find enough strength in his aching muscles to bring Agnes to safety and locate the rest of his friends.

Marcus dodged through shrieking, weeping crowds on his way back. Rain fell in light spurts. He passed Roland Rapler in the streets, directing his men in the assistance of the injured and the rescue of survivors, looking every inch the great commander in his uniform. Their eyes met and they nodded at each other. The air smelled like ashes.

When Marcus reached the Common, she was not where he had left her. His heart raced. He called out for her hoarsely, then ran to the deer park, where the animals were frantically trying to find a way out of their pen, and then on to the Frog Pond.

"Agnes!" he shouted again, pausing to listen for her voice in response, hearing instead only his own rough breathing.

A commotion had begun across from the Common near the State House, and somehow he knew. He moved toward the crowd, dread rising in his throat. As he tried to push his way through, he could just glimpse the legs of a fragile figure in yellow lifted from near a pile of bricks. Not her. Anyone but her.

A dark fog enveloped him. He could not reconcile the crumpled form with Agnes Turner laughing, Agnes Turner splashing with the children, her eyes alive with curiosity and warmth and faith. He heard indistinctly snatches of breathless conversation, bystanders repeating the story of two children, a boy and a girl, their clothes soaked, running toward a building that was swaying dangerously, a young lady chasing after them before a large wood plank came twirling through the air, smashing against her head.

He tried again to get closer but policemen held him back. He shouted and struggled and called out for her, but then she was carried inches from his face.

Into the sea of people he dropped, down to his knees.

XLV

Nil Desperandum

WILL BLAIKIE WINCED as he raised his arm to the knocker. Could they not install a doorbell, with all their bloated grants from the legislature? In the morning's catastrophe, Blaikie had been walking down Washington Street when a mob marinated in panic had trampled him. His wrist nearly snapped under the weight of one man's heel. His anger at the unknown trampler mixed together with his already burning rage at the Tech boys who had assaulted him on the Charles, had humiliated him in front of the Med Fac, and had, if he were to hazard a guess, been the ones to run up a bill at the shop of a tailor who was dunning him for payment for three suits that were too large for him.

Blaikie had been wronged. Blaikie was a man not to wrong.

"Well? What do you want?" the great man himself asked as he opened his office door.

"Professor Agassiz," Blaikie said. "I wish to have a word, if you please."

"Tell me again, if you have told me before, you are . . . ?"

"William Blaikie, sir, Harvard Class of '68. President of the Christian Brethren."

"Oh! Mr. Blaikie, how excellent of you," Agassiz said, beaming. "Come in, come in and sit down." Blaikie was ushered into the scientist's veritable palace of bugs. By now, he was well aware of Agassiz's appointment as consultant to the police, and sure enough, behind the professor was one of the police officers he had seen walking through the college yard with Representative Hale. He had also heard that all the theories Agassiz had produced for the police so far, having to do with changes in the chemical and magnetic composition of the earth below

Massachusetts—or something of the kind—had come to naught since the latest disaster.

"We need more societies like yours at Harvard—not that dreadful Med Fac, which I understand was involved in some secret disturbance just the other night. In the middle of the night, when good Christians sleep!"

"Sir," Blaikie agreed halfheartedly.

"They should abolish such rubbish, and ship out anyone who feels the need to create a life of fantasy instead of the grand world of nature placed before us. You have come to discuss, I presume, my request that your society assist in refuting the monstrous notions of Darwinism. You know, Blaikie—is it Blaikie?—fanciful theories are merely conjectural, and not even the best conjecture. It is by looking at the great complex of the animal world that we shall reach its hidden meaning. I have recently received the skeleton of a racehorse; would you like to examine it for yourself?"

"I have the evidence you need."

"Evidence refuting the Darwinites?" Agassiz asked with a condescending laugh.

"No, Professor Agassiz," Blaikie said. "Regarding what has happened in Boston."

The police officer looked over at the newcomer with sudden interest. Blaikie held up the sack he had brought with him, and then emptied it onto a table, revealing scraps of iron and several well-used compasses, magnets, and compass needles, as well as what appeared to be long lists of chemical compounds.

"These were taken from the rooms of a student from the Institute of Technology."

"Whose rooms?" Sergeant Carlton asked.

Blaikie paused. "They were brought to me anonymously, in my position as the president of our Society of Christian Brethren, Officer." He could have given a name—insufferable Plymouth Richards or that poseur Mansfield, who thought himself enough of a swell to be seen at the opera, the high-handed savage! But he had sworn to himself the night of the Med Fac debacle that he would find a way to bring down the whole

Institute of Technology, not just one or two of their deluded boys. He would fire his best shot, and then relish watching their feathers fly.

"The Institute has aimed to produce controversialists, not observers," Agassiz said, bristling. "I have long feared science will ultimately suffer most in the hands of its devotees."

"You will notice some of these pages are stamped with the seal of the Institute, I believe. I am a scholar, not a scientist, not a policeman. But I believe these might show a connection with the catastrophic events perpetrated in the city, Professor. Those are the facts."

"Facts," said Agassiz, "are stupid things, Mr.—Blake?—stupid things until brought into connection with general laws. Do not snatch a crown before you have fought and won your battle."

"Blaikie."

"You said stamped from the Institute of Technology?" Agassiz began to examine the papers, revealing a sense of awe. "Could it be? Could the nefarious uses of science be mustered with such strength? Sergeant Carlton, you must call for the chief of police at once. Why, the details contained in this are too accurate, too intimate to be known by any but . . . Danner! Bring me my magnifying glass and a pencil. I shall examine these at once. A pencil is one of the best weapons in the arsenal of scientific inquiry."

Blaikie did his best not to smile.

XLVI

Torn

Professor Eliot had a strange sensation the next morning as he entered his private study, which was located on the half story between the third and fourth floors of the Institute. When news of the latest catastrophe spread, and word reached the faculty that the explosions were being attributed to citywide boiler explosions, Darwin Fogg had been instructed to shut down all the machinery in the boiler room and classes were canceled for the next day. The building was empty, but Eliot did not feel alone.

The turmoil the city and the Institute found themselves joined in was paired with opportunity. Folded inside his oblong chemical case, he carried the latest confidential financial papers drawn up by the Harvard Corporation.

Eliot hated that he had to sneak around to do this. But there could be no question, especially *now,* that the Institute needed vision and new foundations to survive. There was so much blind loyalty to Rogers, Eliot sometimes felt himself to be the only man of the dozen faculty members there with his eyes open, with a few scattered and silent sympathizers, such as his fellow chemistry instructor Francis Storer, Eliot's co-author on a manual for chemistry classes that could revolutionize the field, who sadly lacked the will to act. Eliot, unlike some of the others, saw the Institute not merely as an educational manifestation of Rogers. Nor was the Institute about the fifteen members of the Class of 1868, or, for that matter, the thirty-five or so boys (and, misguidedly, one young woman) in the other three classes. It was about all their future students, for generations to come.

"Daughter of Eve!" Eliot cried, jumping out of his chair almost as soon as he lit the lamps and sat down behind the desk. In a dark corner of the study, there stood William Barton Rogers, leaning heavily on his cane and balanced against a chair behind him. His strong features looked softer, his skin pale and dry.

"Why, my dear President, is it really you?" he asked, a little stupidly. "Are you well?"

"I am not," Rogers said, shaking his head sadly and pressing a finger against his bottom lip. Rogers's gestures always seemed methodical, the movements of a man accustomed to being in the public eye. "I asked Mrs. Rogers to bring me here as soon as we arrived back from Philadelphia. The doctors told me I should not go anywhere, certainly not to Boston at this time of turmoil. So, yes, I am here and I am unwell. Do you know, my dear Eliot, that it took me more than forty minutes to be carried out of my brother's house? Not to mention negotiating the latest exodus of carriages and riders leaving Boston in a panic. I have been here for over an hour."

"You mustn't strain yourself on a day like today, after what happened in the city yesterday. And then to be carried all the way up so many flights of stairs!"

"Something had to be done, though," Rogers said, frowning.

"I suppose all the faculty will meet in your office for the occasion," Eliot said as a sort of suggestion.

"No," Rogers said. "Not until you and I speak first in private on the subject of Harvard."

Eliot paused, looked away, but then with a deliberate, steady expression met the president's gaze. "You've spoken to young Mr. Hoyt, I see."

Rogers raised a single silver eyebrow. "Edwin Hoyt? Nothing of the kind. Remember, many of the Institute's loyal financial sympathizers maintain relations with Harvard, as well. For some months before my late collapse, I've heard vague details of the proposal you were developing, though I have not had the distinct pleasure of reading it myself. I must assume in my illness you have only increased your resolve."

"President Rogers, I understand well if you dissent, and disapprove of what I do. Please understand it is for the sake of the Institute that I pursue this union. Imagine, a grand university, not a college that must struggle every day to pay its faculty and beg its students to pay fees on time to receive this kind of education. We needn't be the refuge of these students, shirks and stragglers from the better colleges, any longer, the safe harbor for young men who lack the wit and vigor to be elsewhere, and whose laziness and stupidity poison our classrooms. Think of it this way. With all that is going on out there, with the dark clouds that grew darker even yesterday, we can yet save our college."

"Save it?"

"Certainly you must grasp the dire position we find ourselves in, my dear President. Our college is a dead carcass, and I regret to say you and other members of the faculty have turned a deaf ear to my earnest warnings for too long. Technical education is the most costly kind, what with all the apparatus that is required. I think if you consider it, you will see my side."

"I will frankly say, Professor, that I am convinced that any such a connection with Harvard would be a decided disadvantage to the Institute, which owes its life in great measure to the fact that it has stood entirely unconnected with other institutions, both as to its scheme of education and to its government. No contribution of funds or support would justify consenting to a change. I wonder if you truly wish to bring the Institute to Harvard, or desire more to bring yourself back to Harvard, with the Institute as your leverage."

Rogers adjusted the position of his cane and moved away from the chair as he made the allegation. At least the awkward meeting would end. Eliot took a step in to assist the older man, but stopped short.

"President Rogers!" Behind where Rogers had stood, five cartridges rested on the chair, tied into a bundle. "What is that?"

"Seventy-five percent nitroglycerin, twenty-five percent porous silica," he said, a dry smile lighting up his face. "Better than the mythic Greek fire. Ever since reading the paper Mr. Nobel presented at the last meeting of the British Association, I have wanted to prepare it myself. Even a block of granite can be split with a single cartridge. Remarkable, don't you believe so?"

Eliot crossed his arms over his chest and stared angrily. "President Rogers, I demand to know why you have brought dynamite into my study."

"Because, Charles, I want you to understand, with no doubt in your mind, that I would rather blow this building to shreds than release even a single brick of the Institute of Technology or my brood of adopted sons into the control of the Harvard Corporation. If I am to die, at least I shall die with my harness on."

"This constitutes a physical threat!" Eliot's voice was shrill and shaky. "I shall have you know, President Rogers—" The chemistry professor gasped as Rogers laid a hand carelessly on the chair that held the dynamite.

"Hush up your blubbering, Charles."

"If you continue on your current course, this entire college shall be a blot in the pages of history! Do you really think anything you can do can save it now?"

"Perhaps not. But I have not lost hope that I have had some small part in inspiring the courage of another who might be doing so as we speak."

"What do you mean?"

Rogers waved the topic into the air with his hand. "You are a fine teacher of chemistry and I welcome you here as long as you'd like. But should you wish to teach for Harvard instead, you may leave whenever you wish. I believe you know your way over the river. But know that Harvard is Harvard, Cambridge is Cambridge, Boston is Boston, and the Institute is the Institute, and shall remain so. I'll leave you to your study."

Eliot could only stare, slack-jawed, as Rogers made his way slowly out of the room.

"Wait! You cannot leave *this*," he called out.

"I think you'll find dismantling it fine mental work, Professor."

* * *

AS HE PROCEEDED SLOWLY to the top of the stairs from Eliot's office, President Rogers reflected on the conversation he had had with Runkle earlier that morning. Before coming to the Institute, he had stopped at Runkle's house to ensure he and his family had not been hurt in the latest incident. He found them undisturbed, and Runkle recovering well from his earlier injuries. The doctor said he now believed Runkle would recover fully, but it would no doubt take a few months.

When they had a moment of privacy while Runkle's wife fetched some water, Runkle drew Rogers closer and whispered, "The police are not the only ones investigating what happened in the city. Mansfield—perhaps aided by one or more friends—strive."

That was all he could say before Mrs. Runkle returned, but Rogers understood at once. Marcus Mansfield, as he had hoped, had taken his papers on the day of his last attack of paralysis, when he had called the college senior to his home to ask whether he would be willing to help him investigate what was happening in Boston. Mansfield and his friends, if they succeeded, could prove everything the Institute stood for in making humankind safer, and Rogers was determined to help them as a partner and belated leader.

Rogers reached the stairs and struck his cane three times on the floor, the signal for his wife, Emma, Darwin, and his driver to come with a chair to carry him back downstairs. He was exhausted from being out of the house, but now, with the thrill of confronting Eliot over, he was confident he *was* getting better. During the last few weeks at his brother's house in Philadelphia, as his recovery steadily impressed his doctors and even Emma, he had begun to pick up a pen, swirling the tip in ink, tempted to draw a circle, as he used to do on the blackboards of the Institute. But he did not try. What if his medley of ailments, his faintness, his seizures, left his grip permanently shaky? He could not bear to gaze upon an imperfect circle. He really was, it seemed, sixty-four years of age. Ashamed of his vanity, he would tuck the pen and ink away before the temptation to try could take over. Let him but have patience and give his brain rest for a little longer, and all would go right.

Clack—clack—clack—clack—clack. Too many footsteps on the stairs, too strong a march. Rogers remained impassive as chief of police John Kurtz, several additional police officers, and Louis Agassiz, with his toothy grin, rounded the landing and climbed the last flight to join him.

"Another visit of inspection?" Rogers asked.

"Not this time. The Massachusetts Institute of Technology is now officially under investigation, I'm afraid, sir," Chief Kurtz growled.

"It cannot be. Why?" Rogers replied.

"Because you have finally gone too far in seeking the knowledge you covet, and *someone* here has turned it to deadly use," Agassiz replied, as Kurtz was snapping instructions to his officers to search the offices. Sergeant Carlton stood stock-still for an instant, almost in awe, before he followed. There were soon noises of cabinets being forced open and drawers ransacked.

Rogers knew in that heartbreaking moment there would be no way to assist Marcus and his friends in their endeavor without endangering them. But if there could just be enough time for them, there was hope.

"Agassiz, if this is about unfinished business and prejudices between us, I urge you to change course."

"Nothing of the kind, Professor—President, wasn't it?—Rogers. This is about the truth."

"Where are they going?" Rogers demanded, seeing the police scatter to all ends of the building.

"Worry not about that," Agassiz answered. "The Institute is ours now, President Rogers."

* * *

BY EIGHT O'CLOCK Wednesday morning, the Institute of Technology was under siege. The final edition of the *Telegraph* the night before had revealed the latest facts: Esteemed Harvard professor of zoology and natural history Louis Agassiz, consulting with the Boston Police, had come upon strong evidence that the Institute may have in some manner, directly or indirectly, purposefully or accidentally, been responsible for the recent series of catastrophes in Boston. The Institute deserved further blame, the newspaper opined, "for educating a young woman in the technical arts and employing a man manifestly so ignorant as the Negro Darwin C. Fogg in a position of superintendence, in all likelihood only because his name seemed sympathetic with the personal beliefs of the college government." Even their popular inventions were now targets of criticism; the automatic street lamps had been reported as flickering or being completely dead over the last few days, though some speculated that was the result of sabotage by the rougher elements of the trade unions. The newspapers further reported that the state legislature was now debating withdrawing the college's charter altogether, which would have the effect of permanently shutting it down.

When the students arrived, the building was surrounded by policemen as well as Roland Rapler's labor reformers, who were shouting and singing belligerent songs. They were joined by other workmen, who had been in the factories and mills when the boilers across the city exploded, Sloucher George among them, and weeping survivors and family members of the victims of the disasters. "I told you all, machines will overtake man!" Rapler called out. "Now watch as the creature devours its creator!" An effigy labeled WILLIAM B. ROGERS that had been stuffed with straw and set aflame was brandished like a weapon. As a group of Tech sophomores scurried through the front doors, a window was hit by a hurled boot and glass came down on them from above.

Bob, who had just slipped inside minutes before, helped pull the sophomores in to safety, cursing himself for all the times he'd teased sophs or freshes or stuffed one upside-down into a storage closet; they were all one now. Two masked men, one carrying a miniature of the Institute building under his arm, then brushed past him and ran out the doors before Bob could try to stop them. Bob climbed to the Architecture Department and found the Boston Junior display smashed and smoldering, with one of the architecture freshes on the floor in the corner of the room weeping, babbling that their city had been burned. Darwin Fogg was extinguishing the flames on the model.

"Has he been hurt very badly?" Bob asked after failing to shake the freshman back to his senses.

"Not physically. He got pushed when he tried to stop them," said Darwin, shaking his head. "These boys worked almost two years on building this, you know."

Bob worried it would look like he was also crying, since the smoldering plaster was making his eyes water—and the very worry and the pang of sadness it brought him made him feel as though he would indeed burst out in sobs alongside the fresh.

He descended the stairs rapidly, but his reliable energy was utterly taken away. When he reached the dim corridors of the basement, he saw from a distance a cloaked figure painting on the door to Ellen's laboratory. The first line read:

Witch of Boston!

At least this time the invader was caught red-handed. Bob threw himself forward and grabbed the man by the collar, spinning him around. Albert Hall's flabby face was as white as a sheet.

Bob couldn't believe his eyes. "Hall . . . You! What are you doing?"

"Richards!" Albert gasped, having equal trouble finding words. "I—you don't know how it is! You can't!"

"You," Bob repeated with disgust. "Of all people. Albert Hall, the great master of the rules, the overseer of order!"

"I have followed the rules!" Albert insisted. "Every one of them, from the first day I entered the Institute! No, from the day I was born! I had to, Richards, or I would never have been taken by any college at all. I followed the rules to get here, and now my future is still being taken away from me. It's charity scholars like me and Mansfield, whether the blasted fool realizes it or not, who will be hurt most by the Institute going under. If Swallow can be blamed, at least—why, someone must be blamed for all that has happened, so why not her! She never should have been here in the first place, and cannot benefit from an education meant for men!"

"You've been the one doing these tricks on her the last few months," Bob said with astonishment. "A senior, taunting a helpless fresh."

"No, you're wrong. Everyone has been doing it, Richards, at one time or another. All of us. Why do you think they can never find who it is, however hard they try? The college was cursed the moment they permitted her to step inside. She would have never succeeded out there if she had been allowed to go forward, so what does it matter? She has no business here, and you've made it worse by being seen with her."

"Not all of us, Hall," Bob said. "Not all of us."

"You're going to hit me, aren't you?" Albert's hands were trembling and he was starting to cry. Sweat poured down his brow. Humbled, he was coming apart. "I saved your lives the other day!"

Bob took a step closer and Albert gasped for breath. He realized how much Albert hated himself for this, and though this made Bob no less angry he felt a twinge of forgiveness. He placed his hand firmly on his upper arm. "You'll be all right, Hall. We all will. Just clean that up, before she sees it."

"What difference could it make to you, Richards?" he whined as he began scraping off the paint. "What difference does it make to anyone? The whole place is doomed now!"

"It makes a difference, Hall, even if this building crumbles around our ears," Bob said. "She deserves better."

* * *

BOB FOUND THAT THE REST of the Technologists, all except Hammie, had made it through the obstacles scattered in and around the Institute and had gathered at their basement laboratory, though hardly a word of greeting passed among them.

"What was all that commotion down the hall?" Ellen asked.

"Nothing," Bob said with an uneasy shrug as he took off his coat. "Some rowdies destroyed the architecture students' model of Boston upstairs. They doused it with kerosene and lit it on fire. I have it, Eddy: The next scoundrels who come in"—a gleam returned to his eyes—"yes, the very next ones, we'll sprinkle iodide of nitrogen on the floor. When they walk over it—pop, pop pop! They'll think the soles of their boots are on fire! Do you remember, Eddy? What a grand dodge it was sophomore year when we did it during the military drill march, after General Moore dismissed you from the squad."

"I was exempted from duty, not dismissed. Anyway, it's not a time for practical jokes. It won't help."

"It will help me, Eddy!"

"It won't help, Bob!" Edwin seemed angrier than Bob could remember ever seeing him.

"I didn't know you were made of such stern stuff, Eddy Hoyt," Bob sniffed.

"Maybe you don't know the first thing about what I'm made of, Bob! Have you ever thought of that?"

"Well, someone took a pile of notes I kept in my laboratory," Ellen said. "And I had once thought of those small rooms as my sanctuary. I'm going to go back in to look for them."

"Wait!" Bob said hastily, impeding her exit with his body. "When did you last see them?"

"Well, I suppose I have not looked at them for a week or so."

"Perhaps you simply misplaced them. It might still be dangerous out there."

"Mr. Richards, must we go over this again? I have not yet shown my full strength to you or anyone. I am not afraid. Let me through."

"You mustn't."

Ellen inclined her head as she studied him. "Mr. Richards, need I ask if *you* have seen my notes?"

He felt as if he had been punched in the gut. "Professor—"

"It appears you do not wish me to search for them," Ellen said sharply.

"You mustn't imagine . . . Professor, you know I would not—"

"What I know is that you wanted to continue our investigations despite impossible circumstances, and perhaps you believed my notes could help your own private analysis. What I also know is you have shown enough disrespect for me in the past that you might not think twice about pilfering them."

"Very well, go!" He stepped aside and gestured at the door. "See for yourself what is out there in the corridor. . . . See for yourself what messages await you! Enjoy!"

They stared at each other for a moment and her expression softened, her shoulders slumping. She turned and resumed her seat.

"I heard President Rogers was here yesterday," Edwin said with a transparent attempt to change the spirit of the room. "Perhaps he will come back and help us."

"I doubt that," Ellen said. "Not after the papers, and the police, and this mob descended on us. The crowd out there is increasing faster than rabbits. Our trying to contact him about all that has happened would only put him under more scrutiny."

"I walked by Temple Place; it was surrounded by police. There's nothing Rogers can do here anyway, Eddy," Bob said. "Nothing anyone can." He added softly, "Mansfield."

Bob looked over at Marcus, who was sitting by himself in the corner. Since Monday night, after he told them of his devastating odyssey across the city, he had been mostly silent, sitting withdrawn and broken in a corner of the laboratory. Now he lifted his head slightly, but then returned it to its place buried in his hands.

"I am afraid," Edwin admitted. "Very afraid. What if the experimenter strikes again today, or tomorrow? Maybe if we try to explain one more time to the police what the city is facing—"

"It won't help anything," said Bob. "The police didn't listen to anything we have to say. They wouldn't on Monday, they wouldn't now. Not now, with the Institute directly under a cloud of suspicion! Just our being from Tech would discredit what we say."

"Stop."

The others all looked to Marcus and waited.

"Stop what, Marcus?" Edwin asked gingerly.

"We started our experiments to find out the source of these assaults. To show that science could *help* the city. But what this lunatic is doing isn't about science. No. What happened Monday shows it."

"Shows what?" Edwin asked.

"This is about pure destruction, about tearing Boston into pieces." Marcus stood and looked at each of his three friends. "The die is already cast. So let us come to a stop. Stop presuming that our good intentions, our knowledge, will ever make a difference."

"There must be something else to try!"

"What, Bob? People have died despite all our efforts. Look what is happening around us to this Institute. By attempting to counter such savagery with our theories and experiments, we have only made things worse on all counts. If she had not been with me there in the first place—"

"You don't know where Miss Turner might have been, Mr. Mansfield," Ellen said.

"You mustn't blame yourself, Mansfield," Bob agreed.

Marcus dropped it, then went on. "I said I could do this, could stop it, I vowed to succeed, and I failed. I was wrong. Flat wrong! I've racked my brains hour in and hour out. We tried to investigate on our own, we tried going to the police. But the jaws of hell still yawned. Well, I raise the white flag. Frank Brewer saved my life at Smith Prison by agreeing to enslave himself to a Southern factory, and he nearly lost his life Monday because we couldn't find the right method to stop this. And

Aggie . . . well, shouldn't I blame myself? Can't we all? You should have talked to us first, Bob, before you did it."

"What do you mean?" Bob asked, offended before he knew why he should be.

"Blasting through the door of the experimenter's laboratory. Maybe that provoked the villain to unleash the next attack earlier than he intended to."

"That's a damned cat's cradle, and you know it! I did what I had to, and we found the laboratory because of it! Don't turn the tables on me, Mansfield. You took long enough to tell us about that Cheshire fellow. What if he had talked to the press about us?"

"He didn't."

"He damned well might have before he was barbecued! What were you planning to do to stop him that you didn't want us to know about?"

"I didn't know how closely we were being watched. . . . Do you imply that *I* was the one to blow the man up?" Marcus laughed.

"How do I know you didn't, Mansfield?" Bob asked, his anger transforming all his feelings about his friends, himself, and the whole situation they were mired in. "You were always so desperate to keep hold of your place as a collegey—you might do anything to feed your ambitions!"

"Well," Marcus said. "We all made our beds, and we are lying in them."

Marcus exited without another word. Bob turned for support to Edwin and Ellen, who looked back equivocally.

"Mr. Richards, it is no use fighting among ourselves," Ellen offered.

"Why not tell that to him? I'm utterly exhausted by his dark ghouls and goblins. I have my own to contend with. Well, thank you for supporting me, both of you. I don't have the need for two more false friends."

"Bob!" Edwin cried. "Don't behave like a child!"

"Do you hear that?" Bob asked. "Quickly!"

There were sounds of a new commotion coming from the first floor. Bob rushed out and up the stairs. When he reached the vestibule, his head still steaming, he burst out of the stairwell ready to take no prisoners. But he stopped dead when he saw a group of Tech students gathered in the vestibule. In the middle was Will Blaikie, his wrist wrapped in a bandage.

"Old Plymouth!" he bellowed, smiling at Bob's entrance. "I mean, Mr. Richards," he intoned with exaggerated deference. "Join us, will you? I was just about to inform your peers of some very good tidings from Harvard during this trying time."

Bob glared at him and, trying to stop himself from yelling, barely pushed his words out through his tightly clenched jaw. "What are you doing here, Blaikie?"

Blaikie smiled at the onlookers. "I'd think that I would be welcomed heartily."

"Think again. You're decidedly *not* welcome at Tech. Ever," said Bob.

"I'm rather certain that's not true at the moment, old salt. You see, I've come to tell all of you about a special arrangement. We at Harvard are absolutely crestfallen about what is now plaguing our infant neighbor, your institute, in light of these terrible catastrophes and the *apparent* connections to this place. To this end, at the suggestion of some well-regarded students—I include myself in that, if I may be bold enough—the Harvard faculty has this morning voted to extend an offer, and they have sent me, as First Scholar of the Harvard Class of 1868, to tell you about it." The emissary swept his gaze around the group, letting the suspense build. "If any of you good gentlemen"—he paused when he saw Ellen had by now appeared from downstairs and joined the group—"if any of you fine *gentlemen* who are currently enrolled at Technology in good standing wish to come to Cambridge and switch over to Harvard College, and study under the celebrated Professor Agassiz, the faculty is prepared to do its best to accommodate you in the spirit of fellowship due in these unusual circumstances."

A general murmur ran through the entrance hall.

Blaikie continued even more brashly. "Those of you who are seniors would study for an extra term, freshes would start that year again in the fall, and the rest would be one year behind. If there are any who should wish to discuss possibilities with a representative of our college, you may drive back with me in a comfortable private coach to Cambridge. We shall be a merry caravan, over the river, across the bridge to your futures."

"We'd rather lay our heads on a railroad track and let the train cars run over them!" cried Bob, no longer holding back the power of his voice.

Bryant Tilden stepped forward. "Say, I'll look into it. Why not?" he added lightly to nobody in particular. "Conny, come on—think what your kin back in old Kentucky would say to know you're a Harvard man. What do you say? Hall, you're not going to let all your dreams die for a lost cause? Come on."

"You have some nerve, Tilden," said Conny.

"No, Tilden!" Albert declared. "This is where I belong. You, too!"

"Back to the factory with you, Albert. I'm certain I won't be alone in this for long."

"You traitor!" Bob shouted. "You're killing it! You're killing Tech—we're all it has left!"

"What will *we* have left—tell me that!" Tilden said. "Nobody here ever took me seriously. Nobody thought I was smart enough. Well, blast you all! I take myself seriously. This place is a tomb."

"It is only a tomb for the old system of colleges that *he* represents!" Bob retorted, pointing at Blaikie, who chuckled at the notion.

"It's my future and I wish it to be assured," Tilden replied. "Damn you and your high horse to hell, Richards."

"Scrub! Dirty snake in the grass!" Bob threw himself at Tilden.

"No, Bob!" Hammie said, pulling him off.

"Brace up now, Richards—it won't help Tech!" cried Conny, taking hold of his other arm.

As he was split up from Tilden, Bob was thrown backward in the general fracas. As he struggled to push his classmates off him, he could see Blaikie speaking quietly to Edwin. He would not watch his friend fight his fight for him.

"Stay away from him," Bob cried as he pushed himself to his feet.

"You mean Mr. Hoyt?" Blaikie asked innocently. "Why should I do that, when the prodigal son returns?"

"What are you talking about?"

"I mean Hoyt here—coming back to Harvard," Blaikie announced.

Edwin was looking at his feet. He cleared his throat twice before glancing sideways at Bob and saying, with another pained glance downward, "I am going with him, Bob. I'm . . . I'm sorry."

"He can't do that. He took an oath to Tech!" Hammie complained.

"Eddy . . . no . . ." Bob didn't know what to say. If Edwin had given up on Tech after all they had been through, then what chance did Tech have? A few underclassmen began inching forward toward Blaikie and Edwin. "Eddy, you're a Top Scholar. Don't you see? They'll start following you."

"I'm . . . sorry . . . really . . ."

"Hoyt has more ambition than you gave him credit for," Blaikie said, putting a hand on Edwin's shoulder. "You think everyone just wants to follow your lead, but people like Hoyt think for themselves."

"Bob, please, you have to understand . . ." Edwin said, but then was pulled away by a cheerful Tilden with a congratulatory handshake.

"I told you I'd win," Blaikie said softly as he leaned in to Bob's ear. "Admit it. It takes the usual fellow four years to finish college. This time, your whole college has finished itself in four years."

"I'd rather my limbs be torn from my body then see Eddy go with you," Bob said, writhing against the continued restraint of his classmates. "Let go, you blockheads—do you hear? You'll eat your words, Blaikie!" He finally managed to pull himself free.

"We could even see what we could do for you, my good fellow," Blaikie said pleasantly to Marcus, who was standing on his own, away from the group, watching. "You won't be blackballed, old grudges aside."

Bob waited. Marcus would not allow this to go on. Marcus took a step forward, staring at Blaikie, who flinched, with Tilden cowering at his side. But then he brushed past them, past Bob and Edwin and the whole group, and strode out the front entrance.

Bob followed out and onto the steps. "Where are you going? Mansfield, wait! You cannot leave all of us behind like this!"

"Why not, Bob?" He did not slow down.

"Because you made a promise! What about Miss Swallow? What about me, what about the Institute and the Technologists? And Rogers?"

Marcus shook his head. "College was never a place that I was meant to be. A machine man; a man without a father. I was a fool to believe otherwise, and you were a fool to believe in me. Why not go dun Edwin instead? He's the one switching to Harvard."

"Eddy's frightened. He fears what his father will say."

"There shall be no one disappointed in me—is that what you mean?

There is no one who cares whether I am a machine hand or a college man."

"You promised to see this through!" Bob grabbed his arm and tried to pull him back up the steps.

"Do not press me further, Richards!" Marcus said, a flash of anger altering his voice.

"Or what? You'll strike me instead of striking that arrogant swell in there like you should?"

"There's nothing left to stop me. No rules, no restrictions on how to be a college gentleman."

His face flushed, Bob shoved him hard. Marcus steadied himself by pushing back, sending Bob tumbling down, sprawled out on the steps, and hitting his knee on the granite edge. A spot of blood slowly enlarged on his pant leg.

"Mansfield . . ." Bob said in quiet disbelief, not seriously injured, but wounded deeply. "Wait! Where are you going? Finish this!"

"It is finished."

XLVII

Prove Thyself a Mother to Me

P RAYING TO HOLY MARY, the young woman waited patiently while the bread was soaking up the milk. Carrying the soft bread to the bed-side, she gently opened the lips of the patient and carefully placed it inside her mouth, moving her jaw up and down until the bread was chewed and swallowed. With her other hand, she wiped the girl's fore-head with a clean white cloth.

"Holy Mary, my advocate and patroness, pray for her," whispered the caretaker, face uplifted, kneeling by the bed. For the next five minutes, she sprinkled holy water on the girl's face and body.

"Madame Louise." It was the Sister Superior, Alphonse Marie, enter-ing the infirmary from the adjoining study.

The other nun bowed her head to her superior.

"Changes?" the older woman asked in French. Many of the nuns here, even after years in America, had learned only a few basic words in English, and spoke exclusively in French.

Sister Louise shook her head. "No."

"*He* is outside," said the Sister Superior.

"Still?"

"I am afraid so."

"He has been there for three hours! Perhaps—"

"No," the Sister Superior interrupted before the younger woman could finish her thought. "Madame Louise, you know our rules must be followed without exception at all times. For all we know, that . . . that rowdy, that ruffian from the Institute is partially responsible for what happened to this poor chambermaid. If he does not leave at once, I shall send for police to arrest him."

"Yes, Sister Superior." Louise knew that was not likely. The Sisters of Notre Dame could expect little assistance from most members of the Boston Police.

"I must return to my class," said the Sister Superior. "The girls are scared out of their wits. Will you stay?"

"I'd like to pray for her a while longer."

The Sister Superior nodded her permission. "Pray for all of Boston, Madame Louise."

* * *

HE HAD JUST COME FROM FRANK'S LODGING HOUSE. To his surprise, he had learned from the garrulous landlady that rather than recovering in bed, Frank had been ordered by Hammond to return to the works to help repair the damaged buildings.

"What?" Marcus replied. "I cannot believe it."

"Yes, I pray I never again have a factory hand as a boarder," she said.

"What do you mean?" asked Marcus.

"They are too prone to injury around those diabolical machines, and then who shall pay me what I am owed for his room if one dies? And if they are not lamed or crippled, sooner or later they'll squander their wages in taverns."

"Not all men who work in factories are the same."

"A factory hand is a factory hand is a factory hand, young man—and never shall be gentlemanly! In my house, I look for true gentlemen—lawyers' clerks, for instance. They speak so nicely at the table, too. I will put an advertisement for more lawyers' clerks."

He excused himself, leaving a card for Frank, not having the energy to argue. He walked by Temple Place but found Bob had been right—there were police in front, in back, in the windows of Rogers's home. There would be no use trying to speak with Rogers, so he left.

Now he was pacing along the gate to the convent and the Notre Dame Academy, a few lots away from the Institute. There was an expression of pure determination hardened on his face, though his luck here so far was no better than at Frank's boardinghouse or Temple Place.

"They will never allow you inside."

Marcus turned and saw Lilly Maguire approaching.

"It is a strict rule. No man over the age of ten may enter the convent," the kitchen girl added, stopping a few feet away and still not looking in his face. "Except the police and the authorities, of course."

"If I stand out here long enough, they will let me in."

"Heigh-ho!" Lilly said mockingly. "These are French Catholic sisters. They are as single-minded as the hot-water pipes, Mr. Mansfield, and maybe, if I am not too bold, as single-minded as you. What I mean is, I shouldn't hold my breath if I were you."

"You have been to see her, though? Tell me how she is, Miss Maguire."

Lilly clutched her bright coral rosary beads. "Poor Aggie has been thrown into a 'coma.' "

"A coma?" Marcus's heart ached at how it sounded even before he understood it.

"Yes. The doctors say it is a name for a state of stupor caused by pressure on the brain, or some such thing. What it all means is simple. Poor Aggie is asleep and does not wake up. They said there are cases where a person remains sleeping for years before . . . well, sometimes, they awaken, which can happen anytime, even years later, and are their old selves again. And sometimes they do not, or are changed from what they were forever. Aggie's father arranged with the invalid ward of the Channing Home to take her, but President Rogers spoke to Sister Superior, who agreed she be kept here, in their infirmary, instead. Madame Louise attends to her and tries to soothe her little head, and calls her God's sleeping wonder."

"I only want to see her. Even for a minute." Marcus nearly fell to the ground, propping himself up on the spires of the gate. "She would have been safe, if we had solved it all with enough time."

"What?"

Marcus ignored her. "Which room is she in?"

"Are you as mad as you seem? I've told you they will never admit you. Will you scale the wall, Romeo?"

"Is it one of these windows?"

Lilly shook her head. "Mr. Mansfield, there is no way—"

"Will you see her again? Tell her I came, at least. Please." He was nearly begging her.

"Mr. Mansfield, she is in a state of insensibility," Lilly insisted. "Please."

The maid considered this. After she peered around for nuns, she held her chin up and looked at him squarely. "You know, it is said there is much to recommend even a Protestant marrying a Catholic girl trained in the religious community, that they are women who are most gentle and refined. I mean to say that for my cousin, for Aggie would be too proper to say so for herself."

"I may test your theory, Miss Maguire."

Lilly left him there alone. He finally abandoned his place at the gate an hour later. Sister Louise, standing behind the curtain at the window, watched him as he departed through the gardens, his shoulders hunched in defeat.

* * *

AT THE INSTITUTE, classes had been suspended temporarily, some said permanently this time. There were rumors that the building had already been sold to an insurance company, that the charter had been stripped by the commonwealth, that John Runkle in a fit of madness had blown himself to bits in his laboratory, that President Rogers had died in his library in Temple Place of an acute attack of despondency, and, alternately, that the old man had been dragged out of his home by the police, with his wrists in irons.

Standing in front of the building, Marcus was holding a dagger, checking the the blade against the toughest part of his palm. Sharp enough, yet he waited another second before lifting it, which caused a drop of blood to run down his palm. Satisfied, he marched across the grounds. After spending half the night walking the city end to end, thinking of all that had happened, Marcus had retrieved his belongings and his carpetbags from Bob's rooms that morning. As he carried them through the streets, a carriage belonging to the Campbell family drew near, the pretty face of Lydia Campbell herself peering out. As their eyes met, the horses picked up speed, the sash of the window was closed, and mud and dirt kicked up. His heart sank, not for the strained smile of Miss Campbell, which he never wanted to see again, but for Agnes, who was all she was not.

Dagger at the ready, Marcus stopped at a young tree, grabbed the lowest branch strong enough to hold him, pulled himself up, and cut down the charred straw figure of William Rogers. With the Institute emptied, and a fair number of the building's windows broken over the last few days, the mobs were apparently content enough with the damage they had done to go on their way, at least for now.

"You're still here?" Hammie approached forlornly, his hands digging in his pockets, as Marcus stood staring at the once-gleaming building. "I'm guilty of the same crime, obviously. What's your excuse?"

"I suppose I'm not certain where to go," Marcus said.

"I thought you were chumming with Richards at his boarding-house?"

"No. Not anymore."

"I see. Mansfield, you can chum with me for a while, if you'd like."

He didn't reply.

"I am just on the wing for our cottage in Nahant, actually," Hammie went on. "There is plenty of space and it's quiet, if you wish to come. Perhaps it will be a relief to loaf a little away from the city."

"I can imagine that." Just weeks earlier, he really wouldn't have considered it a relief to strand himself with Hammie. But then again, everything had changed.

"There's sailing, and the cook is handy preparing clam suppers. The sea serpent even comes to the beach to eat the fish in our bay every few years," Hammie said with a grin. "What do you say?"

"I might be needed here." Marcus was staring in the direction of Notre Dame.

"Well, Nahant is only half an hour from Boston, maybe a little more."

"I do not wish to be a pest." But he knew a quiet watering place was by far a better option than going back to Newburyport to face the scrutiny of his mother and stepfather, who would have been reading the newspaper reports that confirmed all the general suspicions they had gathered about the Institute over the last four years—that its purpose was unnatural, artificial, and risky and, worst of all, a waste of time for a young man who could be earning a steady wage breaking his back.

"You think me very unsocial," Hammie said.

Marcus considered the strange comment, but could muster only a shrug.

"Father always says I ought to have more guests of my own. Besides, the Technologists Society must stay together, somehow, don't you think?"

The truth was that Hammie's eccentric detachment was far preferable at the moment to Bob's rootless optimism, which no longer had anything to latch on to; Edwin's profound despondency, which had carried him back to Harvard; or Ellen's doomed brilliance. All of it only reminded him of his own powerless rage for all that had gone wrong, for Agnes.

"The Technologists, Hammie, are no more." He heaved the straw-stuffed mock-up of Rogers up into the air, far away from their onetime sanctuary.

XLVIII

Nahant

"THE WATER WARMEST FOR SWIMMING is that way," Hammie said, pointing with his fishing rod. "You do like swimming?"

Marcus said he did. Hammie smiled broadly, obviously relieved. "Sometimes, Mansfield, the water in Nahant during the summer season can be practically boiling. The waves come in violently on the coasts. Visitors have even been swept under! No need to worry, though, since you're with me," he said earnestly.

Marcus said he was glad for it.

They had taken the thirty-minute train together north from Boston about twelve miles and then hailed a coach at the Lynn terminal to drive to the rocky peninsula. The Hammond family kept a cottage near the fashionable east end of Nahant, and Mr. Hammond was due to come from the city to join them in a few days, depending on his business obligations, which had been multiplied this week after the damage to his buildings from the ghastly boiler explosions.

Hammie and Marcus had gone out almost immediately after arriving for a sail on the smaller of two pleasure yachts berthed near the cottage. Marcus was surprised by just how pleased Hammie seemed by his somber and moody company, but it occurred to him that simply having company here was enough of a novelty to Hammie to count as amusement.

"See there, Mansfield?" His host was pointing to a row of flat rocks jutting out into the water. "When I was a child, I was an awful bore. Do you believe it? Nothing could coax me away from books."

"Not so different today."

Hammie erupted in his gurgling laugh. "My parents would *make* me go outside. So I would. I would sit on those slippery rocks, but I'd smuggle out a book in my clothing in spite of them, usually two, in case I finished the first one. One day, sitting right on that very rock there in the middle, I overheard one of the servants say that I wasn't expected to survive past ten years old, because I was so weak and pale and refused to eat meat, and only read my books and sorted postage stamps and coins. I cleaned each coin in my collection with a stiff toothbrush and a good solution of oxalic acid."

He paused for a reaction. Marcus nodded, which seemed approval enough for the odd companion.

"I never said anything about what I heard. The servant would surely have been summarily shipped away had I done so. I didn't want that to happen. I wanted him to eat his words. I began to sail, to climb, and to work on my grandfather's farm. I ate even the most exotic meat with the greatest of relish. Then do you know what happened?"

"What?"

"Why, I lived, Mansfield," he said, smiling broadly. "When they completed the telegraph cable across the Atlantic, I led a procession of all my cousins in a circle around the farm in commemoration. Do you know what? I was the last one of us to tire of the marching. Last summer, I spent ten days climbing the White Mountains."

Hammie described an incident when he was a boy and went with schoolmates to see a lecture by Professor Fowler, one of two brothers who were popularizing the pseudoscience of phrenology. Calling him up on the stage, the demonstrator ran his fingers through little Hammie's untamed hair and said, "This boy has the engineering head, with which one day he will set the river on fire." Not long after, Hammie chased down a lost dog through half of Nahant, knowing it would yield at least a five-dollar reward from the grateful family. Without telling his father, he purchased a box filled with glass tubes and flasks and started a small laboratory in the attic of their cottage.

"That was my true start in science. What about you, Mansfield?"

"My aunt owned a boardinghouse in Lawrence and arranged for me to be on a tour of one of the mills when I was a boy. I separated from the group and discovered that when I held my fingers near one of the main belts, I could draw a stream three or four inches long of electric fire. When I moved my hand, the electric stream moved, too. The foreman came running and grabbed me away, but I had known that I was in control, not the machine. I never forgot how that felt."

"Didn't you fight in the War of Rebellion?"

The cliff-lined scenery of Nahant had succeeded in keeping Marcus's mind off bleaker topics. He had no intention of talking of war.

Taking the silence as a yes, Hammie nodded his head in pensive camaraderie. "Father would not allow me to consider volunteering. He said I was too young and too frail, and paid your friend Frank as a substitute to go in my place so that I could never be drafted. But whenever there was a train to Boston bringing back wounded men, I would watch them being lifted out, and would not close my eyes, no matter their condition and disfigurement. Whenever my cousin was on furlough I would try on his uniform, and I tell you it fit me as if it were tailored for my body. He let me keep it after the war. Say, is it true, what they say about you?"

"What?"

"That your father abandoned you when you were just a lad. Sad feeling that must be, Mansfield, being alone in the world."

Marcus stared at him.

"Say, I bet you don't know how many gills there are in fifty-five gallons." Before Marcus could respond, Hammie answered himself: one thousand seven hundred and sixty.

Marcus understood more than ever why the other Tech students felt it difficult to do anything with Hammie beyond attend class. On their train ride out of the city, Hammie had counted the rails to himself for nearly an hour. But the quixotic way he had about him did not irk Marcus as much as it did many of the others; even bringing up Marcus's father was done not with malicious intent, but only as more observation of data. It was as challenging to remain angry with Hammie as it was to stay friendly. He was genuine and highly intelligent, at least, and those were qualities that made Marcus tolerant.

Hammie excitedly reeled up three fish, and released each of them back into the water, as well as those Marcus caught. Then, after an hour of vigorous swimming, Hammie climbed up on a large black rock that darkened the sea.

He shook the water from his thick hair. "Go back on the boat for a minute, Mansfield."

"Where are you going?"

"Don't follow. Understand?"

Hammie climbed over a jagged bridge of rocks into the mouth of a cave but Marcus did not feel like returning to the boat. After waiting in the refreshing water for what felt like twenty minutes, he climbed onto the rock for a better view. The tide had risen, and within a few seconds the mouth of the cave was almost entirely flooded, splashing salty water into his mouth. The breeze played in his wet hair and he felt a thousand miles from everything.

"Hammie!" he called. "All right in there?"

His voice echoed back but there was no answer. He moved closer to the cave. He considered swimming into it, but the water was still rising.

"Hammie!"

The surf crashed into the rocks, drowning out his calls. Maybe Hammie knew another way out from the cave. Marcus dove back into the water and, though dragged by the current the opposite way, swam to the anchored boat. He'd try to sail around the back of the cave to look for him.

As he clambered up the ladder hanging over the yacht's rail, he admired the beauty of the vessel, its immaculate appointments. The only sign of wear and tear were a series of scrapes marring the paint along the side. Even the lettering of its name was exceptionally stylish. *Grace.* That suited the small yacht.

After several minutes preparing the yacht, Marcus looked over at the cave, which had been completely flooded by this point, and decided to ring the distress bell aboard. But another sound interrupted him before he could. Out of the cave, a rush of foam and bubbles churned in a straight line. A large whitish hump broke through the surface of the water, which streamed down its strangely ridged skin.

As he stared, the shape swerved and slowed, drifting to a stop alongside the boat. With a metallic sound, a hatch in the hump began to revolve. The iron lid slowly lifted and his classmate craned his neck out.

"Surprised?" Hammie asked, as the whirring of motors and propellers rose up from below him. "I always surprise everyone I meet before it's over and done."

XLIX

My Flaming Sword

"I**T TOOK ME TWO YEARS,** and five or six trial designs," Hammie explained. "I purchased a torpedo boat that was built during wartime but had never functioned, and based my new design on the ones I have read about from Germany and France. Only with great improvements, of course."

"It can stay underwater?" Marcus marveled at the audacious machine bobbing up and down in the water.

"Almost three hours!" Hammie crowed as he lashed the vessel to the yacht. "It is thirty feet long and weighs five tons. Can you believe it?"

"We could have used this recently," he said, as much to himself as to Hammie, who paid no attention.

"Come aboard," Hammie called out, beaming. "You've never seen a boat like this. I had planned on christening it *Brobdingnag,* but instead I call it the *White Whale* after *Moby-Dick.*" When he showed no sign of recognition, Hammie added, "Herman Melville. It was published when we were boys. Most writers in these modern times are just jugglers of words, but not Mr. Melville."

"I think a whale might be frightened seeing this come up to it, Hammie."

"I think you're right! I keep the *White Whale* inside the Spouting Horn—that is the name of that cave—so it is not molested while I perfect it. Everyone around here knows the Horn floods without warning, so nobody swims inside for fear of drowning. Are you surprised? 'Machinery strikes strange dread into the human heart, as some living, panting Behemoth might'—that is something Melville wrote."

"You recite that from memory?"

"I tend to remember whatever I read." Hammie made the observation without any boastfulness about the talent. "Look inside at the controls!"

"I think I'd rather be high up in a balloon instead of trapped below the water in the steel belly of that thing, Hammie."

"Nonsense! Come, I'll reform you in no time."

Marcus cautiously climbed inside the hump of the machine and sat on what felt like a big easy chair. Hammie showed him how to maintain and direct the propulsion of the vessel with various pumps and faucets. "This, over here, this crank, operates the torpedo boat's propeller. It is best to keep the machine moving forward rather than downward. The lower it goes, the longer it takes to rise up. Mansfield?"

Marcus was gazing out a portal window that from outside had looked like the eye of a giant shark.

"She was pretty," Hammie said.

"Who?" Marcus asked.

"I saw her when she was being brought into the infirmary at the Catholic convent. The Irish lass. She was pretty. Awful pretty."

Marcus thought this was his way of saying he was sorry about what had happened to Agnes. However lost Hammie might have seemed in his own introspection, he'd noticed Marcus's grief.

"Thank you, Hammie."

"I did notice at the opera other misses who seemed like they fancied your favor," Hammie said with a paternal interest. "But I know that a heavy heart does not love easily. Where would you like to go next, Mansfield?"

"Can we take this to see the lighthouse you told me about?"

"The lighthouse, then."

As Hammie made a series of adjustments in his controls, Marcus ventured to ask, "You have been in love yourself, have you?"

"At twenty-one years old, certainly I have!" Hammie said indignantly. "She loves, too—but she loves another."

"You mean the girl you fancy already has a beau? I'm sorry for it, Hammie."

"Well, one cannot fairly compete with Bob Richards!"

Marcus marveled at the comment. "What in the deuce do you mean?"

"Don't tell me you don't notice when the two of them are together in the laboratory?"

"You couldn't mean to say Bob and *Ellen Swallow*, could you, Hammie?"

"I mean it and I say it! Plain as a full moon in the sky! She would surrender her heart to him at his slightest desire. She is a rather unique creature, whom most people will never understand. Do you think she sees beyond the rake Richards presents to people? Now, are you ready to launch?"

A sound like howling suddenly came from around the propeller and prevented Marcus from further questioning Hammie's remarkable statement. The machine quickly descended a few inches.

"Not again! A leak! Well, you see, Mansfield, I have not actually been able to quite keep it operating for more than a few minutes before it begins to, well . . ." Then, blushing, he trailed off.

"Sink?"

"Just some trivial adjustments to make now, indeed! Quickly, help me get it back into Spouting Horn," he said more urgently, "or we'll be popped out like Champagne corks in a minute."

After hastily maneuvering the *White Whale* back into its resting place, they continued their explorations by foot.

Over the next days, Hammie introduced Marcus to all the byways and hidden corners of the peninsula. Nahant was quiet. There was no busy village square. There were a few hotels and old brown cottages dotting the coast, with most of their residents preferring seclusion. This was not one of the resorts that relied on a social whirl. Nahant was a dream of unadorned ocean and sky: not exactly beautiful, but fully contained.

It was also subject to violent storms that could be seen coming from far out at sea, and it was an especially sudden one that charged in from the east one afternoon, sending them running over the rocks into the family cottage. They settled in to wait out the weather, which continued for two days. Hammie entertained his companion by demonstrating a steel doormat boot scraper he had invented; they spent hours watching his two pet green snakes, which he'd trained to wrap themselves around his neck; and in a separate structure behind the house, Hammie unveiled an assortment of rifles, including a Whitfield that he boasted was better than a French or Enfield, with heavier bullets and a target sight, and a wide array of topnotch sporting gear. On the third day, the classmates played checkers and cards on the covered terrace, watching the sheets of rain hammer the ocean and growing accustomed to the earthshaking thunder. Hammie concentrated on every move in each game as though his life depended on it, but despite Hammie's appetite for conversation, Marcus felt suddenly overwhelmed by loneliness.

Without quite realizing he was doing it, he reclined on an inviting hammock while waiting for Hammie's next move. When he woke, he was alone on the terrace and inside found only some servants. The rain had stopped. Marcus wandered upstairs into Hammie's bedroom, where he surveyed the enormous collection of scientific books, most of them in foreign languages. He noticed a rope dangling above him and pulled open the entrance to the attic.

Lighting a candle, he climbed up and crawled into the upper chamber, remembering Hammie's stories about starting a secret laboratory there as a child. Tacked on to the wall was the same list Edwin had made of impossible scientific feats, copied in Hammie's handwriting—with the initial "H." by each and every item. At the bottom of the page Hammie had added: "Make them eat their words." Beneath that, resting on a steamer trunk, he noticed stacks of class notes, and, curious, stopped for a closer look.

Here is what struck him first. The notes were beautifully complex—not really class notes as he thought about them. Hammie drew out conclusions far beyond the scope of their experiments. And there was something still more remarkable. All the notes at the top of the pile—he shuffled through more and more, faster and faster, until the formulas seemed to dance and transform—were on an assortment of other topics. Magnetic deviation. The uses of barium. Double fluorides. Chloride of lime. Topics that had been on the tips of their tongues every hour in the last weeks. Topics directly involved in the catastrophes that had shaken Boston and changed Marcus's life.

Then he focused on the steamer trunk itself and dropped the papers he had been examining. He scrambled down from the attic and outside to the shed, fumbling through the rifle rack. As he seized one, a glimmer of metal caught his eye and he moved deeper into the shed to investigate. What he found looked like a monstrous human skeleton, hung by its wrists from the wall, a silk hat perched atop its head.

He circumspectly moved closer. The figure was constructed of iron and other metals. It must have been almost eight feet tall, its legs covered with cranks and levers, its chest and back bursting with gauges and vents, all partially covered by something like a suit, which Marcus had to feel between his fingers to believe.

"He took it," he said to himself.

The monster's hat, on closer inspection, enclosed a steam stack. The face had been molded into lifelike features, complete with a mustache and facsimiles of teeth formed into a wide, innocent smile; in the center of the teeth was a steam whistle. *The steam man!* The humanlike machine with the body of a steam engine that Hammie had described and drawn at one of the college exhibitions, producing so much consternation and disapproval.

Hurrying back into the cottage and up the stairs into Hammie's room, Marcus pulled out his carpetbag, took apart the rifle, and stored the parts inside. He heard the front door below opening and shutting.

"Mansfield, old boy, are you here?" It was Hammie, suddenly affecting a Bob Richards imitation.

He hurried into the attic and piled Hammie's class papers back into some order, dropping himself back down and closing the attic only seconds before Hammie entered the room.

"There you are," Hammie greeted him, his peculiar smile looking at the moment as though he'd just heard a joke too vulgar to repeat. "You must be famished. The cook is just coming in from his quarters to begin supper—fish chowder as usual, I'd wager."

"Thank you, Hammie."

"I was thinking, Mansfield, when I was out—say, Mr. Van Winkle, you sleep like a top, don't you?—I made some adjustments to the *White Whale* and moved it to a more protected place for now, in case the squall starts up again. As I say, I was thinking, Van Winkle, it is a shame about the Technologists Society. A shame about Tech, too. I can't even imagine what I'll do now. Something wrong, Mansfield?"

"Nothing," he said a little too quickly.

"I know," he went on, as he dried his neck and hair with a towel, "that this whole week you have been thinking of that poor girl Miss Turner."

Marcus nodded.

"Someone out there will avenge what has happened," he continued, abstractedly. "Do you remember what he said to us?"

"Who?"

"That man, what was his name? Joseph Cheshire. The man in front of the Institute. 'I am the avenging angel and my tongue is my flaming sword.' It sounds like something out of a Bible sermon. Do you know I attended church every Sunday from the time I was a child, even when I was at my sickliest?"

"Yes, Hammie, that was his name. Joseph Cheshire."

L

Mind

Y THE TIME HE REACHED WHITNEY'S HOTEL, Marcus had formulated
his plan.

"I need to send a telegram," he said.

The telegraph operator prepared a form for him. "But you should
know, young fellow, we have been having some disconnections the last
few days. It might take longer than usual."

"The storms?"

The man blinked indifferently at Marcus's question and returned to
a book he was reading.

"This is important," Marcus said. "If there is any way I could be en-
sured the transmission will be made as soon as possible, I would be
grateful. I will be waiting here at the hotel for an answer. Can you find
me when it comes?"

"Are you a guest here, young man?" The operator squinted at him.

"No, sir." Nor did he have the money for a room.

"You are sending a wire at nine o'clock! Will you wait here all night
for an answer?"

"If I have to."

"But you are not a guest."

"I am a customer of the telegraph office of the hotel, aren't I?" This
seemed indisputable.

It was not yet the busy season of the summer, but the place was already buzzing with families wanting to get far away, physically and mentally, from the events that had plagued Boston. He found a chair in the
public parlor of the hotel and for the remainder of the night alternated
between sitting restlessly and pacing the length of the room, to the con-

sternation of the hotel staff. A kind chambermaid brought him some coffee and a blanket, and he dozed fitfully.

In the morning, he was startled by gentle eyes and a familiar face leaning over him.

"Edwin!"

"Marcus, what in the land brings you here?" Edwin gleefully took hold of his hand.

"I was chumming with Hammie," he said, gesturing vaguely in the direction of the Hammond cottage. "Why are you here?"

"My family likes this hotel when they wish to leave Boston. Did you know the poet Longfellow has a cottage not far from here? Nahant is a small rock, and the people a gossipy sort, but there is always something to do. Since I don't seem to have graduating examinations to study for . . ." He stopped, stricken, and paused to collect himself. "About what happened with Blaikie . . ."

"Don't finish your sentence," said Marcus. "I understand."

"No, you do not, Marcus! While Bob was being restrained from starting a row in the vestibule, Blaikie pulled me aside. He told me that if I didn't agree to come back to Harvard then and there, he had the means to tie you and Bob directly to the catastrophes and have you arrested!"

"He lies."

"But he also has Agassiz's willing ear and we do not," Edwin said. "I saw no choice but to consent."

"You went with him to Harvard?"

"I rode in the carriage with him. For a moment, I confess it, Marcus, I felt a sensation of great relief sweep over me. No more fighting for people to believe in me and my college. I would be a Harvard man again, and all the respect that comes with it. I thought of my father, and how pleased he would be. All this lasted but a minute before I was so sick with disgust in myself and in Blaikie that I couldn't say a word. Then Blaikie started asking about you. Questions about your temperament, your disposition, and so on, as if you had just fallen from the sky. I realized, Marcus, that he feared you. Too much so to ever make good on his threats against you and Bob. I told the driver to let me out, and I walked all the way home. Though Bob first refused to speak to me, I finally waylaid him in the street and he forgave me in grand fashion.

"Mother and Father heard all that has happened at the Institute, and that I rejected a chance to return to Harvard. Naturally, they think I am suffering from some kind of nervous attack," he continued, smiling. "They hoped the waters here would improve my health. Come, we'll continue talking out there."

"Where are you going now, Edwin?"

"To have breakfast on the piazza. Do join us. My family is dull, but the seed cakes are fine."

"Would they mind if you skipped breakfast?"

Edwin's expression turned unaccountably sad. "I suppose they wouldn't mind, in fact. Is it very important, Marcus?"

"I risk being seen if I sit outside. I must speak to you right now."

"Marcus, something new has happened, hasn't it? You must tell me."

"I will. I should also not want your family to become too curious, my friend. Breakfast with them. But eat quickly."

When Edwin rejoined Marcus fifteen minutes later, they continued their conversation in the hotel library with the door closed.

"Brace yourself, Edwin. Hammie is far more ingenious than any of us knew. He has become a sort of technology vampire. He even built a submarine vessel. It does not work, but it's damned impressive nevertheless and he did it on his free time. You know how he always seemed bored at Tech? Well, he was. I think he had a constant need to find additional ways to occupy his mind."

Edwin fidgeted at Marcus's obvious awe of Hammie's intelligence, but couldn't disagree. "When we were sophomores, I chanced to come upon Hammie while attending the opera. There he was, Marcus, attending the performance and at the same time busy with his notes and his schoolwork. Then, another time, when Bob dragged me into one of his preferred parlor houses, there was Hammie again, a young girl in disordered dress on one side, and a scientific book on the other. I knew no matter how industrious I was, how many hours I studied, I could never surpass a fellow doing three-dimensional analytical geometry between acts of *Fra Diavolo* or, well, more involved pastimes. What is it you've discovered, exactly?"

"Remember Joseph Cheshire?"

"Yes."

"It was Hammie who was with me the day he came to the Institute. Besides Runkle, he was the only other one who heard Cheshire's threats against our group."

"But he wouldn't have known what meaning Cheshire's words contained, or who the fellow was."

"I thought not at the time. But last night, when I was at the cottage, Hammie said his name."

"Whose?"

"Cheshire's. Cheshire never told us his name."

"Hammie could have read about him in the newspaper after Chesire died, as you did."

Marcus admitted the point. "Only I don't think that's it, Edwin. And Hammie was in Runkle's private study before I was—and Runkle, or 'Uncle Johnny,' as Hammie calls him, revealed to him that he had also heard Cheshire's words. All of that, the same day as Runkle's drawer exploded, almost taking our heads clean off."

"You don't think Hammie would have . . ." Edwin stopped himself, shook his head. "Why?"

"To protect himself from Cheshire's inquiries. In his attic compartment in the Hammond cottage, I found his notes from Tech—pages and pages with formulas and chemical combinations related to how all three of the disasters were engineered. Edwin: The traveling trunk he had in his attic was identical to the trunk we found holding the pieces of iron with the electromagnetic wires on the seabed! Then, in an outbuilding, I came upon his steam man: You remember—Hammie had the idea to build a machine in the shape of a man to perform heavy labor."

Edwin listened, his mouth agape. "Yes, I do. But what does that have to do with it?"

"Because parts of its covering were made from the machine suits we built for our diving expedition. He was the one who took the suits!"

"No!"

Marcus nodded, continuing. "I've been over it all night. On the side of his yacht, the *Grace,* there are these scrapings, the same kind that would be made by lowering a trunk so filled with heavy cargo—like iron—that it could not be lowered straight down even by a strong grappling hook. Edwin."

"Yes?"

Marcus seemed uncomfortable. "Edwin, I was wrong to turn my back on all of you in our laboratory. On the Technologists. I am sorry to have abandoned you."

"Sometimes you must let go of the reins of your team, before they run away with you."

At that moment, the telegraph operator knocked, and, upon being admitted, handed Marcus a message, bowing to Edwin, the rightful hotel guest.

"What is it, Marcus?" Edwin asked, watching as his friend unfolded the message, then closed his eyes, his expression grim.

"It's him. It is. It's *Hammie,*" he said, the enormity of the words belied by his tone of quiet astonishment. "Hammie is the experimenter."

"What do you mean? What does it say?"

Marcus told Edwin how after first having left a brief note for Hammie that he had to return to Boston, he had sent a wire to Daniel French, the freshman at Tech he had coached. He asked French to look into a question of the ownership of the private laboratory that had collapsed around them.

"But we tried to find that already," Edwin said.

"No. We'd tried—unsuccessfully—to find the name of the *tenant,* thinking what mattered was who occupied that laboratory. I asked Mr. French to inquire at the city records into the ownership of the *building* itself. Hammie would have been able to see exactly which laboratories were vacant and exactly when—because that building as well as several other properties in that district are owned by the Hammond Corporation."

Edwin stared at the message himself as he reflected on everything he had been told. "Why?"

"We can speculate. He felt isolated from other students, bored to the point of madness by his classwork, chastened by his father, and replaced by a factory hand—my own Frank—during a war where he thought he could have proven his worth and heroism. Why would he do it all? To prove he could do more than anyone expected. To prove to all of Boston and the world and especially to his father that knowledge was power, and that he had more of it than anyone imagined—that he held the power to conjure a tempest in a teapot."

"And if you're right, Marcus, then what? What should we do?"

"If he was the one who harmed Agnes, then heaven save Chauncy Hammond, Jr., from me."

Book 5

EXPERIMENTAL PHYSICS

LI

Class Feeling

T HE BUILDING WAS A DECAYING ANCIENT CASTLE this muggy morning, Back Bay a scorched desert island robbed of life, at least in his eyes. Bob leaned back on the granite front steps, where only two weeks earlier, dozens of students had eaten their midday meals, laughing and gossiping, and did his best to conjure the cheerful images that somehow seemed so distant.

"A game of football? Very well, fellows," Bob agreed, juggling a ball that he had found abandoned on the grounds. "Hurrah! Three cheers for Tech." He kicked the ball away hard. In the distance, the muddy tide was washing into its inlet. Not far away, Bob spotted the old organ grinder who liked to play his music outside their windows while his monkey climbed up to collect coins from the students.

"Maurice! Say, Maurice, how about some melodies?" Bob called out. The musician gathered up his monkey and hurried in the other direction. "How is that for loyalty?" Bob pondered to himself. "What do you say, Bacon? Come, Newton. Heathen Archimedes, stop drawing in the sand and put your head together with old Mr. Franklin to solve our little problems." The names invoked were chiseled in raised stone along the granite frieze that ran above the grand Corinthian columns on the face of the building.

He found his own name represented—much smaller—as initials carved into the brick foundation along the outside of the basement when the building was under construction. His freshman year had been a time of trepidation, adjustment, and excitement; the second and third years comfortable and fulfilling, as though he had been here forever and would stay forever. Senior year, from the very start, had had the feeling of something momentous and, perhaps, impossible to fully realize. He practically shouted, "What should we do with all this now?"

"I'd always hoped they'd plant more trees and flowers in front of the building. I suppose nobody would stop us now."

He wheeled around at the sound of the voice. "Professor Swallow!"

Ellen sauntered slowly toward the steps. She wore her usual long black dress and plain black bonnet, which had to be stifling in the sun, though she did not show it.

"Professor, but what are you doing here?"

"The same thing as you."

"Remembering," Bob said, nodding thoughtfully. She sat on the other end of his step, which somehow made things better, as though the old gathering place were again populated by the usual fellows—even though she wasn't really a "fellow." "Do you know the gymnasium on Eliot Street, Professor Swallow? Oh, it is filled with the usual parallel and horizontal bars, clubs, wall weights, you know. Whitney Conant was always there, and of course I'd convinced Mansfield and Eddy to come. Conny, he was experimenting with photographs then, and he took a photo of Mansfield, Eddy, and myself as a human pyramid, with me on my hands on top of their backs, feet in the air! We had to be completely still, Professor, for a full eleven seconds! Can you imagine headstrong old Mansfield that way? That settles it. I'm going to throw myself into exercising again, maybe try fencing again."

After he located the appropriate stick to represent a foil, Bob shouted, "Guard!" and pointed his weapon upward so the tip was level with his chin. Ellen wasted no time in finding her own branch and assumed perfect posture opposite him.

"You, a fencer?"

"I have studied many of the arts usually reserved for men, you know."

"Care to try?" asked Bob agreeably.

"Advance!" she declared, and they went through several movements and parries, laughing and shouting the command words as they did.

"Do you know where he is now?" she asked in the middle of their match.

"He?" Bob thrust his branch forward and she stepped back.

"Mr. Mansfield," she said softly.

He lowered the branch. "Where, indeed. I suppose we grew too warm at each other after everything that happened."

"He did seem out of spirits."

"He left a note at Mrs. Page's and took his things with him. He's gone out of the city, I think. I suppose you must summer and winter with a man before you know him, as they say. It is a hard punishment for me to take. I was drawn to Mansfield the first time I saw him. But for these four years, I have never looked at the old fellow without a pang of shame."

"Why?"

"You will think me cowardly," Bob said with uncharacteristic bashfulness.

"I will not, Robert."

He liked the sound of her saying his name. He owed her something for it, so he sat down and began his story. "Marcus Mansfield was in the Union army, you see. I wasn't. I wasn't chosen in the draft, mind you, but I also did not volunteer. Only one of my four brothers served, in fact. Baby brother Harry was too young. The oldest and next oldest paid for substitutes to go in their places, and I waited. And waited. How I wanted to fight more than anything!"

"Why didn't you?"

"I tell you I was a chicken-heart. Every time I imagined being in uniform, I thought, What if a man in my regiment was in danger and I failed him? I was too much of a coward to take that risk. I wasn't ready."

"Not volunteering does not make you cowardly."

"No? Then what?"

"Patient."

He laughed. "I patiently waited until Lee's surrender. Mansfield, meanwhile, was rotting in a prison camp. I tell you, there is stuff in that quiet fellow. The other prisoners appointed him their 'police chief,' giving him charge of protecting the weaker ones and punishing the wicked ones. I'd have given worlds to have been there by his side. One can only imagine—well, perhaps I always felt I owed him something for that. Though he never talked about it to me but once, when he had too much drink. Do you know, Saturday is decreed the first Decoration Day? They will have it every year from now on, I hear, on the thirtieth of May, to honor the soldiers. There will be parades, music festivals, plays, jubilees. Wreaths will be placed at cemeteries on the soldiers' graves. I had asked Mansfield to go with me."

"I'm sorry he has left. He is not a man for Boston, perhaps, but I found he is strictly of the New England character."

"Do you think so?"

"Yes. I never fully realized how much a New England birth in itself was worth, but I am happy that that was my lot. I have felt it so keenly these last few days. Dear old New England, with all her sternness and uncompromising opinions: the home of all that is good and noble. That is Mr. Mansfield, too."

He sank his chin into his hands. "It's a wonder anyone still remains in Boston. What shall I do without him?"

"I would like to go."

"To the Decoration Day festival?"

"Yes."

"You would?" he asked, brightening. "Would you allow me to escort you?"

"On the condition that you don't call me Professor or Ellencyclopedia anymore."

"No, no, it's 'Ellepedia.' Anyway, 'Miss Swallow' sounds so formal and frightening."

"I'd hoped to be treated equally at Tech," she said wistfully. "If I am to call you 'Robert,' you must call me 'Nellie.' If there is nobody else around, of course. Otherwise, 'Miss Swallow' and 'Mr. Richards' will have to do."

"Sold! Nellie, let us have our day at the festival, then. We both deserve a grand time, I'd say. We all do."

"Sold."

After Ellen continued on her way, Bob did not want to go back to his quiet room bereft of the company of Marcus. He ended up at a beer shop in the neighborhood known as Little Dublin, and stumbled home in the middle of the night, quite "plucked," as the college boys said, and beyond noticing Marcus's absence, or thinking about the faces of Boston's dying and injured during the weeks of catastrophe, or about the fact there'd be no graduation next month for the Class of 1868. No graduation ever at their Institute. How tired he was in his bones, yet he could not find a way to sleep. "I'll do it, Mansfield," he heard himself say, half conscious of what he meant. "I promise I will."

Nor had Ellen really wanted to return to her room at Mrs. Blodgett's after she continued on her way. She went to the public library instead, and drafted letters to private chemists, asking to be considered for any open positions. She then took the letters and deposited them around the city. She did not know if mentioning the Institute helped her or if her affiliation with it would be worn as her own scientific scarlet letter, but did it matter? She knew she would not be asked in for any of the positions when they saw the name of a woman at the bottom of the paper. She had given so much thought to her plan of life at the Institute, the result of cool, deliberate judgment, and she had been very satisfied with the fruits. How noble Robert Richards looked, keeping vigil on the steps of the Institute building, the guardian of lost causes.

By the time she began to make her way to her boardinghouse, darkness had fallen, the streets in the frightened city uncharacteristically deserted. As she was hurrying home, she thought she heard a lone footfall, and sensed a menace. She removed the pearl-handled revolver from the pocket of her coat and spun around, her hand trembling, remembering incongruously how she hadn't told Bob of her revolver when he'd asked on the roof of her building, not wishing him to think her fearful of living in Boston. Walking backward, she cocked the revolver and shouted, "I will fire, sir, I will fire if I must!" But nobody was there.

At last she reached home, her lips quivering, and threw herself, sobbing, onto her bed. She was thankful her mother was not present to see her behaving like a silly schoolgirl, instead of a woman prepared to face the trials of life unwavering. Baby curled up behind Ellen's head and wrapped his paws around her hair like a crown.

* * *

THE SMALL ROW OF ELM TREES lent a somewhat less severe appearance to the grounds, but only somewhat. This was not really a cemetery, nothing like the fashioned gardens of Mount Auburn over the river in Cambridge; this was a burying yard, cold-blooded and forgetful. The gates of granite and iron would make any visitor doubt whether his visit was any more welcomed by the dead than by their keepers, especially at such a late hour.

The reluctant caller held his lantern out and swept it over the unevenly shaped gravestones, which were mostly of flimsy sandstone or cracked marble. At least the ancient, haunting character of the place would keep away vagabonds—well, all but the one he sought, he hoped. He lost his step on the overgrown path and stumbled, almost falling flat onto a grave. Damn those beers, and blast the lack of sleep.

The noise he produced sent a shape scurrying past him through the dark. Regaining his balance, Bob shined the smoky light on the moss-covered tomb where the scurrying had come to a stop.

"Hold on there! Don't be afraid!" Bob whispered.

The shape darted again, this time on all fours, behind a line of jagged graves that led back to the chapel. He ran after it, but the shape was small and quicker.

"I said wait! I'm a friend, damn it! Theophilus!"

The running stopped again at another tomb. A fearful young voice emerged. "Who are you? Did he send you for me?"

"No," said Bob. "No one sent me."

"How'd you find me, then?"

Bob couldn't tell exactly which tomb was speaking to him. He kept his distance so he would not scare the boy into running again. "I've been looking for you all night. I'm not the only one: Some of the shops nearby say you've been stealing bits of meat and fruit the last few days."

"Are you here to arrest me for it?" More rustling, preparations for another run.

"Goodness, no! But if you don't want to be noticed, don't steal, for heaven's sake. One of the merchants had been asking around for you, and heard you had been seen sneaking around one of the burial yards. I climbed into the Copp's Hill and Granary burial yards without finding any sign of you, so I thought I must be getting close here. I brought you something to eat."

"No thanks!" The sound of sniffing. "You have meat?"

"Boiled pork, well browned, smothered in sauce. That's right."

Theo leaned his head out from behind the dilapidated charnel house, a full ten feet from where Bob had been standing. Bob marveled at how deftly the boy had eluded him.

"How long have you been sleeping here?"

"Dunno. Weeks."

"Weeks! For goodness sake," said Bob. "Well, you're going home to-night."

"Not with the likes of you, I ain't! Not if he sent you to bring me!"

"I already told you . . ." Bob began, growing impatient.

"Say, I remember you!"

"Good boy. That's right—we had a fine conversation together on State Street."

"You called me a scamp."

"I hardly would think you would remember that, of all things."

"The other fellow, with the mustache. He was awful kind. Where is he?"

Bob cringed at the question and just shook his head. "You're safe now, Theophilus. Do you have somewhere to go?"

"'Pose not," the boy mumbled, taking a tentative step closer.

In the halo of his lantern, Bob looked the refugee over. His skin was pale and dirty, his greasy head bare, and he was only partially covered by a ragged suit of clothes lined in filth. His hands were lodged deep inside his pockets. "Goodness! Don't you have parents to care for you?"

"Aye, and four brothers and three sisters, and if I don't come with any earnings from employment, my father will show me what is what with a rod. I was making believe this was my castle, and each of these stones, one of my knights defending me."

"What are you hiding in your pockets? Go on. Let me see your hands."

"No chance!"

"Why not? You can't eat this if your hands are hidden away. Come on, both hands now."

With a huff, he slowly withdrew his hands. The hand that had been injured in the catastrophe trembled.

"Just don't try to get my hands, you hear?"

"Tell me, what happened to make you run off? Why make camp here, of all places, man?"

"He told me I had to! That if I didn't, he'd . . ." Theo made a cutting motion with his hand.

"You mean the stockbroker, Joseph Cheshire?"

"Villain!" he replied with emotion. "He chased me into an alleyway and threatened to cut my fingers off my good hand! He would have, too, I vow it! But I must have fainted, and when I woke I was in the back of his carriage wrapped in a blanket. He said only cowardly boys fainted, and he needn't waste his time with a coward, and told me to stay here in this burying yard until he said different, so I could look at the tombs and remember what would happen if I blabbed ever again! He said he'd bury me right here if I didn't keep mum or tried to take wing."

"This was the first burial yard established in all of Boston," said Bob. "No one has been buried here for a long time. Imagine, Theophilus, my little friend, that one of the first things the settlers in Boston realized they needed to build was a burial yard. Well, that scoundrel won't be bothering you ever again."

"Really?" he asked timidly.

"That's a promise."

"It's Thee-a-fil-is, by the by, not Theo-folis!"

Bob lowered himself down, perching on the edge of an ancient grave marker carved with a large skull. "You know, about our last conversation," he said sullenly. "I know I owe you an apology. You had only been trying to help us and you were in great pain at the time, and I was thinking about myself, and not granting you the respect you earned. But blast it all, Mansfield, even at such an evil hour, there must be more to do!"

The boy stared at him with big, glassy eyes, his hands now resting on his hips.

"Say, Theo," Bob said, fighting off the fresh wave of exhaustion and regret, "how fares the arm and hand? The injuries, I mean."

Theo shrugged. "I guess it'll never be better enough to be the man I could have been."

"I'd wager my best scarf it will indeed. In fact . . . Watch out, man!"

He tossed the paper bag into the air. Theo took a few steps back and caught it to his chest, sticking half his face into the bag for his first bite of meat.

"There!" Bob cried out, laughing.

"Why, you're cracked in the head, too!" Theo said, surplus pork flying out of his mouth as he spoke. "What's the great joke, mister?"

"You caught that with your right hand, Theo!"

"Say!" the boy marveled when he realized it, his face coloring with pride. "Say, just a week ago, I couldn't have done that!"

"Come, you'll eat on the way. I owe you this, too." He wrapped his scarf, which was thick and black with gold stripes, around Theo's neck.

"Where will I go?"

"You'll stay in my rooms tonight, and in the morning I'll convince some uncle or cousin he needs a smart apprentice like you in his office."

"You think you can, mister?" he asked, in awe of the idea.

"I am as sure as a gun."

LII

In Harness

M ARCUS WAITED until Edwin could get away from his family again without attracting undue attention. He did not want to confront Hammie without an ally by his side. Who could guess Hammie's reaction upon being accused? And even if he confessed, Marcus would need a witness. Not that he expected Hammie to make it easy.

They embarked on their grim mission, following the picturesque embankment from the hotel to the cottage. Suddenly Marcus stopped dead, halfway up the path.

Standing by the water was the unmistakable figure of Louis Agassiz, with his handsome dome-shaped head and broad frame. He appeared to have been waiting in the same spot for some time.

"Back up slowly, Edwin," Marcus whispered. "We'll go around the other way."

"Marcus! Look."

With a swift movement, the Harvard professor took one step into a pool between the rocks, bent down, and ran a small net through the water, lifting it up with a dainty fish inside. Even at a distance, they could see his face was beaming with joy.

"He does not know who we are, Marcus," Edwin said. "Why, he probably wouldn't remember me as being a former student were I pick-led in one of his jars. Agassiz has had a cottage here for years, so that he could study the sea life and such. He comes with his family."

Despite all that was going on, Marcus was struck by Agassiz's joy at finding what he had been looking for in the fickle flow of nature. It seemed like an eternity since he had seen someone truly happy.

As they stood there watching the Harvard professor, something green slithered over Marcus's boot. "It's one of Hammie's pet snakes," Marcus said with alarm, lifting it up from the ground. "Gawain and Bartleby, I think they are called."

"So?"

"Hammie must have set them free, Edwin," Marcus said. "He trained them, he named them. Who would do that and then set them free?"

He quickened his pace now, Edwin trying to keep up behind him.

"Say, you boys! What kind of snake is that you have there?" Agassiz called out. He made as if to follow them, shouting questions, but shortly turned back to his own pursuits.

"I hope you are certain about this. We *must* be before we act," Edwin said to Marcus.

"Hammie will have his chance to tell his side of things and answer our questions. Do you have doubts?"

"No, no, I cannot see another way, either. But we must be one hundred percent certain of our course. If we prove that a student at Technology was responsible for all these horrific events, for all those senseless deaths and injuries, for the perversion of scientific knowledge, you must realize any glimmer of hope that the college had to survive before this hour will be instantly dashed! The Institute will be broken up forever, and perhaps there will never be another like it allowed to exist."

"It is too late for Tech," Marcus said. "It is better for it to have disappeared than to watch it die by inches."

As they arrived at the cottage, the door opened and a policeman stepped onto the stoop, frowning as soon as he saw them. "What do you want?" he demanded.

"I believe the young gentlemen are here to help me," Chauncy Hammond, Sr., said, emerging from behind the officer.

"As you wish, Mr. Hammond," said the policeman, returning inside.

"Mr. Mansfield and . . ." Hammond turned to Edwin.

"This is Edwin Hoyt, sir," Marcus said.

"Of course. I have seen you before at Institute events and around the village here, and I believe I have met your father in the course of business. The perpetual rival for Junior's class ranking, aren't you? Well, I wish I could greet you both in happier times. You'll spend a few minutes with me inside, won't you? I have something important to talk to you about."

Marcus and Edwin followed the magnate inside. The servants seemed agitated as they fluttered around them, and there was no sign of Hammie. Declining the offer of cigars and brandies, the visitors took chairs in Hammond's richly decorated study where he insisted they take some tea from a shimmering silver teapot.

Hammond gave a rusty sigh before beginning. "Mr. Mansfield, Mr. Hoyt. I am glad you are here. I need your help more than anything in the world."

"Mr. Hammond, what has happened?" Marcus asked, though he thought he knew. "Why are the police here?"

"Junior has disappeared." The elder Hammond had never seemed to bear much resemblance to Hammie before, his features plainer and more regular, but now his worried coffee-colored eyes and dust-colored skin could have been those of his son.

"Couldn't he be in the village?" Marcus proposed.

"He took everything with him. His clothing, his favorite books, his class notes. He even released his snakes."

Marcus stared at the ground and silently cursed himself. He had waited too long and had given as clever an operator as Hammie too many warning signs. Their classmate had guessed that he had been found out.

"He is a tender boy and at times I have been too hard with him," Hammond continued. "I never wanted him to be spoiled by easy surroundings. He has brain power in spades, but he has a fragile constitution."

"Perhaps not as fragile as we'd believed," Marcus said cryptically.

"Has he spoken to you about his mother?" the businessman asked.

"You mean Mrs. Hammond?"

"No, no, Mr. Hoyt—my present wife and I have been married only the past five and a half years. Junior's mother died when he was but thirteen. When he was a boy and lied or committed some other small sin, she would lock him in the closet. One day, a day not unlike this, he vanished. We looked everywhere, turned the house and stables upside down for any trace of the boy. Finally, as we sat in the house frantic and desperate, thinking what to do next, we heard the sound of sobbing coming from the closet! We had already looked there, but he had buried himself deep inside. He had shut himself in for saying some naughty oath to himself, and announced to his mother that all was right now because he had duly punished himself. Despite her harshness with him, when she died he seemed to lose even that unhappy mooring."

"He is a sensitive spirit," Edwin mustered as response.

"A genius, that's what he is, Mr. Hoyt," Hammond replied firmly. "Geniuses take blame or credit on their shoulders for everything around them. I am a common man, by contrast, whose only genius is in his determination. When I was your age I had no higher interest than wrestling and riding with friends. Junior has never had much in the way of fellowship. He has spoken of you both, and one or two others. You may be his only friends, and that you are here is providential. That is why I have asked you inside. I need your help bringing him back to me. You needn't understand everything about him, you needn't even like him, but know that he needs our protection now more than ever."

"Won't the police be able to find him?" Edwin asked.

"I'm afraid I must not divulge too much, but his disappearance may be related to the recent catastrophes in Boston, and there are reasons I cannot share that fact with the police. You know the whole city has been flipped like a flapjack. But I must bring him to safety. As Junior's peers, I'd hope you might have a better sense of where he might be."

Hammond proceeded to give them a list of Hammie's favorite spots. The magnate said that, meanwhile, he was already gathering a group to search every last inch of Nahant.

"We will find him, Mr. Hammond," Marcus promised. *And see him punished, however you try to shield him.*

"Thank you for your loyalty," Hammond said, taking Marcus's hand and pumping it. "You have repaid my faith in you all these years."

As they were walking away from the cottage, Edwin pulled Marcus aside, out of hearing of a search party that was convening nearby. "There is the policeman again. Let us tell him at once what we know about Hammie!"

"Chauncy Hammond is a man of power and fortune, Edwin. I have been in his employ. I know how he is."

"So?"

"You heard what he said about protecting Hammie and not giving information to the police. If our allegations take wind, he will delay any course of action we might take until Hammie has completely disappeared from reach. We have to find him *before* anyone else can bring him back under the protection of his father."

* * *

"SERGEANT CARLTON, I thought you should see this. It was found among the papers of the man killed in the sewer explosion."

"You mean the disfigured gentleman, Joseph—"

"Yes. Mr. Joseph Cheshire."

Sergeant Carlton beckoned for the patrolman to sit down across from his desk in the central police station of Boston. He was already exhausted from dealing with the mountain of scientific raw materials, documents, and equipment they had carried out of the Institute of Technology, and Louis Agassiz's hysterical insistence that every item be considered important evidence of the college's misdeeds. Carlton had learned his lesson from the Harvard scientist's failed theory on landmass shifts, which had drained so many of their resources. As a matter of fact, he had begun to be profoundly impressed and fascinated with the studies at the Institute—at least what he could understand of them. They struck him as modern in a way that made Agassiz seem thoroughly ancient. He had encouraged Agassiz to leave the city to better reflect on the events, and was determined to find what he needed to carry out the conclusion of the case on his own before the imperious professor returned. "What is this to me?" Carlton now asked, after studying the patrolman's slip of paper.

"You see, Sergeant, before he died Cheshire appears to have written down the names of some of the students at the Institute of Technology, addressing a note to one of the newspapers. This was crumpled and discarded, likely after writing in neater hand. His hand is not easy to read. He claims—well, *claimed,* I should say—that those polytechnikers have important information about the disasters. Taken together with Professor Agassiz's discovery of those instruments and materials connected with the very same Institute, I thought—"

"Yes, I follow your drift," Carlton said, inspecting the piece of paper more closely. "Rather awful handwriting, isn't it?"

"Sir."

"Yes, rather. Marcus Mansfield, Robert Richards, Edwin Hoyt, Ellen . . . Swallow, does that read? Wretched cramped hand."

"True enough, sir. Not easy to make out."

"This Cheshire seemed to have reason to believe these collegies were conducting their own investiation of sorts. Have you looked for these individuals yet?"

"Indeed, sir. Mansfield does not have an address listed in our directory. Ellen Swallow is not a name listed in the catalog of the Institute, nor in the last two Boston directories. The others have domiciles listed, but are not now present at them."

There was a knock at the office door and after a few moments the patrolman returned and whispered in Carlton's ear.

"God save the mark!" Carlton said. "Bring him in."

The patrolman escorted in a tall young man.

"I'm Sergeant Carlton. You say you have important information related to the disasters?"

"I think I do, sir."

"Well? Speak up already, man."

"I think a friend of mine knows something."

"You think he is responsible, Mr.— What was your name? You think your friend has something to do with these evil deeds?"

"No, sir! Not a chance!" said the tall young man, who swallowed hard at the insinuation. "My name is Frank Brewer, I am a machine man at the locomotive works. No, it's only that my friend—his name is Marcus Mansfield—had come to me asking for some materials from the foundry, and, well, there have been other odd facts since, like when he came to try to stop our being hurt in the boiler explosions, and I have been awful worried that he has been trying to investigate the occurrences on his own, perhaps with the help of his friends. You see, he is a student at the Institute of Technology, where I hope to attend next term, and he has a special knack for the most advanced new sciences because of it. The lot of them do. They are masters in the mechanic and chemical arts."

"Marcus Mansfield again!" Carlton said. "Have a seat."

"Thanks much," Frank said, lowering himself into a chair after a brief hesitation. "I think he has come so far that he is able to anticipate what will happen next and can discover the resolution."

Frank jumped back onto his feet again and wrung his hands with consternation.

"You are doing what is right," said Carlton.

"I feel such a traitor at the moment, Officer. My hands shake because of it. But I cannot help thinking he must not believe the police would accept their help, and feels he has nowhere to turn. Promise me you would not punish him for trying to help with this on his own!"

"At this point, if they can help, I shall deputize him myself for the rest of his days," said the sergeant.

Then he pulled aside the other policeman. "Patrolman, put those names from Cheshire's note in a circular to be distributed across the whole department. Forget old Agassiz, he has been trapped by his own rusty principles. It may be the Institute is not our enemy in this, but our only salvation. I want Mansfield, Richards, Hoyt, and Swallow brought to me in irons, if necessary. And if Chief Kurtz or anyone from City Hall asks, mention nothing of the Institute."

"Yes, sir."

LIII

What Hath God Wrought

THEY WERE THE FIRST ONES waiting to board the first train back for Boston in the morning. Marcus had wanted to leave the evening before but found to his displeasure that they were trapped in Nahant. "There isn't even a steamship?" he had asked when Edwin told him there were no night trains and that they would have to stay overnight in his family's rooms.

"When the visiting season starts in the next weeks, there are two each day. But at this time of the month there isn't another train or ship until tomorrow," Edwin replied. "In the meantime, should we look in the places Mr. Hammond suggested?"

"Hammie's not in Nahant, Edwin. Not if he wishes to hide—it's too small."

Now, as they rocked back and forth in their seats on an Eastern Railroad car from Lynn, Marcus was relieved to see the craggy scenery disappear behind them. It had rained during the night, the air was now hazy and still, and an almost summer heat had descended across New England, a foretaste of the relentless temperatures certain to come. To find Hammie, they would have to decide where he would hide in the city. With the secret laboratory demolished, Marcus felt confident he knew where he would go next: the Hammond Locomotive Works.

"But that is in plain sight," Edwin replied.

"Most of it will still be closed from the damage done by the boiler explosions. And think of it from his perspective, Edwin. It is entirely private and Hammie knows the place inside and out. He was practically raised there. He might not stay long, but if he's been there, we might be able to find some trace as to where he will be headed."

When they drew closer to the city, Marcus lifted his bag and excused himself. When he returned to his seat, he was wearing a faded blue uniform with brass buttons that didn't seem to have been dulled by time. Edwin appeared transfixed by the sight.

"It's Decoration Day," Marcus explained, a little shy at his classmate's awestruck expression. "Bob had wanted to take me with him to some of the festivities. There will be former soldiers in their uniforms all across the city. This will help us."

"How?"

"Because I won't stand out as much carrying this." Marcus held open his carpetbag to reveal the disassembled rifle he had taken from the Hammond collection.

When the train reached the station closest to Hammond's works, somewhat remote from the city center, they found a messenger and sent notes to Bob and Ellen. They had tried sending a wire through the telegraph office of Whitney's Hotel the night before, but by that time the operator at the hotel informed them disruptions had forced him to cease sending out any new messages altogether.

Marcus and Edwin approached the avenue that divided the two rows of buildings comprising the Hammond Locomotive Works. The usually bustling compound seemed uncomfortably quiet and still without the rumbling thunder of machines and the combined roar of boilers, furnaces, and supervisors and workers trying to meet schedules or fill urgent orders. Marcus thought there should be piles of scrap iron around the corner that they could use to break through one of the boarded windows in the lower machine shop that had been shattered by the explosions.

"Marcus, hold on!" Edwin whispered as he began making his way behind the buildings.

Marcus turned and saw that he had opened the street door to the business office in the main building.

"Not locked?" he asked softly, joining Edwin in the threshold.

"Someone must be inside."

"It's *him*. He's here right now."

"What if Hammie left it ajar on purpose? A booby trap, like at his private laboratory?"

Marcus gave this less thought than Edwin might have hoped. "Then we will finish our business with him here and now."

Edwin wiped his brow with his handkerchief and patted his pocket Bible. "I wish Bob were with you, Marcus, I do. He could help you more than I could, for he is never chicken-hearted."

"You are a man of good courage, Edwin, as much as anyone I know. Bob would say the same. Keep cool and all will come out all right."

Edwin forced a nod, and the two moved cautiously through the dark business office, which was stocked with plans for new locomotive orders. Marcus lit a small lantern and swept it across each hallway, motioning for Edwin to follow. Barely breathing, they sprang into chamber after chamber, prepared to confront Hammie, whose form they saw in every shadow, whose whisper they heard in the passing breeze, then they repeated their steps into the corridor and then through the next department, and then all over again.

As they walked among the massive machinery of the foundry, they were captivated by an unexpected sense of wonder. The machines at rest resembled slumbering beasts, ready to be roused by a single misstep on their part as they walked through. It was an eerily dynamic netherworld, still warmed by the artificial heat of industry that could never properly be removed through even the most advanced system of ventilation.

"Do you smell that?"

"What?" Edwin asked.

"Tobacco smoke."

Edwin sniffed. "Are you certain?"

Marcus gestured for Edwin to follow him to the threshold of the boiler shop, from which thin curls of smoke emerged. He took one step inside, raising the rifle and peering through the target sight. "Hammie!"

Chauncy Hammond, Sr., turned around, a cigar crimped between his lips, his eyes alive with surprise. He was feeding papers into the stomach of a furnace lit bright red.

"Mr. Hammond," Marcus blurted out, lowering the weapon. "How . . ."

He was going to ask how he had reached Boston before they did, but he knew the question was foolish before he finished it. Hammond did not need to rely on the railroad schedule—he *was* the railroad. Edwin joined Marcus in the passageway to the shop.

"Boys, forgive me. I fear I cannot take visitors in here at the moment," Hammond said, smiling at them wearily. "You haven't found my son, have you? Isn't that my Whitfield rifle? Why have you brought it here? What's the matter?"

The gaslights were flickering above them.

Edwin leaped to his own conclusion. "You cannot do this, not even for Hammie's sake, Mr. Hammond. It constitutes destroying the evidence!"

"You don't understand—I *need* to do this," the industrialist snapped. "It is the only way to stop this, Mr. Hoyt. To rescue everything and everyone I care about. Now, Mr. Mansfield, Mr. Hoyt, please do as I ask and find my Junior, so we can all be safe!"

"Hammie must not be protected anymore," Marcus said.

"I'd give my life for my child, just as every good parent would. What are you trying to do? I thought you wished to help! I thought you were his friends. I see my mistake now." Hammond's face tightened. Just like the flames of the furnace, the magnate's anger seemed to gather itself and then literally flare up within him. He put down the bundle of papers and whistled two sharp notes.

Through the dim halls of the next chamber came a gigantic figure, bearing down on them through the aisle of furnaces. The light revealed Sloucher George, the enormous machinist. He had bandages on his face and neck, which Marcus presumed were from injuries suffered during the boiler explosions.

"You didn't bolt the door, you ape," Hammond groused. Though he kept his eyes on Marcus and Edwin as he spoke, the reprimand was addressed to the machinist, whose big face reddened as he joined his employer. "Please help our friends find the exit while I finish my work here."

Sloucher George blocked the way as Marcus moved closer to Hammond. "You hard of hearing, Mansfield? Mr. Hammond said you can't be here right now. I wouldn't have expected you'd try something like this. You still remember your way out, I'd wager. You can give me that rifle."

"George, my friend and I need to speak to Mr. Hammond right now."

Hammond, back to his task, was once again the brusque business-man. "Mr. Mansfield, I must repeat that I am at some very urgent busi-ness just now. Take Mr. Hoyt, be on your way. I promise we will speak later—come to my offices tomorrow morning."

Marcus didn't move.

"You pigheaded whelp! I've always wanted a good excuse to lick you, Mansfield," George said, his huge hand landing on Marcus's shoulder. "Try to interfere with Mr. Hammond's plans, and you'll give me one."

"Careful," Edwin said, leaning in toward the machinist bravely. "Just the other day my friend licked a whole gang of Harvard men who started a row!"

Sloucher George laughed and raised his massive fist. "I ain't no col-legey, little fellow," he replied.

"We haven't time for polite conversation," Hammond said quietly, nodding a signal at his man. "Now!"

George pitched his body into Marcus, grabbing the rifle out of his hands even as he raised it, and throwing it across the boiler shop. George picked up Edwin by the collar and tossed him like a pebble across the greasy floor. Marcus came up swinging but was easily blocked by the machinist, who delivered a rapid series of body blows in return.

Staggering backward, Marcus recovered himself enough to stumble into the foundry toward Edwin, who was still on the floor. Before he could reach him, the large steam hammer plummeted down, sending sparks of fire shooting into the air over their heads. Marcus ducked, shielding his face.

Sloucher George, at the handle of the machine, laughed harshly. As Edwin tried to rise, George maneuvered the small hammer into posi-tion and snapped its iron arm down ferociously into the floor, sending Edwin back onto the floorboards.

"Ready to leave now, fellows?" the machinist yelled happily over the noise of the machine.

"You have to help us, or we'll all be at risk!" Edwin shouted to the machinist. "You can't let him shield Hammie!"

"Shield Hammie! What does Hammie have to do with it?"

"You don't know, George?" Marcus asked, regaining his footing and his confidence. "You will be under the threat of arrest for destroying evidence of serious crimes."

"What don't I know? Crimes? Boss Hammond told me we had to destroy the plans for a new locomotive engine before Globe Locomotive tried to steal them while our operations were still down. It's those wretched commercial thieves I'm here to guard against!" George spun around to face Hammond, who stood in the entryway, taking in the exchange.

"Hold your tongue, boy," Hammond said, pointing threateningly at his employee. "As long as you work for me, you do exactly as I say."

"First tell me what these fools talk about! What is this about Hammie?"

"Nothing of your concern. Get back to the steam hammers and do as you've been instructed. Clear them out."

George hesitated, wringing his hands and clenching his teeth. "Mr. Hammond, I want to know what Mansfield is talking about first," George shot back.

"I believed you a loyal man, George!"

"When Mr. Rapler tried to recruit me at the beer hall to organize against you, I told him to jump off a bridge. But he was right. You're dishonest with your workers! You aren't telling me the truth—I can smell it," Sloucher George roared, swinging his body back and forth between Hammond and Marcus as if unsure where to turn or whom to hurt.

Hammond pressed a hand wearily to his temple. "It seems you boys have all forgotten your places. I'm sorry it now comes to this. I never would have wanted any of you to be harmed."

Seizing Edwin by the shoulders, George was suddenly shaking him. "Someone's going to give me answers. You! What is all this about Hammie? What's that little swell done?"

Edwin wheezed for breath in the frantic machinist's clutches. As Marcus leaped forward to pull him off, the lights in the large chamber of machines flickered off. The three young men groped in the dark to find their bearings, Sloucher George shouting for Hammond to restore the lights.

"Marcus!" Edwin called out.

"I'm over here, Edwin. Don't move— Oh, God. I think he's—"

With a flash of fiery sparks, a revolving shaft of a suddenly live machine clutched Sloucher George by the jacket and threw him twenty feet into the air.

"Marcus, what's happening?" Edwin cried out.

"George! George, where are you?" Marcus called, but there was no reply and no trace of him in the pitch-black cavern of the foundry. He began to grope his way across the wall in the direction of the tossed workman. Massive machinery whirred and clicked all around them. Marcus called out again to Edwin to stay still as he braved one methodical step after another, following his memory of the arrangement of the foundry. A slight lapse, a momentary brush with the wrong machinery in action, could rip an arm off a shoulder in a flash, or separate head from neck.

He followed the groans now coming from the fallen machinist. Just before he reached George, the floorboards, damaged by the boiler explosions, gave way, and Marcus crashed through the floor down into the planing room.

"Marcus! No!" Edwin screamed.

Marcus landed on his back on the top of the enormous wheel lathe, thirty feet above the floor and now activated at full strength. Light was streaming in from a boarded-up breach in the brick wall. When the dust clouds cleared, he drew his head up and assessed his situation. At first relieved his fall was broken, once he realized where he was he was horrified.

Edwin, dashing down the stairs from the foundry into the planing room, stopped short of the machine, now staring up from below at his fallen friend.

"I need help, Edwin," Marcus said as calmly as he could manage.

"Can you jump down?" Edwin asked. But even if Marcus could survive the fall, the wheels on the machine were spinning below and would likely catch him and sweep him under the lathe. "You'll have to climb down the wheel, Marcus."

"I can't. If I move more than an inch up here, it will mimic the operator inserting a plane of wood—the wheel I'm on will turn and I'll be thrown right into the moving parts of the machine."

"Then I'll find a rope and pull you up from above."

Marcus shook his head. "The boards are all broken on the foundry floor—you won't be able to get close enough. Edwin, I need you to shut the machine down as quickly and carefully as you can, but without jolting anything."

Edwin hurried to the other side of the wheel lathe, where the controls were operated under a hood. The massive wheel on which Marcus balanced was shifting back and forth as he tried to keep his weight centered between the sharp wheel spokes.

"Edwin!" The wheel creaked and shivered.

"Don't speak, Marcus! Try not to move a single muscle! I'm going to stop it! I won't fail!"

Even as he said the words, both Tech students knew the truth: Even the blessed brain of Edwin Hoyt could not train itself on the controls of the sophisticated machine in the next thirty seconds. That was all the time remaining to Marcus—sixty seconds, maybe, at most—before his weight would inexorably trigger its movement and he would be crushed under the wheel, swept into the machinery, or thrown into one of the other heartless machines now activated by Hammond.

If he jumped he'd have a chance, however slim, of surviving. He closed his eyes and prepared himself. And then the machine sputtered and groaned and came to a screeching stop below. Lifting his head slightly, Marcus stared in amazement at what he saw.

"Edwin!" he cried in distress.

Edwin had lodged his body into the main gears that were turning the engine. "Marcus, you're clear! Climb down!" Edwin shouted, followed by a rush of tears as he watched blood flow down his own flank. Marcus launched himself down the spikes of the now-fixed wheel and yanked Edwin's body out of the machinery. His suit had been torn to shreds all along his side. Marcus ripped the sleeve from his uniform and wrapped it around his friend's bloody abdomen.

"Edwin, what have you done?"

"Find him," Edwin said, coughing and spitting blood. "You need to find Hammie!"

"Come on." Marcus pulled him to his feet. Miraculously, they found he was walking with less pain than they had expected and dreaded.

"I'm not dead," Edwin cried, marveling. He clung to Marcus's shoulder.

"You're hurt, Edwin."

"But I'm not dying, Marcus!"

They came to a sudden stop.

"What's wrong?" Edwin asked, trying to pull him forward. "We haven't any time to lose. I can keep up."

"Edwin—think," Marcus said quietly, then with a burst of realization. "All the clues we discovered. The set of steamer trunks were owned by the Hammond *family*, it was the Hammond yacht that went out with the iron, it was Mr. *Hammond's* laboratory building in South Boston. What if he isn't protecting Hammie? What if he is protecting *himself*?"

"That's impossible. Chauncy Hammond! He's supported the Institute from the start."

"He didn't come here trying to protect Hammie," Marcus said, now certain of it.

"I can't follow it."

"He wasn't even looking for Hammie. He was distracting us, sending us on a mission to find Hammie because we were getting too close, while he was preparing to get away free and clear, and to destroy all traces of what he'd done."

As they neared the machine shop again, the main engines were roaring at intervals, drowning out their conversation.

"I don't believe it," Edwin said finally. "I cannot"—the roar of the engines again, then a blast of cool air from the machine cooling the cylinders and wheels—"I will not believe it, Marcus, not in this lifetime!"

As they crossed the threshold into the shop, a solitary figure stepped forward. Chauncy Hammond raised the Whitfield at them with the target sight to his eye. There was no running—Edwin was too badly injured to move quickly enough, too easy a target.

"Get down!" Marcus shouted, shoving him to the floor and throwing himself on top, braced for the worst.

When he looked back up, Hammond had vanished completely from sight. Simply vanished.

"Where—"

"Up above!" Edwin called.

A whirring drew their gazes to the immense crane built to lift fifty tons of iron or steel at a time. Hanging from the hook by the collar, twenty feet in the air, was Chauncy Hammond, who kicked and writhed and tried to keep a grip on the rifle until it slipped from his hands and crashed to the floor.

Marcus ran over to the controls and stared at their current operator.

"Now, who said I was too clever to ever be a good machinist?" asked Hammie, glaring at his father as he lowered him down to the floor. "Father, I believe it's time we have a true talk."

LIV

Witnesses

"YOU DESTROYED THE INSTITUTE where your own namesake was a student," Marcus said in disbelief.

"It was Rogers who ruined it!" Hammond protested, then faltered as he looked back for his son. "Hammie, I was merely trying to find you—because if you were in Boston, you were in danger."

Hammie unhooked his father, who was slightly bruised, from the grip of the crane. "You should have trusted me enough to tell me that you were investigating this, too, Mansfield!" Hammie said to Marcus, making no attempt to conceal his hurt pride. "I thought we were true friends. I brought you to Nahant so I could confide my suspicions about my father, and then you ran away."

"No! Junior, listen to me, not these blackguards!" urged the senior Hammond. "I made Marcus Mansfield what he is and now he turns against both of us. You cannot take his side, son. Think of our family name—you'll destroy it."

"No, I will not," Hammie replied. "Doing what I now must do, Father, is the only way left to salvage the name Chauncy Hammond. That's my name, too. Not yours alone!"

"I cannot understand it, Hammie," Edwin said, keeping his elbow close to his lacerated side as he picked up the rifle dropped by Hammond. "Why would your father have had anything to do with causing the disasters?"

Hammie frowned and swallowed hard. "I believe I've discovered the answer in the last weeks, Hoyt. During the war, the company received contracts to produce locomotive engines for the government, cannons and ammunition, so on. It was a lucrative time, and he gambled. Gambled that the fighting would continue for several years longer by converting large parts of his locomotive works to war production. Investments were made accordingly. When the war ended, it all went to waste. The company stood in grave debt and remains so."

"Junior, how dare you spread lies! You have it all wrong!"

"Father, don't try fooling me! I have already thoroughly inspected the ledgers you were so eagerly casting into the furnace to hide your tracks! I know. I know you mortgaged the works to your creditors. I know how desperate you've become—I've seen the change in you. But still. That you would unleash a Frankenstein's monster of technology . . . facilitate mayhem and murder, Father! And to think you are the one who has led to the breaking up of our Institute."

"You said it was President Rogers's doing," Marcus said to the businessman. "What did you mean?"

Hammond's eyes remained locked on his son. "Breaking up the Institute!" he repeated. "Break it. Why, I was the Institute's greatest financial friend from the time Rogers incorporated on the very brink of the war! I allowed you, my only son, to be trumpeted as among its first pupils, for the world to see! But the Institute had enormous expenses and few students or supporters. It has permitted free scholars like you, Mr. Mansfield, and the young woman, Miss Swallow, to attend without the usual fees, and was crippled by the costs of its building. Even so, every invention produced by the Institute represented its own vast fortune. I offered to purchase and patent them, to sell them far and wide and share profits with the Institute. I was hardly the only one who recognized this opportunity for the Institute to thrive and for industry to be advanced. Your president stubbornly refused to sell anything to anyone. He wanted the inventions to be open and free for all; he refused to use them as means for profit, even as revenues for the college shrank. He was committing financial suicide and dragging your entire college down with him!"

Hammie removed a thick packet of papers from his coat. "These are applications for patents for inventions produced at the Institute. I found them several weeks ago in his office vault. Hundreds of them. Prepared by Father's lawyer."

"You wanted to discredit the Institute," Edwin said in astonishment. "So that you could be the one to control all of its inventions!"

Hammond looked down petulantly. "You are all damned fools. Just like Roland Rapler and his agitators, every single day convincing more of the workers of the city to rebel—they are the true Frankenstein's monsters, given life and force by our factories. How long before all industry finds itself bankrupt? Ten years from now, it will not be a question of how many men you employ, but only how many ideas you own. With the inventions to come, the railroad and the telegraph will seem as silly and prosaic to your sons as stagecoaches do to you."

Hammie had handed the papers to Edwin. "You see, Hoyt, if the Institute closed, its inventions would become freely available—that is, until Father's corporation claimed control over them before anyone else could do so."

"How did he know that the Institute would be blamed for the disasters?" Marcus asked Hammie.

"Suspicions of the new sciences were already strong—this was a push over a cliff," Hammie said. "Cyrus Hale and the other hack politicians in the legislature. They serve as the satellites of all big business, and are easily guided. Once Professor Agassiz was appointed to consult for the police, with his own private grudges against President Rogers, the Institute's fate was written."

"You would take lives for this? You would cause catastrophe in your own city to save your fortune?" Marcus demanded, looming over the man to whom he had owed so much.

"No, no! What Rogers dreamed of presented danger to every one of us. Imagine the public in control of the railroad. Imagine each citizen with a steam engine of his own, a telegraph wire at his disposal at his parlor table—the vast Pandora's box that would be opened by the destructive decisions and incompetence. Corporations such as mine manage the forces of science for the benefit—for the safety—of all. To grant free access to technology: That is the fatal danger. I wanted to salvage our city—our country and its citizenry—from that doomsday!"

"You will answer for every life that has been lost," Marcus said, unmoved.

"None of that is my fault," Hammond complained; then, sheepishly, he added, "Not directly, I mean."

"How can you expect us to believe that?"

"Because *my* modest plan was never enacted, Mr. Mansfield! I stand here ruined. But I have been your benefactor. If only for that reason, at least listen to what I have to say. Do you think I would blow my own locomotive works to pieces when I was trying with every fiber of my frame to restore its success? I have been trying to stop all of this, just like you! We fight on the same side!"

The students exchanged freshly confused glances.

The magnate, emboldened by having gained their attention, continued. "You have it all partially right. But my sole aim in all this was to shake the name of the Institute just enough that their fragile financial circumstances would convince them to grant me permission to control their inventions. Or if the Institute could no longer continue, so be it. The result would be the same; I would apply for the patents, and it would be a benefit to progress and man. I merely wished to demonstrate to the public the confusion that ensued when technology was spread without *clear* and *proper* control. It was never my plan to harm a single person!"

Marcus stared at Hammond, as realization, and a new dread, dawned. "You didn't act alone."

"Listen," Hammond pleaded, losing the last trace of defiance. "That is what I am trying to say. I engaged an engineer to create a series of demonstrations. Mere *demonstrations*—harmless exercises, as a sort of counter to those the Institute arranged for the public. That was the beginning and end of my plan. I granted the engineer use of an empty laboratory that a failed commercial tenant had abandoned, leaving it fully equipped, and free use of our yachts and supplies, yes. I trusted him to follow my orders, as he had done in the past. But I hadn't realized . . . his hatred, his bile . . . his actions were beyond my control from the very start, as soon as he had a taste. He said the project was his God-given 'mission.' . . . The manipulation of the compasses was intended merely to be reported by sailors to the police and the newspapers, but he chose to unleash it during a thick influx of fog, and the wreckage was beyond what I could have imagined. I thanked God that no one was killed. I visited the hospitals and paid the bills for the injured individuals. Then, when that poor young actress died on State Street, I was beside myself. Junior, you remember. My nerves grew to a perfect pitch during that very week, and I could hardly hold a conversation or meeting without giving in to my temper. I ordered the madman to stop, demanded it, threatened him, even offered him money. But he refused. He said that if I dared to tell the authorities or anyone else about him he would present evidence to implicate me, and he would do personal harm to me and to Junior. And then, before I could think what to do, he went even further, created an even more horrific catastrophe, exploding the boilers across the city, including my own works!"

"Give us his name!" Marcus said. When Hammond remained silent, he demanded, "If anything you say is true, why protect him?"

"If I tell you—don't you understand, this fellow knows no bounds. He could seek me out, he could find my wife. He could do harm to you, Junior, my greatest fear in the world! With all my resources, I cannot protect everyone at all times, not from him. We are all in danger, even now!"

For the first time in the encounter, Hammie looked chastened, shaken by the degree of his father's concern for him.

Marcus grabbed Hammond by the shoulders. "The name! Now!"

"He's falling to pieces!" Edwin said, dropping the rifle and pulling Marcus off.

Hammond opened his mouth to speak again but shuddered as a multitude of alarms rose outside in the distance. The magnate's eyes rolled back and his body slumped to the floor.

"Stay with him," Marcus said to Edwin as he eased the man's head and neck to the floor. Then, to Hammie, "Can you shut off all of the machines?"

As Hammie complied, Marcus seized a sledgehammer from a rack on the wall and broke through a boarded window, revealing the suddenly blackening sky above Boston and the first signs of the new disaster that awaited them.

LV

Thy Sons to the Jubilee Throng

B OSTON'S JUBILEE WAS IN FULL SWING across the city. Earlier, proces-
sions that included uniformed regiments had conveyed flowers and
wreaths to the cemeteries to the graves of soldiers. Now, the celebra-
tions had begun, though with only about a third of the attendees than
originally planned, since so many families had gone away from Boston
in the last month. Bob and Ellen had rendezvoused at the Boston Common, where the programs of plays and brass bands were under way on
the outdoor stages.

"What a stupendous celebration!" Bob cried out. *"Pygmalion!"*

"Where?" Ellen asked. She disliked the cacophony of drums and
horns and had been covering her ears.

"On the stage, dear lady, I believe they are beginning a rendition of
Pygmalion. Let us go watch. What would you like to eat?"

Ellen declined the offer.

"Come now, you must want something on Decoration Day," Bob
said, finishing the contents of his cup.

"Yes. Cotton for my ears. I do not eat food from a tent. I should prefer
to sit somewhere quiet and enjoy our first true spring day."

"I shall have more beer."

"It is still daylight, Mr. Richards."

" 'Mr. Richards'? We got on bravely with each other for a while. What
happened to 'Robert'?" he guffawed drunkenly.

"I am not certain where he is at the moment."

"Wait here," he said, not hearing, or not listening. "I will get us something more to your liking. Say, wouldn't the Tech boys have enjoyed
this, Nellie? Wouldn't they?"

Ellen frowned and considered taking French leave and letting him enjoy his drinking alone. She wasn't certain Bob, in his current state of mind, would care. She watched the other young women, delicate little dolls who were dutiful slaves to Boston society and fashion. They donned bows and ribbons, while she wore her black silk dress with lace sleeves, not a stitch of color. She had spent twenty minutes braiding flowers into her hair, but she did not think he had noticed. She looked at the husbands and wives as they passed, playfully hand in hand, and the shouting children, and wondered very seriously: Would she ever sacrifice part of her life to have that? It was difficult to imagine subjecting herself to the will of a man, especially in light of the current behavior of the one gentleman who, against all her wiser instincts, she thought the most of in Boston.

Everyone at the jubilee was trying to hide in some way, Bob included. Hide from the fear of what had happened over the last two months, hide from the secret, selfish relief they had felt during the war that violence had never touched Boston directly. On a day when they gave tribute to peace and remembered war, there *was* something that besieged them, something invisible but palpable in the air, felt powerfully by every citizen who stubbornly remained inside the confines of the city—the unknown future.

Bob returned and urged her to share his plate of beans, brown bread, mince pie, and watermelon. She declined again.

"Well, you're a quiet little thing today."

"I am the same Nellie as of old, full of business, never seeing a leisure hour, never finding time to study or read half as much as I want."

"Perhaps you don't wish to be here with me, then. Perhaps you wish to be reading in your rooms alone, pining away for the Institute?"

She regretted her implication. "No, it is not that. It is my nature that I always study causes and effects wherever I am, so I must also criticize sometimes, Mr. Richards. I find it to be my greatest fault that I go against the grain even where it is not necessary. Can you understand?"

From behind her, a large man, his bare head bald except for two bands of thin silver wisps, wearing the uniform of an army musician, portly but long in the limbs, wrapped one of his elongated arms around Ellen's waist, lifting her off the ground. "The devil's inside! I know! Force him out!" He spat on her with each word, as Ellen shrieked and struggled to free herself.

"Unhand her instantly, you lunatic!" Bob cried, jumping on the man's neck and pulling him down. The man fell on top of Bob, who only managed to push the bulky assailant off with great effort. The man, his wild eyes bulging, lifted himself to his feet from a puddle of mud and began stumbling through the alarmed crowd, his head twisting to one side, his hands and legs convulsing violently, but his movements rapid, like a wounded animal with nowhere to hide.

"Who was that man?" he asked, catching his breath.

"I've never seen him! We must find a doctor at once."

"Are you hurt?"

"Not for me."

"You don't mean fetching a doctor for that lunatic? He assaulted you!"

"Something was wrong with him, very wrong . . ." she said, looking through the crowd until she saw a policeman. "Officer!" She beckoned to him, though he had already been coming their way.

"Ellen Swallow. Robert Richards." The policeman said their names in a dreary monotone.

"What?" Bob squinted at him. "How do you know—"

She interrupted. "Sir, a man needs help over there!" But now she couldn't locate her assailant.

"Ellen Swallow? Robert Richards?" the policeman repeated mechanically.

Bob snatched the circular the officer was holding in his hands and studied it. The piece of paper notified all members of the police department that Bob and Ellen, as well as Marcus and Edwin, were to be taken into custody on sight and brought to the station house for questioning about the death of Joseph Cheshire and the attacks on the city of Boston.

"Ellen Swallow? Robert Richards? Not so much noise, if you please," whispered the policeman, putting a hand to his temple. "Softly."

"That man over there is in trouble!" she cried again.

"Softly, softly, young lady. Not so loud. Softly." The policeman reached out a trembling hand, as his legs suddenly collapsed beneath him. He writhed on the ground, his limbs flailing.

Another man, and then a woman, and now a second woman were stricken, and soon everywhere she looked in the Common people of all ages were convulsing in similar ways.

"Nellie, we must find Mansfield immediately . . ." Bob began.

She swept her hand violently across Bob's cheek, sending his food and beer flying. He gawked at her, stunned.

"It's the wheat," she said. "Oh, Robert, it's ergotism—from fungus in the wheat. I've tested it before in my laboratory, and my conclusions showed it causes delusion and hallucination, and even can induce labor in women who are with child. It could be in everything here—the pie, the bread, the crackers, the . . . the *beer*. Half of everyone remaining in Boston will be poisoned if the ergot was introduced into the festival wares!"

People began stumbling about blindly, screaming about demons and shadows chasing them, or that the sky was dissolving into pieces over their heads. A visibly pregnant woman dropped to the ground and gripped her bulging stomach as she screamed.

"My notes," Ellen gasped. "My notes on it were among those stolen from my rooms at the Institute." Then it wasn't mere vandals who took her notes; it had to be the experimenter—probably days before she found them missing, around the time when the explosive was arranged for Runkle and their diving suits removed. Someone who had been inside the Institute without being conspicuous, but who? Once the villain understood ergot poisoning, all that he would have to do was contaminate the wheat at the suppliers of bread and beer for Decoration Day, and here was the result.

Even as she stared into them, Bob's eyes became glassy and his skin dripped with sweat.

* * *

AS HE LOOKED DOWN from the roof of the Hammond Locomotive Works, where he had climbed for a better view, Marcus gripped the railing so hard his hands throbbed. Panic-stricken crowds of people with limbs twisting inhumanly stumbled in groups through the street, many falling down along the way. In the distance, a heavy cloud of smoke floated into the sky—and expanded toward them with remarkable velocity.

He took the stairs back down, two at a time.

"What's happening?" asked Edwin as he passed him.

"I don't know," Marcus answered. "We have to get out there and help."

"Wait, Mansfield!" shouted Hammie from the far side of the chambers, but Marcus was already plunging out the street door.

He didn't go far before he found himself jostled and pushed by swarms of people running in no particular direction. They were not only hysterical but blindly so, shouting out strings of nonsense and strange prayerlike exclamations. Above, the monstrous black cloud was rolling toward them. Edwin and Hammie were close on his heels.

Hammie caught up with Marcus and grabbed for his arm. "Mansfield, my father—"

"Hammie, your father's engineer did this. He has found a way to assault people directly now—men, women, and children alike."

Hammie shook his head that Marcus did not understand him. "Father woke from his fainting spell while you were up on the roof. He told me more. He came here today to remove all traces of his involvement and then to find me. He planned for me to leave Boston with him before anything else happened—that's why he wanted me to go to Nahant in the first place. I believe what he has said. He's not in any control of what has been happening, not since the very beginning, and by the time of the boiler disaster he knew nothing at all of what was planned!"

"So you believe your father has no idea what is happening now?"

"None. But I made him tell me who the engineer was."

"Who is he, Hammie?" Edwin asked, trying to keep up between his two classmates while applying pressure over his abdominal wounds.

"He has been working for my father, and was engaged secretly in this. Father says he was stationed at Smith Prison during the war and was notorious among the Rebels for the damage his clever devices and inventions did to Union troops."

"Smith Prison," Marcus repeated, his eyes filling with rage, as though Captain Denzler stood before them. "Impossible." *Denzler had vowed he would destroy the Yankees himself if he had to do it with his own brain.* "I look out and see his face," Frank, his fear visible and increasing, had told Marcus at the beer hall about spotting Denzler in Boston, and he hadn't listened.

"He had gained experience planning attacks against the Federal army during the war, before my father hired him. . . . Hold a moment. Heavens above, Mansfield!"

"What is it?" Marcus asked.

"There!" Hammie said, pointing. "He's here! That's him!"

Marcus burned with anticipation. For a moment, he actually looked forward to laying eyes on Denzler and unleashing years of slumbering rage; years of trying to repair all that had been broken in that hellish place. He turned and scanned the crowd for the hated figure before his eyes stopped on a different familiar face.

"That's him!" repeated Hammie. "Your friend from the machine shop, Mansfield. The blasted machinist my father sent to war to fight in *my* place."

There stood Frank Brewer, clad in his army tunic and trousers. He seemed to be looking right at them, smiling slightly.

"What do you mean?" Marcus asked. He grabbed Hammie by the collar and pushed him hard against a lamppost. "Damn you, Hammie, what do you mean that's him? I'll break every bone in your body!"

"Brewer is the engineer!"

"Hold your tongue! You're a miserable, lying cheat, just like your father! You hate Frank, hate him for fighting in your place, you made him sculpt you in uniform as if you had been a soldier. You were humiliated that he beat you in whist on Inspection Day at Tech! I saw what you wrote about making everyone eat their words. Tell me the truth!"

"It's Frank Brewer!" Hammie choked out, struggling for breath and prying Marcus's hands from his neck. "The Ichabod Crane machinist from the locomotive works. That's who Father found to help him with his plan! I didn't ask him to sculpt me, and he didn't beat me in whist! He left the study room just a few minutes after you did, and when he came back he told me to come with him to the basement!"

"What?"

"He said you told him that you needed help cleaning your supplies, and after I let him into our laboratory in the basement he took one of those machine suits you had been working on, and I said I could use some material from the other one for my steam man, so he said I should take the other one. That you had told him you didn't want them any longer. It was the skeptics about my steam men I wanted to eat their words. Let go of me, you gump!"

Marcus gradually loosened his grip and Edwin caught Hammie as he stumbled backward. Marcus turned in to the crowd, but as he pushed through the tumultuous pack of distorted faces, he lost sight of Frank. His head swam as he felt himself carried away by the masses, stepping left, then right to avoid being trampled. Frank. He wasn't playing whist because he was planting the explosive in Runkle's office, before stealing the diving suit to use in order to introduce his compound into the city water supply. Now he had managed to poison half the city. Frank. How could it be him—why would he?

"Frank!" he bellowed. "Frank, come back here!" His plea sounded like more nonsense lost in the babel of voices.

Suddenly, he was directly in the line of the oncoming cloud of smoke and could see its source: a freight train on fire rumbling toward them, creaking slowly but steadily ahead. The freight cars were entirely enveloped in flames, which shot up into the sky in what seemed to be an unending series of explosions.

"You're too close!" Edwin shouted, yanking him away from the tracks. "All right, Marcus?" he asked. "We have to get everyone away from here!"

"Edwin. We must stop Frank."

*   *   *

THEY NEEDED THE COMPLETE RAILROAD MAPS for the area, which Hammie assured them they'd find in the locomotive works offices. After they locked Hammond senior in one of the back rooms, Marcus sent Edwin to a nearby boardinghouse where some of the Tech students had rooms; from there, Edwin brought Whitney Conant and Albert Hall. They tried to send for more of their classmates, but the telegraph wires were still down.

"I'll help in whatever way you want," said Sloucher George, whom they had found in the foundry, nursing an injury to his head.

"For one, make certain Boss Hammond doesn't flee—we need him," said Marcus.

"Happily, Mansfield." George cracked his knuckles.

"What in the devil goes on out there, Mansfield?" Albert demanded with a terrified expression. "What are we doing here? Does this have something to do with what you were doing when the carbon gas leaked?"

Marcus clasped his shoulder. "We'll explain everything when there's time, Hall. For now we're going to try to avert a disaster, and we must put aside all of our differences. With the telegraph wires down, there will be no way to stop other trains from their routes—a train colliding with that burning freight would be so combustible it could obliterate hundreds of people in a single blast. Hammie, you and George trace the trajectory of the freight train on this map and find the first bridge it is going to cross that we can get to from here. While it is in flames nobody can get on that train to reach the brake, and if they could, it would still require a distance of a quarter of a mile to stop a train even with the engine shut off. Edwin: You, Conny, and Hall help me make a plan to blow up the bridge with materials we can find in the machine shop or the foundry or anywhere in the works we can access. Remember Squirty Watson's models."

"It would take weeks to draw up an effective plan to demolish a bridge," Albert protested.

"We're not at the Institute," Marcus said. "This isn't a thesis, Hall—it must be done *now*. Make haste! We don't have a second to lose."

By the time they had gathered an assortment of materials from around the works, Hammie had identified a bridge that would have to be their best chance. The student engineers were familiar enough with its structure to debate how they could most quickly bring the bridge down at the point of the keystone, or at the pier.

"If we can use this gunpowder to build two or three mines, and we can transport them safely . . . Marcus, do you think four charges of gunpowder will be sufficient?" Edwin asked.

"No, no, Hoyt, that won't work on *that* structure," Conny objected.

Marcus picked up the sledgehammer he had used on the window and became meditative. "Keep at it, men."

Crossing over into the machine shop, Marcus tried Frank's drawer under their old workbench and found that it was locked. Swinging the hammer in three quick strikes, he cracked the lock and pulled out the large drawer. He found a ledger with gold-rimmed pages, just as Bob had described seeing in the South Boston laboratory. He thumbed through the volume, recognizing formulas and diagrams behind the catastrophes. Five or six pages after this had been torn out, pages that might have given them the key to what they were facing now. Also in the drawer were a group of sculptures in Frank's style, each with faces Marcus knew well: Chauncy Hammond, Sr., William Barton Rogers, Roland Rapler, Sloucher George—all wearing military uniforms. Some were in fighting position, others cowering in fear as though facing a superior enemy or a firing squad. And there he himself was, Marcus Mansfield in miniature, held in the torment of the stocks, his broken spirit etched on his face, his head crushed. Marcus's heart lurched at his misery—and Frank's—made manifest.

"Marcus, what is it?" Edwin said, following him to the workbench.

Marcus took him by the arm. "Edwin, I don't think this is it."

"What?"

"The freight train!" Marcus cried. "I don't think that's the chief danger."

"The train? Marcus, when that train collides with another—"

"It's awfully dangerous—there's no question—but I think he's using it and whatever he did to poison those people as a distraction for something bigger. We—and the authorities—are supposed to be occupied with the runaway train, confused by the afflicted people. But the telegraph wires are down, and the newspapers have been reporting failing street lamps for weeks. Don't you see? People once feared the idea of locomotive engines, steam shovels, factory machines, even as everyone would fear Hammie's idea for a steam man, yet now they hardly notice the common technology around them—because they can see them in operation, they can watch the wheels and pistons. These disasters Frank has engineered all create a fear of science as an invisible face—a ghost and an unseen master that controls us without our knowing how or why or when—the compasses twisted by the air, the windows melted seemingly from the very particles within, the boilers blown apart by the very water running through them."

Edwin thought about it, then paled. "The telegraph and lampposts—why, they're both electrical circuits."

"Circuits. I'd bet a year's wages that Frank has been wiring the telegraph and street-lamp circuits into one massive circuit spanning the entire city—but for his own purpose. Currents that surround us, until we stop noticing them altogether: invisible yet everywhere. Remember, the lamps' circuits aren't yet complete."

"The train . . . it's going to complete the circuit!"

"And I think the circuit will set off explosions all over Boston—the city as we know it will be blasted away."

"But how could he have engineered that by himself, to span the whole city?"

"If he located the chief points of the circuit to alter, he would have had little trouble. When the train reaches the right spot, he will finally bring on the doomsday he's been working toward. Boston will go up in smoke."

"Thunder and lightning!" Edwin grabbed Marcus's arm. "The streetlight circuit was still being expanded along the outskirts, right? From front to back, the train will completely cover the area that was not yet completed. And with the speed we've estimated it is now moving, we have only forty minutes, forty-five at the most, before it happens!"

"We have to go now."

"But the train will reach the end of the circuit before it reaches the bridge where we can intercept it. There's nowhere to stop it before that!"

"Then I have to get to the origin point of the circuit instead," Marcus replied.

"That could be anywhere!"

"Edwin, think of it. The telegraph wires' circuit is too spread out to manipulate easily. The answer must be the streetlights. The Institute began the circuit outside our own building. That must be what he'd use to initiate the current. But even if I can stop it there, you'll still have to stop the freight train before it collides with another train or the terminal station—you have to get to that bridge."

"Edwin, we have it. A plan to throw down the bridge!" Albert interjected, running over with Whitney Conant, the rest of the group close behind them. "If we were able to bore a cylindrical hole two inches in diameter with a strong drill, fill it with water, and plug it, one blow with a steam hammer might break it apart. Well, what do you think?"

"It might just work! But how could we have the power out there for the drill and hammer?" Edwin asked.

Albert looked down at his feet. "Well, we haven't exactly . . . That is to say, perhaps . . ."

"We don't have time for hypotheses, Albert!" Edwin cried.

"I think I know how to blow the bridge." Sloucher George stepped forward. "Follow me!"

"Hurrah for George!" shouted the group in unison, falling in behind the machinist.

Edwin turned to Marcus with a look of solemn worry. "Where could Bob and Miss Swallow be?"

"They must not have received our messages," Marcus said.

"You don't think they could be . . . hurt?"

Marcus closed his eyes. "I don't know, Edwin. But if they're out there, they're helping, one way or another."

"Of course!" said Hammie, joining them. "They're Technologists, after all."

LVI

Babel

Frank Brewer has been working in the shoe manufactory a mile outside of Richmond for two weeks when Captain Denzler appears at his chamber. Denzler informs him that the Confederates are forming new regiments of engineers that Frank is to be part of, as Denzler's own assistant instead of being a lowly servant to the shoe manufacturer. When Frank asks why he should go with him, Denzler gestures to the two soldiers behind him, one of whom has cocked his pistol and now aims it at him. "We will shoot you if not, and report a hair's-breadth escape attempt."

"I am a fast runner," Frank finds himself saying.

"But your friends in Smith haven't anywhere to run," says Denzler, smiling, as Frank's defiant posture deflates. "If you escape, I assure you they will not, and I will personally bring them into the yard and watch them suffer."

The engineering office at the top of Smith Prison, far removed from the sight of the prisoners, is only a little better than a cell for Frank, who still wears his Union colors and will be shot immediately upon any attempt to escape. At first, he is assigned to aid in drawing up plans to repair railroad tracks and improve the design of the floating bridges, as well as to prepare maps for distribution to Confederate soldiers. It is a surprise when Denzler asks Frank to carve a statuette of him and even offers to sit for the purpose. Denzler has found the little wood carvings Frank does in his spare time between assignments. Denzler has also begun to praise Frank's sketches and maps. Denzler tells him about his family, his heritage: One ancestor was a great Hessian warrior during the American Revolution, and Denzler had always known he would one day fight for the noble cause of the United States. Frank's mind is spinning around in *circles: Here is a man he hates with every drop of his blood, confiding in him and befriending him, and he hates himself for allowing it.*

Denzler even takes Frank into his confidence about secret assignments he has been given by the Confederate authorities. You are the only one in all the engineering corps with enough brains to assist me, he tells Frank. Denzler confers with him about a plan to spread smallpox using contaminated blankets; ideas to poison the water and food supply of major Northern cities; calculations to determine whether unmanned hot-air balloons could, as one scientist's unproven theory insisted, attract meteorites to land at strategic points; and a plot, called "Request Number 44" in the official papers, to burn all of New York City to the ground and poison its main reservoir so that it could never be inhabited again. There is also the design of an exploding shell that would release a fatal mixture of chemical powders in quantities large enough that everyone in a small town would suffocate within an hour of its detonation. "You see, Frank, the principles in technology live even if we all die. That is the power of the engineer, to control everything around him without ever being seen. Technology lives, Frank!"

The engineering work Frank is forced to do contributes to improving the Southern army's gunpowder by increasing the proportion of charcoal in it, and later he designs a more effective earthworks to be used as a fortification.

He also devises a thousand ways in his head each and every week to murder Denzler using the chemicals and materials at his disposal. Each time, he becomes stuck on how he could escape after Denzler's death. He also imagines the expression on Denzler's face if he were to live long enough to know that Frank was responsible for a successful attack on him: Would Denzler feel betrayal? Nonsense, this man keeps him prisoner and tortured him and Marcus and their comrades!

Yet there is a palpable feeling of camaraderie when Denzler, disheveled and nearly in tears, tells him that the Confederate government has decided not to authorize the more destructive and brutal techniques they have been engineering. Request Number 44 and all the others are dead. But even their more modest endeavors together have done their work against the Union.

And then one day, without ceremony, a guard comes to his small cell.

"*You, Ichabod, get your haversack and come with us. Make haste.*" He is being released. Frank looks around for Denzler. When he does not see him, he calls out. His captor steps out from the corridor.

"*Your name is listed as part of a detachment being exchanged for a detachment of our soldiers being held in Union prisons,*" Denzler explains. "*I know you will not tell anyone what you have been doing, for they will hang you if you do. I am afraid I have no further say in the matter.*"

"*Then I am really going back to my family,*" Frank says, astounded and afraid at the idea.

"*Your friend, what is his name?*"

"*Who?*"

"*With the Roman name and the Roman sense of heroism: Lucius? Nay, Marcus, isn't it? Your friend who conspired with you here, snipping apart our machinery, the so-called chief of police of the basement. I am glad it was you here, instead of him.*"

"*Why?*" Frank feels strangely touched at the comment.

"*Because he would have tried to kill me for enslaving him, if given all the chances you have had while here. I do not doubt that, even if it cost him his life. The boy became a warrior while under our watch. Yet, here I am alive, even flourishing, in my new position. I thank you, Brewer, for you have remained the same level-headed Yank you were before ever witnessing a single bloody battle. You will have a fine future one day as the foreman of a machine shop, I haven't a doubt in my head.*"

The words continue to echo in Frank's mind even once he has been living and working in Boston. The disdainful face of Denzler follows him, appearing in flashes within large crowds at Quincy Market, in the corners of subterranean taverns and brothels, in windows of buildings or passing trains. Then vanishing before he can give chase or remind himself that, no, that is not possible, Denzler has fled the country. The face itself is unchanging, the maddening expression of violent superiority he himself had carved from wood in the engineering office at Smith. At first, he rejects the voice, argues with it, cries under the assault of its taunts. He sculpts more faces and figures of people who are not Denzler, who do not imprison or abandon him. But, more and more, they, too, become soldiers imprisoned in war. More and more, toiling twelve hours a day in the machine shop, remembering and dreaming of wartime, of what he did for Denzler, *of what he did against his own comrades, against the commonwealth of Massachusetts, Frank Brewer is imprisoned and abandoned.*

One February day, a day with a dry bracing cold, on his way to his lodgings after work, at the side of the road stops a two-horse carriage. Frank recognizes that it belongs to Chauncy Hammond, Sr. The driver calls him over and says that Hammond has sent him to drive Frank. The driver puts a blanket down so Frank does not have to step in the slush as he climbs up from the curb. During the ride, Frank feels content and privileged at this special treatment—long overdue since he took upon his shoulders Hammie's place in the war—but also ashamed that the other machine men from the works would be trudging home in the cold. But the carriage crosses over into Charlestown—this is not the way to his lodgings—and soon they are stopped at the foot of the Bunker Hill Monument. The driver tells him to climb to the observatory, and at his questioning stare explains only that this was what Hammond requested.

Frank marches up the narrow, winding staircase inside the hollow shaft, sliding periodically on top of the ice and mud left behind by previous boots. Up and up to the small chamber beneath the apex of the tower. Hammond waits, looking out one of the windows.

"Did you know this is one of the finest views in the world? Even on a winter night, you can see hundreds of miles away. It is like a painting—a painting of the past and the future. You can see the ships as they float in and out of the harbor, and the lights from the railroads that once were only a dream, my dream, that have allowed young men like you to come from all over to live in Boston."

Hammond turns around, a tight nod the only greeting and acknowledgment of Frank's making the treacherous climb. "There are some important conversations that should not be overheard by any others. This is one. Are you prepared for that, Brewer?"

He nods.

"Good," continues the businessman. "The Institute of Technology. You know something about it, I presume?"

"Marcus Mansfield is to be graduated from there this summer," he answers sullenly. "He's given up four years of wages to play the part of a collegey, but I for one can't be convinced anyone in Boston will see him as anything more than a factory hand. Anything more than me."

"*The Institute's leaders believe that all scientific innovation belongs to the masses,*" says the older man. "*Their professors guide brilliant young fellows like my Junior without an awareness of the danger that this sort of thinking entails. I financed that place before it had a single cornerstone laid down, yet they squander away the fruits of their labor! They squander away the future! For my own reasons, Brewer, I should like to see those innovations fall under private control. After pressing them to this end, it seems I must instead stoke that outcome more directly.*"

"*Why speak to me about it, sir?*"

The magnate rests a hand on one of the two brass cannons displayed there, under which is the inscription SACRED TO LIBERTY. "*I know what you did with Captain Denzler at Smith Prison.*"

"*How . . . ?*"

"*I will explain another time. You needn't be afraid, Brewer, I promise! You had no choice, and it is not in my interest to tell anyone what you were made to do. Why, if Junior had been in your place, well, I cannot conceive his fate. Let us apply the skills you received from that scoundrel Denzler to better use. Let us give Boston a small scare or two, and in doing so shake the stubborn will of Tech to my purposes. What say you, my boy?*"

"*Yes,*" answers Frank, faster than he ever would have imagined.

LVII

White Whale

"IT'S SO COLD." Bob's head twisted into his shoulder. "Nellie, Nellie! Nellie, it's cold. Where are you? I can't see you!"

"Stay calm—don't try to walk!" Ellen cried, putting her arms around him to prevent him from falling. "The ergot produces convulsions in the joints. Can you hear me? Lie down on the grass. As long as you understand what is happening, you need not be frightened by it. Your vision may be affected, and you might see things—shadows and shapes—that aren't there. Listen to me! You will feel tingling in your hands and feet, and you will feel hungry, but you mustn't try to move or eat until your body is cleansed of the effects. Robert, can you hear me? Robert Richards?"

"Thank heavens it's you," he groaned.

"What?"

"If I am to die—"

"You're not going to die!"

"Thank heavens it's you. You can save me."

As she loosened his neckcloth, she said lightly, in an attempt to calm him, "I am only a mere woman of the weaker sex, remember."

"I love you," he mumbled, his lips curling into a strange smile. "Not only a woman, the best woman. I love Ellen Swallow."

"Really! Robert, must a man wait until he is delirious to declare such a thing?"

"I love your hands. The tips of your fingers. They are such a delicate shade of—purple, is it?"

"Yes, I was working with iodide of potassium and chlorine gas earlier."

"Ellen Swallow *Richards.*"

"Excuse me!" she gasped at the presumption.

A young woman in a frilly dress fell only feet from them, while others ran in all directions, attempting to escape the wrath of an assailant already inside their skin.

Pulling Bob out of the way of being trampled, Ellen rushed into the crowd, waving her arms. "Throw down your beer! Your food! If you feel sick, lie down on the grass and don't move!"

"Why should we listen to you, woman?" groused a doctor who was tending to the mysteriously ill.

"My name is Ellen Henrietta Swallow. I am a student at the Institute of Technology, and if you listen to me, you'll save lives."

As she shouted this back at the chastened man, a black column of smoke shot into the sky in the distance.

* * *

GEORGE PROPOSED using a wire rope on a pulley from a steam engine to transmit the power they needed to drill the holes. He explained that they had used a similar scheme before to bring power from the machine shop to some of the outer buildings where the materials were too combustible to maintain engines nearby. He knew of a mill not half a mile from the bridge with an engine that could be easily accessed.

Marcus detached a great black-and-white mare from Chauncy Hammond's team. He ran his hand across her eyes and over her wide nose to familiarize her senses with him. The rest of his cohorts were finishing loading the wire rope and pulley, and pushing Mr. Hammond inside his carriage with them.

Hammie helped steady the lone horse for Marcus to mount it.

"I should be at your side, Mansfield. It was my father who started this all in motion."

He shook his head. "Get them safely to the bridge with the materials, and have one of the men bring your father to the police station to tell them exactly how all of this was started. Whatever happens, if I succeed, or if I fail to stop Frank today, the world must learn the Institute was not to blame. It's vitally important, Hammie."

Hammie considered this momentarily before resigning himself to climb into the carriage with the others.

Marcus called out: "Hammie! I always swear by Tech and always mean to."

He smiled back at Marcus with his wide, off-center grin. "I always swear by Tech and always mean to! No daredevilry now, Mansfield," he added.

Marcus prodded the horse onto the street and kept his heels in position for maximum speed.

As he traveled over its gravel streets, Back Bay seemed more a deserted island than ever. When he reached the massive Institute building, he dismounted at the central streetlight in front. Unlatching the box at the bottom of the lamppost, which ran into the ground, he caught his breath as he saw the vast array of coils and devices that had been inserted among the electrical cables and the wheel. He put his rifle down on the ground. Here was confirmation of Frank's plan—but how to stop it?

He stared at the configuration, feeling the time slip away as he studied it, and then set doggedly to work. After fifteen minutes of sustained effort, his hands buried within the tightly packed wiring, he cursed as he shredded the skin on his knuckle on a sharp edge, and sat back, hand to his mouth, to stanch the flow of blood. His fingers were throbbing, aching, and swelling red to the point where his right hand would be useless in a matter of minutes. He tried to form a fist and flinched at the agony in his joints, falling to his knees and crying aloud in pain.

"Well, I see you've discovered my circuit. What a place to build a college! You have to be very careful with circuit closers here, with the tide in these marshlands."

Marcus turned and saw Frank approaching. With his hands hooked over his pockets as though he were a gentleman of leisure on an afternoon stroll: his uniform on, posture tall and proud, he looked nothing like the tired machine man he had been.

"Here, let me help you up," Frank offered. "You must be careful with that hand."

"Don't touch me," Marcus snapped.

Frank looked to be deeply injured. "Marcus? Why, I thought you'd be grateful."

Marcus shook his head in confusion and disgust. "What have you done, Frank?"

"Oh, how I wanted so much to tell you all about it when you came with your class to the machine shop! I actually believed you'd understand it, and appreciate it, more than anybody in the land! Then, when you asked me to bring those iron samples to the beer hall, I realized what you were doing, already trying to stop me. I knew then I would have to prove to you I was up to snuff before I told you the truth."

"The truth?" Marcus said, so astounded he almost broke into laughter. "What do you mean?"

"That I was saving your college."

"What?"

"Hammond wanted to damage it, possibly even see it disappear for his own purposes. But I realized right off I could do something about it, that I did not have to merely vanish into the dark corner of a machine shop any longer. I would show Boston that they needed the Institute—that their money and family names were no longer a shield—not from the weapons you and I possess. Not from the highest intelligence: not from technology. Starting today, the city will finally reach the point where they realize they will have to beg the Institute for help, they will have to crown it, guard it, celebrate it, as they have done for Harvard for hundreds of foolish years!"

Marcus was flabbergasted. "Why?"

Now Frank laughed as though Marcus was joking. "Why? Didn't I tell you? When you came with your class to the shop, I told you I was ready for something better. Because it was finally my chance, my chance to leave the machines and do something by joining the Institute—and I wasn't about to let Hammond take that away!"

"You could have refused him then!"

"He would simply have found someone else to do his bidding! The Institute was finally giving men like you and me a chance, but the college was always being kicked around by someone. How long before the distrust and stupidity of the legislature or the public brought down the Institute? No, this was bigger than Hammond—by proving to Boston that they had nowhere else to turn, I've given the Institute the freedom to be more powerful than any institution ever before!"

Marcus squinted at him as if he were a mile away and he was trying to identify him as friend or enemy. "What do you think is going to happen now, Frank? Look me in the eye and tell me!"

"Boston is slow to change, slow to act. I need not tell you! The people of Boston turned their back on us when we were imprisoned at Smith."

"They did nothing like that."

"Oh, but they did! My family, my regiment, my government, they all knew where I was, only a poor lad, and nobody did the least thing about it. Rich boys like Hammie paid for substitutes like me to go and be killed or captured instead of them. As long as they felt safe, we were forgotten, as good as dead. Boston cannot pretend to be safe now, Marcus. Today we prove to them they cannot protect themselves, and then the Institute will be uplifted! Why, I know for a fact the police are already coming to the conclusion that the city must bow to the college, and after the damage today they will bow at your feet for you to stop what's next—which we will make certain you do. You will be graduated, I will begin as a freshman, and we will be respected. This will be my examination for admission! Come, give me your hand, old friend. We will finish this together."

Marcus examined the outstretched hand for a moment, then looked back at Frank's face, a face that had brought him so much comfort over the years. His teeth were showing in an excited grin and he was nodding. Marcus took a step back.

"You didn't leave the prison camp as a shoemaker, did you?" he asked.

"Indeed I did," Frank corrected him calmly. "And Captain Denzler was in a fury about my release. That monster found some value in me. He came to me at the shoemaker's and said I must assist him as an engineer or be executed right there, and be responsible for others to be executed, too. For you and the other men in Smith to be executed. I did it, Marcus. I used my abilities to make better bullets for the Rebels. To explode mines and collapse bridges underneath our soldiers' feet."

"You betrayed your army."

"Betrayal, did you say? Look at the fate they left me to, Marcus! Then to offer to exchange us like we were worthless cows at the market. Do you know how many 'simple soldiers' like you and me they counted as worth one officer? Ten . . . twenty, sometimes even more.

"Chauncy Hammond had heard what I had done in the war from a man he had hired to design an engine part, an engineer from the South who recognized me from when he had visited Denzler's office during the war. Hammond chose me, recruited me, just as Denzler did, this time to craft demonstrations to shape the public mind against technology and force Tech into selling their inventions. But I did what Hammond couldn't dare imagine. I finally taught Boston the superiority of technology over all else! I've done that myself, my friend, not anyone at your Institute, not any of your brilliant companions from your classes! Those who can't recognize and reward our special knowledge and accept our power over them, I say damn them all. Damn Hammond, too. He was too weak-kneed to understand the scope of his own mission and that's why I had to turn the tables on him. And damn Hammie more than all of 'em."

"Shame on you, Frank."

Frank fidgeted, his hand slipping back into his pocket. "He never deserved to be the heir to a man of innovation—that is why his father chose me to wear the uniform in his place!"

"You even let Hammond's locomotive works be damaged, and knew where to be to avoid serious injury from the boiler explosions. You murdered Joseph Cheshire. You've hurt innocent people. You've hurt Runkle, and . . ." Marcus paused, his back teeth clenched on his next phrase.

Frank bowed his head. "You know she was an accidental casualty. I wept for her. And for you. That scoundrel Cheshire, well, he nearly nabbed me removing evidence from the yacht Boss Hammond gave me use of, and when I realized he had also found you, he had to be finished. Then I couldn't risk the superintendent at the private laboratory becoming suspicious after your friend Bob showed up. Runkle was getting too close, as well. I had agreed to come to the Institute for Inspection Day; I heard when Hammie told you what Runkle said to him."

"You might have killed me with that explosion, instead of injuring Runkle."

"I didn't know you'd go to Runkle's office, Marcus!"

Marcus shuddered with a new thought. "And you lifted him from my arms—you would have finished him in cold blood. Was that your plan?"

Frank shrugged. "If that Negro janitor had not scooped him up, I would have had my chance. But you'd admit the blast safely removed Runkle from being any trouble, anyway."

"Bob and Ellen. Where are they? If you've harmed them—"

"I don't know where your new friends are! I suppose they might have been at the Decoration Day festivals, with the rest of Boston, poisoned into a daze as they gorged themselves on the memory of real soldiers. Always trying to control his friends, trying to protect them—that's Marcus Mansfield. Marcus Mansfield, who thinks he is the chief of police for the world, the arm and hand of God. Well, if you can't see this is the right way, then damn you for it, too!"

"Frank, this isn't you! Hammond tried to use the Institute and he used you, to make up for his own greed and his mistakes during the war."

"No. Hammond pointed the way, gave me a sip of true power. I found I liked the taste of it very much, Marcus, and I drank deeply."

"You could have left me when your laboratory building collapsed. You should have let me be crushed."

"You still don't understand! I have looked forward to this moment, Marcus, more than anything. For you to come to finally understand that running away to Tech did not make you the better man, did not make you my superior, that I am just as good as you. That I could be the one to make the world finally give the Institute its due!"

"I never said I was superior!"

"You asked me to serve you, to bring you iron bars, but you didn't ask for the help of my mind!"

"That's not it, Frank—" Marcus protested.

Frank did not let him finish. "Four years ago, you left me behind quickly enough! You thought going to Tech made you special—improved—that you'd left your previous life behind. Left behind the machine shop, the twelve-hour days, Smith Prison, me. You heard what your friend Albert said, that Tech no longer could help charity scholars—you got lucky, as usual, to join while you could, and I would still have been trapped on the machines. Now you see the truth. You cannot escape the station you are born to, but we can prove to the world how we are better and stronger than any Boston gentlemen. It's too late, far too late to stop this. This had to come to pass, whether by me or someone else. This is the future. You do understand that now?" Frank held out a pocket watch where Marcus could see it. "The circuit will be completed by the train just two minutes from now. I saved your life at Smith, Marcus, but it was still *you* people respected, *you* who they thought had brass. I'll save you again. Come with me, we'll be safe inside the Institute. I would not stand outside when that train completes the circuit, it will be Judgment Day in Boston."

Marcus looked behind him at the Institute. The building was a battered shade of its magnificent former self, a relic of empty classrooms behind shattered windows. Frank's vision of bringing it to life again by tearing apart Boston chilled him to the bone because Marcus knew it could work. There could reach a moment where Boston had no other choice but to turn to the Institute for protection.

"This is over. Your circuit will not work, Frank. You'll have to answer for what you've done, even if I have to drag you all the way to the police station. Hammond is there telling them everything."

"Come now!" Frank laughed joyously, throwing his head back. He had never looked so pleased, so strong and so free in his body. "You shouldn't have tried so hard, not with that weak hand of yours. Did you know how much worse it was getting, and that you wouldn't have a choice but to leave the machine shop sooner or later? You weren't the brave one I believed for going to Tech—you just couldn't admit even a little weakness, even admit it to yourself. Tell me. What would you have done with your diploma, once your hand was fully lame? Even an engineer needs both hands, I'd venture. Well, do not blame yourself. Nobody could cut the circuit the way I've managed to arrange it—not in twenty minutes, not in ten hours. Nobody. That includes you."

"You're wrong, Frank. A Tech man could and has. I've done it already. Hammie and my friends are going to stop the train once it gets to the first bridge. I've stopped your circuit. There was one thing you failed to realize in all this, Frank. One better way to bring the Institute into a new light than all the horrors you concocted."

"What is that, exactly?" Frank asked.

"To show the world that a group of Tech students could stop your destruction."

"I don't believe you," Frank said, his eyes narrowing. "You were always willing to die for a cause."

"Believe what you want. Don't touch that box, Frank. I warn you. Stop right now!"

Frank took his place at the circuit box.

Marcus launched himself at his former comrade.

To Frank's own apparent surprise, he was able to fend Marcus off with one hard push, which dropped him to the ground. As though finally overcome with exhaustion years in the making, Marcus got back on his feet slowly, brushing the dust off his tattered, bloody uniform.

"You took it all upon your shoulders. To save a city that cares nothing for you. Look at you. You haven't slept, you've barely eaten. Now you're too weak to do anything, Marcus." Frank examined the contents of the circuit box for a few moments and then laughed. "Why, I knew it. So much for the genius of a Tech boy. You weren't able to cut the circuit!"

"You're right. You engineered it in there too well to cut," Marcus admitted, then began to back away. "You engineered it too well to stop the circuit, because you thought someone—maybe the police, maybe Hammond, maybe me or my friends—might find out the truth about you and try to cut it. But you never thought of stopping someone from reversing the electric current."

"What do you mean?" Then he realized. He dug his nimble fingers into the wiring and went to work with remarkable speed.

"Get away, Frank! Right now!"

"No, you can't!" Marcus's old friend delivered an awful scream, then his eyes went wide. Far across the city, the fiery train was making its passage over a portion of track where, with its wheels hitting the first and last rails, it connected the incomplete portion of the circuit. But instead of blowing half of Boston to shreds, a massive jolt of electricity shot in one direction back through the cables to the origin point and into the sculptor's fingertips. With an awful buzzing sound, his eyes bulged and his body flew ten feet into the air.

To Marcus's surprise, as he fell to the ground aflame, he struggled to get back to his feet, gurgling blood, every inch of visible skin charred.

Marcus stood transfixed, as Frank seemed to reach out, to move toward him with open arms. Marcus thought of running, but knew Frank was gone already even as he gasped for a final breath of air, then folded into Marcus's arms.

* * *

THE TRAIN GREW LARGER AND LARGER within the circle as it pushed toward the outskirts of the city, throwing off flames along its wobbly path.

"It's coming," whispered Edwin to himself, lowering the spyglass. Then, to the others, "It's gone past the end of the circuit and it's still coming! Marcus did it! He stopped the detonation!"

Cheers rose up from the four young men. They were at the railroad bridge where the train would have to cross over the Charles River. After the moment of joy for their classmate's success passed, a flurry of urgent activity resumed. Now it would fall to Edwin and the others. This bridge between Boston and Cambridge was the place of last hope to stop the freight before it could reach another train, or the terminal station, and end in a massive, possibly deadly, explosion.

Whitney Conant had split off from the group near the police station so he could escort Chauncy Hammond inside to confess his story. The remaining four had divided themselves up once they had reached the bridge. Edwin and Sloucher George worked together on the Boston side. Across the river on the Cambridge end, there were Hammie and Albert Hall.

Both teams successfully drilled holes into the main braces at both ends of the bridge. They had to study the structure of the trusses meticulously, since, by their calculations, destroying the counterbraces would fail to bring the bridge down. The respective teams were now fitting the holes with the powder-infused cylinders they'd hastily put together. Hammie and Hall finished on their end first, laying out the fuse across the bridge.

"Are you finished yet?" Albert called out. "We're ready to light it!"

"Not yet, Albert!" Edwin called back. He fitted the device into the hole in the brace, then passed the fuse line to his partner. They rushed off the bridge to the safety of the Boston side of the river. "We're off!" he yelled to their collaborators.

George took out his cigar lighter and positioned himself flat on the ground with the end of the fuse in his other hand. "All right," he said quietly, steadying his hand.

"All right," Edwin called to the other duo. "George is ready to light it, fellows!"

"So are we. On my count," Hammie said. "Three . . . two . . . one . . . go!"

The fuses on both ends of the bridge were lit and the small flames ate through them. On the Cambridge side of the river, the cylinder gave off a loud pop, the brace immediately fractured, and the whole bridge shook. Hammie laughed nervously. But on Edwin's side, when the burning fuse reached the cylinder, there was a muted fizzle. Then nothing. The bridge, shaking in an unstable fashion, still remained intact.

"What happened, Hoyt?" Hammie shouted to them.

"Something's wrong with our fuse!"

"Can we light the cylinder up close?" George asked.

"No. We wouldn't be able to get off the bridge in time if it worked," Edwin said. "The whole thing would come down under our feet."

"Stay here—I'm going to try!" George said stoutly.

"No, George—I won't allow it!" Edwin cried, physically restraining the larger man.

"What do you care about it? I was going to lick you an hour ago."

"Listen to him, George!" Hammie called out from across the river. "It's too dangerous to light by hand. The bridge *might* still come down from the weight of the train alone, even without it."

"But it might not, Hammie," Albert objected. "And if we allow the train to pass over the bridge, there's nowhere else to stop it for miles. We have to find another way to take this bridge down *now*."

"How much longer do we have?" asked George.

"Five minutes, maybe four," replied Edwin grimly.

Everyone spoke over one another, offering conflicting and desperate ideas about how to complete the task in the allotted time.

"Greek fire," Edwin shouted across the river. "Hammie, do you have enough materials in Albert's case to make your Greek fire, like we used against the Med Fac?"

"More fire?" Albert asked. "There's a train filled with flaming petro-leum bearing down on us. Fire is the whole problem, Hoyt!"

"Listen to me! Forget bringing the bridge down—we've run out of time—but if we derail the train right here, it will land in the water and be rendered harmless," Edwin explained.

The others fell silent and considered. Hammie rummaged through the contents of Hall's chemical case.

"Hurry!" Edwin cried.

"There's an empty cylinder I can use as the container," Hammie said. "It's not ideal, but . . . yes . . . I can improvise something, Hoyt!"

"If we can dislodge just one set of the wheels, the whole train should tip over," said Edwin.

"Do you think it will work?" George asked.

"George, you're addressing Edwin Hoyt—the smartest fellow at the Massachusetts Institute of Technology!" Hammie answered.

As Hammie worked feverishly, a mechanical roar pierced the air. Edwin and George glanced at each other. The train was so close they could even smell it burning. Edwin stood on higher ground with his spyglass raised.

"I can see it coming!" he cried. Then, bringing down the spyglass, he saw it was close enough that he could see it now with his naked eye, and said, "Oh, no!"

"Almost through here," Hammie promised, directing Albert to hand him the various materials. "Another second and . . . done!"

"Put it on the tracks, Hammie!" Edwin cried.

"I can't!"

"What? Why in the land not?"

"I'd say there is a twenty-two to twenty-five percent chance the dam-age already done to the bridge could cause the train to be raised off the tracks and land on our side of the river without touching the portion of tracks on our end—it would fly over this cylinder and plow right into the heart of Harvard Square before there's time to do anything else. The cylinder needs to be near the front of the bridge. *Your* end."

"How the deuce could he know the chances so perfectly?" George sniffed.

"Because," said Edwin, "*he's* the Top Scholar at the Institute of Technology."

"I'm going to throw the cylinder to your side," Hammie called out.

"Won't that thing blow up?" George asked with a gasp.

"I haven't sealed the cylinder. The pressure should remain stable if you catch it," said Hammie. "Still, I wouldn't let it drop, if I were you."

"Thanks for the advice," George muttered.

"George, are you ready?"

"You ought to catch it," the giant machinist said meekly to Edwin.

"I?" Edwin laughed morbidly.

"The vision in my left eye is clouded," George explained, then dropped to an embarrassed whisper. "That's why I am slower at the machine shop than the others, why some of them think me a slouch. I've never told anyone."

The snorting of the runaway train came closer and closer and the ground underneath their feet shook hard.

"Very well," Edwin said, wrapping his coat tighter around the wound in his flank, which he had covered during their carriage ride over. "Hammie, on my count, then! Three . . . two . . . one . . . go!"

Hammie drew his arm back and launched the cylinder in the air. Edwin steadied himself, reached up, and plucked it from the sky, the deep concentration and sudden pain from his wounds almost knocking him backward. He quickly sealed the top of the cylinder tight, then turned around to put it in place.

Before he could, there was a sound like an animal's howling, only it was a man. A portly man, military uniform covered in hardened mud and filth, his eyes red as fire, sprang onto the embankment and grabbed Edwin.

"The devil's come for us! The devil's come!" the man shrieked, his strong hands clutching the first thing they could, which happened to be Edwin's arms.

"Get away from me!" shouted Edwin, while struggling to hold on to the cylinder.

"The train's coming!" Albert screamed from the other side of the bridge.

"You fool! You'll kill us all!" George screamed, trying to loosen the lunatic's powerful hold.

"I don't care what you say!" the stranger said in garbled tongue. "I'll punch the devil right in the face!" He seemed to address this to either Edwin or the cylinder.

"Hoyt, give me the cylinder!" George said as the three wrestled.

Edwin pushed against the man's viselike grip on his wrists as George pulled on the stranger's arms.

"Hurry!" was repeatedly shouted from across the water.

Finally, George screamed and kicked the man hard in the belly. As he was propelled away from Edwin, and tumbled into the trees behind them, the cylinder went flying into the air. The heat of the train was now bearing down on them.

Edwin and George tumbled down the embankment as fast as they could, and Hammie and Albert did the same on the other end. Just at that moment, the lead carriage of the train slammed across the tracks, remaining in a steady forward charge. The cylinder landed near the threshold and ignited with a brilliant flame across the first carriage's wheels. The bridge shimmied and shook as the train continued to the halfway mark and across before a single wheel flew off, and the nose of the train turned off the tracks, its flaming freight now lifted in the air, its shadow laid out on the surface of the water and growing fast.

Book 6

BUILDING AND ARCHITECTURE

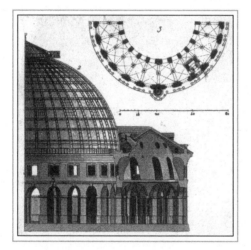

LVIII

Twelve Days Later

H E ROLLED from his toes to the balls of his feet and back as he waited. After a few minutes, the door creaked slightly open and a woman's slender fingers beckoned him.

"Be quiet and be quick. Upstairs, the second room on your right."

He hurried up the stairs, his friend close behind him. As they entered the room indicated, he froze at the sight of the motionless girl in her bed. She was more beautiful than he had ever appreciated, and his heart raced.

There was a stool next to the bed where the nuns would sit when feeding Agnes or reading to her from the small Bible that sat on a nearby table. He had waited so long to speak to her, but Marcus suddenly didn't know what to say.

Quiet and quick, Sister Louise had instructed, but he didn't know if he could be either, now that he saw her.

"Aggie," he whispered, "I can't stay very long. I promised. You always wanted to meet Ellen Swallow, our female scholar. Miss Turner, may I present Miss Swallow."

Ellen bowed a little.

"Madame Louise said I could not come to your room without a woman accompanying me, so here we are. Even then, the madame is very bold allowing a visit without informing the other sisters. It is against the rules here."

"Miss Turner, as soon as you have recovered your health, I will coach you in science if you wish," said Ellen softly. "In fact, I intend to speak to our president about admitting students of chemistry without any regard to sex, and would think you might be a candidate."

"Miss Swallow, may I . . ."

"Of course," she said, turning her back to give Marcus some privacy.

"I've been wanting to see you, Aggie." He paused, as if Agnes would reply. Of course, she couldn't, and as that realization stung him, and she seemed so delicate-looking, the momentary joy at reunion vanished. "I wish more than anything we could talk. I miss you more than I know how to say. When I close my eyes you are there, and when I open them you are not. More than anybody else, I wanted you to know that we've done it. The other boys of '68 and myself are to be graduated next week at the Institute. I think of you all the time, and I think of Frank, but when I dream of the past, I am no longer in it. I wanted to tell you that." What could he say, really? How he wished he had never left her side that day. How he would spend every waking hour with her in this infirmary if he were permitted by the strict Catholic sisters. "And it was because of Miss Swallow that many lives were saved when she was the first to realize that Frank had poisoned the wheat at the three major bakeries and the brewery company that were supplying the city on Decoration Day, and she knew what the victims had to do to begin to recover."

"Mr. Mansfield!" Sister Louise whispered from the corridor, where she was watching the strong young man fighting back tears. "The others are returning from chapel. You must go."

"Aggie, I will be back for you." He took her hand and pressed his lips against it as a tear escaped his eye against his will. He knew the madame would not approve, but he couldn't help himself. She gave him a kind frown and shook her finger at the stairs. He rushed out. Ellen followed, but stopped midstride as two of the other nuns appeared from around the corner before she could reach the entrance to the stairwell.

"Sister," they both greeted Ellen. She blushed, realizing her usual drab outfit served as the perfect costume, and followed Marcus's path down the stairs.

Sister Louise returned to the room, filled with relief that her weakness for the college student's ardor had not been found out by the Sister Superior. The Sister Superior would have compared her action to something in a fiction novel by some Protestant author, and would remind Louise once more that the fatal consequences of fiction reading had been proven time and again.

She picked up the Bible and began to read once more to her patient. Agnes's lovely eyes fluttered. It was only for a moment, and it was so fleeting Louise might have imagined it, but if it really did just happen, it had been the first movement since her accident. Louise sprang to her feet and ran. She ran through the corridor and into the stairwell, chasing after the young man, faster surely than any nun at the convent had ever run before.

LIX

'68 (Forever)

THE FOURTEEN MEMBERS of the Class of 1868 sat on the wooden benches in front of the president's office at the Massachusetts Institute of Technology, brimming over with excitement. One at a time, they were called in by President William Barton Rogers, and one at a time each young man exited, proudly flourishing a plain but instantly cherished diploma, lettered with great care by fellow graduate Albert Hall. And each time three cheers were raised.

With all their fellowship toward one another, today of all days, there was a special emotion of gratitude and anticipation attending the next name that would be called on the alphabetical roster. After all, he had found a way to stop the catastrophes that had shaken Boston and almost swallowed up the Institute and all of their futures. So it was no surprise, after Edwin returned to the hall, his face bright red, hugging his diploma close to his chest, and limping only a little despite the heavy bandaging in which he was still wrapped under his suit two weeks after his injury, that when "Marcus Mansfield" was pronounced by Rogers, all the fellows stood up and slapped him on the back and shook his hand heartily. Bob threw his arms around Marcus's neck and gave him a long embrace, then Hammie—First Scholar of the class—did the same.

After Rogers closed the door to his office behind him, Marcus took the waiting chair.

"I hope you and your friends are not disappointed that there are no flowers or festivals, as there are at Harvard. Well, it is not our way, you know. At least, it is not my way."

He was surprised to notice that President Rogers appeared to be agitated, almost distraught, on this day.

"I cannot say how deeply sorry I am, Mr. Mansfield," Rogers continued, looking down at his desk.

"President Rogers?"

"I shall come out with it, for I do not know how to put what I have to say into words. I cannot give you a diploma today," he said, finally looking up and meeting Marcus's eyes.

"Why?"

"I cannot let you be graduated, my dear boy."

He was speechless for a moment. "I don't understand, President Rogers. If I have done something—"

"Something. Something, Mr. Mansfield, yes. You saved our Institute from extinction! You represent all I dreamed the Institute might produce in time. You remember I've mentioned our original charter from the state legislature? Please." Rogers handed him a square sheet of parchment, dated 1861. "There is a special provision put in to appease those elements frightened of the new sciences. The public peace and harmony clause. You can find it at the bottom. You see, Mr. Mansfield, that it states that at no time should any individual affiliated with the Institute use his expertise in science and practical arts to harm another citizen of the commonwealth."

Marcus stared at the provision and allowed the implications to sink in.

Rogers went on. "The story of your heroic actions has been in every newspaper in Boston. Every major paper in the world, thanks to the telegraphic columns! I'm afraid Harvard has threatened that if we allow you to be graduated, they will use their influence to insist that the legislature revoke our charter because your defeat of Mr. Brewer would constitute a clear violation of that provision."

"They cannot do that."

"I fear they can, technically. The clause contains no exceptions, and your actions are a matter of public record. It is petty revenge on their part. But it is lawful."

"Is Agassiz behind it?"

Rogers shook his head. "Agassiz believes he is right in every matter of science, and cannot suffer the offense of anyone believing he is wrong, but he is still a true scientist—he does not seek glory or power or money, only to prove time and again the supremacy of natural law. No, it is not Agassiz, but a new president of the college. He has just been elected by the Harvard Corporation," Rogers said, pausing solemnly.

"A new president?"

"Charles Eliot, our own chemistry professor—ex-professor. He makes it plain that the moment I sign my name to your degree, the legislature will revoke all of our powers as a university. Our enemy was before our eyes all along. I am not afraid of Eliot; he is a shallow fellow to think he can run us down, and I will stand my ground to him as I have done before. It is because of you that no additional people were harmed. It is because of the actions of you and your classmates, as well as Miss Swallow, to save the city and stop Hammond's engineer, that the legislature has offered us their commendation. It is because of you, indeed, that we sit here today with our first graduates, in a city with peace restored. I will fight Eliot with every fiber of my being, in the legislature, in the courts, in Washington, if I must."

Marcus sat in silence, his expression composed, the only outward sign of emotion the tightening of his hands clasped in his lap. "No, sir," he said finally.

"What?"

"My sincere thanks, President Rogers, but I cannot allow the risk to the future of the Institute. Why would I fight so hard for its survival if

I could? I do not wish you to fight them—not over this. There are far more important battles to win."

"Then I shall fight those, while I find some way to win this one, too, without giving Eliot the chance to put the Institute at risk. And if I cannot give you a degree today I give you my hand," Rogers said, reaching out to him. "The survivors of the catastrophes you prevented will always be with you."

"The dead are with me, too, President Rogers."

"What have the doctors said of your hand?"

He grimaced, hesitating to reply. His right hand was in a specially made glove with extra cushioning along the fingers and joints. "I must give it more time."

"Mr. Mansfield, I do possess some good news. I have a letter here, from the Northern Pacific Railway. They read about you and have offered you a position. It is for immediate employment, Mr. Mansfield, and you would leave at once for Montana to claim it, with or without a degree—it matters not to them. They've included tickets for your passage, of course."

"Montana?"

"It is a first-rate opportunity for a young engineer, with excellent pay. They're waiting for you as we speak. You merely have to show yourself there. I think you should accept it."

Marcus deliberated for a few moments and then smiled slightly at his benefactor and nodded. "I'm sorry, President Rogers."

Rogers was startled at the response. "But, Mr. Mansfield—"

"The nun who attends Miss Turner has been reporting to me the improvements she is making almost every day, improvements the doctors consider a miracle. She just began speaking a little this morning, and is now expected to recover fully with time. I must be here for that day."

"Mr. Mansfield, an opportunity like this must not be taken lightly."

"I would not. But I have made my decision."

Rogers considered this, then nodded affectionately. "Very well, Mr. Mansfield. Then I have another idea, perhaps less adventuresome, but still worthwhile. Stay here."

"To study?"

"No! To teach. You will be close to Miss Turner, and will help the students, as you have proven you can do in singular fashion."

Marcus replied, wide-eyed, "A professor?"

Rogers laughed. "Not yet! But a professor's assistant. We need many more of them, as demand for enrollment in the next freshman class is enormous since news of your triumphs. But one day, perhaps, a professor you shall be if that is what you wish. Do you know, Mr. Mansfield, why we have always been so careful to prohibit gambling and cards at the Institute? Not for the usual reasons alone. With their special skills and analytical techniques some of the students will inevitably face the temptation to cheat, first at cards, then to leave behind their fellow man in life. It must fall to us to instill the right approach in the young men still to come. As far as I am concerned, you are not only a member of the first class, you are the first son of Tech, and welcome here always. Together we have built something never seen before."

They stood and shook hands again.

"President Rogers," Marcus said with hesitation, "there is one thing more."

"Yes?"

"If I walk out there without my diploma . . ." he started. "Well, they are all so excited out there to have them, they are holding them up, passing them around, reading them aloud, even kissing them! They are a loyal group. If I have to tell them right now what's happened with Harvard, in the rush of their excitement, they will insist on fighting it. They may not accept their own degrees if I do not receive one. Well, I'd wager that's what Bob Richards would insist upon."

"Yes, I could imagine he might."

"Some, at least, will put their own degrees at risk for mine."

"You are their leader."

"Chiefly their friend, I hope. But I want to have time to explain it to them individually, and keep their heads level."

Laughter scattered through the corridor.

"This should be their time to celebrate," Marcus continued.

"I understand, my son. What would you like to do? I can give you another paper to carry out."

"No. I would not like to deceive them, and they will see if it is not real." After a moment, he gestured to the window with a grin. The president questioned whether he would be injured, but after some gently reassuring promises from his pupil he opened the sash.

The older man watched from the window as Marcus landed on his feet. He began walking up empty Boylston Street toward the center of Boston, and then his step grew faster, buoyant, hopeful. Rogers, smiling to himself at the momentous day, closed the window, and as he watched, the glass fogged under his breath. He traced his finger on the glass pane around the figure of his newest member of the faculty as the image of Marcus Mansfield gradually became smaller.

"A perfect circle," he whispered to himself, taking a step back.

Returning to the hallway once he had mastered his emotions, Rogers called out the next name. "Robert Hallowell Richards."

Bob jumped to his feet, looking up and down the hall and then peering into the president's office. "But where's Mansfield?"

Rogers offered a bemused expression as though the question were incomprehensible. The new graduates exchanged glances of confusion.

The president cleared his throat. "Robert Hallowell Richards. You *are* coming in to receive your diploma, my son?"

As the other students whispered among themselves, Bob looked to Edwin and Hammie, who stood as if to start a search party for their fellow Technologist. Bob began to step into the office but paused at the threshold. He wheeled back around to his classmates.

"Three cheers for Marcus Mansfield. No: Three times three for Mansfield!"

President Rogers was almost as loud as Bob as they all roared at the top of their voices, loud enough for Marcus to hear as he walked along the sidewalk toward the sanctuary of Agnes Turner.

Charley

I T WAS TOO HOT A SUMMER DAY out on the Charles for such strenuous activity, but Will Blaikie did not rest his squadron. They had more preparation to do for their trip to England and their race against Oxford for the Grand Prix of university rowing in less than three weeks' time, and after the rainy spring they were sorely lagging. Their mission was far too important to Harvard, of which Blaikie was (almost) one of the newest alumni, and too important to Boston itself, to be interrupted.

"The Institute of Technology is beginning to make itself heard," said one of the Harvard junior-class rowers out of the blue.

"What do you mean by that, Smithy?" Blaikie demanded.

"I mean, in the newspapers, after they managed to resolve that line of disasters before our own Agassiz did, even while under their own cloud of suspicion. Of course, I'll always swear by Harvard," he added hastily. "I hear old Bob Richards stayed there and is instructing metallurgy in the fall, while that Mansfield helps with teaching mechanical engineering. And I hear that Richards got down on his knee in the laboratory and proposed marriage to that lady scientist who was rumored to be studying there! That's what the gossips say, anyway. Of course, they also say that a ten-foot-high man made of iron and fueled by steam assisted them in taking down the bridge to sink that runaway train, but that seems a tale."

Ignoring the junior, Blaikie turned to the rower behind him, the recruit from the hated place, whom he had invited to row since his doctor had ordered Blaikie to continue to rest his injured wrist, and recited:

Thou heard'st the creaking gate, the moaning trees
Between the palaces;
Saw'st how, in clear-cold air of Jove, the snows
To icy coating froze.

"The harmonious treatment of the body as well as the soul is the only condition under which man's mind may thrive," the stroke oar said in a matter-of-fact voice. His wrist had also prevented him from completing his senior examinations, which meant he had not technically been graduated yet and was not yet (though really *almost*) an alumnus, a title he had looked forward to boasting since his childhood. "Smithy there pays too much attention to sentimental gossip, as you can tell. Every week, to sharpen our mental valor, we learn ten odes of Horace by heart, and recite them to one another during our rowing."

"I swing the Indian club fifty times before breakfast," Bryant Tilden offered, though this did not seem to impress the leader.

"Who do you think the better general was, newy? Washington or Napoleon?" asked another rower, renewing what seemed to be an old debate.

"Well, Washington was the American, wasn't he?" Tilden responded forthrightly.

"Now that the faculty agreed to your admission, old salt," Blaikie said to Tilden, "you must be able to sing 'Fair Harvard' by heart."

"Oh?"

"Don't you know it after a month here?"

"I suppose not by heart," the new man said with the air of uncomfortable confession.

"Fellows, shall we repair the newy's ignorance?" Blaikie asked. "Tilden, it's sung to the tune of 'Believe Me If All Those Endearing Young Charms,' by Thomas Moore."

As they sang in time with their powerful strokes—*"Fair Harvard, thy sons to thy jubilee throng!"*—the rippling water began to bubble up from underneath them in a strange manner. Soon they could hardly pull through the water, and then the current seemed to suck their craft backward.

"Freighted with treasure thoughts, friendships and hopes, thou didst launch us on Destiny's sea . . ." The lyrics melted away as all eyes rested on the powerfully swirling water beneath them, under which something solid seemed to slowly take shape.

"If I didn't know better . . ." started one of the Harvard six.

"Don't!" Blaikie barked at him, not wanting to hear a word about Charley, the sea monster they'd often alluded to as a means of frightening strangers or freshes.

From beneath them, a shiny ridge thrust the boat into the air, sending the team tumbling up and out in all directions. As they flailed about, they watched the back of a bright white beast, which looked much like a whale—though shinier than any whale spied by man—as it sprayed a torrent of water into their faces. It then sped away faster than any Harvard six had ever rowed.

"Is that a propeller on its back?" Blaikie demanded. "What was that? Newy! What are you smiling at? I'm speaking to you—what in the deuce was that?"

"Hurrah to the nineteenth century!" proclaimed Tilden, who could not help but enjoy the spectacle. "I'm smiling, Captain, at the future!"

The History and Future of the Tech Boys

O N MAY 25, 1868, the following special act was passed by the legislature of the commonwealth of Massachusetts:

> *Section 1. The Massachusetts Institute of Technology is hereby authorized and empowered to award and confer degrees appropriate to the several courses of study pursued in said institution, on such conditions as are usually prescribed in universities and colleges in the United States, and according to such tests of proficiency, as shall best promote the interests of sound education in this Commonwealth.*

> *Section 2. This act shall take effect upon its passage.*

Section 2 may read like legal boilerplate, but it was important. It meant MIT's degree power was granted just weeks before its first graduation, despite the fact that this was seven years after founder William Barton Rogers had incorporated the college. It sparked my interest to think what was behind this timing: the resistance to the college's fight for legitimacy at a time when the concept of technology and scientific education was considered unorthodox, even dangerous.

The initial image that came to me for the novel was a scene in which MIT students rowing the Charles River are pushed aside by a polished Harvard crew team. I'm not sure why this materialized before other moments, but I think for me it captured the daunting race with our futures we begin when we are young adults. The first "Tech" boys really had the weight of the world on their shoulders. Their futures depended on a radical new school that couldn't promise them degrees, and that school's longevity hinged on these students' uncertain futures.

Besides transporting me into some of my favorite parts of nineteenth-century Boston, this novel also gave me a chance to build on my own modest ties to the world of science and the history of technology. My great-grandfather Louis Pearl was an inventor and manufacturer in Brooklyn, New York; another relative, Professor Richard Pearl, was once one of the country's leading geologists and an expert in meteorites; and another relative, Harold Howard Hirsch, was a powder metallurgist at Los Alamos when he witnessed the first test of the atomic bomb, remarking later that he believed it would lead to the cessation of all wars. During my years at Harvard College, my roommates (a group that included mathematicians and a physicist—a somewhat unusual crowd for an English major) and I lived in Eliot House, named after Charles Eliot, one of the original chemistry professors at MIT. One of my wife's ancestors, a Bostonian named Edward Tobey, was a chief fund-raiser for MIT, and he appears in this novel advising the faculty (she also happened to attend the John D. Runkle elementary school in Brookline, Massachusetts, named after MIT's original mathematics professor).

The "picked-up lot" of MIT's inaugural Class of 1868 offered me a colorful cast from which to select my main characters. Robert Hallowell Richards and William Edwin Hoyt were real students. Bryant Tilden's disciplinary scrapes remain on record in the MIT archives, as do Albert Hall's immaculate class notes, which allowed me to "enroll" in the original curriculum. Marcus Mansfield and Chauncy Hammond, Jr. ("Hammie"), are fictional, but in them can be seen composites of other Tech boys I researched. Marcus's closest counterparts in history are Charles Augustus Smith, a son of a sailor who commuted every day from Newburyport to MIT and worked as a railroad leveler and assistant engineer to earn money for college expenses; Civil War veteran Channing Whitaker, who worked in a machine shop before going to MIT and ended up as a professor there for many years; and John Ripley Freeman, who came to MIT from a farm and traveled each day to and from Lawrence, except during busy periods of study, when he, like Marcus, boarded in Boston.

Hammie is partially derived from Frank Firth, probably the most aloof member of the first group of MIT students; Hammie's plan for a "steam man" comes from an invention patented in 1868 by a young mechanic in Newark, New Jersey. Ellen Swallow was a few classes behind the '68 boys, sequestered in her own lab and not permitted to attend classes. She would later teach at MIT, where she was a renowned pioneer in women's education and in environmental and nutritional sciences, working alongside her husband, Professor Bob Richards (who indeed proposed to her in one of the MIT laboratories). Daniel Chester French, appearing in this novel in his freshman year before he failed out of MIT, later became a celebrated artist, responsible for the Lincoln Memorial in Washington, D.C., and chosen (over all Harvard alumni) to create the statue of John Harvard. Whenever possible, the experiences, language, and spirit of those people on whom my characters are based have been incorporated, especially those who left behind records of their time at MIT.

The disasters that plague Boston in my novel are my creation; however, each one has a basis in real technologies developed at the time (often at MIT), and my research binders are thick with articles about train wrecks, destructive boiler explosions, early divers and submarines (including the *Alligator* and the *Intelligent Whale* of the 1860s, on which Hammie's *White Whale* is based) and compass-related shipwrecks that allowed me to craft the relevant scenes in context. In addition, the fear and anxiety about the strange concept (and the strange word, at the time) of *technology,* and by extension the Institute, are grounded in fact; even the statement the Rogers character makes that the Institute of Technology, being such a vague concept, is seen by some as a front for some kind of brothel, comes out of the historical record. Edwin's list of "unsolvable" scientific problems is derived from a contest promoted by a contemporary scientific journal.

The MIT building on Boylston Street in Back Bay was for many years called the Rogers Building, though modesty would never have allowed Rogers to condone that in his lifetime. I've attempted to re-create the original building's details by studying photographs, drawings, elevations filed with the municipal records, and student accounts. In

1938, twenty-two years after MIT moved to Cambridge, the remarkable Boylston Street building was demolished to make way for an insurance office building, which stands there today.

Rogers returned to MIT to deliver the commencement address to the Class of 1882. Midway through his speech, he paused, leaned forward, and collapsed. Here were some of Rogers's last words, delivered to the new graduates and their families:

I confess to being an enthusiast on the subject of the Institute, but I am not ashamed of this enthusiasm when I see what it has come to be. It is true that we commenced in a small way, with a few earnest students, while the tides rose and fell twice daily where we now are. Our early labors with the legislature in behalf of the Institute were sometimes met not only with repulse but with ridicule, yet we were encouraged and sustained by the great interest manifested by many in the enterprise. Formerly a wide separation existed between theory and practice; now in every fabric that is made, in every structure that is reared, they are closely united into one interlocking system—the practical is based upon the scientific, and the scientific is solidly built upon the practical. You have not been treated here today to anything in the nature of oratorical display; no decorations, no flowers, no music, but you have seen in what careful and painstaking manner these young men and women have been prepared for their future occupations in life.

ACKNOWLEDGMENTS

As always, incredible people inside and outside publishing deserve thanks for making this novel possible and making it better. Suzanne Gluck, Raffaella De Angelis, Tracy Fisher, Alicia Gordon, Cathryn Summerhayes, Eugenie Furniss, Michelle Feehan, Erin Malone, Sarah Ceglarski, Caroline Donofrio, Liz Tingue, Mina Shaghaghi, Eve Attermann and their fantastic colleagues at William Morris Endeavor Entertainment; Jennifer Hershey, Tracy Devine, Gina Centrello, Tom Perry, Jane von Mehren, Erika Greber, Amy Edelman, Vincent La Scala, Richard Elman, Courtney Moran, Jessica Waters, and the dedicated team at Random House, as well as Stuart Williams and his colleagues at Harvill Secker; my secret society of readers/brainstormers Eric Bennett, Kevin Birmingham, Benjamin Cavell, Joseph Gangemi, Julie Park Haubner, Marcus Padow, Cynthia Posillico, and Scott Weinger, as well as tireless supporters Marsha Helmstadter, Susan Pearl, Warren Pearl, and Ian Pearl.

My research assistant Gabriella Gage once again used her exemplary skills to help me uncover layer upon layer of great historical material. Gail Lippincott, Joyce Miles, and Pam Swallow were among the scholars who lent aid in searching out rare material on Ellen Swallow Richards. Nora Murphy at the MIT archives, Frank Conahan at the MIT Museum General Collections, Peter Bebergal at the MIT Technology Licensing Office, and David Kaiser of the MIT Program in Science, Technology and Society each were helpful and generous with their time and expertise. The early history of MIT was first recorded thoroughly by Samuel Prescott in *When MIT Was Boston Tech*, later enriched by Julius Stratton and Loretta H. Mannix in *Mind and Hand: The Birth of MIT* and in a recent volume of essays Professor Kaiser edited called *Becoming MIT*. Along with Robert Hallowell Richards's memoir, *His Mark*, these sources proved to be among the most valuable.

Finally, my wife and son provided inspiration and perspective on a daily basis and gave me a reason to come back from the nineteenth century.

ABOUT THE AUTHOR

MATTHEW PEARL is the *New York Times* bestselling author of *The Dante Club, The Poe Shadow,* and *The Last Dickens,* and the editor of the Modern Library editions of Dante's *Inferno* (translated by Henry Wadsworth Longfellow), Edgar Allan Poe's *The Murders in the Rue Morgue: The Dupin Tales,* and Charles Dickens's *The Mystery of Edwin Drood.* His novels have been published in more than thirty languages and forty countries around the world.

www.matthewpearl.com

ABOUT THE TYPE

This book was set in Bulmer, a typeface designed in the late eighteenth century by the London type-cutter William Martin. The typeface was created especially for the Shakespeare Press, directed by William Bulmer; hence, the font's name. Bulmer is considered to be a transitional typeface, containing characteristics of old-style and modern designs. It is recognized for its elegantly proportioned letters, with their long ascenders and descenders.